I0818898

THE YOUNG WILL REMEMBER

OTHER TITLES BY EVE J. CHUNG

Daughters of Shandong

THE YOUNG WILL REMEMBER

EVE J. CHUNG

BERKLEY
New York

BERKLEY
An imprint of Penguin Random House LLC
1745 Broadway, New York, NY 10019
penguinrandomhouse.com

Book design by George Towne

Library of Congress Cataloging-in-Publication Data

Names: Chung, Eve J., author
Title: The young will remember / Eve J. Chung.
Description: New York : Berkley, 2026.
Identifiers: LCCN 2025023410 (print) | LCCN 2025023411 (ebook) |
ISBN 9780593640562 (hardcover) | ISBN 9780593640586 (ebook)
Subjects: LCSH: Korean War, 1950-1953--Fiction | Women--Fiction |
LCGFT: War fiction | Fiction | Novels
Classification: LCC PS3603.H85334 Y68 2026 (print) | LCC PS3603.H85334 (ebook)
LC record available at https://lccn.loc.gov/2025023410
LC ebook record available at https://lccn.loc.gov/2025023411

Printed in the United States of America
1st Printing

The authorized representative in the EU for product safety and compliance is
Penguin Random House Ireland, Morrison Chambers, 32 Nassau Street,
Dublin D02 YH68, Ireland, https://eu-contact.penguin.ie.

For the women's human rights defenders all over the world.
Thank you for refusing to stand down,
for refusing to shut up, and for refusing to surrender.

And, as always, for my children—my Chinese-Korean-American children—who have shown me what it means to love like a mom. I would not have been able to write this book without that gift.

THE YOUNG WILL REMEMBER

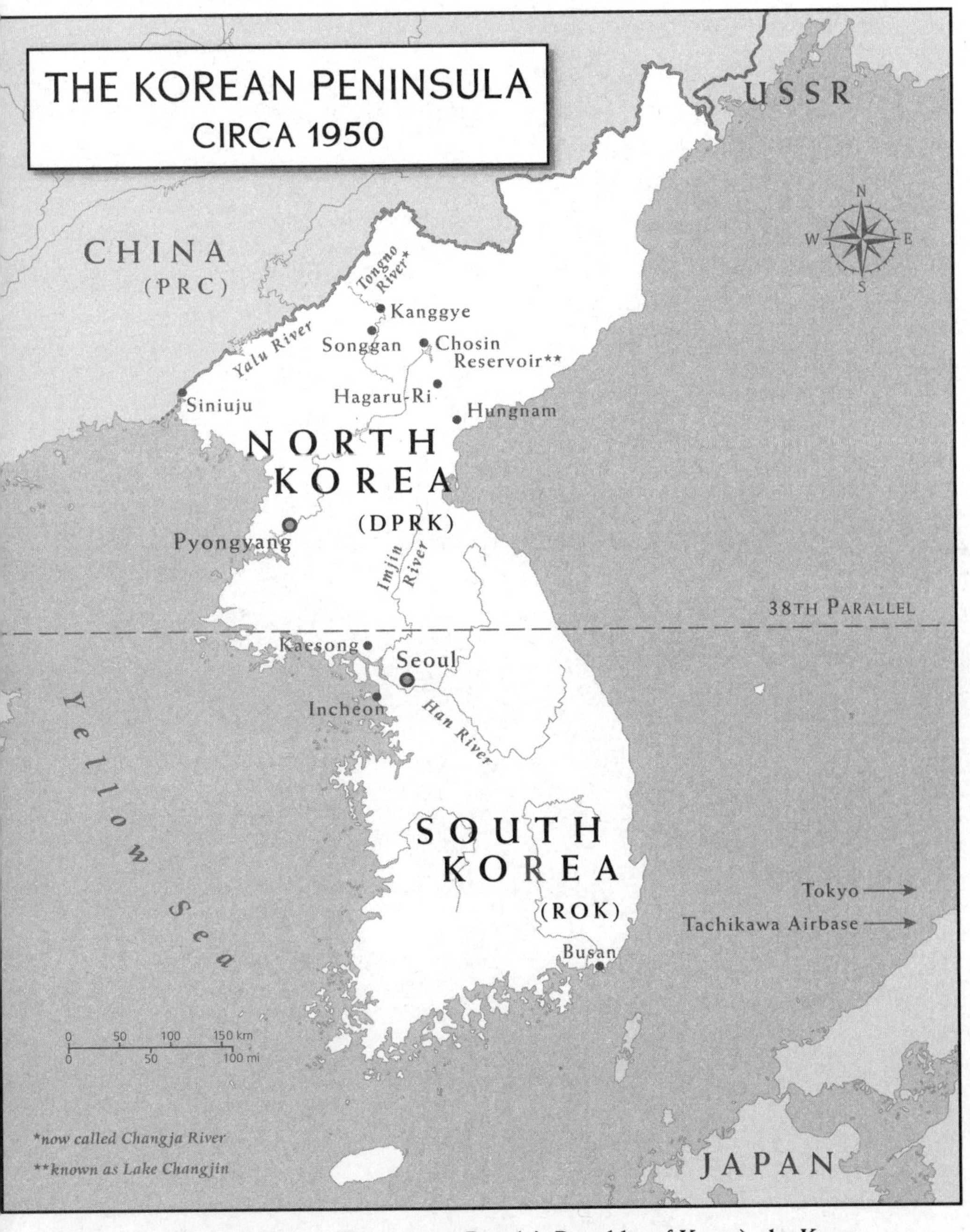

The army of North Korea (Democratic People's Republic of Korea), the Korean People's Army (KPA), is assisted by the People's Republic of China's People's Volunteer Army (PVA) and supported by the Soviet Union.

The army of South Korea (Republic of Korea), the Republic of Korea Army (ROKA), is assisted by the United Nations Command (UNC), led by the United States of America.

1

TOUCHDOWN

August 12, 2019

Seoul is unrecognizable.

I press my forehead against the plane's window, my breath fogging the view of this flamboyant metropolis. It is silver, with bridges that leap over rivers and roads that whip into mountains, claiming a horizon that was once viridescent. A few years ago, NASA shared an image of the Korean peninsula from space, its southern half flaring with light while the north lay engulfed in darkness. Though I have seen that iconic photo, I am still unprepared to be here.

My son's fingers graze my hand. "Are you okay, Mom?"

A deluge of emotions converge within me, and I cannot tell what I feel, only that it is overwhelming.

"Do you want some water?" he asks, raising his voice and enunciating each word. "*Wah-ter?*"

This is our first plane ride together, and he believes that he is my chaperone. Though he has his own years mapped in the wrinkles across his face, I don't want to speak until I am steady. Children get upset when they see their parents cry, no matter how old they are.

I wait for the ache in my throat to go away, but the immensity of everything that I've never told him hardens that knot. While I've known my son for his whole life, he has known me for only part of mine. He tells people that I am terrified of flying, but seventy years ago I was traipsing around airfields with my typewriter tucked under my arm, begging pilots to take me to the front lines. Back then, I was a correspondent for the *Global Tribune*.

I have seen Seoul from the sky at least a hundred times.

I don't talk much about the war, but since then, I have tried my best to live well. The fear of disappointing *her* has held me hostage.

A tone dings as the FASTEN SEAT BELT sign comes on.

"Mom?" My son shakes my arm with urgency.

We are about to touch down.

2

HOME BY CHRISTMAS

"Recently catastrophic events in the Far East suggest strongly that . . . we are on the brink of, if not already involved in, World War III . . ."

—Lt. Gen. Albert C. Wedemeyer,
San Francisco, November 16, 1950

December 5, 1950

General MacArthur had promised our troops that they would be home for Christmas, but it was clear now that if any of them were going back to America, it was going to be on a stretcher or in a coffin. The six a.m. sun, already weary from winter, cast lukewarm rays over Tachikawa Airfield, where technicians towed a C-47 onto the runway. Mount Fuji arched in the background, a snow-cloaked spirit serene beneath its crown of clouds. On the tarmac, half a dozen flight nurses gathered, their arms crossed in their thick air force–issued coats. Though they had the day off, they had arrived early, and were stewing as they waited for the next pilot.

Nothing excited me more than angry women who had gotten organized.

In my own corner, I squatted with my back against the wall, balancing my typewriter on my knees. With a biscuit between my teeth and red bean mochi in my pocket, I began typing:

In North Korea's Chosin Reservoir, our haggard survivors are stripping their dead comrades of their clothing and stacking up corpses to block the gales. Though the Soviets aren't formally fighting in Korea, the blizzard blowing down from Siberia is its own horrifying army. At minus 40 degrees, soldiers' blackened toes are breaking off in their boots and carbines are jamming.

Chairman Mao had warned us not to cross into North Korea, but General MacArthur was arrogant.

My fingers slowed to a halt. Was that last sentence too abrasive?

Letting my biscuit fall from my lips, I uncapped my pen and slashed a line through "arrogant," perusing a mental list of synonyms. "Confident," maybe? I started writing in "confident," but I'd barely crossed the "t" before Barbara, one of the flight nurses, yanked the paper from my feed roller.

"We have boys in Korea who still have no winter uniforms!" she exclaimed, flipping her bangs up from her forehead. "It's *December.* If that's not arrogant, I don't know what is!"

Her chestnut hair, usually back-combed and bombastically curled, hung limp over her freckled cheeks. She pulled out her own pen and scribbled furiously over "confident," her lines as jagged as a lightning bolt. In all capitals, she wrote *ARROGANT* with so much force that she punctured the paper.

"Give that back!" I cried, surging to my feet. My ankles tingled from squatting. "The *Global Tribune* already got a warning from MacArthur's office. If I get us another, we might get blocked from the embassy briefings!"

Censorship was supposed to be patriotic, but Barbara wasn't with the press. Unrepentantly, she underlined *ARROGANT* before returning my article, her thumbprint smudged into the ink. I shooed her away, smoothing the crinkled paper before inserting it back into my typewriter.

Barbara and I had arrived in Japan on the same flight in July 1950, shortly after the North Korean People's Army—KPA for short—invaded South Korea, and the US initiated a "police action" under the United Nations. I'd been covering the Korean War for the past five months, but while every other correspondent was chasing MacArthur's top officers, I had been hanging around with Barbara and the other flight nurses of the Medical Air Evacuation Squadron. Being a female war correspondent was hard enough. It was even harder when you looked like the enemy.

Though I was born and raised in San Francisco, I was ethnically Chinese, with straight black hair and eyes that folded at the corners. My nose was small but broad like my father's, and my lips were plump like my mother's. Despite my perfect English and my Californian slang, American officers often balked when I tried to talk to them, let alone press them for information.

It was annoying, but at twenty-eight I had spent most of my life prying open side doors when the entrance was blocked. Many correspondents can attack a front-page story head-on, shark-style, but some of us can advance only if we get really good at picking the glitter from the dust. I began my career by writing about the Women Air Force Service Pilots, which few other outlets covered in detail. Through that series, I shone enough to get an assignment abroad. Though my bosses were initially reluctant to send a woman to a war zone, no one else at the *Global Tribune* was fluent in Japanese and Mandarin, as I was. My language skills—and my promise to use them to get scoops like no other—finally tipped the scales in my favor.

Over the past months, I'd made friends. The flight nurses helped me arrange interviews with patients, and the pilots let me hitch rides to Korea. Because of them, I was churning out stories on every major battle. Today, however, was going to be different.

"There he is!" Barbara shrieked when the office door squeaked open. "There's George!"

I snapped my head up so quickly that a joint in my neck popped.

George Miyashita slumped into the hangar, so exhausted that he wobbled, his sparse mustache a stain on his upper lip. Among the pilots, he was my favorite. He spent most of his free time at the pool on base and had the broad shoulders of a swimmer—and washboard abs if you caught him at the right angle.

The technicians who had been loading fuel barrels into the cargo hold slowed to stare. When George saw us, he recoiled. "No!" he yelled. "I told you all no!"

George and the other pilots had been flying nonstop for five days, because our leaders had underestimated a Communist "bandit" and his "peasant army." "We're going all the way to the Yalu," one of the generals had said. "Don't let a bunch of Chinese laundrymen stop you!" Though the police action was supposed to end at the 38th parallel—the line separating the two Koreas—MacArthur had sent our boys surging into the North so quickly that they had had to spread themselves thin along narrow mountain roads. Pilots had airdropped turkeys and potatoes near the Chinese border so that troops could celebrate Thanksgiving.

No one had noticed that the trees were moving.

No one had believed that a "peasant army" would tiptoe through the forests, under white sheets to camouflage with the snow, until they surrounded every single road; until their bugles sounded in the middle of the night and entire platoons disappeared as if swallowed, a bloodbath that verged on annihilation. Air force escorts had had to blast napalm on the path to help the survivors eke out a retreat, over five days, to our base at Hagaru-ri. Thousands of critically wounded soldiers now needed evacuation, but the mission was so hazardous that nurses were forbidden from flying.

Most of the women understood, but the "abrasive" ones were livid.

"We're air force too!" Barbara cried, leading the charge. She pointed to the logo on her jacket as the women encircled George. "Patients need us. You need us. You're going to lose men in flight otherwise!"

George huffed in exasperation. "It's not up to me, okay? I have my orders. The Chosin is too dangerous for you all."

"That's bullshit, and you know it!" said Barbara. "To hell with orders. Just take one of us. Stand up for what you know is right!"

I shoved my typewriter into its case, snapping it shut before gobbling down the rest of my biscuit. "Who's going to care for the patients, George?" I demanded, brushing crumbs off my chin. "On top of being wounded, those boys haven't slept or eaten in five days!"

"Some of us have brothers and boyfriends over there," exclaimed another nurse.

"'No' means 'no,'" said George, pushing past them. "Sorry."

The technicians scattered as George stomped to the ladder

that led to the cockpit of the C-47. I dashed after him, whipping out my bag of mochi, still warm from being tucked in my pocket.

"The orders were 'no flight nurses,' right?" I said, flashing my most persuasive grin. If I strained, I could get a dimple to dot my left cheek. "Not 'no women,' or 'no correspondents,' right, George? In any case, I'm a civilian, so military orders don't apply to me. Right?"

His stride was longer than mine, and I had to pump my arms to keep up with him. "No, Ellie, you can't come either," he said. "And I'm not a dog. You can't bribe me with food."

"But I waited in line for these all morning!" I had been betting that George would succumb to these snacks. Like me, he was from the Bay Area and loved the chewy combination of red bean and sticky rice flour. "They're fresh, from our favorite stand—the one by the bathhouse. Come on, George. California solidarity. No one else from the *Global Tribune* made it to the Chosin. If I can get there, my boss will go wild. The entire team back home will. Please, George. I need this!"

"Go away, Ellie!" George snapped, swatting at the mochi that I dangled by his nose. "I know you think you have to prove yourself, but this is ridiculous, even for you."

Barbara had caught up to us, her boots thudding as the plane's cargo door clanged shut. The other nurses pattered angrily behind her.

"Oh, good Lord," said Barbara. "If you won't take us, at least take Ellie. Let her get her story!"

George whirled around to face us, the bags beneath his bloodshot eyes pronounced. "What is wrong with you all?" he demanded. "Do you have any idea what's happening at Hagaru-ri? The Chinese have the airstrip surrounded. When I fly in, it's going to be with an escort of fighter jets. When I fly out, it's going to be through fire. You should just be grateful that you have the day off. Get some rest. Curl your hair and take a bath."

Barbara flushed so deeply that her freckles faded into her ruddy skin. "Damn you, George. We can help. We *want* to help!"

I leaped between George and the ladder and stretched my arms out. At five feet two, I barely reached his chin, but I clenched the mochi in my fist and let my typewriter dangle from its shoulder strap. "I thought we were friends, George. I always tell you when there's beef jerky at the commissary. I always get you extra mochi at the market, because I know you're too scared of the mochi *obasan* to buy them yourself."

George snatched the mochi bag from me, ripping the top. "I'm not scared of the mochi granny," he said. "And we are friends—good friends. That's why I want you to stay here. You, of all people, should not be at the Chosin right now. You know what I mean, don't you?"

The nurses' outrage dwindled to a hush, and Barbara cocked her head, uncertain. They might have been confused, but I knew exactly what he meant. Of course I did.

If anyone else had referenced my ethnicity, I might have gone ballistic, but George was Japanese American. During World War II, our government had sent his family to an internment camp even though George's father was fighting for us in France. The Miyashitas didn't get released until the last camps closed—just four years ago.

"They're really bloody mad at China over there," George continued. "If I were you, I'd lie low for now. MacArthur's foaming at the mouth. Rumor has it, he's pushing to bomb Manchuria. If it were up to him, we'd go nuclear."

A chill shivered down my spine.

As a woman in this field, I always had to be brave, to work harder and smarter for every scrap and bone—never complain, and above all, never cry. I kept my fear in a box and labeled it *opportunity*, but it was still a slippery beast. Courage and madness were different shades of the same color, and I couldn't tell which I had painted myself with when I said, "I'm willing to take the risk, George. I won't put my life on hold because some jerks can't tell the difference between me and a Red."

I stood my ground, holding my head so high that I had to tilt it back. That was the only way I could look down at someone taller than me.

George rolled his eyes and threw his hand up. "Fine, Ellie. But only because I'm starving, and I need you to feed these to me while I keep my hands on the controls. I swear to God, if you cause any trouble—"

"I won't cause trouble," I cried, bouncing with adrenaline while Barbara and the other nurses cheered. "I'll feed you like you're my firstborn child. Let's go!"

Though I wasn't a flight nurse, when the next pilot came around Barbara was going to argue that George had taken a woman on his plane, so why shouldn't the others too? I couldn't help feeling sorry for George, who was probably going to get an earful upon his return, but I grabbed the rungs of the ladder like it was a lifeline for my career.

George pulled my arm. "Get yourself a thicker jacket. It's cold enough over there to freeze hell over."

"Take mine," said Barbara, unbuttoning her fur-lined leather flight-nurse coat. She threw it over my shoulders and it settled like a cape, the hefty weight as comforting as a hug. While I threaded my arms into the soft sleeves, she stuffed an extra pair of gloves into my pockets.

"Double up on socks," another nurse said, plopping down on the floor so she could rip off her own. Lint clung to her bare feet as she handed me two moist balls of wool, which I seized with gratitude. Giddy, I scrambled up the ladder, my typewriter thumping against my hip.

13 October 1950
Dear Yun-Hee,

The bombing is getting closer to us in Pyongyang, but don't worry, I am safe.

I made dumplings for Jae-Min today. He used to visit me once a month, but since the war started, it's been once a week. Too often! I don't want to see him that much. Men are a chore. If he comes, I have to clean the house and make him a snack.

I try to be nice, but he can be so annoying. He tries to give me money, even though I don't need his help. I am still working, and so far, the factory is still running. Besides, what will people say if they hear that I'm taking money from such a young man, and a student no less? Embarrassing!

I always tell him no, but after he leaves, I find bills stuffed in my coat pockets. Once, he even left a hundred won in my shoe!

So I suppose I should at least feed him. There is no meat anymore, so I filled the dumplings with kimchi and bean noodles. You have to squeeze as much water out of the kimchi as you can and chop it fine for texture. With a bit of mushroom, it almost feels like meat.

I hope you are eating well.

Mom

3

PARCHMENT YELLOW

December 5, 1950

George and I soared, Tachikawa's white and gray buildings scattering below us like seeds. The plane hummed, an aluminum bee. Though I couldn't remember what being in a womb was like, I imagined that it must be something like this. Peace was difficult to find, and even harder to hold on to, but in flight it embraced me. Clearing my head, I let my eyes drink the sky's azure light, mirrored by the sparkling sea.

George's deft hands swept over the control panel of the unheated and unpressurized plane. Dutifully, I held out the mochi while he took big bites, my ears popping with our ascent.

Indignantly, he said, "I can't believe the mochi granny is so nice to you. She doesn't like doing business with Americans."

I laughed, though my fingers were stiffening with the cold.

The mochi granny's name was Hitomi, and she liked me because she thought I was a hard worker—I often woke up before six to beat the crowd at the public bathhouse. Male correspondents could get away with stubble and flea powder, but I risked losing interviews if I wasn't fully coiffed.

"She's okay with Americans," I said, "as long as they aren't military."

"She always pretends she doesn't understand my Japanese."

"You don't use your honorifics. She thinks you're rude."

"She told you that?" he asked, suddenly mortified. "Do you two talk about me?"

"No," I lied. Truthfully, I was a small beast who fed on gossip, and Hitomi liked to chat during the slower hours before the rest of the market opened. She told me that she had lost all five of her children during the firebombing of Tokyo, which was why she was selling mochi at the age of seventy—and also why she hated the American military. In George's case, she was especially hostile, not only because of the honorifics, but also because she considered him a traitor.

I couldn't tell him that last part, though. It hurt to straddle two worlds, and that was a pain I understood well enough to want to shield him from it.

"I wish my parents had taught me more Japanese," George said wistfully as we skimmed past an oblong cloud. "They just wanted me to speak good English. They didn't want me to have an accent, like my grandparents do."

"Neither of my parents taught me their native tongues either."

"Yeah, but they made you learn two other languages."

My parents were ethnic Chinese from Taiwan, a former Japanese colony. They were Hakka and Hokkien speakers who had been born and raised under colonial rule and educated entirely in Japanese, so we spoke Japanese at home. In our neighborhood in California, however, Mandarin was common, and the only Chinese language available to study. "I'm not complaining," I said.

"I'm just saying that our parents try to do what they think is best, and it's hard for them to predict what that will be."

"I guess," George muttered.

I leaned over and grinned. "Well, your English is very good, so at least that worked out."

George snorted. "Jesus Christ, you're smug. Give me another mochi. I have to remember why I'm putting up with you."

Starch coated my frozen fingertips. I dusted them off before putting on Barbara's gloves. "We're cruising now," I said, holding out the bag for him, "so you can feed yourself."

He gave me a petulant side-eye. "Unbelievable." Still, he smiled when he plucked out a second piece, a tender moon in his palm.

It took four hours to get to Korea from Japan, but for me it went by quickly. From above, the Taebaek Mountains ripped through the land like a tiger's spine, flaunting granite peaks streaked with snow. We curved up north, into a low-level storm, our plane bobbing as fighter jets zipped through the flurries. MacArthur had ordered an evacuation by sea, possibly the largest in our military history. Every man who could fire a gun was going to have to fight if our troops were to have any hope of breaking through to the coast. I couldn't believe that I was going to be there to cover it.

I probably should have been scared, but I was so fascinated by military action—by the coordination that allowed hundreds of thousands of people to operate as one, to become an incredible school of fish that conquered not only the sea but also the sky. My parents never understood why I wrote about war when so many immigrants went to America to avoid it. It wasn't that I was apathetic about the devastation; rather, I examined armed conflict like a detective might study a murder. The more we knew about war, the better we would be at preventing it—and, if necessary, winning it. Though I had tried explaining that to my family, my visits home often left me worried that something was wrong with me.

Perhaps that was why I was so drawn to other women in the war zone. There were so few of us, but when I found my flock, I no longer felt like I was programmed defectively but instead with intentionality and purpose.

I leaned over to get a closer look at an F-86 Sabre jet with swept-back wings—an aerodynamic adjustment that made them nearly supersonic. Could you imagine tearing through the air at the speed of *sound*?

There were female pilots who would have killed for a chance to fly one of these, but American women weren't allowed to take combat roles in Korea. Many of my pilot friends had scrambled to enlist when women were allowed into the air force, but they were all grounded in Tokyo now, monitoring the weather. They were going to be jealous that I'd even laid eyes on these jets, fresh from Washington. These women talked about planes like my friends back home talked about boys, gushing about top speeds and salivating over engines. I didn't use to care about jets, but that kind of fanaticism is contagious, so I memorized every curve and angle of that F-86 for bragging rights later.

"Hold on," warned George as our wings rattled.

I clung to my seat as we began our turbulent descent into Hagaru-ri, the clouds lifting layer by layer. Light snowfall veiled the base like gauze. Wind roared as the mountainous crater appeared, a gaping jaw with hills for teeth, each crest mottled with foxholes. Soldiers guarded the perimeter with machine guns and mortars, while fighter jets circled like birds of prey.

Military engineers had labored under floodlights to finish this airstrip, but it was only half the length it was supposed to be, impossibly small and as stark as a minus sign when snow-brushed tents rushed up to meet us. Our wheels smashed against the ground, my seat belt digging into my shoulder as we jolted.

Throughout my body, I hardened my muscles like armor, not for the flesh but for the soul. There was weight in my work, and if I wasn't careful it would drag me under. In the maelstrom of war reporting, I could not be a brittle boat, or even a battleship. I had to be an anchor and sink on my own terms, controlled and unyielding. Only then could I bring myself up again. Only then could I keep coming back again—to watch again and write again.

We screeched to a stop, and George pushed the door open, wind bursting into the cockpit. Weary technicians plodded around to help us disembark. Along the airstrip, grown men had fallen asleep as children do—seated on crates, curled on the ground, one with his forehead on a tin can of hot dogs. A surgeon waited outside the MASH—the mobile army surgical hospital—the smoke from his cigarette swirling over the red cross at the entrance. With ash on his lapel, he handed George a list of patients.

"I'm going to talk to the technicians," George said while soldiers emptied the cargo hold of his plane. "If you need me—"

"I won't need you," I called over my shoulder, already scurrying to the MASH. At every site, I checked in with the nurses first, not only because they were usually friendly to me, but also because they heard almost everything and never sugarcoated the casualties.

Inside the MASH tent, the air was thick with a sickening mix of rust, dirt, and gangrenous flesh. Cots were filled with shredded men, several of whom had swollen feet and missing toes. Wounds often froze shut in the field, but as soon as they thawed indoors, the patients would start gushing blood. The ground squelched beneath my boots, and I wavered.

Though I had visited countless hospitals, I still gagged at the sight of gore. I had gotten better at hiding it, though. With my hand casually over my mouth, I pretended to wipe my runny nose, waiting for my stomach to settle as I stepped carefully over maroon patches.

One nurse, dressed in an olive-green trench coat, sucked on a morphine syrette to defrost it. Her pants bulged with the packets of blood plasma in her underwear, kept in a crotch pack to prevent them from freezing. When she turned toward me and flicked the syrette, I recognized her.

She was someone I had interviewed months ago, in Busan. Back then, she had natural strawberry blond curls—the kind that Barbara spent hours trying to tease out each morning—and a scarlet starlet pout. Now her hair was dull and pulled into a frizzy bun like a rabbit's tail, and her lips were beige.

"Clara?" I said tentatively.

Blinking, the nurse evaluated me with sunken eyes. "Oh." She smiled, revealing a snaggletooth. "You're the lady from . . . the *New York Tribune*?"

"*Global Tribune*. Eleanor Chang."

"Oh yes! Ellie!" She hugged me tightly, like she had missed me, even though we were only acquaintances. In the field, simply surviving was a shared victory. "Sorry," she said. "I've always been awful with names. I can't believe you're here! Are you covering our march south?"

"Yes, if I can."

"Heavens, you're crazy! If I didn't have to be here, I sure wouldn't be."

Another nurse, a glowering brunette with glacial blue irises, made her way past a groaning patient. "Excuse me," she said, "but what are you?"

I patted my typewriter case and showed her my press badge. "I'm a correspondent. Eleanor Chang, *Global Tribune*."

"I mean, where are you from?" she clarified. "Are you a South Korean?"

"Oh, Lucy," Clara began, but I was used to this question. It was annoying, but it happened often enough that I had a response that I could whip out like an umbrella.

"I'm from California," I said. "I'm American, but my parents are from Taiwan." Chiang Kai-shek's Nationalists in Taiwan were America's allies, the "good" Chinese.

"So you are a Chinese," Lucy said. "I thought so. You're more of a parchment yellow than a Japanese. I've read articles on Orientals. I know how to tell you all apart."

"Then why did you ask me if I was South Korean?"

"Because only South Koreans are allowed here."

Before I could probe Lucy on whether she could tell a North Korean and a South Korean apart, Clara jumped in. "Lucy, I know her. Eleanor really is a correspondent, and she's written articles about our work. General Smith is having a press briefing. He wants coverage from here to Hungnam."

"Our patients' safety is our priority," said Lucy, growing shrill. "Who can rest if a Chinese they don't know is lurking around? Even if she isn't a Chinese, no women are allowed on base—except for nurses."

Everyone in the tent was staring now, including a medical technician who had just transferred a patient onto a litter. "I'm sorry, ma'am," he said, straightening to his full height. "No reporters allowed here. You're disturbing the wounded."

Lucy smirked, validated like I was a criminal she had caught red-handed.

The last thing I wanted to do was upset the patients, but I resented being blamed when reporters regularly appeared in the MASH. We were all Americans, yet Lucy reminded me that there were different rules for different people, and back home our communities were still segregated—separate and unequal. Before I had learned to read as a child, I already knew which stores were off-limits, because my anxious mother would drag me away whenever she spotted the signs that forbade "Orientals." It wasn't that I could ever forget that, but Truman had recently ended segregation in the military—though many commanders opposed and ignored the order. Korea was America's first war using integrated units. Times were supposed to be changing.

"I'll see you later, Ellie," Clara said apologetically, sidestepping to the next cot. "Why don't you come back here after the press briefing? I might have a moment to catch up then. I'll treat you to some chewing gum and instant coffee."

My indignance was sticky in my throat, but I swallowed it like a bitter pill. "I'll see you later. Thanks."

It was hard to explain, even to my friends, how a slight like this could make me so afraid. Every day since China had entered the war, I had woken up worried that I might come home to find my family in a camp. Barbara didn't think there would be another internment campaign, because that was something she would never do. She didn't fully understand that people like Lucy were not uncommon, and that they made laws too. Lucy's disdain for me was another cut in a tender place that had long since scarred into a warning: When you look like the enemy in the land of the free, even your children can end up behind barbed wire.

20 October 1950
Dear Yun-Hee,

I left you a note on our door so that if you come home, you will know where to find me.

I didn't want to leave Pyongyang, but Jae-Min said the imperialists are going to bomb it. He still has friends at the train station from when he used to load cargo there, so he got two of the last tickets to Kanggye and barged into our house with them.

So pushy!

I went with him to Kanggye, but I shouldn't have. His mom and I haven't spoken since you left, and it is awkward between us. She knows I am still angry at her, but I am beneath her roof, so I have to be polite. She's got that same big mouth, and I am stuck listening to her rambling. How does she still have so much to say?

She is a slightly better cook now, but only slightly. Do you remember that time she tried to fry zucchini? They were so soggy! What a waste! To make hobak jeon you have to salt the zucchini first. Slice them evenly. Wait for them to sweat, then wipe away the water before you cook them. If you get lazy and skip this step—like Jae-Min's mom always does—you will have soggy hobak jeon and your kids will be as skinny as Jae-Min!

I want to go back to Pyongyang, but now the trains aren't running anymore.

Do you have children yet? You are twenty this year. Best not to start too late.

Mom

4

ADVANCE TO THE REAR

December 5, 1950

The press tent was as plain as any other, conspicuous only because of the officers waiting for the generals to arrive. It was close enough to the perimeter that refugee children waved to us. On the fringe of the base, thousands of Korean civilians had amassed, huddling around barrel fires, their faces red from the slapping wind. Women with blue lips breastfed infants along the snowbanks, some with possessions strapped to their backs or balanced on their heads. These people had carried their children in *podaegi* slings and followed the retreating Americans, hiking up icy roads for the mere chance of making it to South Korea.

At the tent, I presented my badge to the wiry and disgruntled press officer. Moisture from his breath had formed icicles on his beard. He read my name aloud, drawing out each syllable, so that "Eleanor" sounded foreign and "Chang" sounded like a buzz saw: *"Eh-lee-yah-nor Chaaaan-guh."*

I never knew that my name could sound so ugly.

He examined my badge and identification with the meticulous care of an art historian. "This doesn't look like you," he concluded, brushing droplets from his chin. "How old are you?"

"Twenty-eight," I replied.

"You look like a teenager."

"I'm twenty-eight," I said, forcing myself to speak at a lower volume and a higher timbre—a trick to sound more docile. "It says so on the ID that you're holding."

"Do you have anything else to prove you're with the *Global Tribune*?"

I held up my typewriter, which weighed nearly fifteen pounds. Only a journalist would bother lugging it around. "I don't have any other documents. I've never been asked for anything but my press badge before."

"Well, I've never seen you before," he said, glancing at his watch. "I'd certainly remember if I had. This is a highly confidential briefing. How come you've suddenly decided to show up now, when you haven't come to any of the others?"

"I've been to dozens of briefings," I said. "And I'm not just here for this briefing. I'm here to cover our retreat to Hungnam Port."

He stiffened. "We are not retreating. We are simply fighting in a different direction. In any case, there are no facilities for women, so you can't come along. It's just a fact."

"I'll just stay for the briefing, then," I said, as two male correspondents sauntered past us. They didn't even bother to show their press badges before entering the tent. "I came here with Captain George Miyashita, from the air force. He can vouch for me. If you ask him—"

"I don't care if you came with General Douglas MacArthur," said the press officer, squaring his hips. "Women aren't allowed on base for a reason. It's dangerous for you, and a distraction for us. Our boys have to focus on fighting, not flirting."

The reins on my temper snapped. "I am a correspondent with a press badge—an *American* correspondent—and I know the rules! There is no language or policy forbidding women journalists, you ignorant ass!" I knew I'd regret cursing at an officer, but I had swallowed so much anger earlier that I would have vomited if I'd had to hold in any more.

The press officer spat a glob that landed inches from my boot. "You don't have the right clearance," he sneered, snapping his fingers at a soldier to escort me away. "Take this lady back to the airstrip. Make sure she gets on the next flight out, for her own good!"

I fumed as a potbellied man with a beak nose and brown eyes lumbered forward. He tried to take my elbow, but I snatched it away. "I can walk by myself."

The potbellied soldier shrugged. When we were out of earshot, he said, "Don't mind him. We've had a wringer of a week, but my best friend growing up was a Chinese. I know y'all aren't all evil."

I wasn't sure if I had been rejected because of my ethnicity or because of my gender, but when there is shit blocking your path, does it really matter what kind it is? *Don't cry,* I told myself. *You cannot cry. Not just for you, but for every other woman who is going to try to do this job.*

Back at the airstrip, technicians were refueling George's plane and inserting the last of the patient litters into the slots along the walls of the hold. Dejected, I ripped my press badge from my neck and threw it on the ground. George was smoking with another pilot, but he excused himself when I plopped down onto a crate, my elbows on my knees and my cheeks in my hands. He had a thermos full of coffee, and a second cigarette tucked behind his ear.

"You look like you're going to cry," he said, bending over so that his face was close to mine.

"Of course I'm not going to cry," I snapped, even though I was on the brink of tears and it was taking a joint armada of pride and spite to prevent them from spilling over.

"Was it that bad?" He picked up my press badge and wiped off the snow.

"I don't want to talk about it." I was too embarrassed to complain, because George had told me so, and because what happened at the press tent could have been worse. Beyond the airstrip, soldiers were using bulldozers to lower their comrades into a mass grave that they had blasted open with dynamite. Did I have a right to be so upset about a briefing when, back home, there were families about to arrange funerals with no bodies?

That's not the point, a voice inside me cried. *I'm also American. These are my losses too.*

George eased himself onto my crate and handed me my badge and his coffee, a concentrated brew so thick that it made my tongue tingle. "It will get better, Ellie. Maybe not right away, but eventually this hostility will pass."

I sipped the bitter liquid and tucked my badge into my typewriter case. "What if we do go to war with China?" I asked. "The real China—Mao's China, not Chiang Kai-shek's China."

George sighed. "At least, this time around, it's harder to separate the 'good' Asians from the 'bad' Asians. You can't go by nationality, not with two Chinas and two Koreas. And here, at least our soldiers are used to seeing faces like ours. Do you know how hard it was for my father in France? He stuck out like a sore thumb."

I leaned back, the crate creaking under our weight. "Why would you even enlist, George, after everything that happened to your family?"

George tossed the butt of his cigarette onto the tarmac and reached for his lighter, which had the air force logo on it. "Because I'm not here for the government, or for the politicians. I'm here for my country, which is composed of people, most of whom are good, and ideals, most of which are honorable." With his gloves on, he struggled briefly with the flint wheel before a flame bloomed like a teardrop of light. He cupped his hand protectively and lit his next cigarette with one smooth puff. "And the scholarship money. I'm not going to lie. The scholarship money was very persuasive."

Wisps of smoke slithered from his nose and dove into an icy gust. George's family had lost everything during internment, and he had joined the air force straight from high school, with the promise that the government would pay for college after his service.

"Why are you here, Ellie?" he asked. "The salary can't be that good. I heard the benefits are pathetic too. And you have to deal with bullshit, on top of almost getting shot—or bombed, or worse."

I hesitated, my mouth sour from the coffee's acidity. My conviction was clear, but I was worried that it would sound hackneyed if I told George that I believed that I was fighting for a better world—not with arms, but with words—and that in my own way, I considered myself a soldier too.

"Because I believe in telling the truth," I finally said. "And I care about democracy. In order to make the right decisions, and to vote for the right representatives, people have to know what's happening. They deserve to have real information. I'll never be a general or a commander, but I don't mind being a small cog as long as I can keep moving. I have to do *something*."

George dabbed his smoldering cigarette. "I'm a small cog, Ellie. You, on the other hand, are not. People read what you write—thousands of people, probably. You're at least a medium cog. Maybe even a lever, or a pulley."

"Don't be ridiculous, George," I said, though inside, I thawed—a spark of spring. "I'm nothing right now, just someone who blew her whole morning getting kicked out of Antarctica." The snow had abated, but even with two layers of socks and gloves, my extremities were numb.

"You can still do something," said George. "Maybe not go barreling through the valley, but if you want, you can come with me to Hungnam. Scope out the preparations. Write about a ship, or something."

"You aren't going back to Tachikawa?"

"I am, but we're ferrying a squadron of jets to Hungnam. Maybe you can tag along."

I perked up. "Korean civilians are gathering in Hungnam too. Maybe I can interview some of them about what they've seen so far. I don't think any paper has published an article about refugees, at least not in detail." I couldn't speak Korean, but Japan had annexed Korea shortly after taking Taiwan, so many Koreans had been forced to learn Japanese.

"See? There you go," said George, brightly. "Make lemonade."

I smiled, though I always found that saying about making lemonade to be cruel. If life handed you lemons without sugar, all you could make was horribly sour juice. But since it was George saying it, I let it go. He was the type of person who searched for sweetness everywhere, on barren ledges and in life's darkest corners. Meanwhile, I was the type who wouldn't shut up about the sour. I had to warn people. I had to make them see—to show them what was real and raw, unsweetened and uncensored—for without truth, freedom was no more than an illusion, and choice a curated platter. The greatest enemy of democracy was not Communism; it was silence and ignorance, whether willfully undertaken or enforced by law.

That was why I chose to write about war. And that was why I was here, in Korea.

8 November 1950

Dear Yun-Hee,

When you were little, you were scared of thunder, and I used to tell you that it was just the old Gods punishing evil. As long as you were a good girl, thunder couldn't hurt you. I laughed then, but I'm scared of thunder too now. It sounds too much like bombs.

No two wars are the same, but this one reminds me of the last one. When I wake up, I hear footsteps even though they aren't there. I smell iron. I imagine that the Japanese are at our door again.

"You don't have a son," they said. "You don't have a son, so you must give us your daughter."

I hear it again, as I wipe my face.

"You don't have a son, so your daughter must serve."

I hear it loud, so I don't eat breakfast. Their voices make me sick. They won't shut up until I leave the house.

I take a long walk to get them to stop. I repeat my plea: "My daughter is my only child, and I have no living siblings. I beg you, let my daughter serve in a factory here. She is a hard worker. I beg you."

I bump into people because I am not paying attention. I am too busy reliving, rewatching them take you away to join the other girls in the truck.

You say your last words: "Don't worry, Mom. It will be okay."

That's when the voices stop. Instead, I hear truck doors slamming and the engine humming. I am so angry, I see blood. I am in such despair that everything looks like a noose. But then I remember that I cannot leave, or you will have no home to return to. And so I stay.

As long as I can, I will wait for you. Do not give up.

Mom

5

THE COLOR OF MOURNING

December 5, 1950

The plane was so crowded that four more patients sat in the aisle between the litters, which were stacked three to a column. Oxygen masks hung along the wall, and a medical technician named James Porciello was passing out graham crackers. While George scribbled a final tally in his notepad, I unpacked my typewriter from the copilot's seat and tucked a thick stack of envelopes inside my coat. Before boarding, I had stopped by the MASH to chat with Clara, who had asked me for a favor. She had collected letters from patients, some of whom had died under her care.

"I wrote all the addresses in," she had told me. "These last two are mine, one to my parents and one for my grandma. I know you're busy, but if you have time, do you think you could mail them for us?"

Love is abstract and intangible, but sometimes it takes on solid form. I had promised to send the letters out as soon as I touched down, and in turn Clara had told me that there had been more than ten thousand battle casualties, and an additional seven thousand casualties due to the cold alone. Though I wasn't able to go to the press briefing, I still had to send a story out this evening, so I typed these numbers as George jumped into his seat.

There was no door separating the cockpit from the cargo hold, and George swiveled to address the men behind him. "Just a few more hours and you'll have warm food and warm beds. We don't have nurses in flight today, but if you need help, Ellie Chang here will do her best."

My fingers slipped and hit the wrong key. "George!" I cried. "I have no medical training. I can't even keep plants alive, let alone people."

"I said you'd do your best, Ellie. It's a team effort."

The men chewed silently on graham crackers, licking crumbs off their cracked fingers, while Porciello sat with his legs crossed.

Mentally, I tried to wipe today's regrets off my slate, to have a clean canvas on which to imagine tomorrow. Though it hadn't been my first choice, I was getting excited about interviewing civilians in Hungnam. Correspondents reported facts, but every story passed through a human lens. Part of why I was drawn to journalism was because of the power to find and share stories—especially women's stories, which tended to fade when the majority of storytellers were men.

The plane's wheels rumbled as we built up speed, the litters rattling and the patients moaning. With a bellowing of our engine, we shot over pine trees bowed with snow, their tufted needles protruding like cowlicks.

From the back, a patient yelled, "Hey, Nurse! Griggs is having trouble breathing! He looks like he's going to faint."

George's eyes darted to the barometer on the control panel. "It's probably the altitude. I can slow our ascent. Ellie—"

"I'm going," I said, unbuckling my seat belt. I was still aghast that George had volunteered me, but I jumped over the men in the aisle and toward the litter, where Porciello was already crouched.

Griggs was probably a teenager, with arms and legs too long for his body, and a mix of pimples across his cheeks. His lips were blue, and his eyes had rolled back. Removing my gloves, I grabbed an oxygen mask—a guess at best—and passed it to Porciello, who snapped it on Griggs's face and squeezed the attached balloon. Porciello moved with a calm ease that reassured me that he must have done it before.

Thank goodness, I thought.

Griggs gasped, and Porciello pumped the chamber again.

Suddenly, George cursed, jerking the plane up so sharply that I rammed into Porciello and he lost his grip on the balloon. Another patient slid out of his litter, squawking, into the aisle.

"What the hell, George?" I yelled, staggering back to the cockpit.

George had his jaw clenched hard, a vein in his temple bulging. Ignoring me, he forced us higher, patients crying out as they clutched the sides of their litters. Someone retched, filling the cabin with the acrid odor of bile. When George swerved leftward, I finally saw the trails of smoke whirling around us like ribbons.

The air was thick with flak, arching in streaks of light before bursting. My head swam as we lurched again, my pulse spiking with the altimeter. I could hear the shells now, a subtle whistle barely audible over the cacophonous wind. From above, an American jet dove, its screaming engine cutting over our own plane's thrum. The rapid popping of machine-gun fire punctuated the slower, thumping spurts of flak.

George had his radio pressed against his lips, but I couldn't hear him. Terrified, I braced myself in the opening of the cockpit just as our plane bounced and began to spin, throwing me against a wall. One of the litters clattered from its holder, and smoke obscured the windows. In the dark, we hung in the air—only a few seconds before the plane began to plummet.

A scene from my childhood overtook my mind. It was the first time that I saw a sea lion at the wharf, obsidian beneath the frothy waves. Beads of water hung from its whiskers, and it grinned before barking—a sea dog.

My head slammed against the ceiling, but I clung to that memory like a child might cling to her mother's hand.

Patients howled. Someone in the hold prayed, shouting each word like a drill sergeant for God.

Our plane swung again, thrashing as George struggled with the yoke. When gravity yanked me back down, I landed on my belly, knocking my chin on the floor. Another litter jolted from its holder and whacked my temple, right beneath the brim of my hat. My vision went spotty as pain seared through my skull.

The C-47 was not equipped for combat, and it wouldn't take much of an impact for us to crash. I tried not to think of shattered wings and broken propellers.

Sea lions, I told myself. *Think of sea lions. Think of home.* A gray house with a flat roof. An atrium with my dad's good-luck talismans and my mom's excessive collection of orchids. A child's bike that my mom had held on to, because one day we might need it again. Two giant dog bowls, not because we had dogs but because we wanted burglars to think that we did. *Home.*

Gradually, the plane stopped pitching. There was a clunking sound along the right side, by the wing, but we subsided to a gentle bounce. Everyone seemed to exhale simultaneously, and I had to blink hard before my eyes refocused.

The windows were clear, but the sky was hazy. Graham crackers and oxygen masks were scattered across the floor, alongside chunks of vomit, which were also smeared on the walls. Several patients lay crumpled at the back of the hold. Most of the men had managed to stay strapped into their litters, and they peeked out like frightened caterpillars. One flicked through the beads of his rosary, his thumb sliding mechanically.

My face dripped with sweat as I wobbled back to Griggs. He still had his mask on, but his arms were splayed at his sides, his face puce. Even without medical training, something about his eyes, partially open and his lids lopsided, told me that if I checked for his pulse I'd feel no beat.

Porciello wiped the corners of his mouth before bending down to pick up a litter. A Black soldier with a scar on his cheek and with his arm in a sling took the other side of the litter while I scampered to support patients' heads.

In the cockpit, George's fingers tapped across the control panel. "We're down an engine," he called out. "But I can manage with one. We're losing altitude, but I think we can coast out of these mountains. As soon as we see a field, I'll do a belly landing." He spoke casually, as though it were easy.

To stabilize myself, I kept my hand against a wall, and I gasped when my fingers left red prints. Someone was bleeding. Whirling back to the hold, I scanned each man for scrapes on their skin, or dark, wet patches on their clothes. When I wiped my damp brow and my palm came back scarlet, I realized that the blood was coming from me. I touched my temple where the litter handle had hit, and I winced. My hair was sticky, and my skin had split into a deep, stinging cut.

"Jesus!" exclaimed George when he saw me. "Are you okay?"

"It's not as bad as it looks," I said, clawing my way to the copilot's seat. I should have searched for a first aid kit, but I sputtered when I saw that the footwell was empty. "What happened to my typewriter?"

"Here it is," said George. With his chin, he gestured to his lap, where my typewriter was wedged between his thighs. "This thing is like a bowling ball. It socked me right in the gut."

"Oh, I'm so sorry!" I pulled the typewriter from him and cradled it like an infant. "You didn't have to keep holding it, though."

"Yes, I did. Otherwise it could have broken a window—or my skull!"

"Sorry," I muttered again, opening the case to check it for damage. I tested each key tenderly.

"Ellie, is that really your priority now?" asked George.

The landscape below was rocky, but agricultural plots were beginning to appear, flat grids divided by fences and footpaths. "Well, I don't have anything else to do," I said.

"Pray."

"For what?"

"Our survival."

"I thought you said you were going to do a belly landing."

"I am, but I've never done one before!" Biting his lower lip, George turned us toward a snow-covered field as white and flat as a marble slab. "I've had training, but that's not the same. If we die, are you really going to spend your last moments tinkering with your typewriter?"

"All right, all right!" I shut the case and shoved my typewriter underneath my seat. My heart was thumping again. Both of my parents were Buddhists, so I knew some blessings, but over the years I had seen too much hurt and read too much war to believe in the power of prayer. "Do you really think we're going to die?"

George didn't answer.

We'll be okay, I thought. Maybe I had more confidence in George than he did in himself. "We're not going to die," I announced, answering my own question. "We're coming out of this alive, and then we're going to fly a jet to Hungnam."

George swallowed and nodded, his eyes, black like eight balls, locked on the field below. His gloved knuckles were rigid peaks on the yoke as our plane thundered over a set of railroad tracks and past farmland and houses with sloping thatched roofs. For the Chinese, white was a color of mourning, and the snowy ground stretched out to catch us like a shroud. I hadn't thought to pray, but checking my typewriter had been my own stubborn manifestation of hope—of faith that I was still going to need it.

Because I'm going to survive this.

I had no specific scripture, but this conviction was a religion of sorts. I believed in fate, and I believed in myself. For me, that was all that made sense. For me, that was enough.

---

23 November 1950
Dear Yun-Hee,

I am encouraged when I hear about women who are not married but still have a good life. I know it might be difficult for you to find a husband, but remember three things.

First, your husband does not have to know everything about your past.

Second, marriages work better when the man loves the woman more than she loves him.

Third, there are more jobs for women now than there used to be, so if no one wants to marry you, that's okay.

It was hard for me to raise you alone, but it was possible!

I know you don't like talking about your father, but there is something I never told you. All your life, you believed that your father left us, but truthfully, I was the one who left him. I am the one who decided that you'd grow up in a factory compound instead of the pretty house you deserved.

Forgive me for lying. I had been hoping to tell you when you were older.

The other woman was pregnant, and she had a son. He was born a few months before you, but I knew about him early on. That's why you have such a bad temper. In my belly, you soaked in my rage.

The other woman and her son were going to move in with us. She was going to be a concubine, but mother of son outranks wife, and you and I would have been second-class in our own home.

Everyone said I'd curse myself for being so brash, but times were supposed to be changing. I never regretted leaving them, until after the Kempeitai took you. I can't help thinking that if you had a brother for the war, then you'd be with me now.

Is it terrible that I wish you grew up with a boy, so we could have fed him to the Japanese instead?

Maybe, but I want you to know that I would have stayed with your father if that meant I could save you. I would have lived with that woman if that meant that I could have kept you.

Mom

6

CRUEL ANGELS

December 5, 1950

We hit the field with an explosive crunch that knocked my teeth together, bobbing as we careened across a solid layer of ice. The snow bunched up in front of the plane, slowing our motion to a bumpy glide. Slush piled on the windshield, then slid off in a single sheet as dramatically as a curtain opening.

There were scattered applause and whooping for George, who slouched forward when we ground to a halt.

Steep mountains encircled us like sentries, framing a frozen river. Icicles glinted, iridescent along branches and wooden fences.

My throat was parched as I stumbled back to the hold. Griggs was dead, and I chewed on that fact like a bitter cud. If he was going to die anyway, then we might as well have flown higher, out of cannon range.

You can't think like that, I chided myself. *You do the best you can with the information you have.* I had my own slogans, like Band-Aids that I slapped on when I sensed myself wading into despair. There were days when I felt like I was held together by little strips of nothing, a mess of Band-Aids just trying to make it to midnight. No matter what you did, sometimes there would be a what-if that haunted you. Griggs was simply one of those ghosts.

The Black man with the sling, named Henry Carsons, was gently shaking the men who had their eyes closed. "We have to get everyone out of here," he said. "And we better go soon."

George put the radio back into its holder. "No, we have to stay with the plane. The rescue mission won't be able to find us if we leave."

"We came down slow, though," Carsons warned. "I bet the Chinese had eyes on us too. They know where we are, and they're going to find us before the rescue mission does."

Another soldier in a litter propped himself up on his elbows. "I'm with Carsons. They're gonna be on us like piranhas."

"Protocol requires us to stay with the plane," said George, firmly. "I've called Air Control. Rescue is on its way, but if any of you want to take your chances out there, be my guest. Just know that we're locking these doors as soon as they close."

Carsons massaged his arm and leaned against a wall, careful to avoid the foul streaks of vomit. Nobody left, but most of the men could barely stand, let alone walk. I stretched my tense shoulders while George stared up at the sky, his eyes catching on every sliver of cloud that resembled a plane. The absence of fighter jets meant that we were away from the front lines, but the silence from above was disconcerting.

I looked more carefully out the window now. A few hundred yards away, there was a raised road teeming with travelers flowing in both directions. Women mostly wore long skirts in plain colors like white, blue, or gray, while men wore a mix of traditional robes and Western dress. Oxen, laden with supplies, lowed beside their owners. Some children pointed at our plane, but most adults only gave us a cursory glance before hurrying to distance themselves. Wherever we were, it was probably closer to sea level, and slightly warmer, than the Chosin Reservoir.

We were all so focused on the blue horizon, bitten by jagged peaks, that no one was monitoring the road, until horns blared, urgently and repeatedly. Travelers scattered to the snowbanks as a convoy of jeeps with a hodgepodge of artillery jutting from their cargo beds rumbled toward us. The soldiers appeared to be Korean but were bundled up in the long ponchos issued by the American marines.

My heart swelled with relief. It was odd that our rescue would come by truck, but at least it was here. In the third jeep, two Caucasian men dressed in civilian clothing were seated with Chinese soldiers in white, quilted uniforms.

That was strange. Were we taking prisoners of war?

I squinted as the convoy stopped. Travelers' shouting echoed over the snow, and I didn't need to look at George or the others to know that something was wrong. The air around me had changed, and I could feel their terror like it was heat. Beneath my sleeves, every hair on my arms stood on end.

From afar, it was difficult to discern small military insignias, but as the jeeps approached I spotted details that did not match those of any of the UN troops' uniforms.

"Soviets," Carsons whispered. "Reds."

"That's American equipment, though," said another soldier. "Those jeeps might even be from the reservoir. The weapons and jackets too."

Outrage flared within me, augmenting my fear. The Communist soldiers must have pulled ponchos from dead marines and layered them over their own uniforms for warmth. They must have been as unprepared for this winter—the coldest in forty years—as our own troops had been, but this theft felt personal, and more egregious than picking up abandoned grenades. How many naked Americans lay exposed along that cursed reservoir?

The dead don't matter, I told myself. It was the shivering men in this hold that we had to think about.

Smoke puffed from the jeeps' exhaust pipes. A North Korean soldier with a square jaw and an angular nose stepped out of the first truck, slamming the door with swagger.

"Do we have any guns?" asked Carsons, as the patient with the rosary whimpered.

Communist soldiers wearing our clothing stomped through the field. Some of them had stolen boots, but several wore cloth sneakers, which were already soaked. Their noses were inflamed and streaming.

"Or grenades?" asked another man. "If we're going down, we're taking as many of them as we can with us."

No one answered, because everyone in the plane knew that we had nothing—no weapons, and nowhere to hide.

The two Soviets remained in their vehicle, because Stalin, despite funding and advising the KPA, was stringent about avoiding combat with Americans. Until now, I hadn't seen any Soviet officers in Korea at all, which raised a terrifying question. Just how deep in enemy territory had we landed?

George was still holding the radio receiver. "Do we have anything white?" he asked.

"Bandages and gauze," Porciello replied.

Fear overtook my outrage as our enemies formed a crooked semicircle around our plane, carrying bazookas that could punch right through our metal doors.

Though the temperature was below freezing, George unbuttoned his coat and shed every layer until he could pull off his eggshell-colored undershirt. Goose bumps erupted like pox on his pale skin, and he stretched out his undershirt and held it up to the windshield—a white flag, still warm from his body.

Outside, the square-jawed soldier gestured for us to disembark. His cotton coat was torn at the neck, and his fingers bled around the nail beds.

George kept his undershirt raised and said, "You all stay here and update Air Control. I'll go out and see if I can negotiate with them." He hurried to dress, leaving his coat unbuttoned. With his hand on the door, he pleaded at the sky, with desperate eyes, for armed angels to descend and save us.

"I'm coming too," I announced.

"No, Ellie. It's not safe. I need them to understand that we have rights as prisoners of war—or stall them until rescue comes. I can't have you getting in the way."

"But I can speak Mandarin!"

"I don't need you to. The Koreans speak Japanese."

"Not all of them do! Many people outside of the cities never learned it. You won't be able to do anything if you can't communicate with them. Let me come with you as backup, please. I'll be quiet until you tell me to."

George scoffed, but I was right and he knew it. "Fine," he said. "But we're going to have to swallow shit, so dial yourself down, okay?"

"Okay," I said. I wanted to point out that since I was always swallowing some type of shit—whether it was from my bosses or from persnickety commanders in the field—I never lived my life at full volume, but I zipped my lips and stood up to follow him.

Without a ladder, it was a long jump from the cockpit, but George and I took the plunge. We landed in knee-deep snow, our arms up in submission, fingers spread wide. My sleeves slipped, and the wind nibbled my naked wrists before weaseling through my jacket. I was conscious of Clara's letters against my chest, and of the promise that hung over me. At Hagaru-ri, I had never thought to write my own final message, and now I regretted my confidence.

When did I last speak to my family? Was it weeks ago? I'd always said that I didn't have time, but it had been there, sparse like pocket change—available if I had been more organized.

The Communist soldiers pointed their burp guns at us, and the one with the square jaw stepped forward, barking orders in Korean.

George bowed with his back straight like a rod, inclining nearly ninety degrees. His hands were above his head when he said, in Japanese, "I am very sorry. I cannot understand you. I am an American person, not a Korean person."

Square Jaw flinched as though George had made a lewd joke. The other soldiers murmured in a mix of Korean and Mandarin, and I clung on to the Chinese words, trying to decipher their meaning through the chatter. They were wondering "what" George really was, because in this war there were alliances but there were no in-betweens.

Clearing his throat, George continued. "These men are very much hurt. No fighting. We want to go to the hospital. Where is the hospital?"

I cringed. George's Japanese had always been worse than

mine, though I didn't recall its being this stunted. He was scared, and with the soldiers glowering at us, I was too, but even with nerves frayed, I was fluent enough to speak more eloquently than this.

Should I take over? I asked myself. *Will I get in the way if I do?*

A crease appeared between Square Jaw's brows, as deep as a cut. "Ohhh," he said, drawing out the vowel, as if savoring its hollow vibration. "*Ilbon-sekki.*"

George glanced at me questioningly, but the only Korean words I understood were "*annyeong*" and "*gamsahabnida,*" "hello" and "thank you." I had no idea what "*ilbon-sekki*" meant, but other Koreans repeated it, a scattered echo that sounded like a chant.

Finally, someone translated for the Chinese soldiers. "*Riben gou.*"

Japanese dog. It was a slur. George had angled himself between me and the Communists, but I pushed past him. "No!" I said, in Mandarin. "He's American. He's not Japanese. He's American!"

Was being American better? The Korean War was only a few months old, and possibly a small flame compared to decades of Japanese occupation?

"We aren't combatants," I continued, my raised arms sore. "This is a medical evacuation mission. Please. Our plane is damaged and we're waiting for aid. Please, have mercy."

The Chinese soldiers blinked at me, confused. One of them translated for the Koreans, and Square Jaw listened, bemused. With a sneer, he aimed his pistol at George's glistening forehead and said, in accented Japanese, "Get down. Both of you."

My legs buckled, but it was hard to kneel in so much snow. George and I complied as best we could, my hands trembling, my calves stinging as they sank into slush.

Dear Mom and Dad, I thought, *I'm sorry that I didn't write sooner, and that I didn't write often. I always knew this was a possibility, so I can't say that I'm surprised.*

"What is a Japanese man doing with a Chinese woman?" Square Jaw asked, stumbling on some of the words.

"We are both American," said George, in Japanese.

"Yes!" I added, still in Mandarin. "We are the same thing!"

If I die here, I want you to know that I love you. I want you to live well, to be safe, and to be happy.

"What country are your parents from?" asked Square Jaw. "What are they?"

"Our parents are American too," I said. George's were born and raised in California, and mine had become citizens earlier this year.

"Don't lie!" barked Square Jaw. "Japanese are evil, but traitor *chinilpa* are worse."

Try not to be sad. I'm sure we will find a way to meet again.

With all my love, Ellie.

"I'll ask you once more," said Square Jaw. "Are you a Japanese whore? Or are you a whore for the Japanese? Answer me!" When he moved the gun from George's forehead and pressed it to mine, the icy barrel plunged me into panic.

"American!" I squealed, a sound like glass cracking. "I'm not a whore. I'm American!"

Beside me, George shouted, "She's Chinese. Chinese, all Chinese!"

"Bitch!" cried Square Jaw. I thought he was going to fire, but he whipped his gun back to George and dug the barrel beneath George's chin. "And you, you dog? What are you?"

George kept his lips sealed in a tight line. In that moment, he no longer looked afraid, but I couldn't tell what he was thinking or feeling. Was he incensed? At them? Was he disappointed? At me? At life?

A single shot exploded, and George crumpled as though every bone in his body had snapped.

Someone was shrieking, but it wasn't me. My ears were ringing, but I had fallen into a well of silence, thinking about the little badges that my parents had bought during World War II—badges that read, I AM A CHINESE. While our government rounded up our Japanese neighbors, my family wore those badges like religious insignia.

The sight of George, broken in the snow, his arms still up and his brains soft and pink, was too much. Tears stung my cheeks, the salt raw on my chapped lips. When I found the courage to lift my head, I expected to stare down the barrel of a gun, but instead there was a woman in front of me, the back of her white skirt embroidered with columns of yellow chrysanthemums.

Was this how death worked?

I had always assumed that death personified would be a tall man in black—the grim reaper—but it made sense that I'd see someone who looked like my mom: short and Asian, with an apricot mouth and an upturned nose. This woman wore a padded gray coat and carried an embroidered satchel over her shoulder. Her tadpole-shaped eyes had long creases in the corners, and gray and black hair poked out from underneath her fur hat.

She screamed something in Korean, chilling enough for the North Korean soldiers to murmur in alarm. Square Jaw scowled.

A man in a quilted uniform, with a bulbous nose and bushy brows, interpreted for the Chinese. I wasn't sure what his ethnicity was, but many Koreans had fled to China during the Japanese occupation. While some had returned after Japan's surrender, others had fought for Mao's army, and then joined the KPA as seasoned veterans of China's civil war.

Confused, the interpreter said, "The auntie is . . . very angry. She wants High Comrade Jung to release this . . . child?"

I touched my temple again, where my wound was still unbandaged. Did I have a concussion?

Turning to me, the woman smiled. Her words, though incomprehensible, were gentle and reassuring. She swiveled back to Square Jaw—High Comrade Jung—and then the two of them began to argue. The interpreter struggled to keep up, and stammered something unintelligible. His Mandarin had a thick accent, but it didn't seem like he was fluent in Korean either.

"This, uh . . . this girl is a Japanese prisoner," explained the interpreter. "Taken and . . . drafted during the . . . War to Resist Japanese Aggression. It is not her fault that she is a prostitute. Japan started a war and forced this girl to go to China."

Now I could tell which soldiers were Chinese and which were Korean by whom they directed their attention to, but I still couldn't make any sense of this conversation. My anxiety thrummed as the woman shouted, but the interpreter just repeated insults and slurs.

A Chinese man crossed his arms and said, "So these two ladies know each other?"

"Can't be," said another Chinese soldier. "This girl isn't even Korean."

"You don't have to be Korean to be friends with a Korean. Just look at us."

"Well, it's different when you're fighting together."

I crouched lower in the snow, hyperventilating. The icy air

was burning my lungs as the Chinese debated "what" I really was. *I'm Chinese,* I wanted to say, but it felt like I'd be betraying George if I did—like I'd be agreeing that he deserved to die and I deserved to live.

"Ahh," said the interpreter, after listening carefully. "High Comrade Jung says that Auntie is mistaken. This woman here is a prostitute for the Americans, not a prostitute for the Japanese."

I bristled at the fact that they both seemed to agree that I was a prostitute, but I also understood that this woman was trying to help me—maybe to cover for me so I could escape. But why? She was a complete stranger, yet here she was, between me and automatic guns that could fire nine hundred rounds a minute.

Chest puffed, the Korean woman stomped her foot, her rubber work boots peeking from beneath the hem of her skirt as she scolded High Comrade Jung, shrilly and scathingly.

The interpreter said, "Auntie says that this girl is a slave. This girl belongs to her. The Japanese dogs stole this girl from her sixty years—wait, no, six years ago—and if we take this girl now, we are as bad as the Japanese dogs."

I shuddered again at that slur. Blood had spread beneath the remnants of George's head and pooled in the indentations of his footprints.

"I thought slavery was illegal in Korea," said one of the Chinese soldiers. "Wasn't it banned years ago?"

The interpreter kept using the word "slave," which surely was a translation error, but the woman had both her hands slanted toward her chest like she was making some kind of claim on me.

"The government can ban whatever they want," said another Chinese soldier, "but people can still do it."

High Comrade Jung lowered his gun, examining me with a

mix of pity and disdain, like I was both frail and radioactive. I knew nothing about slavery in Korea, but it disheartened me that this well-dressed woman might be fighting so hard for me simply because she thought I was her property.

Narrowing his eyes, Comrade Jung asked me a question in Korean that might as well have been gibberish.

My confusion magnified my terror, and I began to weep anew. Sniffling with my head down, I waited for the interpreter, but he too had paused.

Huffing, the woman flung her arms around me. She was close enough that I could see that one of her molars was missing. With her chin on my head, she snapped fiercely at High Comrade Jung.

The interpreter inhaled sharply. "Auntie says, if we want this girl, it will have to be through her own dead body!"

Beside me, the woman took on a feral stance, her shoulders hunched and her fists curled tight, one leg forward like she was ready to lunge. Her ferocity was astonishing. I couldn't believe she would stick her neck out for me and bluff with such bravado, property or not.

Or perhaps this is death, I thought, swinging back to doubt, *a dream before my brain shuts down, to ease the transition between this world and the next.* My uncertainty was dizzying as I hovered between gratitude for a random Good Samaritan and fear that I had lost my mind.

High Comrade Jung began a retort, but one of the Soviet advisors, with a blond mustache, shouted in Russian. From the jeep, the advisor pointed to the sky before holding both hands up, seeming annoyed and perplexed.

There was a domino effect of interpretation, as one of the Koreans shouted back in Russian, another explained in Korean, and the Chinese interpreter finally said, "American devils are coming. How can we waste our time arguing over a prostitute when there are combatants in that plane?"

"They're not combatants anymore!" I interjected. "They're wounded men who need care!"

The Korean woman pinched me, her fingers biting through Barbara's coat like pliers. She muttered something, but the Communists had boiled into a mélange of languages—instructions in Russian, orders in Korean, and arguments in Mandarin. In the chaos, I could no longer follow what was happening.

Finally, High Comrade Jung spat and said, "*Gah!*"

The Korean woman's grip tightened on my arm, with such force that I almost lost my balance.

"*Gah!*" High Comrade Jung repeated angrily. "*Bbali!*"

Trembling, the Korean woman whispered to me, and I glanced desperately at the interpreter, but found him stone-faced. I braced myself for the worst, but then the woman snapped forward at the waist.

"Oh!" I cried, thinking that she had fallen, but when she rose and inclined again, I realized that she was bowing—fervently and repeatedly, like a bird pecking at the ground.

"*Gamsahabnida!*" she exclaimed, starting to sob. "*Gamsahabnida!*" Slapping her hand over her heart, she laughed with her mouth wide-open, an unhinged and guttural sound. It unsettled me, but not more than the Communist soldiers did, with their legs apart and their burp guns lifted.

The woman pulled me up to standing. "*Gahja,*" she said, wiping her eyes with the back of her glove. "*Bbali! Bbali!*"

I was uncertain, but she tugged me toward her like I was a kite that she had to fight the wind for. For the first time since she appeared, I began to wonder if she was unwell—if it wasn't I who had lost my mind, but she who had arrived without hers.

She is just acting, I assured myself as the Communist soldiers stepped aside. Without looking back at George or the plane, I allowed the Korean woman to lead me away, my legs still numb.

The Soviet advisors gave us a stern nod, their eyes pebble gray, while we traipsed around their jeep and onto the frozen road. I was a willing puppet, raising one foot after the other to join the throng of travelers, one more drop in a frantic stream.

What was going to happen to the patients? And where was this woman taking me? I wondered if I should try to escape from her now that we had distanced ourselves, but I didn't know where else to go in this bitter cold. She was walking as though she had a train to catch, patting my arm as we sped ahead of everyone else. I leaned heavily on her, and though she panted from the exertion of carrying me, that didn't stop her from talking, a narrative long like a ribbon that unrolled from her gut. Occasionally she paused and waited for me to reply, and when I didn't, she only squeezed my hand, smiled, and said, "*Genchana.*"

The road was clamorous, with slapping steps and grumbling wheels, and we didn't make it far before the sputtering of machine-gun fire cut through it all. It was the signature *braaap* that gave burp guns their moniker, and though I heard no screams, I knew the sound of lead against metal. Everyone around us halted, as though time itself had surrendered, people's eyes widening until their irises became small, quivering dots.

The Korean woman, however, only quickened her pace, and whispered, "*Genchana. Genchana.*" She repeated that word, a hypnotic mantra. Within my head, I had my own silent song: *I'm sorry. I'm sorry.* I felt traitorous for leaving, selfish for living. If she was bringing me to death, perhaps I deserved it.

Several paths split from the main road, and when the woman took me around a sharp turn, I held on to her and climbed away from the crowd, into a dense pine forest. With my boots clomping on ice, I lumbered between tree trunks, their whorls like mouths that caught the snow. Branches, evergreen, swallowed the sunlight in their outstretched canopies. In these woods there were no creatures in sight, not even birds with their varied warbles. Only the metal jets had wings, and they roared unchallenged.

---

1 December 1950
Dear Yun-Hee,

There was a time when you would call "Mom" incessantly. Mom, I'm hungry. Mom, I'm cold. Mom, I tripped. Mom, Mom, an endless loop with no reprieve. Look at this, Mom. I found a coin, Mom. Mom, I want new shoes.

There were days when I just didn't want to hear it, but now it has been a long time since anyone has called me Mom.

In that silent world, I often wonder, am I still a mom? Or can I only say, "I was a mom?"

7

EMMA

December 5, 1950

The Korean woman noticed my unease as we slogged farther up the mountain, where the temperature dropped once more. It was so steep that someone had built a wooden railing, and everything was covered with ice. Before we began our climb, she patted her chest.

"Emma," she said, introducing herself. "Emma. *Genchana*. Emma *yoh-gissoh*."

I wasn't sure if that was her real name. In the South, some Koreans had chosen English names for themselves, which were easier for the Americans to pronounce. Perhaps "Emma" was hers?

Though a name was not a soul, there was something human about having one, and a connection came from sharing it. Surely this wasn't how a mistress would treat her servant. It reassured me that she was indeed trying to help, and whatever slave story she had spouted had been part of an act.

"Emma," I repeated. Then I patted my chest too. "Ellie."

After what had happened to George, I was too afraid to attempt Japanese again, so I stuck with gestures. It was unclear whether she had understood me, or whether she even cared to know who I was, but I wanted to tell her, more for myself than for anyone else. Remembering one's own name was a marker of sanity, wasn't it?

On the slippery path, I stepped in the oval wells of other people's footprints. Snow built up on my pants and boots, sucking me down, so that I had to throw my back into each stride. At one narrow turn, Emma and I had to walk single file, but she never let go of me. My knuckles ached from her grip.

The sun had dipped below a peak, the sky dimming to a steel-toned blue. Houses appeared on the mountainside, stubborn huts with wooden walls and thatched roofs. Under Japanese rule, Korea had been functionally divided, with industries and mines in the North and agriculture in the South. After the country split at the 38th parallel, the North was cut off from its food source, while parts of the South lost their electricity and irrigation. People in this village seemed to have demarcated gardens, and perhaps they had adapted to growing their own crops.

Emma urged me onward until we reached a house that was slightly larger than the others, with a slate roof, a detached shed, and a covered porch.

Was this where she lived? It wasn't as opulent as I expected, given her ornate skirt. Emma unlatched the heavy wooden door, worn with age. The hinges screeched, and I balked, uncertain of what might be waiting inside. Police? From what I'd heard, the North Korean authorities didn't just make arrests; they made entire families disappear.

Emma shoved me past the threshold, stomping to dislodge

the snow from her rubber shoes. There were several pairs of men's and women's footwear lining a wooden hallway that led to three rooms and a kitchen. Warm air caressed my face with such tenderness that my knees grew weak.

Succumbing to the seduction of shelter, I pulled off my gloves and unlaced my boots, breaking fragments of ice from the leather. Some type of heat was channeled up from the stone floor, and I closed my eyes so I could savor the warmth through my soles.

The house was pungent with garlic and a hint of smoke. At the entrance, there was a poster of Kim Il-Sung, and discoloration was on the walls where other pictures might have hung. Cautiously, I surveyed the room that was closest to us. It was sparse, with only a bookshelf, a cabinet, and mats over the oilpaper-lined floor. In the center, there was a *kotatsu*—a heated table with a blanket—and two men, one Emma's age and one closer to mine, who were seated at it with their legs crossed. Both wore thick knit sweaters, and the younger one quickly tucked his book under the blanket and folded his hands. While the older man seemed inquisitive, the younger one was rigid with disapprobation.

Were they Emma's husband and son?

Emma removed her hat, her heavy bun flopping onto her shoulder like a skein of yarn. When she unfurled her hair, it tumbled to her waist, jet-black with a streak of silver on the right side. She greeted the men exuberantly before repinning it.

In the kitchen, dishware clattered, and another woman scurried out. She was taller and possibly older than Emma, with a graceful neck, deep-set eyes, and a wide forehead. Her hair was mostly white and pulled into a tight bun, and her face was smooth, with high cheekbones and a prominent nose. Though she was well-groomed, her clothing was baggy on her skeletal frame.

Emma draped her arm around my shoulder, grinning as

though she had brought me to a surprise party. She gestured to the other three and began to introduce them, saying each name like it was a question. "*Moksanim?*" The older man, with a strong chin, large nostrils, and wire-rimmed glasses, stood up. "*Sahmonim* . . . Imo?" She was the woman by the kitchen, and she grasped Moksanim's arm, staring at the air force logo on my jacket like it was a tarantula. "Jae-Min?" The younger man towered over the couple, and though thin, he was muscular. From his resemblance to Imo—the same deep-set eyes, high cheekbones, and nose—I guessed that the three of them were a family.

How did Emma fit in with them?

Emma prodded me, but I wasn't sure what she wanted. Was I supposed to say something?

"*Genchana,*" Emma said. Facing the three, she launched into a monologue in Korean. Moksanim's lips scrunched with worry, but Imo's curled with anger. Jae-Min's face paled to match the shirt collar that protruded over his sweater.

I squirmed. Did Emma tell them I was American? Was that why they were so upset?

Imo was the first to speak, softly but firmly. The two men chimed their agreement, but Emma put her hands on her hips, her words louder and faster than before.

It was dangerous for civilians here to be associated with their "enemy," but I couldn't explain that I wasn't with the military without confirming that I was a foreigner. My cavernous stomach grumbled, and my soaked legs were weak from the hike here. The warmth that had initially seemed so welcoming made me wary when the four of them began to argue, just like Emma had with High Comrade Jung.

I tried to deduce what was happening, nervous that I was akin to a frog that had leaped into a pot of water and those around me were turning up the heat. Imo and the men kept shaking their heads, while Emma's cheeks flushed. I edged toward the door, sweat collecting in the underarms of my coat. Once night fell, the cold outside would be lethal, but these people could be scheming to murder me, for all I knew.

Suddenly, Emma stepped in front of me, like she had with the Communist soldiers, and she put her arms up, a fragile but threatening barricade. It seemed that Emma was still trying to protect me, but she was outnumbered—and even though she was the best dressed, the way she bowed to the other two adults indicated that she had less authority.

The others probably want to report me, I thought, which was not so different from killing me outright. Americans who had been taken as prisoners of war were forced to march to camps up north, and many died in transit.

Damn it, Ellie, think! I had to get out of here, but to where?

I shouldn't have followed this crazy stranger in the first place. This was my punishment for leaving the plane, and for leaving those men. I thought about George, and how he had kept my typewriter clamped between his knees; I couldn't picture his face without smelling his blood. For the rest of my life I would torture myself, not with the image of his brains but with his last, inscrutable expression before the gunshot sounded.

"Aniyo!" Jae-Min roared. His outburst was so startling that I jumped back and his elders recoiled. Whatever he was bellowing must have crossed a line, because Emma turned a deeper shade of plum. With a strangled cry, she flew at Jae-Min, slapping his chest, her arms circling like windmills as she began to bawl.

Moksanim tried to restrain Emma, but she wiggled from his grasp.

Jae-Min lowered his head and did nothing to block Emma's

blows, but Imo charged in front of her son, shrieking with bulging eyes. When Imo raised her hand to strike, I rushed between the two women. I couldn't let Emma get hurt because of me—not after she had saved me, and not with the guilt that I already carried. Covering my face, I braced for the sting of Imo's bony fingers, but Jae-Min's arm lashed out like a whip.

He snatched his mother's wrist. *"Hajima-seyo, Eomma-ni."*

Imo scolded him and struggled to pry his fingers loose, but she wilted at the sheen of tears in his eyes.

Jae-Min let her limp wrist go. *"Eomma-ni,"* he said, and then continued in Korean that sounded strained. Emma blubbered despondently, and Jae-Min was on the verge of losing his composure too. I concentrated hard on his words, as though I might comprehend them through willpower alone. At first, I thought that he was telling Imo not to hit Emma, but he also seemed to be calling Imo "Emma," like that was her name too.

Did I mishear? Was "Emma-ni" the same as "Emma"?

When I focused on that word, I began to hear it clearly. Sometimes Jae-Min said *"Oh-mah."* Sometimes it was *"Uh-mah."* Regardless of the variations, I cursed my own idiocy when I finally understood.

"Emma"—or *"Eomma"*—was not a name at all. It was a title. It meant "Mom."

Chinese call their mothers *"Ma"* or *"Niang."* I had never had any reason to think about the Korean equivalent, but when Emma sank to her knees and wailed, anguished and unrelenting, I felt awful. Somehow, this woman had believed that I was her daughter, and I had failed to correct her.

Imo shot me a blistering glare, her tar-black eyes so potent that my insides shriveled. She shoved me aside so she could rub

Emma's back, which she did contemptuously, as though comfort was a rare commodity.

Moksanim kneaded the bridge of his nose, where his glasses had left two dents. He muttered something before asking me a stern-sounding question. Under his gaze I shrank further, but then he tapped his temple and pointed to my head.

At first, I thought he was calling me stupid, but then I remembered my wound. I had completely forgotten about it since leaving the crash site. Though it no longer hurt, blood had trickled down to my jaw and stained my coat's fur collar. Dried flakes, like slivers of rust, peeled off when I touched my cheek. I must have been a ghastly sight.

Moksanim repeated his question, more loudly this time. Emma hiccuped and began to reply, but he shushed her with a brusque word.

I wasn't sure what was safe to admit. On the wall, Kim Il-Sung leered forebodingly, as if he were sentencing me to death. Mortified, I plucked out the Korean words I knew and forced them together like mismatched puzzle pieces. *"Hanguk . . . aniyo."*

Everyone's expressions, including Emma's, withered. I had meant to say that I couldn't speak Korean, but Imo sneered, and Jae-Min blushed.

Moksanim, however, chuckled. Unlike the others, he recovered quickly from his initial shock. "So you are indeed American," he said, in English. His *R*s were slightly muted, and he lingered on his vowels, but he seemed confident with the language. "You speak through your nose, like a Westerner. You sound like the missionaries who used to live here, when I was a boy."

I licked my chapped lips, afraid to respond in case this was a trick. With a keener eye, I examined Moksanim again. Unlike his son, he was only a few inches taller than me, the same height as his wife, and fit for his age. He carried himself like someone who was accustomed to deference—the kind that was earned, not seized.

"Who are you?" asked Moksanim. "And why are you here?"

I wanted to ask him the same thing. As a Chinese American, I had grown up holding ties to different countries, but lately I'd felt like I was on the verge of being drawn and quartered. Was this man similarly a person between worlds?

"I'm Eleanor Chang," I finally whispered, bracing for condemnation. "Ellie Chang. I'm a correspondent. I was riding with a medical evacuation mission, but our plane got shot down and we made an emergency landing nearby."

Emma's eyes and cheeks were smeared with tears, and she pressed her hands to her chest like I had smashed it.

Beside her, Imo's sallow face had contracted, her every muscle drawn in sharp, quivering lines. In my career I had caused trouble, but I'd never had anyone stare at me like Imo did, with such abject hatred, bordering on horror. It was like she thought I was the Devil, or perhaps death personified—a bomb disguised as a woman between worlds, who lived a life that she couldn't possibly understand.

8

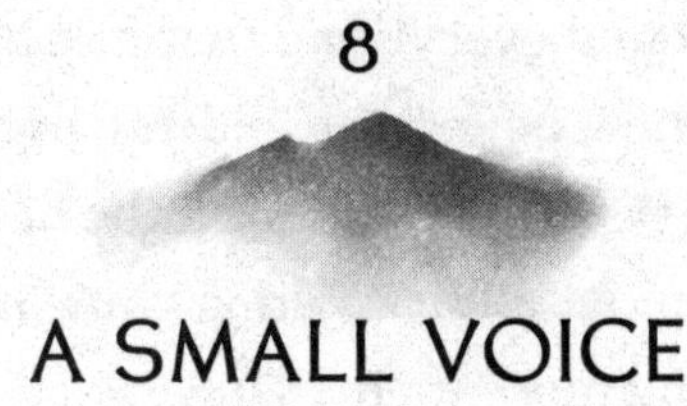

A SMALL VOICE

December 5, 1950

The man I had thought was named Moksanim was a Baptist pastor named Pak Sung-Ho, educated by American missionaries and previously employed at a Christian school in Pyongyang. Having come from a long line of scholars, he also spoke some Mandarin, as Korean academics used to, and both he and his son had studied the Bible in English.

Pastor Pak and Jae-Min beckoned for me to sit by the table, while his wife pulled a still-disconsolate Emma into a bedroom, giving me one last blistering glare before snapping the shoji screen shut. Through the paper, I couldn't tell whether Imo—who still hadn't told me her name—was reassuring Emma or chastising her, but Emma continued to keen, her breath hitching with each word.

I chewed my lip and tried to tune her out. Flames crackled boisterously as a log in the stove split with a pop. Jae-Min went to the kitchen, which was cramped because of the pipes that curved out from the stove to heat the *ondol* flooring.

While Pastor Pak perused his cabinet for tins of ointment and bandages, I regurgitated everything that had happened to me on the plane and with the Communist soldiers, in rambling segments that revolved around George yet skirted the details of his murder. I couldn't replay him out loud, couldn't show him to strangers to whom he was nothing more than a sad story.

"I'm sorry," I said, as Pastor Pak pulled my hair back to examine my cut. "I didn't mean to mislead her."

Jae-Min returned with a basin of boiled water and a cup of barley tea.

"It is not your fault," Pastor Pak said, wetting a cloth and dabbing at my wound. The hot water prickled, but it was also soothing. "Moon Hwa-Ja has not been well for some time. I don't believe she has ever had an episode like this before, but the War for Liberation has been hard on her—on all of us, but especially on her. She has no family, and she is in an unfamiliar place."

It took a second for me to register that "War for Liberation" was the North Korean name for the Korean War, and that similarly, "War to Resist Japanese Aggression" was the Chinese name for World War II. Names alone revealed so much, and though I wasn't taught this in school, I knew from my own parents that learning a new language helped to open your ears and, by extension, your mind.

Jae-Min pressed the tea into my unwashed hands. His accent was thicker than his father's, possibly because he had spent less time with the missionaries—the Japanese authorities had deported any remaining Americans in Korea prior to World War II. "You don't look like Yun-Hee," Jae-Min said accusingly. "Yun-Hee was taller than you too, and very beautiful."

"Yes, exceptionally beautiful," Pastor Pak agreed.

I cupped the glazed teal mug, inhaling the barley's nutty fragrance. "Who is Yun-Hee?" I asked, trying not to be offended by their assurance that I was too ugly to be this woman.

"Why, she's Auntie Moon's daughter, of course," said Pastor Pak. "We have been talking about her this entire time."

A fresh wave of guilt washed over me at their confirmation that Emma had indeed believed that I was her daughter. Though I hadn't intended to, I had essentially taken advantage of someone who was unwell, and possibly exacerbated whatever illness she had. "I can't understand any of you when you speak in Korean," I reminded Pastor Pak timidly, using my higher-pitched, nice-girl tone.

I still wasn't sure what these men were planning to do with me, and I desperately needed them to like me more than Imo seemed to.

"Ah, that's right," said Pastor Pak. "Song Yun-Hee was Auntie Moon's only child. We usually try not to talk about her—not because we don't miss her, but because we must help Auntie Moon. Auntie Moon and my son both live in Pyongyang, but they came to stay with my wife and me when the war reached the capital."

"Yun-Hee disappeared during the last war," Jae-Min explained. "The Japanese military conscripted her for the *cheongshindae*, and she never came home."

Yun-Hee. It was a pretty name, and now that I'd heard it a few times, I recognized it among Emma's utterances on our way to this house: *"Genchana, Yun-Hee yah. Eomma yoh-gissoh."* "It's okay, Yun-Hee. Mom is here."

I swallowed a lump in my throat and calculated the passing time. "That must have been at least six years ago?"

Jae-Min's eyes flipped up as he counted. "Yes. There were a few rounds of *cheongshindae*, but Yun-Hee was taken in August 1944."

"*Cheongshindae* is the Women's Volunteer Labor Corps," Pastor Pak clarified. "But it wasn't voluntary. It had a draft, just like for the boy soldiers. The Kempeitai—the Japanese military police—took girls from people's homes for labor. Yun-Hee had turned fourteen in July. That was the minimum age for factory work."

I thought about everything else that Emma had told the Communist soldiers—or at least what I had been able to decipher through the interpreter. "So Yun-Hee went to a factory?"

"Yes," said Jae.

"We aren't sure," admitted Pastor Pak, swirling the soiled cloth in the basin. "Auntie Moon never heard from her after the Kempeitai took her away. No one did."

"Chances are, she was sent to a factory in Japan," Jae-Min said. "I know girls who went to make airplanes and machine guns there. My high school was shut down and converted to an ammunition factory, so I was allowed to stay in Korea. I had to load the cargo, but most people were on some kind of assembly line. There was plenty of industrial work to be done."

Though Jae-Min sounded certain, I couldn't discount what I had heard back in the snowy field. "Auntie Moon kept saying that I was a slave. I guess that she confused me for her daughter, but that means she thinks her daughter was a slave? I don't know if I'm missing something."

The two men exchanged an ominous look.

"The factory workers weren't paid," said Jae-Min, "so in that sense, I suppose she was a slave."

"But—" I hesitated, uncertain if I could say the word "prostitute" out loud when we were talking about a girl these men clearly cared for. With the pieces that I had gleaned thus far, I was starting to string together what Emma had been raving about, in part because my relatives in Taiwan had already told me about the *ianfu*—"comfort women" whom Japanese soldiers could have sex with in stations throughout their occupied territories. Many of these women had been forcibly taken from Japan's colonies, including Taiwan.

"Auntie Moon said that the Japanese took her daughter to China," I said, paying attention to Jae-Min's tense lips. "I don't think the Imperial Army sent women there for factory work, did they?"

Pastor Pak popped open a tin of red ointment and slathered it over my cut. "We don't know where Yun-Hee went. She never wrote to anyone after she was drafted. She might have been in China, but there is no proof at all."

"Auntie Moon has always been dramatic," said Jae-Min. "Even when Yun-Hee was young, Auntie Moon was overprotective, smothering. She often assumes the worst."

"Jae-Min-ah," said Pastor Pak, in warning. "That is not the way to talk about your elders."

Chastened, Jae-Min said, "Auntie Moon has her theory, and we have ours. It's sensitive between our families."

"Is that why Auntie Moon started hitting you?" I asked. "Because you said you don't believe that Yun-Hee was . . . in China?"

Jae-Min's eye twitched. "No. It was because I said that Yun-Hee is dead."

"Oh."

He lowered his head. "I shouldn't have said it. Even if it's true, and we all know it, it is a terrible thing to shout at Auntie Moon. She was coming to terms with Yun-Hee's death, but when the bombing started, she got worse. She started talking about her daughter all the time, and insisting that she is alive." Focusing on his lap, Jae-Min fiddled with the frayed edge of the blanket, then pretended that the bandages needed organizing.

Pastor Pak unlatched a lunch box that was filled with thread and a mess of sewing supplies. "The last war ended five years ago," he said, plucking out a needle. "Other girls have returned. Some are missing; some are dead. Some might simply have new lives. We cannot be sure of anything."

"No, *Appa*," Jae-Min bristled. "A girl like Yun-Hee would have come home. She was like Auntie Moon, really stubborn. If she was alive, she would have found a way—" Jae-Min shut his mouth, his eyes welling again.

I winced as Pastor Pak's needle pierced my swollen skin and he pulled the thread taut.

"Jae-Min-ah," Pastor Pak said, "the Lord works in mysterious ways. It is hard to understand, but we have to try."

Sighing, Jae-Min muttered what I guessed was a prayer in Korean, while Pastor Pak continued stitching. I was surprised that the two of them were so open about their faith when religion was now banned in North Korea. Perhaps they assumed that all Americans were Christian, and thus I was too.

American missionaries used to have a major presence here, to the extent that they had dubbed Pyongyang "the Jerusalem of the East." Last month I interviewed missionaries in the South, and they had told me that Pyongyang used to have the largest Christian community on the entire peninsula, until Kim Il-Sung started burning the churches—with their followers inside them.

Pastor Pak washed my hair and wrapped a bandage around my head. "Thank the Lord, your cut is not deep. It should heal soon."

I bowed to him sheepishly, with my shoulders curved. "Thank you for your help. I hate to ask you for more, but would it be all right if I slept on your floor, just for tonight? As soon as the sun rises, I can head to Pyongyang." The UN Command still held the capital, so from there I could probably hitch a ride to Japan.

"Pyongyang?" repeated Pastor Pak. "Oh no, you cannot go to Pyongyang now. The trains are not running anymore."

"You Americans bombed all the stations," said Jae-Min, his expression as acerbic as his mother's.

"I wasn't planning to take the train," I said slowly, unsure of how to respond to Jae-Min's enmity. "I don't have any money for fare, and I don't speak Korean. It's probably best for me to walk there, right?"

Pastor Pak's mouth fell open, and he and Jae-Min exchanged another one of their coded looks. "Do you know where you are?" asked Jae-Min.

"I guess not," I said. "I thought maybe a suburb around Pyongyang, since you and Auntie Moon live there."

"Like my father explained," said Jae-Min, "we used to have a train that ran all the way from Sinuiju to Busan. Koreans aren't all peasants, you know."

"You are close to Kanggye," said Pastor Pak, gently. "It's about three hundred kilometers to Pyongyang."

My heart sank. "Oh God, no."

I had assumed that the wind had pushed my plane south, but Kanggye was even farther north than Hagaru-ri—only twenty miles to the Chinese border. Kim Il-Sung had moved his headquarters to Kanggye following his retreat from Pyongyang, and last I heard, both Chinese and North Korean soldiers were reconvening deeper in the mountains—these mountains—to avoid American bombs. I wasn't just stuck in North Korea; I had landed in a Communist hive!

I cursed, my thoughts churning frantically. *I can't even beg in the native language, and it's so damned cold that I can't sleep on the streets.* It was impossible for me to get back to Hagaru-ri before the Americans evacuated, especially with no provisions, no money, and nothing to barter.

Seeing me ruminate, Pastor Pak said, "Don't be so scared, child. We have another mat, another bowl, and another pair of chopsticks. Take time to think. We have no need to push you out, so there is no need to despair."

"Really?" I asked, skeptical of his generosity. "Won't I cause trouble for you, since I'm an American? Doesn't your government punish . . . sympathizers?"

Pastor Pak waved his hand. "I am a man of God first, and the law second. I have hidden too many troublemakers to count. How do you think I learned how to treat wounds? So many Korean rebels came to me when the Japanese were after them. What is one more?"

"Well, I won't be a troublemaker," I said, "and I'm definitely not a rebel. I'll lie low until I find a way to Pyongyang. I promise."

Pastor Pak laughed. "I am not worried. The Lord Jesus does not care about your country or where you are from. You are a person in need, and he led you to me. God often speaks with a still, small voice, but when we hear him, we must obey. I trust his plan." With a resolute smile, he closed his sewing kit and collected his ointment.

Jae-Min, though less enthusiastic than his father, said, "You can borrow some of our clothes. It will not be difficult to hide you. Everyone will assume you are Korean, like us."

"Or Chinese," said Pastor Pak. "The river is not a wall, after all. There are many Chinese on our side, and many Koreans on theirs, and many mixed people throughout these villages. Just don't try to speak Korean."

"Or English," added Jae-Min. "Use Chinese if you must. No one will look twice at another Chinese girl."

I bowed again. "Thank you. I don't have any money, but in the meantime, I can work."

"Recover first," said Pastor Pak. "We can discuss the rest later. In war, everything changes quickly. Who knows? Only God. Maybe the front lines will shift once more, and your Americans will come back next week." He chuckled, which made it sound like it was all a game, while in the side room Emma and Imo had fallen quiet.

"Maybe," I said, but the knot within me only tightened.

My mere existence here was illegal, and secrecy was a fragile shield. Each person in this house was a crack that could compromise me. Though Pastor Pak was gracious, Jae-Min seemed grudging and Imo was downright mean. As for Emma, she was unpredictable, and possibly angry at me too—but trusting them all was not a choice. Outside of this shelter, death was a certainty.

December 6, 1950, Kanggye
Dear Mom and Dad,

I'm sorry that I haven't written in so long. I don't know if you've started to worry yet, but for now, I'm safe. When I'm scared, I think about the trips we used to take to the wharf, where we'd splurge for fish-and-chips on the dock. Maybe we can go again when I'm back home. I feel a bit silly writing, since I can't even send this letter anytime soon, but I guess I wanted to have some kind of record. Should anything happen to me, maybe someone else can mail my letters in my stead so you know that even at the very end, I was thinking about you.

With all my love,
Ellie

9

HUNGRY HEARTS

December 8, 1950

Pastor Pak told me that his grandfather had built this mountain house when tigers still roamed these forests, and though Pastor Pak had lived in Pyongyang most of his life, he decided to move back to Kanggye after World War II. For the past three days, I'd slept on a mat in Pastor Pak's study, while Jae-Min shared a bedroom with his parents so that Emma could keep to herself in the other. Mostly, I spoke only with Pastor Pak, who asked me enthusiastic questions about America.

"I am old," he joked. "When you get to my age, you have a special love for what reminds you of youth, especially that which is lost."

"The word for that is 'nostalgia,'" I said.

Though I didn't consider myself old, I had it too. I left California after graduating from Berkeley and had moved constantly since, but home was where my parents were. I got a pang from anything that let me relive my childhood in the suburbs between the hills and the sea, where mist rose in the highlands and succulents bloomed in spring.

Pastor Pak told me about his schooling with American missionaries, and I learned that he was not just a humble harborer of troublemakers, as I had thought. His father had converted to Christianity because the churches often supported the Korean independence movement, and Pastor Pak and his brothers were rebels of such renown that everyone in Kanggye knew their family. Two of his brothers were killed by the Kempeitai during protests, and one died in a political prison. Though Pastor Pak was a prominent Christian, the local authorities had enough respect for him, as the sole surviving heir of the Pak family, that they had let him go with a warning and a promise not to practice Christianity.

But Pastor Pak practiced *all the time*.

Despite surrendering his religious texts, he gathered followers under the guise of a "revolutionary choir." Once a month, they all wore red armbands and performed Party songs in Kanggye. Once a week, they had "rehearsals," and worshiped in the *village leader's* home. The village leader's! According to Pastor Pak, hidden Christians were everywhere, including among North Korean officials.

I didn't have a leg to stand on, but his devotion made me nervous, like he had roped me into being an accomplice. Here I was, trying not to be a troublemaker, and Pastor Pak was cathartically confessing how he got around the law—not necessarily because he trusted me, but probably because I couldn't tell the authorities even if I wanted to. I began to consider that Pastor Pak, with his extroverted loquaciousness, could be a worse secret keeper than his wife, who rarely left the house.

Imo still hadn't told me her name, so I continued to call her Imo, which meant "Auntie." The Paks ate twice a day, and Imo limited everyone's meals, scowling when she filled my bowl and making a show of scraping the bottom of every pot. Once, I had peeked into their cellar, at the kimchi pots—*onggi*, large enough to hide a child in—and Imo shooed me away with the ferocity of a hen guarding her enormous eggs.

I was grateful for anything that Imo was willing to share, but I wished that it wasn't with such intense animosity. At night, through the thin shoji screens, I often heard her arguing bitterly with her husband, most likely about me and how long I'd be there. My wound was healing with minimal pus, and Pastor Pak had taken out the stitches, so I resolved to find transportation to Pyongyang as soon as possible.

Winter mornings in the mountain were misty, and I woke up damp and stiff despite sleeping in my coat and under several layers of blankets. After stowing my bedding, I padded softly to the kitchen. Typically, Imo woke first, to revive the fire, but she had passed that task on to me. I didn't mind, since I was used to getting up early, except that Imo always chided me in Korean afterward. It was hard to improve when I couldn't understand her criticism. According to Jae-Min, both Emma and his mother were fluent in Japanese, but when I tried using it with Imo, she'd only become more hostile—in Korean.

Shivering, I grabbed the metal poker, an icicle in my palm, and prodded at yesterday's charred wood. Vermilion embers winked through the ash, and I coaxed them out with kindling. Once the flames gnawed, I tossed in a thick, splintery log and put the cast-iron kettle on to boil.

Only when the heat began rising from the floors did everyone else begin to stir. Pastor Pak would recite the Lord's Prayer in Korean, and, for my benefit, in English too. He did this each dawn, with the regularity, punctuality, and enthusiasm of a rooster, albeit at low volume. Though I was Buddhist and not particularly religious, I said "Amen" out of politeness—and also because I wasn't sure how much of Pastor Pak's goodwill was because he believed that I was a fellow Christian.

It isn't really a lie, I told myself. He never explicitly asked me about any denomination. Maybe he truly didn't care, but I didn't feel safe enough to risk admitting the truth. From living in a predominantly Christian country, I knew enough about the practices to pretend to fit in.

Since I wasn't allowed in the kitchen cabinets, I decided to use the barley that was on the table to make tea for prayer. As soon as I pulled open the drawstring, however, heavy footsteps thumped across the main room. No one but Imo had the gumption to brave the cold house, so I replaced the barley and prepared to nod dumbly at her impending harangue.

"You aren't shutting the stove door quickly enough," someone said in Korean-accented Japanese. "That's why it's so smoky in here."

I turned, surprised to see Emma hunched in the doorway. Her hair hung loosely and tangled, and her button nose was scrunched. She had thick socks stuffed with batting, and she had slipped on a heavy skirt embroidered with gray and orange birds—unusual compared with the plain hanboks most other women wore.

Unsure of how to greet her, I bowed.

Though Emma no longer cried, she took her meals in her bedroom, venturing past me only to go outside, where she disappeared for hours at a time. Jae-Min said she liked hiking through the mountains. Typically, she returned close to dusk, just as Imo finished cooking barley and beans for dinner.

"I'm sorry," I said, closing the stove's door. "I thought that leaving it open would get the fire hot faster."

"The pastor's wife is sensitive to smoke," Emma explained. "She is sensitive to many things, but she had pleurisy when she was young, and never recovered fully, so she is very picky about the air."

"I guess that's why she's been so upset with me every morning."

"Other reasons too," said Emma, coyly. "But yes, early mistakes can ruin the rest of the day."

"Why couldn't she have just told me this herself? I tried asking her about the stove in Japanese. Does she not actually understand the language?"

"Oh!" Emma's brows, light as though painted with watercolor, lifted sharply. "The pastor's wife has the best Japanese, but she is sensitive about that too, since it is so good. You understand?"

I huffed. "No, I don't understand. Why would that be a problem?"

"Because the pastor's wife is part Japanese," Emma replied. "Her maternal grandmother married a Japanese man. Her father was a Korean landowner, but he supported Japan so he could save his own properties. He reported rebels and gave money to the Kempeitai. The Japanese governor-general rewarded him with a position in the administration, and then he registered with his father-in-law's surname so his entire family could pretend to be Japanese—until Japan lost the war, of course. Then, suddenly, they were Korean all along."

"Really?" It hadn't occurred to me that anyone in this village could be part Japanese, even though mixed marriages had never been uncommon, even during the colonial period.

"Yes. That is why the pastor moved back to the mountains. He had such a devoted following in Pyongyang, but his wife's family were infamous *chinilpa*—rich, very rich, *chinilpa*—and

Koreans, whether from the North or South, despise traitors." There was a bitterness with which she emphasized the word "*chinilpa*," which I gathered was a term for Koreans who collaborated with the Japanese. "Here, the pastor's wife has to have a simple life, but she can pass as a normal Korean woman."

Emma opened the pantry and rummaged through the spices. The water in the kettle grumbled, threatening to boil.

"I'm so sorry," I said, shifting away to give her space, "for what happened between us and the soldiers. I didn't mean to mislead you."

Emma found a canister of tea and shook it to see how much was left. It sounded mostly empty. "My heart was hungry, and it snapped at what was in front of it," she said with a doleful smile. "You did nothing wrong."

I lined up the teal cups. "I couldn't understand what you were saying, and I just assumed it was all some kind of act to help me. I didn't know that you thought I was your daughter."

"I didn't at first. When I saw you from the road, I thought you were just a Korean girl. I didn't know why you were with a Japanese, but I know what soldiers do to girls. I knew you were in trouble, and that something awful was going to happen. It wasn't my business, but I couldn't let it go. You weren't my daughter, but I knew there was a mother like me who was waiting for you. I thought about how unfair it would be if you didn't come home—for her to wait for so long with no news. Once my head turned down that road, I slipped. In my mind, there was a soft, warm bed, and I folded myself in. Truthfully, I wanted to believe that I had found her, even if it wasn't real."

I handed Emma the bag of barley, warm from being close to the stove. It was hard for me to imagine in the abstract the depth of her loss. Inevitably, I thought about my own parents, who were blissfully unaware of my situation. They were used to not hearing from me for weeks on end, but then again, I wasn't fourteen. Our lives were no longer intricately intertwined.

"When you said you were *Eomma*, I got confused and thought you said 'Emma,'" I admitted. "That's a popular English name. I keep thinking of you as an Emma, but please tell me what to call you. Maybe Auntie Moon or . . . also Imo?"

Leaving the barley, Emma opened the tea canister, counting out each leaf and plunking them into the cups. They rang faintly against the ceramic. "'Emma'?" She chuckled. "That's funny. I've never had an English name before, but that is a nice one."

"You don't have to be Emma. I'm happy to call you whatever you prefer."

"'Emma' is all right," she said, "as long as I can pick a name for you too."

"A name for me?" I asked. "But I told you my name already."

"Ellie, yes?"

"Short for 'Eleanor.'"

"That is a strange name, and very hard to say."

"'Ellie'? Or 'Eleanor'?"

"Both. I can find a suitable Korean name for you, but I need time. Names are a serious business. If there wasn't a war, I'd consult a professional."

I laughed. No one had ever told me that my English name was unsuitable. My parents had chosen it because Americans often struggled to pronounce their Chinese names. "Sure," I said. "I guess it will be easier for me to blend in here then."

Emma filled each cup, seeming satisfied. Curls of steam rose in sequence, connecting and merging.

The slight scent of jasmine tea summoned Imo like an apparition. She materialized by the kitchen, a crease from her bedding cutting across her cheekbone. Her hanbok was casually tied, but her hair was neatly pinned. Apparently, Imo was forty-five years old—three years younger than Emma and Pastor Pak, yet she looked a decade older.

Scowling, Imo grumbled in Korean, which Emma translated for me. "The pastor's wife doesn't want anyone touching the barley or the tea. You may leave the kitchen now. She thanks you for boiling the water."

I was certain that Emma had made up that last part, but I bowed politely and said, "*Gamsa hamnida*," backing away slowly, like one might retreat from a bear. Now that I knew more about Imo, I could guess why she hated me so much. If it weren't for us Americans defeating Japan, her family would have continued reigning in Pyongyang and she wouldn't be here, rubbing elbows with peasants. Getting money changed people; losing money changed them even more.

I wondered how Pastor Pak, an impassioned resistance fighter, could have married someone who was so embedded in the colonial government. Maybe Imo was an exceptionally devout Christian? Or was Pastor Pak exaggerating his rebel past? Every person had a story, and if I were a cat, I would have run through all nine lives because I got sucked into chasing them. My family never thought of journalism as a serious profession, but once they'd resigned to it being my choice, they began joking that I'd never starve because I was so naturally nosy.

I drummed my fingers in empty air, feeling the phantom weight of my typewriter's keys. How long would it take the *Global Tribune* to replace me if I didn't get back soon? A week? Two? There were bigger threats in this village, and yet I couldn't help but worry about who would rush to fill my place. It had taken years of covering stories no one else wanted just to scramble up this splintery career ladder, and I hated thinking that I had fallen off already.

No, I thought. *I'll get back in time, and with a story like no other.* There had been only a handful of American journalists at Hagaru-ri. How many were there in Kanggye? Probably none!

The KPA routinely detained journalists as prisoners of war, so Western media outlets no longer sent their staff this far north. In Kanggye, I could also scope out travel options to Pyongyang—transportation and a story, two birds with one stone.

"Are you all right?" asked Pastor Pak, as he came out from the bedroom and brushed lint from the sleeves of his sweater. Before he slid his screen shut, I got a glimpse of Jae-Min curled up underneath his blanket. "You were talking to yourself."

"Was I? I guess I was just thinking out loud." I touched the scab on my head. "I'm feeling better, though, and I was thinking that I could go to Kanggye. From your map, it looks like a straightforward walk. There's only one main road, right?"

He removed his glasses and cleaned the lenses with the stretched-out hem of his undershirt. "Ellie-yah, you do not want to go to Kanggye. There is nothing to see anymore, and it is dangerous. The road is full of soldiers. It might be better in the spring. You can try then."

Goodness, I hoped I wouldn't still be stranded here in the *spring*. "I'm going to write about the city," I explained, since he was speaking to me like I was a tourist. "I also need to find a car to Pyongyang."

"Oh, there is nothing to write. And there are no cars. Anyone wealthy enough to have a car left long ago—unless you want to ride with soldiers, and I am sure you do not."

"I wouldn't be opposed to it. That's usually what I do as a correspondent. I'll just have to pretend to be Chinese. I mean, I am

Chinese, but I'll have to say I'm Chinese from China. Mainland China. People's Republic."

The kettle clanged as Imo glided out from the kitchen to give Pastor Pak his tea and me another disapproving frown. Her dress was retied, with such care that the loops on her bow were perfectly symmetrical.

"It is too dangerous, Ellie," said Pastor Pak, after blowing on his tea. "Even if you speak their language, it will not take long for them to know that you are not truly one of them. If you wish, Jae-Min can take you around our village. The weather might be better later, and if it is not cloudy you can go to the lookout point. From there, you can see part of Kanggye, and perhaps write about that."

"That isn't how my type of journalism works," I said. "I'm used to being in a war zone, and I can't just sit here. I'll be careful, I promise."

"Let's discuss tomorrow," he replied. "The wise are cautious and avoid danger; fools plunge ahead with reckless confidence." Serenely, he sipped his tea and went to his *kotatsu*. Our discussion was over, and he had made his decision. Though Pastor Pak was not my boss, he was an elder, and I was in his home, so I was obliged to respect his authority.

He flipped open a leather-bound book titled *The Communist Manifesto,* in bold English letters on the cover—but it was actually a Bible that he had rebound himself. Local authorities continued to conduct house visits, sometimes in the middle of the night, but they couldn't read English. Many of them couldn't read at all. If they were to come while I was here, I was to say that I was a Chinese singer and revolutionary who wanted to start her own choir.

Pastor Pak turned a page, lips moving as he read. According to Karl Marx, religion was "the sigh of the oppressed creature, the heart of a heartless world, and the soul of soulless conditions." If

Christianity in Kanggye was the "opiate of the masses," then Pastor Pak was essentially a drug dealer.

How was what he did any less dangerous than what I wanted to do?

Perhaps if I could fabricate a religious reason to go to Kanggye—a cause that Pastor Pak would deem worthy—he'd allow it. According to his map, there were three churches in Kanggye, and possibly more along the way. Maybe I could write about their closure?

I had asked Pastor Pak why he was still in North Korea, when he couldn't worship openly and so many other pastors had fled. His response had been short: "A place where even the mere freedom to believe is banned is a place where people need something to believe in most."

As I knelt beside the *kotatsu* and Pastor Pak selected a passage for our morning prayer, I wondered what was worse for the North Korean authorities: a silent American woman desperate to leave, or a subversive Christian man determined to stay?

Washington, December 7, 1950; Excerpt from Meeting Between President Truman and Prime Minister Attlee (United Kingdom):

The President said he had just talked with the Prime Minister and that they had discussed the atomic bomb and its use. The President reminded Mr. Attlee that the Governments of the United Kingdom and the United States had always been partners in this matter and that he would not consider the use of the bomb without consulting with the United Kingdom. The Prime Minister asked whether this agreement should be put in writing, and the President replied no that it would not be in writing, that if a man's word wasn't any good it wasn't made any better by writing it down.

(*Foreign Relations of the United States*, 1950, Volume VII, p. 1462)

10

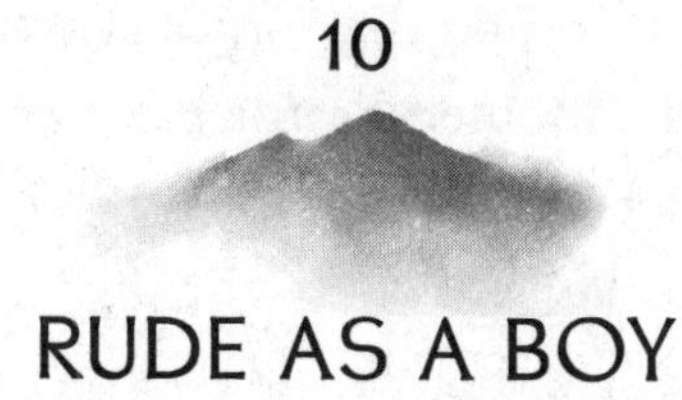

RUDE AS A BOY

December 8, 1950

I didn't need to ask to know that Jae-Min had been in love with Emma's daughter. It was a shadow that he wore on his face, as blatant as a tattoo, as painful as a scar, and as enduring as both. Jae-Min was polite to me, but he kept his distance, giving short, curt answers to any questions I had:

No, I couldn't ride a horse and cart to Pyongyang.

Kanggye was eight kilometers away from the Pak's home.

Yes, his father would be angry if I left the house by myself.

No, it was not possible for me to hitchhike anywhere using just sign language.

Yes, there were police in this village. Spies too.

Restless, I pored over maps. I wasn't a prisoner, but I envied Emma, who came and went as she pleased. Pastor Pak encouraged her to take walks. He said that mountain air could heal the soul, which was why he had moved back here in the first place. Whenever Emma and Jae-Min were away, I would ask Pastor Pak about

Yun-Hee, but the snippets he gave me formed only a scattered outline, like the chalk around the corpse at a crime scene.

Initially, Emma had joined Pastor Pak's church to pray for a child so that her husband wouldn't leave her. God had granted only one of those wishes.

Though Yun-Hee's father also lived in Pyongyang, Yun-Hee had never met him. Pastor Pak used to scold her for telling the other children that her father was dead. Since Emma was both literate and skilled at sewing, she was able to get a job as a supervisor at a textile factory, but money was tight. Still, Yun-Hee had lavishly embroidered outfits that Emma spent months sewing by hand. "She already gets teased for not having a father," Emma used to say. "At least no one can say she looks poor, and no one can say that her mother doesn't care."

Though Jae-Min was two years older than Yun-Hee, they used to play together because Emma and Imo were close friends—so close that Yun-Hee called Imo "Auntie" instead of "*Sahmonim*," which was the title for a pastor's wife. According to Pastor Pak, the two women sat together every Sunday, and they often visited each other during the week, with their children in tow.

"Are they still friends?" I asked.

"Of course," he answered.

It was hard for me to believe that anyone would call their friend a *chinilpa*, but then again, why would Emma be in this house if they weren't on good terms? For a factory supervisor with only basic schooling, Emma had exceptional Japanese, which made me wonder what else Pastor Pak wasn't telling me.

That night, Emma offered to sleep with me so that Jae-Min could have his room back. She and I lay our mats by the kitchen stove, listening as the fire's coarse laughter hushed into a lullaby.

With her eyes half closed, Emma whispered questions to me about my family.

Was I scared? Did I miss them?

I told her that I used to envy only children, because I was the journalist middle child sandwiched between a cardiologist and a general surgeon—a lackluster kind of filling. Though I loved my family, I wished that they could be a little different, that our edges weren't so jagged in ways that were so incompatible. Still, I always missed them when I was traveling, and even more so now that I had no way of contacting them. We weren't Christian, but we loved Christmas, because that was the only time that all of us could take leave and get together. I yearned to go home to them, even if it meant dodging questions about my sad, empty womb.

Emma sighed and said, "I understand what you mean about a sad womb. I got married at seventeen, but it took me eleven years to have a baby. It wasn't that I didn't try, but my in-laws seemed to think I was barren on purpose."

"Did you want to be a mother?"

"Of course," she answered. "It is hard for a child to have no father, though. I tried to be both mother and father, and it worked sometimes. My daughter was a quick learner, but she had a mouth like a bomb, as rude as a boy! There were days when I would pass her school and see her being punished outside—she used to have to hold her arms up in the air, maybe for hours. I'd make her do it again when she came home, because I didn't want people saying that I didn't teach her right. But oh, there are some problems that no amount of discipline can fix. Maybe if there had been a man in our house, it would have been better."

"I doubt it," I said. "I grew up with a father and two brothers, and people think I'm rude too—sometimes."

"Is that why you don't have a husband yet?" she asked, with the gravity of a doctor making a diagnosis.

"Maybe."

"An elegant girl like you? Best not to start too late. Do you at least have suitors?"

"Nope."

"I see." She sounded disappointed, but people are often scarred by what they believe are their biggest mistakes, and by the blank spaces where love was supposed to be. Pastor Pak had said that Emma had planned her life around ensuring a better marriage for her daughter than the one she herself had, and had accumulated a respectable dowry of fine linens, silks, and wools purchased through her factory connections. Last he heard, Emma still hadn't sold the dowry, and occasionally she added to it. "Well," said Emma, shifting optimistically, "you don't have to be scared if no man wants you. There are more jobs for women now, so you can be your own man. It will be all right."

I laughed. It would have been a lie if I said that I wasn't worried at all, so I said, "I'm not *that* worried. I'm here because I *am* working, remember?"

Before Emma could answer, Imo's voice from the other room grew strident. Imo and Pastor Pak were beginning their usual bedtime argument, which was as routine as brushing teeth.

Emma wiggled on her mat, tilting her ear shamelessly toward their screen.

"I feel bad," I whispered, propping myself up on my elbows. "I know they're fighting about me."

Emma snorted. "You think this racket is about you?"

"Is it not? I thought Imo was mad at Pastor Pak for taking me in."

"Bah! No. The pastor is always taking people in. His wife is used to that. Usually it's people with *big* problems, much worse than yours. People who need guidance from the Lord. Alcoholics. Gamblers. Crazy people." She said this righteously, as if she couldn't possibly fall into any of those categories. "Their fight has been going on since weeks before you arrived. Everyone is scared that this war won't end, so the pastor's wife wants to go to Japan—*chinilpa*, after all—but the pastor wants to stay here."

I scooched closer to Emma. "So, what are they saying?"

Under the moonlight wavering through the paper windows, only the outline of Emma's jaw was visible. "The pastor's wife says the Americans will bomb Korea like they bombed Japan, that the imperialists have better bombs now—many bombs. The pastor says Korea is not like Japan. Japan killed millions of people in Asia, then flew across the ocean to attack America. Korea's war is small. We are unifying our own country, not invading our neighbors."

I lay back down, using my own arm as a pillow. News here came mostly from the mandatory Party meetings, so even a scholar like Pastor Pak knew little about America and the Soviet Union's intensifying arms race. Korea's war was by no means small—it was a dogfight between two nuclear superpowers.

"The pastor says America is a Christian country," Emma continued. "His wife says that Christians can be barbarians too. Just look at what they've done to our cities already! The pastor believes the worst is over, but she is sure that it's just beginning."

Pastor Pak and Imo hushed abruptly. Perhaps they could hear us through the screen as well. When they spoke again, it was in whispers, so that it was no longer possible for us to overhear.

I turned to focus on Emma instead. "You came from Pyongyang, didn't you?" I asked. "Jae-Min said that he used to visit you while he was at Pyongyang University, before his classes were suspended."

"Oh yes. He's a very needy boy, but at least he's smart. He was studying civil engineering! I was working at a textile factory, the same one that I've been with since my daughter was born. Everyone was rushing to get out when the Americans came. Our soldiers were laying land mines around the city, so I didn't have much time to pack, but I did bring my sewing machine with me. Even if we're at war, I still have to work. I still have to eat."

The machine, which she kept in the main room, was cast-iron and operated with a hand crank. I had tried picking it up and found it woefully heavy. "Do you get any customers here?"

"Not really. I have to go to Kanggye if I want to be paid with money instead of beans—not that anyone has beans to spare anymore either."

I bolted up on the edge of my mat. "You go all the way to Kanggye? Pastor Pak lets you?"

"Lets me?" Emma scoffed. "Like I said, I still have to work—I don't have a man who can do that for me. I was coming back from Kanggye the day you and I met. I had gone there to see if I could repair uniforms, or wash uniforms, or cook—any kind of job, so that I'm not a burden to the pastor."

I strained to make eye contact with her in the dark. "Are you going to go again? Can I come with you if you are? Please?" In my mental pocket, I had pitches like playing cards lined up to throw out.

"I don't see why not," said Emma. "It's a long walk, but—"

"I am very fit and strong," I announced, which was only partially a lie; I rarely exercised, but I was always running after one plane or another, one source or another. "I can help you carry stuff, and I can speak Chinese. I can talk to the Chinese officers for you. I can't sew, but I can fold clothes and use scissors!"

Emma chuckled. "Good Lord, I already said I'll take you! It'll be nice to have someone to chat with along the way. Even picking up a sheet of paper is nicer together than alone."

"Yes, definitely!" I almost kicked my feet with joy. Maybe Emma could help me speak with someone who could take me to Pyongyang.

"Now go to sleep," said Emma. "The screens are thin, and Imo will get mad if we keep her up." Flopping onto her belly, she turned her face away from me.

"Good night," I said, pulling my covers over my head.

I tried to shut off my whirling brain, but nights had always been hard. When the world was quiet, my mind became a cinema, playing scenes that I didn't want to see. There were memories that I could fight in daylight, but in darkness, they clawed. Even before George's death, I often woke to imaginary gunfire. Now I drifted off to the sound of his voice, interspersed with the tapping of my typewriter and the howling of jets. In dreams, I cut myself on fresh paper and bled ink.

Beside my ear, there was a guttural rattle as Emma began to snore. It reminded me of a burp gun, and yet it was so human that it grounded me. Her body was a gentle mound, and when I focused on its rhythmic rising, the ghosts let go and my own breath deepened. I thought of my mom, smashing cloves of garlic with the flat side of her cleaver, while the room around me faded.

11

ONE OF MY FLOCK

December 10, 1950

With about two weeks until Christmas, I had accepted that I was going to miss the holidays with my family. I'd been stuck at the Paks' house for five days, contemplating how I was going to make it to Hungnam before the Americans evacuated, and realizing that I'd be lucky just to get there alive—forget about being on time. It wouldn't be my first Christmas without my loved ones, but I was distressed about it in a way that I had never been before. Maybe I had taken MacArthur's promise too seriously. Or maybe I was scared that I would never go home at all.

I will eventually, I reassured myself, the scab at my hairline still tender. *This is just an unexpected detour—a rare opportunity, really.* The human mind has its own form of censorship, to bend reality into something more palatable, bearable. There is a kinder word for such delusion: "hope."

On Sunday morning, everyone in the Paks' house was up before dawn, not for worship but because there was a Party meeting in the afternoon. The local authorities held them weekly, to teach Communist ideology, provide updates, and mobilize support for the war. Usually these meetings ended with self-criticism sessions, during which everyone had to confess their failings—little faults, like sleeping in late or shirking chores, that were significant enough for a shaming but not for an arrest.

As a precaution, Imo always prepared a treat or gift to "thank" the comrades, and set aside a portion for who she suspected was the spy. In every neighborhood there were covert people in charge of reporting extravagant behavior, such as eating beef or white rice, or suspicious activity, such as hiding an American imperialist. Today, Imo was making chicken and potato soup, and the rhythmic thudding of her cleaver made me wring my hands.

"It's okay," said Emma, noticing that I had blanched. "The spy lives on the other side of the mountain, and the pastor's wife said he's mostly concerned with getting his childhood bullies arrested first."

"That's a vicious kind of karma," I said, though I was more worried about Imo reporting me than I was about the spy discovering me himself.

When Jae-Min returned from the shed with feathers on his sweater and blood on his hands, Emma announced that I was going to help her take measurements for clothing in Kanggye.

"It's better for the foreigner to be gone while the meeting is being held, don't you think?" she asked Pastor Pak. "The less attention on her, the better, yes?"

For added measure, I said, "I'm going to visit the shuttered churches in Kanggye and write about the persecution of Christians." Though this excuse was mainly to appeal to Pastor Pak's sense of religious obligation, I was excited to see what kind of story I could glean from the city. One can turn off a camera, but not a heart that beats like a typewriter's keys.

Pastor Pak was preoccupied with a chip in the blade of his ax and waved us off with neither approbation nor objection. He had forgotten to chop firewood yesterday and was distressed that he now had to labor on a Sunday to keep us warm.

Relieved by his nonchalance, I rushed for my hat, but Imo stopped me.

"Do not just write about the closure of churches," she said caustically, in Japanese. "Write about their bombing too."

This was the first sentence that Imo had bothered to speak to me in a language I could understand.

Emma had been right. Imo spoke just like the civilians in Tachikawa, with a fluency that was unusual for any Korean, especially women, who generally had lower levels of education. Even Pastor Pak's scholarly Japanese had a noticeable twang.

A petty monster in me wanted to reply in English, but instead I said, "I understand."

From what I'd seen, Imo never left the village, so anything she heard about Kanggye was through her neighbors. She was a secondary source at best, and I was eager to see the city for myself—and hitch a ride to Pyongyang if I could.

Emma lent me one of her plain hanboks, which I wore over my pants, with extra stockings underneath. Instead of wearing my flight-nurse jacket, I borrowed Jae-Min's old coat, even though it was ill fitting. With my hair braided back and my mouth shut, I was a frumpy but passable Korean civilian.

The sun was mostly hidden behind the mountains when Emma and I set out. This partial glimpse, a bare shoulder, still ignited the horizon. Saffron light flared over the treetops, tinting the snow a shade of apricot. I didn't know that these peaks could blush, and for a slice of time as satisfying as butter-soaked bread, I forgot that we were at war.

Emma and I balanced carefully down the terraces, cutting a detour over muddy earth and slippery roots. Emma didn't explain why, but I knew. She didn't want me to see the plane, or the bodies of the men I had left behind. Would they still be there, after all these days?

The footpath meandered past huts and plots, intersecting a forest before meeting the main road, where the Tongno River twisted toward the mighty Yalu. There were still many travelers, and now that I was oriented, I understood that these refugees, with their heavy packs and wagons, were seeking safety in Manchuria. Since President Truman had declared China off-limits to American bombers, the Yalu had become a holy river, demarcating sanctuary.

At our brisk pace, we passed an elderly man with a *jige*, a wooden A-frame carrier, strapped to his back. "I have to tell you the truth," Emma said, keeping her voice low so others couldn't hear our Japanese. "I am not going to Kanggye to sew. I am meeting someone, but not for money."

"What do you mean?" I couldn't imagine anyone making this journey, in this weather, if it wasn't for profit.

"It's just easier for me to tell people that I'm going to Kanggye to sew than to explain something that they wouldn't understand."

"You lied to Pastor Pak so he'd let you go?"

"Of course not!" Her eyes widened in offense, or perhaps in warning. "I just made an adjustment, like when you alter a jacket. Is it a different jacket? Certainly not! Just a different fit."

I wasn't sure how valid that analogy was, but I let it go. "What are you really doing in Kanggye, then?"

Emma hesitated. Then she hitched her satchel higher on her

shoulder, as if daring me to reproach her. "I am going there to look for my daughter."

Internally, I cursed. Emma had seemed lucid when we left, but I didn't know her or her mental state well enough to say for sure. Now I was worried that she had snapped again, or was at risk of doing so. There was no doubt in my mind that Yun-Hee was dead, especially if she was actually a comfort woman, as Emma seemed to think. The mortality rate for comfort women was atrocious. When the Japanese retreated from China, officers slaughtered them as one might sabotage materials of war.

"I'm not crazy," said Emma, "if that's what you're thinking."

"Of course I don't think you're crazy," I lied. *Not a lie, just an adjustment*. "It's just . . . why would your daughter be in Kanggye of all places?"

"Kanggye is on the border with China! If Yun-Hee came back from China, maybe she settled there. Even if she isn't in Kanggye, there are girls like her in Kanggye—girls who might have met her, girls who might know where she is or . . . or what happened to her."

"I see." I relaxed slightly now that her goal seemed more reasonable. "You found former comfort women in Kanggye?"

"Former slaves."

"Excuse me?"

I had almost forgotten about Emma's emphasis on that word during our first encounter.

"Slaves," she repeated. "I don't like saying '*ianfu*,' because it sounds so kind. A mother is a woman who brings comfort, maybe a wife, but these women were slaves. Soldiers with guns forced girls to let men use them. Slaves."

She wasn't wrong. These women were never paid, but "slavery" was so broad, and the Japanese army's subjugation of women for sex was such a specific phenomenon. It was confusing to call these women slaves, especially when there had been chattel slavery in Korea not long ago. Words, however, were my bread and butter, and I understood the importance of—and the power in—choosing the right one.

"Slaves, then," I repeated. "Military sex slaves."

Emma blinked like she hadn't expected me to agree so readily. A smile twitched at the corner of her mouth. "So, I have found someone who has found former slave women in Kanggye, and she has agreed to introduce me. Maybe. It's all very difficult. No one dares to say they were in a sex station, or everyone will know that they slept with hundreds of men—maybe thousands. No one will be friends with them, let alone marry them. There are more jobs for women now, but not for dirty women. It takes a long time, and so many tries, to find survivors, but I have gotten better at it."

"You mean you've done this before?" I asked. Information about Japanese sexual slavery was limited in the US, and the articles available relied on the accounts of Americans who had either seen "comfort stations" or met the women in temporary refugee camps. "Is this something you do regularly?"

"It is something that I started three years ago, when I couldn't stand just waiting around anymore. It is something I will continue to do until I bring my daughter home."

I whistled under my breath. Considering the number of sex stations and how widespread they had been, not just in China but all over East and Southeast Asia, Emma might as well have been searching for a single snowflake in a blizzard—if her daughter was even in this system to begin with.

In the distance, a pair of Soviet MiG-15s glinted. Reflexively, we clapped our hands over our ears, and others around us ducked as they neared. Unlike the droning propeller-based planes of World War II, these jets sounded like they were ripping up the sky.

After they passed, I said, "So, you just ask people if they know Yun-Hee?"

Emma massaged her ears. "Initially, I only wanted to know about my daughter, but many of these women had never spoken to anyone about what had happened to them, and once we started talking, they wouldn't stop. So I started to listen. I set aside time for it, but soon there were too many stories. I was getting them mixed up, so I started to write them down, and now I have a notebook full of them. I think, this way, I can take away some of their pain. It is a tiny footprint, but I want to do anything I can. In a way, they are all my daughters."

Amazed, I threaded my arm through hers. Though I wasn't a mother, I understood this desire to fight, to seize small pockets of power against daunting odds, to throw all one's energy into a single scream with the vain hope that it might resonate. Who knew that Moon Hwa-Ja was akin to a journalist, a bird of a feather and one of my flock? That in these frigid mountains I could find more than just a shared will to live, that I could find a shared way of thinking?

"I want to hear more," I said, "about your project, about your work—everything that you are willing to tell me."

Emma blushed, and swatted my shoulder. "Ah, don't get so excited. It's not work. It's just something that I do in my spare time."

"How many women have you spoken to?" I asked.

"Twenty-six in Pyongyang."

"Twenty-six!" I hadn't expected a double-digit number, let alone one greater than twenty. To my knowledge, no journalists in the US had gotten any interviews with these women at all. "That's astounding!"

"Not really."

"Yes, really!"

"Well, I had help," she said. "I knew other mothers whose daughters were taken during the draft. I'm in a women workers' organization in Pyongyang, and I asked around there. The first women who were willing to talk to me did so only because they heard that I was looking for my daughter. Maybe they knew I wouldn't judge them, and I'd keep their secret. My greatest breakthrough was finding a doctor who told her patients about me. After that, women began showing up at my door—far more than I expected."

"What about Kanggye, then? Do you have connections there?"

"I didn't at first, but I do now." She smiled, the first hint I had through her veil of modesty that she was proud of herself. "During my last trip there, I looked for clinics—for women's doctors. They are the ones that girls like my daughter might be honest with. They can identify these girls, sometimes, by the diseases they have, and by the damage to their bodies. They are the few who can guess how many women exist, all over Korea, pretending that nothing happened."

"That's resourceful," I said. "No, ingenious! But why would you have to hide this from Pastor Pak? I'm sure he'd support this kind of calling."

Emma sighed. "The pastor is a wonderful man, but he is still a man, and he is traditional in many ways. For him, this is not a topic for good women to discuss openly. In my case, he would also think it is an unhealthy obsession, like picking at a scab instead of letting it heal. His advice for this type of hurt is to pray, and seek comfort in the Lord, to forgive—but that does not work for me.

Searching for my daughter—for these women—gives me the courage I need to open my eyes each morning. To leave my bed. To *live*."

"I understand. Believe me—I do." Like Emma, I preferred to harness my anger and ride it like a flaming horse. It burned, it consumed, but it also carried me in a way no other force could. "What about Imo, though? She's a woman too, and a mother, no less."

"Yes, she is a mother," said Emma. "And for that reason, she does not want me to talk about my daughter in her house at all. Her priority is her son. Jae-Min is still young, and he can forget Yun-Hee. In this world, with so many girls, my daughter is replaceable—for everyone except for me." She tilted her face toward the sun, illuminating the faint discoloration of liver spots on her cheeks.

My feet were throbbing, but at least they were dry when we wound around the frozen river bend and reached a flat bank where travelers paused to rest around a fire. A woman and her daughter were hawking roasted yams, the peels cracked teasingly to reveal starchy flesh. There, my stomach rumbled, not for yams roasted whole, but mashed in a casserole with cream and brown sugar and topped with a gooey marshmallow layer—an "abominable" American dish that my parents always condemned as being far too sweet.

Emma brightened at the yams' honeyed smell, seductive and insistent. As if lifted by a memory, she said, "I wish my daughter had a friend like you. She would have liked you, I think."

I smiled, hiding the heaviness that I had soaked in from her story. "I'm sure I would have liked her too. Especially if she was anything like you."

FROM THE DIARIES OF LT. GEN. GEORGE E. STRATEMEYER, FAR EAST AIR FORCES COMMANDER:

November 3, 1950

I also told [MacArthur] that as a lesson we could burn some other towns in North Korea and I indicated the town of Kanggye which I believe is occupied by enemy troops and is a communications center—both rail and road. He said, "Burn it if you so desire," and then said, "Not only that, Strat, but burn and destroy as a lesson any other of those towns that you consider of military value to the enemy."

November 5, 1950

The gist of General MacArthur's instructions are as follows: Every installation, facility, and village in North Korea now becomes a military and tactical target.

—*The Three Wars of Lt. Gen. George E. Stratemeyer*,
edited by William T. Y'Blood

12

FREEDOM

December 10, 1950

Kanggye, like Hagaru-ri, lay in a crater, low and flat like a tea saucer. Mountains, swollen with snowfall, rippled around the perimeter, with a single road large enough for wagons and cars. Emma and I took a footpath, my thighs trembling on yet another steep hike that would end in a screaming drop. The eight kilometers through undulating, rocky terrain was killing me. While I strained to climb, Emma bounded as nimbly as a goat, her embroidered skirt a flash of color against the slush. Along a crevice, she stepped on a loose rock, wavering precariously before hopping to the next ledge.

She landed like a gymnast, with her arms up. "Oh my, I can be clumsy sometimes." She giggled, though I had slipped and fallen too many times to count. Mud stains ran from my hip across my knees, saturating the gray hem of my skirt.

Along the narrow, unpaved path, there were occasionally human bodies. It was unclear what they had succumbed to, whether it was the cold, fatigue, or illness. They frightened me at first, and I hurried to pass them, my stomach flipping frantic catapults. In this weather, the dead had to be repositioned quickly. If no one cared enough to do so, they froze with limbs splayed in disarray. That was how I could tell which ones were soldiers and which ones were civilians.

It was impossible to bury anyone in this rocky soil, but the deceased who had traveled with loved ones were usually covered with snow, moved beneath a tree, or nestled between boulders—arranged with their arms over their chests, or curled as if en-wombed. Soldiers, however, were left where they had fallen, or hastily pushed aside to avoid blocking the path. Often, they were stripped of every possession.

Without uniforms, it was difficult to tell who was on which side. Skin can be blotchy gray, blue, or black when frozen, and race is imperceptible when mud obscures the face. Some men, however, had marks around their wrists—cuts from communication wire, which the KPA used to restrain prisoners of war when they marched them to camps.

I wanted to do something for the fallen UN troops, but I couldn't move them on my own, or change anything about their bodies, now that they were stiff. Moreover, I was afraid of calling attention to myself. What kind of Chinese or North Korean woman would touch a nude dead man, or waste her time scooping snow to cover her enemies?

Emma didn't blink when we passed the corpses, and even children no longer stared. Seeing the first few bodies had been jarring, but after I lost count, I shut my soul's door. Like a horse with blinders, I plodded onward, my senses tingling at the changes in the air as we approached Kanggye's outskirts. While the cold contained the stench of death, it could not hide the smells of smoke and sulfur. Fine ash floated with the wind, which carried the acrid, garlicky stink of white phosphorus—a substance that voraciously burns human fat.

As we climbed up toward the city, my nose warned me before my eyes could see. I pulled my scarf over my face to shield it from the tacky dust that was suddenly abundant, coating everything and catching on my lashes. When we reached the crest of the hill, my knees buckled, and I clenched Emma's gloved hand in both of mine.

On Pastor Pak's map, wrinkled and worn, there was supposed to be a small city here, with about forty thousand inhabitants. Now I understood why he had wanted me to go to the lookout point. It would have saved me this trip, because from there, I would have seen that there was no Kanggye anymore. Everything was gray and charred.

Multilevel buildings were flattened, with mounds of wreckage stretching across the entire crater. The city grid remained, but within each square the blocks were leveled, bare and grim. Slabs of concrete were stacked like tombstones, while store signs in Chinese dangled over broken windows. Gaping craters punctured the streets, lined with mutilated vehicles, strips of rubber, and splintered telephone poles.

My chest tightened as I surveyed the landscape. Other travelers swerved around me, irritated that I was blocking the path. I knew that America had bombed the North, but I hadn't grasped the extent of the damage. Only a few of the residential areas here were intact, forlorn amid stretches of crumbled bricks. There were still people in the streets, but they lumbered over heaps of purple ash.

I had never witnessed the aftermath of a bombing campaign, and black-and-white photos could not convey the solemn atrocity of a skeleton city, the magnitude of the desolation, the invasiveness of the smells, or the harried movements of civilians picking through the ruins for sustenance. Every now and then, human cries echoed with excitement, alarm, despair.

The air scratched my throat like sandpaper, and I pressed Emma's hand against my chest.

Seeing my shock, she said, "The Americans bombed Kanggye a month ago. I don't know why. They'd already captured our capital. They didn't need to destroy this city."

"They were probably looking for Kim Il-Sung," I said, grasping for an explanation. "He moved his headquarters here, didn't he?"

"Our government was in Sinuiju then, and the Americans bombed there too. They bombed everywhere, even the crops and the cattle, so everyone lost their meat and harvest."

I stared at the rubble, grateful that she'd said "Americans" when she could have just as easily said "you people"—because this was my people. I felt no responsibility for the sins of Mao, or for the war crimes of the Chinese, for they did not represent me, but when the government that I had pledged allegiance to and paid taxes to destroyed with such wanton disregard, I could not remain unrepentant.

Within me, there was a spark of hope that Emma was wrong, that maybe Kim Il-Sung, or even Mao or Stalin, had set up a scene for his propaganda. In my heart, however, I knew there was no conspiracy.

"Kanggye burned for days," Emma said. "For weeks, we could smell the smoke, even from Pastor Pak's house, no matter how the wind blew. There are other villages too that are just gone, and so many people have no homes and no food stores for winter. I don't know how many are dead, but it is beyond what we can handle.

The survivors are too worried about where to shelter and what to eat to deal with funerals."

No wonder refugees had flooded these roads. They continued to stream past us as I followed Emma down into the city, pressure building in my kneecaps. An iron stove, glazed with frost, stood solitary over the remnants of its home. A stray cat pounced behind a pile of warped steel.

Amid this wasteland, I wallowed in dread. If this was what the American leadership was willing to do when we were winning, what did they have planned now, in the aftermath of the slaughter of our marines? People often said that "hell hath no fury like a woman scorned," but in our world, so far, there was nothing comparable to the wrath of a man with wounded pride—no amount of suffering, and no level of savagery.

"Come," said Emma. "The clinic is on the other side of this neighborhood."

For the first time, I began to consider that perhaps Imo didn't hate me because America defeated Japan. Maybe she hated me because America bombed Korea—or both.

I forced myself forward, detached from my body, like it was a machine that I had to maneuver. "Are you sure the clinic is still here?" I asked. "There doesn't seem to be anything left."

"The clinic building is gone, but the doctors are working inside the boys' middle school. The classrooms are temporary shelters and medical facilities now. They have some supplies from the Soviets and are doing the best they can with what they have."

Past what might have been a fountain, there were three strips of houses standing, and a church with a shattered steeple. No waste-management systems were functioning, so there were human feces everywhere. The two-story schoolhouse, fenced in with barbed wire, had a small courtyard that had been hastily painted over with an enormous red cross. It was a signal for pilots—a plea.

At the front, there was a slide and a rusty swing set. Under a frayed awning, men smoked Lucky Strikes pilfered from American accessory kits. They grumbled their greetings as we pushed past the red double doors, paint chipping off on my gloves.

The front lobby had at least a hundred people crammed into a space that was meant for no more than a dozen. This waiting area was unheated, but it was warmed by rank human breath. There were patients with frostbite and terrible injuries, but there were seemingly healthy soldiers and civilians too.

Everyone, even some of the sick, cheered jubilantly when we entered the room. A Chinese soldier, with his quilted jacket unbuttoned, pressed a tin cup into my hand. He had large ears with detached lobes, and a long, hooked nose. The fumes from the liquid in the cup were so potent that my eyes watered; it might have been rubbing alcohol and bleach. Gagging, I held it as far away from my face as possible.

Did he know I was American? Was he trying to poison me?

"Mashi-le," said Emma, pointing to my cup. Then she chugged hers in one gulp, sending the soldiers howling and scrambling for a refill.

I gawked, half expecting her to combust.

"Mashi-le!" Emma repeated, holding her second shot to her lips.

Everyone in the room watched me, a few with their own cups raised. The walls behind them were plastered with posters of Stalin and Kim Il-Sung, and a few newer ones of Mao.

Were these cups even clean? Had they been shared by patients with diphtheria or tuberculosis, which were prevalent in the region?

My body didn't process alcohol well, but I couldn't explain this to Emma now. Even if I could, I doubted that this condition was an acceptable excuse not to drink the liquid. Closing my eyes, I knocked my cup back, my tongue searing as fire barreled into my throat and out through my nostrils.

The room exploded with whooping while I coughed, and the Chinese soldier who had given me the cup slapped me on my back. My stomach gurgled, protesting the abuse, but I wiped my lips and grinned like a clown.

"*Gahja,*" said Emma, seeming completely unaffected. She handed our cups back and pulled me toward the hallway, the plaster walls yellowed with age.

After squeezing past the crowd, I asked, quietly, "What's going on here? It's more like a bar than a clinic."

Emma glanced up and down the hallway before answering. "There was a government broadcast yesterday. We took back Pyongyang! The Americans have issued a formal evacuation order. They're leaving the North completely!"

Suddenly, I lost feeling in my lips and fingertips. My heart pumped faster as I processed her words, reciting them to myself. It didn't sound like news; it sounded like an insult. *A slap in the face.*

Emma rapped on one of the classroom doors, while panic sucked me in like quicksand. If there were no more Americans in Pyongyang, then I'd have to go all the way to Seoul for any hope of getting home. I pulled up a mental map of the Korean peninsula. Had our troops made it to Hungnam already? If I was quick, perhaps I could catch up with them there . . . but I was farther north than everyone else was, and traveling on foot!

It's not over, I told myself, fighting the impulse to cry, pushing away images of myself aging in the North Korean mountains, or withering away in one of Kim Il-Sung's prisons. *The UN Command will return.* The front lines here fluctuated as wildly as the weather in San Francisco . . . right?

Emma exclaimed in excitement when a short-haired woman, perhaps in her forties, opened the door. Unlike the other women I saw, she wore pants, which had to be rolled up and cinched at the waist. Her white shirt was wrinkled but clean, her hands chapped from frequent washing.

The woman and Emma spoke briefly in Korean before Emma introduced her as "the stupendous and highly intelligent Dr. Oh."

The stupendous and highly intelligent Dr. Oh was still delivering babies, given that they did not stop for war, but she functioned as a trauma surgeon and social worker now too. Instead of using Pastor Pak's cover about me starting my own revolutionary choir, Emma told Dr. Oh that I was a Chinese woman looking for her fiancé, a People's Volunteer Army (PVA) officer whom I had met when I was a "valiant interpreter" fighting against "evil Japanese aggression." With dramatic flair, Emma added that I was "so very old" and would have no alternative prospects, so it was critical that I find him.

"Aiya, xie xie ni!" said Dr. Oh, dropping a few Chinese words before reverting to Japanese. She bowed. "Our people are as close as lips and teeth! Everlasting honor to your fiancé, and all of the freedom-loving volunteers who have come to our defense!"

"Long live Chairman Mao," said Emma.

"Death to the imperialists and their puppet army," added Dr. Oh.

I didn't know many Communist slogans, so I said, "Freedom is not free."

"Exactly!" said Dr. Oh. "Forward to victory!" She embraced me and ushered us into the classroom.

My mind flashed to the airstrip at Hagaru-ri, and the battered marines dying in a foreign land with the understanding that we were small cogs in the crucial war against Communism. Though I had been with the Paks for only a few days, I was already beginning to understand Korea's struggle in a different light. This perspective didn't make this war better for me, though; if anything, I only found it more atrocious.

The classroom's desks and chairs were pushed into a corner, along with an array of cooking pots filled with water, some still steaming. There was dirt caked along the windowsills, and a basket heaped with soiled rags. Three patients lay on filthy floor mats. Though it was cold, one heavily pregnant woman was bare bottomed, legs spread as she moaned. Her jacket barely covered her belly, and her mat was soaked. When she saw us, she screamed.

"It's okay," said Dr. Oh—not to the pregnant woman, but to Emma and me. "She'll be fine. Her baby is head down, a good size, and this isn't her first delivery. But she's not dilated yet, so it's going to be a long and noisy night."

"Ah, my labor took two days," said Emma, clucking her tongue sympathetically.

"Two days is not bad," said Dr. Oh. "As long as mother and baby come out healthy, it's not bad!" She tilted her chin toward a pale woman who was curled on her side beneath a quilt. "That one I'm worried about. Not even six months, but she's lost blood—lots. I have to decide whether to send her across the border. Better facilities there, but the bumpy ride might make her bleed out."

"How's her baby?" whispered Emma.

"Irrelevant now," said Dr. Oh. "We women have our own wars. Sometimes, just making it out alive—alone—is a victory."

While Dr. Oh poured glasses of hot water for her patients, I sat down at one of the student desks and listened to the boisterous chatter from the waiting area. Someone had broken out in song.

Without meaning to, Emma had planted an idea in my brain. If Pyongyang was back under Communist control, then surely more soldiers were heading there. If I used Emma's lost-fiancé story, maybe I could convince them to take me along.

Dr. Oh gave me a glass of water too. "The woman you are looking for is upstairs," she said to Emma. "She was in a comfort station for three years, close to Beijing. I told her about your daughter, and she is willing to meet with you, but she'll want privacy. As you know, these women were forced to speak Japanese to their captors—to their rapists. I don't know how she feels about the language now, but I am not willing to ask her to revisit such a painful time in anything but her native tongue."

I downed my water, still thirsty from our trek here. "I don't need to go with you," I said. "I'll wait in the lobby."

"Really?" asked Emma.

"Yes. I have my own goals—remember? Maybe I can ask around and see if anyone knows my fiancé."

"Tell them not to get too drunk!" said Dr. Oh. "I might need them to drive someone to the border!"

It might have been too late to keep anyone sober, but I excused myself, emboldened by the moonshine and encouraged by my plan.

Back in the waiting room, people were singing off-key, and two Soviet men in civilian clothing had arrived, one with a typewriter. I was tempted to check whether it was mine, though it was probably in Cyrillic. The Soviets pulled out an unlabeled bottle from their bag and demanded, in Russian, that everyone present their cups. The one with the typewriter pointed at my face, which was probably the color of ketchup, and guffawed.

Ignoring them, I found the big-eared Chinese soldier who had given me my toxic drink earlier. He was seated on the floor, with other men in quilted uniforms, trying to figure out where their shared cup had gone.

"Hello," I said, in Mandarin. "I'm looking for someone, a People's Volunteer. Can you help me?"

He cocked his head at my hanbok, while his friend, a man with a large mole above his lip, borrowed a teacup from a civilian. "You speak Chinese?"

"I am Chinese," I clarified. "I came here to find my fiancé."

"By yourself?" He glanced around me, as if searching for a chaperone. "That's brave. I guess it's true when they say small peppers are spicy."

"I think he might be in Pyongyang," I pushed, "so I need to go there. Is there anyone here who is going and can give me a ride?"

He laughed, while a Soviet filled the cup to the brim. The Chinese soldier with the mole had to suck quickly at the top to prevent it from spilling.

"Slow down," said Big Ears. "What's your lover's name?"

Mole jutted in. "And where's he from, this boy?"

"What division is he with?" asked a third soldier.

I stared back as they waited, in earnest, for me to respond to their reasonable questions. Why hadn't I thought to give my fiancé a backstory?

"His name is Chang Shan-Wei," I said, giving my father's name—the first Chinese man's name that came to mind. "He's from Fujian. As for division, he never told me."

"Oh," said Mole. "Well, there are a few brothers from Fujian in my unit. I can ask them. What hometown?"

Luckily, my face was already red, so they couldn't see me

flush. I had forgotten how important hometowns—*laojia*—were for Chinese people, and I didn't know any cities in Fujian Province because my family had immigrated to Taiwan so many generations ago. "I don't remember," I said. "I met him in Beijing."

"You don't remember your fiancé's hometown?" Mole asked incredulously.

"It's somewhere in the mountains. It's very small, so you probably haven't heard of it."

"Well, do you have a photo of him?" asked Big Ears, wrestling the teacup from Mole.

"We are too poor for photographs," I answered.

"Hmm," said Mole. Turning to another group of Chinese soldiers in the corner, he shouted, "Hey! Attention! Does anyone here know a Chang Shan-Wei, a Fujianese boy? His fiancée is looking for him."

I froze as every Chinese soldier in the room whipped his head around and stared at me. Most of them still had traces of baby fat on their cheeks and were probably in their late teens or early twenties. Half of them were drunk, but they all began talking with urgency, like a child had been kidnapped.

"How tall is he?"

"How old is he?"

"When was he sent over here?"

"Can you draw a picture of him?"

Finally, one stern soldier with thick brows, a spattering of freckles, and eyes that drooped slightly at their outer corners said, "Your fiancé is busy serving the people! You shouldn't be bothering him. Go back home and wait for him there!"

In response to that, the others groaned.

"Come on, Comrade Ying," said Big Ears. "Whoever he is, he's going to want to see her!"

"Yeah," said Mole. "Don't be jealous that no one came looking for you!"

Comrade Ying crossed his arms while another soldier belched. "How did she get from Beijing to Korea anyway? Where is she even staying? Her tagging along will just create trouble."

"It's been a hard journey for me," I snapped, feigning indignation. "But I don't regret it. What if my fiancé is injured? What if he's dead? All I want is to see him one last time!" Sniffing, I dabbed at my eyes with my sleeve.

The soldiers murmured, and Big Ears punched Ying's shoulder. "Stop upsetting her, you bully! If you can't be helpful, just keep your ugly mouth shut."

"We'll figure it out, miss," said Mole, encouragingly. "Not right away, but we'll do our best to find Chang Shan-Wei. But then you have to go back to China. It's not safe for you here, not when the imperialists are raping unaccompanied girls."

"Not just unaccompanied girls," said Comrade Ying, tersely. "They barge into houses and rape them in front of their families. Did you know that before coming here, miss? This is a war zone—a *war zone*, not a fairy tale."

"Of course I know," I said.

Of course I did.

Every woman knows that in every war, on every side, men rape women, cruelly, viciously, and with impunity. American soldiers, and American leadership, were no exception. They turned a blind eye, but American soldiers certainly spoke about it; a few even bragged about it. Outside our bases, soldiers also coerced starving women into having sex in exchange for cigarettes, which could be traded for food to feed their families. But this was a type of story that no domestic paper dared to print—or cared to print—not when we were still at war and speaking ill of our troops was akin to speaking ill of the dead.

"I am pretty sure he's in Pyongyang," I continued. "Can you please take me there? I can cook and do chores. Clean weapons too."

"No way," said Big Ears. "The roads are deadly right now. The imperialists are monitoring them by air, and in some areas they'll gun down anything that moves. If you aren't going to battle, you have to avoid traveling—even for love."

Comrade Ying snorted, and left sulkily to get a drink from the Soviets. They handed him the entire bottle.

Mole burped and said, "There is nothing more terrifying than finding yourself suddenly in shadow, with no cover around and nowhere to run. I'm not sure what hurts more, being strafed with bullets or burned alive with napalm. Either way, it's not a fate your man would want you to have."

"Let's hope your boyfriend is here," said Big Ears, summoning a merry tone. "There are more of us in Kanggye than in Pyongyang. Besides, it's not just bombs that you have to worry about. There are bandits in these mountains. People here have lost everything, and they'll do anything to survive."

Comrade Ying took a swig from the bottle and held it out to me. "Come on. It'll keep you warm." His breath was like gasoline, and his expression was still sour enough to make my mouth pucker. "We will ask about Chang Shan-Wei when we get back to our bunks. I suppose little miracles boost morale. We can all use good news, even if frivolous."

Big Ears elbowed him. "Only a man who has never known love would say it is frivolous."

I accepted the bottle, but only pretended to sip, since I wasn't as skilled a liar as I had thought. If I really got drunk, it would be only a matter of time before I started slurring my way through the Pledge of Allegiance.

Or perhaps I'd just start bawling.

All men looked similar when they were scared and when they were worn. It was easier to think of the Chinese as fanatic robots beholden to Mao than to think of them as the boys they truly were—boys who, like many of our soldiers, came from poor backgrounds and believed wholeheartedly that they were fighting for good, bleeding for a cause. I had read that dying men, regardless of where they were from or what they believed, often called out for their mothers or their wives. In the MASH tents, I'd seen this truth confirmed. There, the American soldiers usually begged for "Mom," because most of them were too young to be married.

Were women the same way? I couldn't help thinking about Yun-Hee, and whom she might have called out for in her last moments. Was it Emma?

Eomma?

---

10 December 1950
Dear Yun-Hee,

Sometimes I wonder if it is selfish for me to pray so hard for your survival.

I've talked with so many women like you, about what they have lived through, and what they are still living through. I cannot erase them, so I carry them constantly. Through them, I understand that there is a difference between a slave and a prostitute, and a difference between how a man will treat a woman he owns versus a woman he pays.

Did you ever try to run away, Yun-Hee? Did they beat you when you did?

I spoke with a woman today who said that she tried to run away and Japanese soldiers burned her between her legs. She said that soldiers stuffed socks in her mouth so she couldn't scream while they used her. She has so many terrible stories about how soldiers tortured women as punishment for catching venereal diseases, and yet what breaks me is when I hear that more than half the girls at her station were killed. Death is not the worst fate, but it is I who cannot bear the loss of you. No matter how bad it was, I hope that you survived, just so we can meet again.

You are not alone, Yun-Hee.

Mom

13

TICKET TO SURRENDER

"The heroic People's Army and guerillas, in close cooperation with the brotherly Chinese People's Volunteers . . . are now continuing a large-scale annihilation programme in pursuit of the enemy who are fleeing southward in confusion."

—Kim Il-Sung, "On the Occasion of the Liberation of Pyongyang," December 9, 1950

December 10, 1950

There were Chinese soldiers heading south to Pyongyang, but no one was willing to take me. I made some Mandarin language mistakes when I tried to argue with them, but everyone just assumed that I was too inebriated to talk, or that they were too inebriated to listen. By the time Emma returned, I'd forgotten most of the details of my fake fiancé, and the soldiers struggled to remember his name. Most of us had drunk on an empty stomach.

Emma rubbed her knuckles, and ink had settled, weblike, in the whorls on her fingertips. She had spent two hours on the school's second floor, interviewing a woman who was originally from Wonsan. The woman had been too ashamed to return to her village, so she had settled in Kanggye and changed her name. She had married, but her husband didn't know about her past. The only reason she had gone to Dr. Oh was because she was unable to have children—a consequence of uterine trauma from repeated and prolonged rape. Irreversible and irreparable.

After accepting another shot of liquor from a KPA soldier, Emma and I sidled out into the bright courtyard. The sun was past its midpoint, poised to plunge like a stone behind the crater's edge.

I was ravenous, and the scab on my head itched, but the moonshine burned, leaving me almost giddy as the wind ripped at my coat. It was disappointing that I couldn't get a ride south, but I was determined to find another way, even if it meant walking. There were hundreds of thousands of refugees doing the exact same thing, including children and the elderly. If they could do it, I could too.

Except they can't do it, I reminded myself. They were dying by roadsides, starving and freezing, strafed and bombed.

Absorbed in my dilemma, I didn't notice Emma's silence until she shattered it, her grating voice startling me.

"I begin every conversation the same way," she announced. "I ask everyone who they are and where they are from. When and where were they taken, and how did it happen. Was it the draft? Were they abducted? Were they tricked?" Emma stepped into a pile of frozen excrement without breaking her pace. "Did you know that there were girls who were sold to the Japanese by their own families? Some people don't deserve to be parents, and yet they have so many kids. It took me more than ten years to have one—just one—and I didn't work hard enough to keep her. I think about that all the time. It's like a horrible song that repeats itself, a song that I can never ever turn off."

Whatever moonshine was in my system evaporated as Emma gnashed her teeth. Her eyes were unfocused, as though she were watching a movie that only she could see, the same kind that played in my own head during the night's dark hours.

"Emma," I said, "let's rest. We've been walking so quickly since we left. My legs are killing me."

"It doesn't matter why someone became a whore," Emma continued. "It just matters that they were used. They brought shame. Most families think that way, so they won't take their daughters back. But we never did things like most families, Yun-Hee and I. Of course, we couldn't—it was just the two of us. She should know that I don't care what she did. She should know that I still want her. How could she not know? How could she not know?"

"Stop," I said, grabbing Emma's elbow.

She slapped my hand through my glove, hard enough that it smarted. "I was a strict mom!" Emma yelled, drawing worried glances from the others in the ruined neighborhood. "But I had to be! I wanted her to have a better life. I wanted her to have a better job and a better husband. I wanted her to marry well, so I taught her well. I told her that girls should be *modest*, that they should be *pure*. I told her that girls who slept around with men were bad girls. That's why Yun-Hee won't come home. She doesn't want to come home. She thinks I will shun her. She thinks—"

"Moon Hwa-Ja!" With all my strength, I clamped my hands down on Emma's shoulders. She pushed like a bull, but I managed to swing myself in front of her and stop her frenzied walking. "That woman at the clinic was not your daughter. She is not Yun-Hee. And there is no way for you to know what Yun-Hee was thinking then or what she might be thinking now."

Yun-Hee is probably dead, I wanted to say, but I bit my tongue. I tasted blood, a rusty salt, and was terrified that Emma was going to snap. If she did, I wouldn't be able to restrain her on my own. Here, she could easily hurt herself, or expose me for who I was—what I was.

"Even if she doesn't marry, she has a place with me," Emma

rambled, oblivious to my words. "We managed, just the two of us, before. We can do it still. Of course I still want her. I will always want her. Always!"

I wrestled Emma's satchel from her shoulder and yanked her notebook out. "I don't know what you heard today, but you have to separate yourself from your work if you want to do it well!" Flipping through the pages, some crinkled and worn, I found the latest entry and held it up to her face. "This is what you wrote. I'm your friend Ellie Chang. We're in Kanggye, but we need to get back to the Paks—or back to the clinic, if we can't make the walk tonight. Either way, we can't go anywhere until you get your head on straight!"

Emma squinted angrily at the paper. Korean, like Chinese, is written vertically, and she ran her finger along the lines, nail scratching the ink. She inhaled as she reread her words, her lips moving silently like Pastor Pak's did when he studied his Bible. It was only natural to blend a stranger's sorrow with that in one's own soul, for misery loves company and pain impairs reason. Her despair as she distinguished her own story from the one she had recorded hurt me too. Emma and I were similar, but ultimately, she was not a journalist. Her work was not an assignment or a project; it was a Herculean pursuit of grief.

Gently, Emma took the notebook from me and pressed it closed between her palms. "Just like I begin every interview with the same question, I always end with the same question," she said. "I ask if they ever met a girl named Song Yun-Hee. Her Japanese name is Machiko. She is one hundred sixty centimeters tall and has eyes like mine. She was born in the year of the horse and was taken from Pyongyang. There's a birthmark on her collarbone, shaped like a gourd. So far, I haven't had any success, but one day I will."

Taking a deep breath, she slid the notebook back into her

satchel. A line of men with *jiges* trudged past us with salvaged scraps for sale. After adjusting her hat, Emma tried to nudge me aside.

"Emma," I began, keeping her blocked, "how are you so certain that Yun-Hee was in a comfort station? Jae-Min said that she never told you where she went. If she was taken in the labor draft, she might have been in a factory. There were so many factories, and far more women in them than in the comfort stations." In that cursed World War, there was any number of ways that a girl like Yun-Hee could have been killed—industrial accidents, infectious diseases, bombings in Japanese cities.

Emma, as if defeated, squatted in the middle of the debris-strewn road. "If it was anywhere but a sex station, she would have told me. She would have been able to write to me. She was fourteen when the Kempeitai took her—old enough for sex to be legal, but young enough to be a virgin. The Imperial Army picked young girls for the stations because virgins don't have venereal diseases. I want to believe Yun-Hee went somewhere else, but I just can't. I wish I didn't know, but I do."

With her elbows on her thighs she resembled a gargoyle, curved and deformed, carved into the architecture of a land marred by too many masters. I knelt beside her, our wet skirts ombré with rings of dirt. One had to separate oneself from one's work in order to do it well, but I had been in North Korea for days and my own boundaries were eroding like lines drawn in sand.

"All right, I believe you." This was partially true. I was still pretty sure that Yun-Hee was dead, but I said, "I believe your daughter was in a comfort station—sex station—and I will help you find her, or find out what happened to her. I can't promise anything, but I will try my best."

Emma wasn't a journalist, but I was, and I had the education, the training, and the experience to expand her search.

"How?" asked Emma. She regarded me quizzically, as if I were the one who had lost her senses.

"I don't know yet. I have to think more about it, but maybe there are records we can request from the temporary refugee camps in China, or even humanitarian organizations we could write to."

Simply speaking English opened up possibilities for me that Emma didn't have. Perhaps Yun-Hee did come back to Korea but was stuck in the South. She might have followed Allied soldiers to the West, as some in refugee camps did. It was all a bunch of scattered crumbs with no clear trail, but digging through chaos was part of my process. The best leads were hard to find, and even harder to follow, but they often led to the most amazing stories.

Americans wouldn't want to read a story about some Korean girl, though, I thought. *Or would they?* So much of the news was controlled by one type of man, but readers were broader than that. My success with the WASPs was largely due to female readers who wrote letters asking for more articles like mine because there were so few about women in war. *There hasn't been any detailed coverage about military sex slaves yet.* Emma's interviews weren't just glitter in the dust; they captured voices that deserved to be heard, to be blasted at full volume.

"Ellie-yah?" said Emma, uncertain. "Are you all right?"

"Of course I'm all right," I said. "Are you?"

"Yes, of course," she said. "But you were mumbling to yourself."

"Was I?"

"In English."

"Oh." It was odd that I hadn't noticed. "I'm tired, I guess. Maybe still a bit drunk. Nothing to worry about, though. As long as you're all right, let's go. The soldiers said there are bandits on these roads, so we should get back before dark."

Emma sniggered. "Bandits? They're ones to talk! Most of the bandits are deserting soldiers, or starving soldiers. If the Americans don't bomb our food, the Chinese will steal it."

"So there are bandits, then?"

"Yes, I suppose." Groaning, Emma arched her back and cracked her neck. "Let's go."

I moved so the two of us could walk side by side. My boots were broken in, but I had blisters on both feet, and my leg muscles were screaming. It wasn't the pain in my body that frightened me, though; it was something that I couldn't get a pulse on, like the fraying on the lining inside a dress, invisible yet obvious against the skin.

On our way up the crater, someone in front of us lost control of a handcart. As Emma and I climbed over a mess of broken ceramic and scattered clothing, a plane purred overhead. There had been intermittent air traffic all day, but this hum was different. I had lingered on enough tarmacs and flown with enough pilots that I could distinguish between the sounds of some aircraft.

"It's American," I said. Scanning the sky, I picked out a lightweight single-engine plane nicknamed the Mosquito. In this war, we used Mosquitoes to mark targets for air strikes. The Mosquito wasn't a bomber, but it often preceded them.

"Do we need to run?" asked Emma, shifting toward a patch of trees. Their winter boughs, bare and laminated with ice, could never shield us from incendiary jelly. Still, I had an animalistic urge to duck beneath them too.

"No," I answered, clinging to my logic. "All our fighter jets should be covering the evacuation at Hungnam, and our bombers won't come here without them. Bombers are expensive to replace, and too slow for the Soviet MiG-15s. We can't afford to let them get shot down, at least not easily."

An alabaster puff resembling a flock of birds burst from the back of the Mosquito. Tens of thousands of papers hung briefly in midair before dispersing into the wind, sashaying as though the clouds were shedding.

"Ppira," sighed Emma, with both relief and annoyance.

Leaflets drifted along the crater, and Emma snatched one as it fell. They were about the size of my palm, twirling before sticking to the damp ground. I bent over and plucked up another, and recognized it as one of our red and white safe-conduct passes.

On one side, it resembled the North Korean one-hundred-won bill, with Korean and Chinese characters. On the other side, it said, in English, "This certificate guarantees good treatment to any enemy soldier desiring to cease fighting. Take this man to your nearest officer and treat him as an honorable prisoner of war. Word as to the type of treatment actually received gets back rapidly and largely determines whether the next man fights or surrenders. Therefore YOU can help YOURSELF by giving enemy troops every reasonable opportunity to surrender and by feeding them, treating them well and allowing them to keep their personal property. REMEMBER, the more of them who give themselves up, the less you have to fight."

Emma sniffed as she read the Korean part. "They're telling our men to desert their units at night and destroy their weapons. If they cross the battle lines with their hands up, they'll get food and shelter. Ha!" She crumpled up the paper and tossed it aside.

"The Americans are retreating, and they're still trying to give us tickets to surrender? What a joke!"

Oh, Emma, I thought, my heart sinking as I searched the sky for additional planes. *Don't you know that the marines do not retreat? That they simply advance in another direction?*

Despite Emma's brash words, there were other civilians on the road who were collecting the passes by the handful, even though they were clearly marked for soldiers. Discreetly, I folded mine until it was as small as a strip of gum and tucked it into my pocket.

More than ever, I was keenly aware that I looked like the enemy, and if I ever crossed back into American territory, I'd have to do it with my arms raised. Women fought for the KPA too, and in the past, KPA soldiers had dressed in South Korean uniforms to sneak into our camps. Would our officers believe me if I said that I was American? It pained me to say that I really wasn't sure. But if they didn't, at least I'd have this pass to buy my safety until I could convince them to trust me.

If I could convince them to trust me.

I tried not to dwell on the possible outcomes. By the time I decided to pick up a few more passes in case I lost this first one, other people had claimed them all. Every leaflet had vanished, like leprechauns' gold. If it wasn't for the few bills winking at me from tree branches beyond my reach, I might have believed that I had hallucinated the entire thing. After all, where else in the world did fake money rain over bombed cities?

WESTERN UNION TELEGRAM

Mr. and Mrs. Shan-Wei Chang

1775 Cedar Drive, Daly City, CA

Deeply regret to inform you that your daughter, Eleanor Chang, is presumed to have been killed on 5 December 1950 at Hagaru-ri, Democratic People's Republic of Korea. Please accept my heartfelt sympathy. Letter to follow.

Mr. Clark Pembroke, Editor-in-Chief, Global Tribune

December 11, 1950

WESTERN UNION TELEGRAM

Mr. Joshua Sterling

570 74th Street, New York, New York

URGENT

Job opening, Tokyo Office. Immediate hire. Interested?

Mr. Clark Pembroke, Editor-in-Chief, Global Tribune

December 7, 1950

14

THE MAN WHO BECAME THE SUN

December 10–14, 1950

When Emma and I finally reached the Paks' house, the sun had set. The risen moon was a sliver, curved like a fisher's hook, and from afar, the snowy land looked like the sea—shimmering, as though nature refused to accept that we were mourning. Again, I soaked in the beauty on offer, as one might tilt a nearly empty cup for its last few drops.

Every day at the Paks' I had prayed for the Americans to come to Kanggye.

Later that evening, they did.

The planes must have flown out from Japan at dusk, just as Emma and I collapsed in front of Imo's stove. Like drunk women, we sprawled on the warm kitchen floor, our wet garments in a twisted pile. We had the house to ourselves, since the Paks were still out, so we forwent decorum. With legs spread wide, I massaged my calves while Emma helped me wash my bleeding feet, which were so numb that I didn't even wince when water seeped into my blisters.

Imo had left us two bowls of barley mixed with chicken soup, and a small dish of corn and kimchi to share. A thin layer of fat had congealed on the surface, a delightfully golden sheen. Too lazy to reach for spoons, we slurped up the bloated grains, savoring the pungent bite of spicy fermented cabbage.

After cleaning, Emma and I unfolded our mats and stretched out side by side. Nights in these mountains were never silent, with the fire's popping and the wind's incessant keening. Each gust was like a nosy neighbor rattling our windows and doors. Emma wasn't nearly as tired as I was, since she was accustomed to long walks and her feet were armored with calluses. She started telling me a story about a man who became the sun, but I fell asleep like I had been drugged, with my cheek plastered against the mat. I didn't hear the Paks come home, but it must have been late.

In middream, I thought I heard drumming.

Did the Gods know that one day humans would learn to package an earthquake and fly with a forest fire?

I bolted up on my mat as dust fell from the rafters. The mountainside was trembling, and the house itself seemed to moan, a vibration that I could feel but not hear over the blasts in the distance. There was so much light outside that it snuck in through the shutters, streaking the floor with flashes of white.

The Paks burst out from their bedrooms, yelling in Korean.

"To the cellar," Emma croaked hoarsely, bunching her blankets up.

There was no way that being underground would save us from napalm, but I rushed to follow them, scraping open a blister as I forced my boots on. When I hobbled past the threshold, I gagged at the smoke that billowed from the north.

Clouds of soot had blotted out the moon and unfurled over the mountains like a vulgar pair of wings. Kanggye's crater was a crucible of fire, boiling red as bomb after bomb hurtled down. My mother once said that shooting stars were just souls leaving for their next life. Somewhere in our skies, there must have been a meteor shower.

Imo slammed the cellar door shut, entombing us all beneath the damp earth. Dirt sprinkled our faces as the mountain continued to jolt from explosions. While wedged between the *onggi*, Pastor Pak began to cry, his sobs reverberating off the stoneware. It was too dark to see anyone's face, but soon Emma and Jae-Min began crying too, and Imo and I were the only ones who weren't hitching and sniffing. As much as my chest hurt, I had to contain the pain, even if I were to burst. How could I grieve with them when I felt like this was my fault? Amid the odor of cabbage and soil, the weight of my shame threatened to suffocate me.

Here I didn't look like the enemy, but I was the enemy.

For the next two days, the amber sky was thick with ash, so hazy that it was impossible to see past the midpoint of the mountain. Even with the doors and windows closed, Imo coughed, a hollow barking that sounded like that of sea lions. Pastor Pak and Jae-Min went to the outskirts of the city to search for survivors, and the villagers opened their homes to the wounded. Most of the people who had remained in Kanggye after the first major bombing were those who had difficulty traveling—the elderly, the infirm, families with small children, and people with disabilities.

Pastor Pak's house was crowded now, harrowing from the burn victims who stank of pus, melted fat, and cauterized skin. I tried not to stare, but they howled when a breeze grazed their raw flesh. There were no analgesics for their pain, and half of them died within the first day. We piled their bodies up in the forest, with a conflicted sense of mourning—I was relieved that they were no longer in agony, but I was also penitent. It felt wrong to herald death as a blessing. When I wasn't washing bandages, I was boiling water, and when Jae-Min wasn't dressing wounds, he was moving corpses.

Nothing was standing in Kanggye anymore, not even the school with the new red cross in its courtyard.

"I understand why they bombed the airfields and the steel factory," said Emma, as Imo rummaged through her cabinets for spare blankets, "but how could they bomb the hospital, or a school?"

I sat between them, cutting already-ruined clothing into strips for bandages. "I don't know," I said, at a loss for an explanation that didn't make Americans sound vindictive or cruel. Most of us, whether civilian or military, were not, and are not, vindictive or cruel. There was, however, a history with poisonous roots, and here in the Pacific, our leadership wanted unconditional surrender.

Unconditional surrender. Our enemies were never allowed to feel safe—to have sanctuary or rest—until they bent to our will, crawled to us on their hands and knees, with a ticket to surrender clenched between their teeth. Our enemies were supposed to feel pain, and nothing hurt as horribly as cradling a child in a shroud. If there was any chance that soldiers were inside a building or a home, we were going to blast it, regardless of its function or how many civilians shared the space. What humanitarians would call a war crime was simply "collateral damage."

I cut the last of the bandages and laid them in a pile for sterilizing.

"*Mwojyo?*" asked Imo. She had made her way to the back of the cabinet, where Emma had hidden Barbara's air force jacket in case the authorities came by for a house check. Imo held it up, pinching each shoulder pad with just the tips of her thumb and pointer finger, like it could be contaminated. Though the jacket wasn't really mine, it was the only item I had to connect me to home, and I didn't want her touching it with such contempt.

"That's mine," I said, quietly, my anger mounting as Imo poked at the fur lining. When she flipped it over to examine the air force logo, the letters from Hagaru-ri tumbled out, landing in disarray on the floor. Addresses were scrawled in Clara's hasty cursive, barely legible except for the states, which she had written in all capitals. *OHIO. GEORGIA. NEW YORK. TENNESSEE. MISSOURI.*

I sprang for them, but Imo dove like a jet. In a single sweep, she scooped up every envelope and stomped toward the kitchen.

"Give them back!" I snarled. The refugees in the hallway stopped their conversations and stared as I scrambled after her. I would have caught up, but Emma's arms lashed around my waist and tightened as though her bones were steel. Kicking my legs, I struggled to pull open her strong seamstress fingers.

"No!" I screamed, in English, as Imo wrenched open the stove's door. Summoning all my strength, I knocked Emma over just as Imo threw the entire stack of letters into the fire. The edges of the envelopes curled as the flames licked them obscenely. They were just paper, but in my heart, that ink was blood and each line was holy.

"I was supposed to mail those!" I exploded, too livid to speak anything other than my native language. "I promised I'd mail those! There are families waiting for them. I *promised*!"

Imo hissed in Korean, and I faced her head-on, unafraid. Everyone in the house was watching us, and I was ready to punch her, regardless of her family's hospitality. I was so focused on Imo's skinny, brittle nose that I didn't see Emma's open palm. It cracked like a paddle against my cheekbone, sending me reeling.

"Enough!" said Emma, in Japanese. "How could you exchange letters with that boy, and lie to us about it? Didn't I tell you that he's from a bad family? I take you in, and Imo feeds you, and you repay us with disobedience? A woman's reputation is a vase, and it breaks easily! Who's going to marry you now?"

Imo launched into a tirade in Korean, picking up her poker and rattling it at me.

Was she threatening to *spank* me?

I hated not being able to understand Korean, and I was so furious that I was ready to fight anyone—even Emma. My cheek stung, and the tears that I had been holding back brimmed. Through that blurry sheen, I saw my spectators. Among them was a woman whose entire torso was wrapped in bandages. She held her two children, both of whom had burns on their faces. On the mats behind her there was an old man whose hair had been incinerated to the scalp, and a son who had just moved his father's body to the mass grave among the pines. Everyone here had lost someone in the bombing, and they whispered, concerned.

I touched my face, still throbbing where Emma had hit me. She had covered for me once again. Obviously, I couldn't have those letters here, not with all these strangers around, exploring and prying. If anyone knew I was American, the Paks and Emma would be in danger, not just from the authorities but from the civilians, who were starting to despise America too.

Imo stood over me like an executioner, holding her poker as if it were a sword. As the hot tide of my rage subsided, I was embarrassed about losing control, and worried about what I might have revealed. Bowing to Imo, I mumbled an apology before excusing myself and running outside, desperate for the crisp air to cool me.

I dashed past men loading firewood, and ducked behind the shed. There, I unplugged myself and wailed into the wind, crying like Pastor Pak had in the cellar. *I am going to die in North Korea, like the marines who wrote those letters.* My parents would have no body to bury, and like Emma, they would always wonder what had happened.

Usually I could talk myself out of despair, but I had lost my library of encouraging words. With all the lies that Emma and the Paks had invented to explain my presence, I had lost myself. I was a Chinese woman searching for her fiancé. A revolutionary singer. A Japanese interpreter for the Allied Powers. Adopted. A spy. I couldn't keep track of it anymore!

In the end, I was an American woman who was going to be killed by American bombs.

I was certain that more death was coming. In the forest surrounding the Paks' village, families were cutting the pine trees down to make temporary shelters. Many of these people had relocated multiple times already. Was there even a point in rebuilding?

With my back pressed against the wooden shed, I could hear the chickens clucking softly. Farther out, children gathered twigs for kindling. Some of the older ones wore their red Patriotic Youth League scarves and built traps for mice and rabbits. Imo had spared some provisions for the wounded, but she made it clear that everyone else had to fend for themselves. Pastor Pak, meanwhile, was a leaky pot. When his wife wasn't looking, he slipped handfuls of millet or corn to everyone around his house.

A peal of laughter cut through the air. The smaller children had found enough pebbles to play *gonggi*, a game similar to jacks. They threw a pebble up and scooped another before catching the tossed pebble in their fists. It was hard to do with mittens on, so they all had their fingers bare, accessories strewn carelessly in the snow. Their lips were cracked from the cold, but they shrieked with joy when one boy tossed the pebble too high and it hit him on the forehead.

Hugging myself for warmth, I watched the children take turns in their game until one of the adults chided them, perhaps for not finishing their chores.

"*Neeeh!*" the children exclaimed, scattering like gulls. They left a squishy trail of footprints in the mud, their voices ringing with the timbre of bells.

My own lips were probably blue. When I thought I was calm enough to fake a smile, I slunk back into the house to boil the bandages and hang them to dry by the stove. The refugees who had witnessed my outburst greeted me sympathetically, strangely kind despite my behavior. I found Emma at the *kotatsu*, sewing up Barbara's jacket.

She glanced up as she poked her needle through the fabric. "It was ripped," she said. "A tough fix, but I'm almost done."

Imo ignored me, but no one else seemed upset, or even wary.

"How did you explain my English to them?" I whispered, wondering what story she had spun up now.

Emma chuckled and reinforced her final stitch. "I didn't. I told them you were speaking Russian. Most people here won't know the difference between one Western language and another, at least not when you yell it like a madwoman."

She laid the jacket flat on the table, tugging tightly at her knot.

At the right breast, where the US Air Force logo had been,

there was now a crimson circle with a Korean slogan embroidered in bright yellow. In the center, Emma had pinned a button similar to the "I am a Chinese" ones that my family had worn during World War II, except that this one had a portrait of a stern Kim Il-Sung on it.

"I'm sorry I did a bad job," said Emma, "but this was all I could manage with what we had. It would be a shame to throw away a fur-lined coat over a small tear, wouldn't it?"

I had thought that I was calm enough to fake a smile, but all I could do was breathe, blink, and force myself to contain my devastation. From the depths of my memory, the bedtime story that Emma had told me began to resurface—the one about the man who became the sun.

Hidden Christians were everywhere in North Korea, but none were as audacious as Kim Sung-Ju, a Presbyterian whose grandfather was a minister and whose father was a teacher at schools run by American missionaries. The Kims were also independence activists, and they fled to escape Japanese persecution. In the rugged mountains of Manchuria, Sung-Ju became a guerilla fighter with the Chinese Communist Party and changed his name to Kim Il-Sung: "Kim becomes the sun." He was only thirty-six when the Soviets pushed him into power.

The Sun said that the Japanese used to call him the Tiger.

The Sun said that his people are his eyes.

The Sun said he is a servant of the motherland, a warrior of the fatherland, and the only pathway to liberation.

There had been other independence activists competing with Kim, many of whom were Christians with strong support from various churches. By purging the North of religion, the Sun not only eliminated his greatest challengers; he also erased anyone who remembered him as little Sung-Ju—a child who prayed, and a person beholden to a power above his own.

Emma had said, "The Sun understands that it is better to be feared than to be loved, because if people fear you they will pretend to love you, and isn't that enough?"

She never gave me her opinions on America, but daily I was seeing hatred seep from the fresh graves in the forest. The smaller the victims, the greater the enmity. For every civilian our bombers killed, at least two more concluded that the West was as evil as the Sun claimed it was. They were forgetting how much they feared *him*, and beginning to agree that America had to be eliminated for Korea to survive, let alone prosper.

I thanked Emma and tried the jacket on, noting that she had sewn her circle tightly over the original logo without piercing the leather. The fur was soothing against my skin, while Kim Il-Sung was triumphant on my chest. This jacket was now my most expensive item, augmented in value because I had nothing else. Emma had managed to salvage it so I could wear it without reprisal, yet somehow I still felt like it was gone.

But then again, it had never really been mine to begin with.

PRESIDENT TRUMAN'S NEWS CONFERENCE

November 30, 1950

THE PRESIDENT: We will take whatever steps are necessary to meet the military situation, just as we always have.

QUESTION: Will that include the atomic bomb?

THE PRESIDENT: That includes every weapon that we have.

WESTERN UNION TELEGRAM

Mr. Clark Pembroke

The Global Tribune

830 East Broadway, New York, NY

URGENT

Gen. MacArthur has requested Pentagon for commander's discretion to use atomic weapons. Story to follow.

Mr. Joshua Sterling, Special Correspondent (Tokyo)

December 9, 1950

15

INSIDE INFORMATION

December 15, 1950

All the communication towers were destroyed, and there was no more electricity. Neighbors said the Americans were now concentrated in Hungnam, but I wasn't sure what to believe. As someone who was once part of "the news," I thirsted for information, but every tap was either dry or potentially poisoned. In Kanggye's mountains, I was the only one who "didn't know" that the South Korean "puppet army" had started the "Fatherland Liberation War," and the North had "acted in self-defense."

When I was alone, I reminded myself that I was a news correspondent, and that I had personally spoken with American military staff who had been in Seoul when the KPA came screaming across the 38th parallel. There were photos of it all. Yes, *they* had started it! But when everyone around me was vehemently insisting on a different story, I couldn't help questioning my sanity.

I was in the kitchen, helping Emma fill a steel tub for the children to bathe in, when Pastor Pak asked me to accompany him on a walk. No one just "walked" anymore, when everyone was hungry and there was so much to do, so I prepared myself for an awkward conversation. Zipping up my Kim Il-Sung jacket, I met the pastor outside.

Over the past days, he had lost weight from sharing his own portions with eleven new guests. Imo kept the cellar locked and stood guard in her kitchen, doling out occasional gifts like the most stringent ration officer. Aside from Jae-Min, no one was even allowed to glance at her grains or sniff her fermented vegetables. The dried anchovies may as well have been silver-plated, and the garlic made of pearls. Others in the house grumbled that war had shriveled Imo's already hardened heart, rendering it small and dense—like a bullet.

Pastor Pak's skin sagged from the rapid loss of fat around his face, aging him. He had his hands stuffed humbly in his pockets when he said, "Ellie-yah, I have an important question to ask you, maybe the most important question that I have asked anyone in a long time."

We hiked up the mountain, passing a neighbor who was loading a handcart with blankets and sacks of millet. "All right," I said. "What do you want to know?"

He was my elder, but now he stared at me with childlike inquisitiveness. "Will the Americans really use an atomic bomb on Korea?"

Internally, I heaved a leaden sigh. "How am I supposed to know? I've been here at your house, remember?"

"You must know something," said Pastor Pak, stepping carefully to avoid loose stones. "People here are worried. They think that America is only rushing to evacuate the North because they are planning to drop atomic bombs on it."

Some of the refugees had anxiously packed what little they

had and set out for Manchuria. I was nervous too, but Manchuria wasn't an option for me. The US had no diplomatic relations with mainland China, and it would have been even more difficult for me to get home from there than from Kanggye. For a Korean, however, it was a great plan. Emma told me that Imo had been pushing to flee, but to her teeth-gnashing frustration, Pastor Pak remained as stubborn as the mountains he clung to.

"You and I hear the same rumors," I said, "the same news."

He frowned as though I were being uncooperative. "We live in a fallen world. It is harder to be a Christian now than it used to be. It will get harder still, but we must stand firm in our faith."

We passed the last houses in the village, their thatched roofs piled with snow. Sheets of rock led to a hazy clearing, which was the lookout point that Pastor Pak had told me about before. The sky had faded from a rusty orange to a lemon gray, but we still couldn't see past the mountainside.

"Is that why you don't want to leave here?" I asked. "Because you think God will protect you from the bombs?"

Pastor Pak laughed, a robust sound that echoed over the treetops, which were dusky in the ochre light. "No, Ellie, that is not what I meant."

"Then how come you don't want to go to China? It seems like the safest option. The Americans won't cross the Yalu River."

Unless we declare war on China too.

"I have thought about going to Manchuria," admitted Pastor Pak. "Not just now, but throughout my life. My father and my brothers were murdered by the Kempeitai for protesting the occupation." He pointed to the Kim Il-Sung button on my jacket. "I knew most of the Christian rebels in Pyongyang, including the supreme leader's father. He was a well-respected man who also had a bounty on his head, but unlike my father, he took his family and ran away to Manchuria. That is how the supreme leader joined the Chinese Communist Party and trained with the Soviet army. Kim Il-Sung is a Chinese Soviet, not a true Korean."

"Okay, but that doesn't answer my question."

"Ellie-yah, I am getting there. If you ask a complicated question, you must listen to a complicated answer."

"All right. I'm sorry."

"Don't be sorry; just be patient. Now, my point is, Kim Il-Sung came back to Korea after being gone for twenty-six years—more than two thirds of his life. Rhee Syngman is also a stranger," he said, about South Korea's president, who had assassinated rivals and put hundreds of thousands of his own people into prisons and reeducation centers. "Rhee came back here with the American military after living in America for forty years. He is an American dog, with a sharp bite. Both Rhee and Kim care only for their own power, when real Koreans just want our country to be independent and unified—without foreign influence, whether Soviet or American. And yet we've been partitioned under the protégés of our occupiers. What do you think will happen to Korea if people like me leave?"

With both hands, Pastor Pak made a sweeping motion to encompass the area below us. "Several generations of my family are buried in these mountains, including my parents and my brothers. The Paks could have gone abroad anytime, like the Kims, but we didn't. We have always stayed. We have always fought—here, in Korea—even during Japanese rule. Here, in Korea, where we were, and still are, needed most. The Lord has a plan for this country, but he also helps those who help themselves. That requires sacrifice. I will not abandon Korea, and that is what I mean when I talk about faith. Do you understand me?"

"Kind of."

I sympathized with wanting to live for a cause, and for that reason, I typically ran toward instead of away from conflict. However, I was the daughter of emigrants—people who did exactly what Pastor Pak seemed so scornful of—and as a result, I identified with the country that I was raised in more than the roots of my family. Sometimes I wondered what I would have been like had I grown up in Taiwan or China. Would I have joined the Communist Party? Would I still have become a correspondent?

"This is not a terrain for the faint of heart," said Pastor Pak, disappointed by my lackluster response, "or a time for wavering. If you live here long enough, perhaps you will see. You will change."

I shuddered whenever anyone mentioned my long-term boarding. While others were heading to Manchuria, I had shifted my goal to Seoul, which I was betting on the Americans to hold like the balance of the world depended on it—because, in the realm of our rivalry with the Soviets, it did.

When we returned to the Paks' house, Imo was bidding goodbye to yet another family. Upon seeing us, she cast her signature scathing side-eye not at me but at her husband.

Pastor Pak pretended not to notice and crab-walked stiffly past her.

"When you can," he said to me, "tell my wife that you don't believe there will be any nuclear bombs. She won't listen to me when I say she is overreacting, but she'll believe you, an American."

Seething in his own subtle way, Pastor Pak retreated to his bedroom, leaving me confused. What part of my conversation with him had indicated that I agreed with his decision to stay here? Hadn't I explicitly said that, despite being American, I had no idea what America would do?

Pastor Pak and Imo usually tried to avoid fighting when they had a full house, but that night they had a shouting match. The blue light of their kerosene lantern shone through the shoji screen so that everyone could see their shadowy figures animated behind the paper.

I wondered if Pastor Pak was using something that I'd said, or that he thought I'd said, as leverage. I was starting to feel like everything here was my fault, or that I wasn't doing enough to help. My gut twisted with consternation as I lay on my mat, which I shared with Emma since she had given hers to another family. Emma had lost weight too, but her back still had meat on it and radiated heat. The two of us used one blanket, overlaid with my fur-lined coat, which kept us warm even as the fire dwindled.

I knew Emma wasn't asleep, because of the absence of snoring, but I was startled when she whirled around to face me. Her nose was inches from mine, and the faint lantern light caught her features, each wrinkle drawn into a net of worry.

"Ellie-yah," she said, low yet urgently, "we don't have to listen to the pastor, or stay with the Paks. We can make our own plans, you know—you and I."

"Really?" I asked, surprised by her offer. Since the recent bombing, I had been mired in a sense of solitude, even as the Paks' home became more crowded. I never expected anyone to include me in anything, let alone an invitation to run away. Despite our differences, she had recognized that I was as afraid as she was, and that touched me more than she realized.

In the other room, Jae-Min sounded like he was reprimanding both of his parents.

"What's he saying?" I asked.

"Oh, Jae-Min says they will starve if they go to China. There are too many refugees there already, and Mao doesn't even have enough food for his own people."

"So Jae-Min also wants to stay here?"

"No, he wants to go back to Pyongyang," said Emma, listening and translating simultaneously. "He says the government is building air-raid shelters there and will provide relief packages too—not that the Paks really need relief, mind you, but you know how it is. If everyone is starving, it's only a matter of time before they eat the rich—or relatively rich."

"Jae-Min said that?"

"No, that last part is from me. Jae-Min is saying that the Americans didn't use nuclear weapons on Tokyo. He thinks they'll avoid using them on our capital too, but I'm not so sure."

"No one can be sure," I said, irritated. Speculation about a matter of this magnitude was hubris.

"Only God knows," Emma agreed. "As for us, we just have to make our best guess."

"We just need to get out of North Korea. If you and I are to make a plan, that's it."

"So you want to go to China too?"

"No, I want to go to South Korea." I paused. "I *have* to go to South Korea."

"South Korea? Do you know how far that is?"

"I am heartbroken by how far it is, but at this point I can't stall anymore. When I first arrived at this house, I thought I was more likely to die if I left on my own. I can't speak Korean, and there are so many risks on the road, but now it seems like we're all going to die if we stay. I can't waste more days wavering. It's time to just start walking."

"Aigo," said Emma. "Do you remember how torn up your feet were after we got back from Kanggye? Imagine ten times that distance. Twenty!"

"I'm not going to do it overnight. It will probably take me a month, but I have no other choice. No one is going to save us." Seeing her uncertainty, I added, "You don't have to come with me. In fact, I don't think you should. Manchuria is closer, and probably safer than the South is."

"Ha, that's a guess too, isn't it?"

It was probably just as arrogant for me to assume that I could make it to the South unscathed as it had been for Jae-Min to predict where the bombs were going to fall, but as the Paks continued sniping, I realized that perhaps I'd been overly defensive with the pastor earlier. I was cautious of being associated with the enemy, but I had been following the American air force ever since I got my first press badge, during World War II. As I stared up at the rafters, indiscernible in the dark, I grasped at every conversation I'd had with our pilots in the past months, hoping they could guide me now.

Everyone in Tachikawa knew that Truman had already ordered atomic-capable B-29s to Guam, carrying assembled nuclear bombs. Off duty in the lounges, Barbara and I had debated whether Truman would actually authorize their use. Pilots and other nurses had weighed in, and soon the discussion had devolved into an argument over whether Japan had "deserved it." Barbara and George were so similar in that, first and foremost, they saw light—they saw good. Both of them were convinced that Hiroshima and Nagasaki had left too deep a scar for Truman to pull the trigger now, but that was before China had entered the war.

George's last words on the tarmac in Tachikawa were etched in me, in red: *MacArthur's pushing to bomb Manchuria. If it were up to him, we'd go nuclear.*

I turned to face Emma again, certain that the wrath in Washington had not yet abated. "I'm not guessing," I said. "But I was wrong when I said that Manchuria is safe. I don't know what type of bomb our military will use, but I know—I *know*—that we will annihilate your country. Even if it isn't nuclear, it's going to be horrific, and there's a good chance that not even the Yalu River can contain it. So while I don't know what the Paks will do, if it's you and me, we need to go to South Korea. And we need to leave as soon as possible, with as much as Imo will let us carry."

Emma's eyes grew wide and childlike, the whites tinted blue from the kerosene light. "But what about Yun-Hee?" she whispered. "What if she's trying to come home? I left a note for her on my door, telling her that I came here with Jae-Min. If I go south, she'll never find me. What about Pyongyang instead? There is shelter for us, and I have some food stored in the pantry. I agree with Jae-Min. The Americans won't drop an atomic bomb on a capital city, and this way I can make sure I won't miss her."

Are you stupid? I wanted to shake Emma until her head rattled. *Yun-Hee is dead, dead!* How could such a decision possibly revolve around her? Suddenly, I felt the phantom sandy texture of red bean on my tongue, and the silken mochi hand kneaded by Hitomi in Tachikawa.

"Emma," I said, "we never used nuclear weapons on Tokyo, but we firebombed the hell out of it. Within the next month, Pyongyang will be a city of ruins, a giant grave. Forgive me, but if your daughter was in the North, and she really wanted to come home, she would have done so already. And you will never find her elsewhere if you are dead. We can stop in Pyongyang to rest, but we cannot linger. We might not survive the trip to Seoul, but you will never see your daughter again if you stay in North Korea. Never. That is not a guess; it is a promise."

The Paks had stopped arguing, leaving my words standing out above the wind and the fire, a lone act on an empty stage. *Was that too abrasive?* Sometimes, even when I tried to dial myself down, I came across as too harsh, too loud.

"I'm sorry," I began, but Emma stopped me.

"Don't be. I trust you." The mat shifted as she rolled over, her back to me once again. "You're a smart girl, and a brave girl too."

Emma was quiet, but I could tell from the strain in her breath that she was hurt. The fear that Yun-Hee had decided never to return was too fresh in her heart. Could I have gotten my point across without being so blunt?

I replayed my arguments and reimagined them even as others around me drifted off to sleep. Being persuasive yet respectful, strong but not obnoxious, was a mental tightrope that I struggled with. For every article that I wrote, my time was cleaved into three parts: writing the article, revising the article, and then regretting something about the article—either something I said or something I should have said. As I got older I got better, but I also became bolder. I cared less about public figures and their disapprobation now, but Emma was different. She was my friend, and I wished that I had done a better job at winning this fight.

December 16, 1950, Kanggye
Dear Mom and Dad,

I've been afraid to write to you, but I don't know when I'll have another opportunity. Imo burned all of my other letters, except the first one that I wrote to you, because I had that stashed in Jae-Min's jacket. I'm about to set out for South Korea, and though I'm afraid of what's to come, I am looking forward to getting away from Imo. I have to keep this short, because if she catches me writing again she'll shred this letter too.

I've studied and written so much about war, but nothing can prepare you for actually being in it—trapped in it. I know you never wanted me to come to Korea, and that you must be so worried now, maybe disappointed too.

Was it Confucius who said that the worst crime a child can commit is to die before his parents? I can't remember, but please know that I'm doing everything I can to get home. When I'm at my worst, knowing that you are waiting for me forces me to keep my head up and eyes forward.

With all my love,
Ellie

16

PAPER PLANES

December 16, 1950

We often woke up to American leaflets, which settled overnight like frost, soggy paper in an increasingly barren forest. They ranged from the size of an index card to that of a newspaper sheet, and were directed at soldiers, many of whom had fled into the mountains following the bombing of Kanggye. Some leaflets gave instructions for surrender, while others warned that Mao was plotting to annex North Korea. A few had no text, and were just caricatures of Stalin and Kim Il-Sung, fat and cackling while emaciated villagers watched them feast.

Imo used the paper for kindling, while children collected them and made planes: "Korea's gallant warbirds!"

The prolific waste of paper was bizarre. We could have buried the North in anti-Soviet messaging, and everyone, young and old, would still have remembered one simple fact: Because of Stalin's fighter jets, the American bombers no longer flew during the day. There was sunlight again. There was some reprieve, and it was thanks to the only country that was strong enough to stand up to the "imperialist marauders."

Emma and I didn't have much to pack, but I wanted to speak with Pastor Pak one more time; I couldn't leave without trying to change his mind about staying. Though I had rehearsed my words and prepared for an argument, the heavens intervened. While Pastor Pak was out tending to the three chickens that remained in his shed, his God spoke to him, not with a still, small voice but with a deluge from the sky.

It was rare for leaflets to fall during the day, and Jae-Min was the first to run back inside, with a *jige* strapped to his back. Imo was boiling water for another round of bandages, and one mother she had taken a liking to sat beside the fire with her toddler, warming her feet while smacking her son's hand whenever he tried to touch the stove.

"Eomma-ni!" Jae-Min cried, waving a piece of paper the size of a magazine cover. Without removing his shoes, he dashed into the kitchen, leaving muddy ovals on the mats. His *jige*, half filled with firewood, clunked as he ran. Emma and I were disassembling her sewing machine—we had just dislodged the hand-cranked wheel—when Jae-Min launched into a string of Korean, gesturing animatedly.

No matter how old or big someone is, everyone sounds small when they are scared.

Emma was usually quick to translate, but she gasped in shock as the other women began to jabber. I loathed these minutes of limbo, when I was helpless while everyone else was already reacting.

"What's going on?" I asked impatiently.

Jae-Min whirled around, wood clattering onto the kitchen tiles, and clomped over and shoved the leaflet into my face. It was a drawing of a house with four missiles overhead, about to strike. Huge Korean letters were printed in red, but I didn't have to be literate to get the message.

"It says, 'Warning: Save your life,'" seethed Jae-Min. He crumpled up the paper. "How much time do you think we have?"

The heavy door slammed as Pastor Pak and three other men entered, each with their own leaflets, as though the one that Jae-Min had crushed had been resurrected and multiplied.

"Ellie!" exclaimed Pastor Pak, holding his hatchet. "How serious is this? Do we really need to evacuate?"

"Why would anyone bomb these mountains?" asked Jae-Min. "There's nothing here but houses and farms!"

The refugees didn't know I was American, and most of them didn't speak Japanese either, but all three of the Paks were looking at me as if I had personally ordered the leaflet drop.

"I'm not sure," I said, even though I was familiar with the map of the military mind. With Kanggye destroyed, the enemy would retreat into the mountains. Perhaps they were crouched in peasants' cellars or camped among the pines, and in the warm homes of simple families, Communists were hiding and breeding—as insidious as cancer and as contagious as pox. "Maybe they're after the soldiers," I offered.

"Most of the soldiers went across the border!" yelled Jae-Min. "And the ones who are here can read those bloody papers just as well as we can. You think they'll stay, like idiots? The Americans are going to destroy this village, but the soldiers will just get shelter elsewhere. What about us? Even if we survive, we'll have nothing! No home, no food!" He loomed over me, the *jige* adding to his height.

The gleam of Pastor Pak's hatchet blade, silver like the ash that now coated the snow, caught my eye. Laws of war were convenient when it was decided that the mere possibility of soldiers rendered anything and everything a military target. How many civilian lives were we willing to trade for each Red? It was a question that I wanted to scream, with an answer that I already knew. As this war dragged on, that number would approach infinity, a limitless line of bodies stretching to victory.

"Leave her alone!" Emma cried, linking her arm through mine. Her fingers were threaded through the iron spokes of her sewing machine's wheel. "She has nothing to do with this!"

"Don't yell at my son!" snapped Imo. "We don't have time for you to be a mother hen, Hwa-Ja. Ellie isn't even your daughter."

"She doesn't have to be my daughter for me to care. She's a civilian like us, and you're being unfair!"

"Worry about yourself," retorted Imo. "No one's going to coddle you if you lose your mind again, least of all me!" Turning on her heels, Imo reverted to Korean and started shouting at Pastor Pak and Jae-Min, both of whom shouted back.

So many people were speaking, voices overlapping, but Emma was quiet, her arm limp in mine. She had the heavy wheel resting on her abdomen, her wrists crossed.

I put my arm around her solid, wide shoulders—those of a woman who was accustomed to lifting heavy loads, often alone. "You have nothing to be ashamed of," I said. "You will be all right, but if you're not, I will help you. We have our own plan, you and I—remember?"

The two of us were already packed. As soon as we finished dismantling the sewing machine, we could set out, before the roads became completely mobbed.

Emma wiped her eyes and said, "I don't want to be a burden to anyone."

"You are not a burden," I said. "I need you. How am I going

to make it through this country when I can't speak the language? I don't even know where I'm going. I'm the burden, not you. If you don't mind helping me, then I don't mind helping you."

One family was already at the door, with nothing but the clothing on their backs. They bowed to Pastor Pak on their way out, and bounded to the mountain path. Others were throwing their belongings together, but there were still three wounded people in Jae-Min's bedroom, with injuries serious enough that they wouldn't be able to make it out unassisted.

Emma lowered the wheel, glancing at the sewing machine and a bag of millet that Imo had given her. "How much time do we have?" she asked.

"Not much." Now that I wasn't the subject of an inquisition, I was able to focus, able to think. "Every flight is a risk, but during daytime especially so. The Americans wouldn't send a man over enemy territory for nothing. The plane that dropped these leaflets is probably marking targets, and my guess is that a bomber squad will fly out this evening. They usually leave at dusk, from Yokota, so we need to get as far away as we can before nightfall."

From the kitchen, a child screamed—sharp and bloodcurdling. It was the toddler who had reached for the stove earlier. His mother had rushed to start packing, and he had wandered back to the kitchen alone. He wailed in front of the stove's door, his two palms crimson as blisters erupted on his small fingers.

His mother shrieked, leaping over people's bags to pick him up. Her hair tumbled over his downy head as he cried.

"*Genchana,*" she said, bouncing and rocking him while Imo ran for balm. "*Eomma yoh-gissoh. Eomma yoh-gissoh.*" "Mom is here. Mom is here."

17

SENTIMENTAL OBSESSIONS

"We are facing an army of barbarians in Korea, but they are barbarians as trained, as relentless, as reckless of life, and as skilled in the tactics of the kind of war they fight as the hordes of Genghis Khan."

—Hanson W. Baldwin, *The New York Times*,
July 14, 1950

December 16, 1950

The mountain's central path was packed, dark heads bobbing, an endless snake slithering toward the valley. Everyone else was heading for Manchuria, but Pastor Pak maintained that he would never leave Korea. He gave his handcart to the wounded so their families could push them across the border, and he grudgingly agreed to relocate to Pyongyang, where he had lived for most of his life.

Though Emma and I had had our own plan, the Paks decided to travel with us because Imo needed help carrying the contents of her cellar, and Emma and I were eager to comply in exchange for a share of their provisions. Within the house, the floors trembled as everyone scurried to collect their belongings, squabbling over who had brought what. Women pulled reluctant children away from the warm mats and hoisted them onto their backs, while Imo flitted around like a hummingbird.

In the kitchen, Imo sorted through her cookware, metal clanging. The hem of her skirt fanned up when she bent to collect her silver chopsticks, which tinkled like chimes. She plunged her arms into the cabinet, then stopped as though she had been stung.

Gingerly, she lifted out a porcelain bowl painted with blue and white peonies. Even through a layer of dust, it shone when she caressed its delicate sides, as one might a lover's cheek. When she noticed me, she gasped like I had caught her in the nude. "What are you doing just gawking?" she snapped. "Go help Hwa-Ja!"

"Yes, Imo," I sputtered. Blushing, I backed up so quickly that I nearly tripped over someone's bag.

Imo returned the bowl to its place in the cabinet, a resolute grimace splitting her face, and grabbed a cast-iron pot instead.

Outside, the chickens squawked, and Jae-Min stumbled from the shed with a gash on his forearm and with a basket tied shut with twine. After brushing the dirt from his coat, he hustled to gather his father's tools and fastened them to his *jige*.

I hid my discomfort by searching for something to fold, while Pastor Pak unwrapped a worn quilt that was full of picture frames. At first I thought they were family photos, but when he lined them up on the mat I saw that they were prints of Jesus at various stages of his life, from his birth in Bethlehem to his resurrection in Jerusalem. The shapes and sizes of these simple frames matched the faded rectangles on the walls.

Among the prints, Pastor Pak selected one of Christ's crucifixion—a particularly gruesome rendition in which Jesus's ribs jutted out like a cage and his bloodied wrists were painted to contrast sharply against his skin. Before Pastor Pak could add it to his "keep" pile, Imo descended.

"We don't have space for sentimental obsessions," she said. "If you can't eat it or use it, don't take it."

"But this was a wedding gift," Pastor Pak protested, "from my favorite teacher. He's the reason I chose this calling and—"

"You're already taking your ancestral genealogy albums!" Imo snapped, while dropping three bags, of barley, millet, and corn, into Emma's lap. "I don't want any whining about the weight, all right? We are lucky to have so much to take!"

"No one's complaining," said Emma, stuffing the grains beside her sewing machine parts.

Forlornly, Pastor Pak stacked his Jesus prints and laid them in the blanket, with a wooden cross on top. Swaddling the package like an infant, he said, "Maybe I can bury them."

"No time!" Imo cried before scuttling to the bedroom. "Put them in the cellar and hope for the best."

Pastor Pak grumbled in Korean, and Emma chuckled.

"They have a good marriage," she said, as Pastor Pak headed for the cellar. "I hope you find a man like Pastor Pak—and that you'll be more grateful for it than Imo is."

Emma often forgot that I was almost thirty, and spoke to me like my life had not yet started.

My own elders also fretted about my getting married. They became more belligerent with each year, warning me that though there were plenty of fish in the sea, one had only so much bait. I tried to explain that times were changing, that women had more choices now; while love was something I wanted, it wasn't the only thing.

When the last of the refugees departed and Imo deemed that we were ready, Pastor Pak locked the door and beseeched the Lord for a blessing. We set out like snails, with Jae-Min carrying the heaviest items in the *jige* and the rest of us stooped under our bags, secured with strips of cloth that crossed over our chests.

Jae-Min and Imo turned to look back at their house, but Pastor Pak kept his face forward, leaning on a cane that had belonged to his father.

"Jesus fled to Egypt when he was just a baby, to escape King Herod," Pastor Pak declared as we joined the stream of families winding their way down the mountain. "And long before that, Moses fled from Egypt to Midian, and Abraham left Ur of the Chaldees to go to the land of Canaan. Sometimes a journey can be a good thing. I have faith in the Lord." He grinned, but something about the way he bared his teeth unnerved me.

In the valley, the main road was crowded, but the villagers here had less than the earlier refugees did. Almost everyone was making their way to Manchuria, and we jumped in with the vigor of fish swimming against the current. Shoulders and bags bumped against me, threatening to knock me back as I pushed southward. There were no oxen, and few other travelers had boots or heavy coats like ours. One man had managed to tie an enormous *onggi* to his back, and when he stumbled, the lid came loose and shattered. He tried to dive for it, but frenzied feet crushed the clay pieces.

I shivered, missing home with an urgency that overtook every other sensation: San Francisco, where there was no gold, but there were wide streets and rolling hills far gentler than the jagged Taebaeks; California, where "cold" meant layered clothing but no snow, and "windy" excluded Korea's rabid, biting gale; where there were strawberries and citrus fruit, milkshakes and movies, and my parents' house perched on its own small hill a few minutes from the highway.

Thinking of my family crying over my disappearance jolted

me. Did they think I was dead? If not, how long would they wait before giving up? Was there a normal length of time to mourn the loss of a child?

I imagined grief to be akin to the hills and mountains. In some forms, it was softer and could be surmounted with patience. In other forms, it ripped through the soul like a tiger's spine, as stubborn as granite and as expansive as pine forests.

I'm not dead, I reminded myself. *And I'm not going to die anytime soon.* I had faith too. It kept a plug on my despair, like the lid on an *onggi*.

Ahead, the muddy road fell into the curves of the Tongno as if pulled into a dance. Earth and shimmering ice meandered together like two locks of hair. From the opposite shore, villagers ventured onto the frozen river, tapping its surface with their feet cautiously before transferring their weight forward. At the next bend, families surged up from the bank.

"Stay close to us," said Jae-Min, quietly, in English. "If you get separated, it will be impossible for you to find us again in this crowd."

He had learned English primarily through reading, and though he often pronounced words wrong, his vocabulary was expansive.

"Thank you," I replied in English, astonished that he cared. Using my native tongue was akin to taking a mouthful of comfort food. It was as savory as the first bite of freshly fried chicken—a thigh, not a breast—slippery with grease, with juices running clear. Beneath my hanbok, my pants hung loose and my stomach ached with longing. "I'll make sure to keep up."

"Auntie Moon has really taken a liking to you," Jae-Min continued, in a whisper. "If anything happens to you here, I'm sure she'll blame me—even though you are my elder and I really shouldn't be responsible for you."

He sounded resentful, but I wasn't going to complain. It was rare for Jae-Min to initiate a conversation with me, and though I had never intended to steal Yun-Hee's identity, or the love earmarked for her, to him I was an impostor—maybe even a fraud. Speaking English here was dangerous, but it was also a connection. Now that we had a moment together, perhaps I could smooth out some of his animosity.

"I'm sorry," I said.

"For what?" he asked.

"For the inconvenience that I've caused. I know that it's already a terrible time, and I'm making it harder by reminding you of . . ."

I couldn't say her name. She was a secret code, a type of bomb. Though I tried to leave her blank, she was potent enough to seep into that silent space.

"She has nothing to do with you," he said, brusquely. "You don't have to be sorry, because your being here does not matter."

"Oh. Well, that's good."

Jae-Min's answer should have been a relief, but it had come with a flaying. My olive branch hung limp before barbed wire, and I felt foolish for attempting to patch such a chasm.

There had been so many planes today that the cries of their engines were now as unremarkable as the buzzing of cicadas in the summer. Still, I latched onto a trio of MiG-15s, sleek as they flew south. Where were the front lines now? Hungnam, from where the Americans were about to evacuate by sea? Or maybe even farther, at the 38th parallel?

Jae-Min tracked the planes too, his eyes following them until they slipped behind cloud cover. He let out a soft breath like the flapping of a white flag. "Everything reminds me of Yun-Hee," he said. "Our mothers were close, so she and I were two seeds that grew in the same pot. She was always in my view, always underfoot. It used to bother me, but now I can't look at anything without noticing her absence."

"I thought you were avoiding me," I admitted, "since you always seemed like you were in a rush to leave whatever room I was in."

"That's because you're always with Auntie Moon. If there is anyone who's hard for me to be around, it's her. The two of them look alike, and in Auntie Moon I see what Yun-Hee might have been, and what she will never be."

Ahead, Emma had pulled her knit hat down over her ears. People from the riverbank were hoisting their baggage onto the road, lifting their children and passing them to others before clambering up to follow. A teenage girl tumbled backward, knocking an elderly woman down behind her.

"I thought you and Auntie Moon got along," I said, while the girl and the elderly woman helped each other rise anew.

"We did. Or at least my mom and Auntie Moon did. Now it's hard for them to be in the same room together, but it's been better since you arrived." Jae-Min smiled slightly. "With you here, Auntie Moon is less angry. Less sad, really. And for my mom, you are like a lightning rod. If it wasn't for you, they probably would have had a big fight by now."

I had been so preoccupied with avoiding Imo that it never occurred to me that Emma might have been doing the same. "What happened between them?"

"It's . . . complicated," said Jae-Min, glancing sheepishly at Imo. "Auntie Moon blames my mom for what happened to Yun-Hee, because my mom is part Japanese. When the Japanese began the labor drafts, most Koreans didn't know that girls would be forced into brothels, but Auntie Moon thinks that the local Japanese knew, and that my mom secretly did too."

"Did she?"

Jae-Min bristled. "Definitely not! My grandfather worked for the Japanese authorities, but he disowned my mom after she married my dad. She hasn't spoken to her parents since I was a baby. I've explained this to Auntie Moon a hundred times, but she won't listen. Or maybe she doesn't care."

"She's been through a lot," I said, compelled to defend her.

"We all have. Yun-Hee is not just Auntie Moon's loss, but Auntie Moon is possessive of her grief—even though there is plenty to spare."

I wondered if it would be too abrasive for me to say that a boyfriend wasn't the same as a mother. In my book there was no comparison, but maybe I just failed to grasp the full extent of romantic love. It saddened me to think that there was a range of emotion that I couldn't access, and high notes that I'd never sing.

"I think you're misjudging her," I finally said. "She probably doesn't know how much you're still hurting. Maybe if you told her—"

"I can't. If I bring up Yun-Hee at all, it just turns into a trial for my mom. I don't want to cycle through these arguments anymore, so Yun-Hee is someone we simply don't talk about. She is one of many things we don't talk about. We've all become icebergs, and beneath the surface, it's dark. There's bad blood here, enough to dye this river."

His angry steps sank into the mud while I envisioned crimson water, and Emma's belly swollen with grudge.

Scattered cries broke out ahead, where the olive turrets of Soviet tanks rose like spires. A line of armed vehicles parted the crowd as deftly as Moses might have split the sea. KPA soldiers were crowded on top of each tank, shouting while waving their arms toward the railroad tracks.

"They want us to clear out," explained Jae-Min, switching to Japanese, his fear stretched over each whispered syllable. "There's only one big road between the Chinese border and Pyongyang, and the army cannot operate with us all over it."

"Right." I cowered, avoiding eye contact with the men on the tanks, afraid that the soldiers might identify me as American, even among this crowd.

Everyone trundled into the bare shrubbery, which had grown unhindered along the space between the road and the train tracks. Emma beckoned for me to catch up, so I trotted quickly, my skirt snapping icicles and catching on low branches. It was hard to move between the rails. One mother walked with her breast hanging out, a red-cheeked infant latched onto it as she balanced over the wooden railroad ties.

"*Bbali, bbali!*" barked a soldier who could not have been older than twelve. His face was doughy, and his uniform was so baggy that he had to cuff his sleeves and pants. Mittens, which he had taken off so he could hold his weapon properly, stuck out from his pockets. In his small hands, his gun almost looked like a toy. *Almost.*

I am a civilian, I reminded myself. *I don't have to pretend.* And yet I felt like a spy. My anger was a burning itch in my throat, for me to scratch at my own risk. Terror kept me cautious, but ultimately it was pity that reined me in. I couldn't send my hate toward a child in a costume.

Even if he had lurked amid the snowbanks of the Chosin.

Even if he had managed to fire that gun and hit my men.

Did that make me a traitor?

Did it mean that I wasn't American? The weight of this war was too much to bear, too much to keep. My chest was compressed with layers of stolen grief from innumerable losses. When the night sky in the North erupted with bombs that burst high among the mountain peaks, no one said a word. Ancient pine, once home to tigers, still home to humans, went up in flame like nothing more than matchsticks. We pretended it was thunder and just kept walking. Within my depths, a glacier was forming.

THE GLOBAL TRIBUNE

President Truman Proclaims a State of Emergency

December 16, 1950

Citing the recent events in Korea as a grave threat to the peace of the world, President Truman has proclaimed a national emergency that requires the military, naval, air, and civilian defenses of this country be strengthened as speedily as possible . . .

18

THE BIRD AND THE MOUSE

December 18, 1950

When Pastor Pak was younger, he used to make the thirty-kilometer trek between Kanggye and Songgan in a single afternoon. He had some close friends there, and had been hoping that we could rest with them before continuing onward. Our group, however, oozed like tar, because Imo could not endure the strain of the cold and the residual smoke. Even with all of us carrying portions of her load, she wheezed through the day, coughed through the night, and stopped constantly to catch her breath. Mucus clogged her lungs, but she was too proud to spit in public; instead, she gagged until she managed to choke it down with a queasy grimace.

It took us three days to reach Songgan Station, which had been bombed beyond repair, with only two crumbling walls remaining. Wind howled straight through the center, but travelers still gathered between this semblance of shelter, and cooked beside exposed wires. Along the tracks, there were makeshift encampments, many nothing more than cardboard boxes and blankets over poles. Some enterprising individuals had cobbled together crooked wooden hovels that were now businesses in which one could exchange food or cigarettes for a few hours of warmth. We had counted out corn kernels, hard and yellow like teeth, as though we were paying the tooth fairy to buy Imo reprieve, but people smoked so much in these shacks that she coughed even harder inside.

We slogged past the station, with Pastor Pak swinging his arms for momentum. The anticipation of meeting old friends, some of whom had been arrested with him while protesting the colonial government, buoyed him like a hymn. "We might not need to go to Pyongyang after all," he said. "Brothers behind bars are like brothers in arms. They'll let us stay for as long as we need to, maybe even until we can go back home."

No one ventured to correct him. Fire had slid down Pastor Pak's beloved mountainside, its blinding light reflected in his irises until black clouds shrouded the pine forests, and yet he spoke as though his house was still there—waiting like a lover.

Or maybe a mother.

I was eager for the protection of a real roof and walls, but Songgan proper was now a garrison, which the KPA was fortifying as part of their supply chain. Soldiers had commandeered the undamaged residential areas, and most of the inhabitants had fled, including Pastor Pak's friends.

A commander shooed us away, while his contingent filled potholes with gravel and rolled antiaircraft guns into Songgan's former square.

Emma discreetly interpreted for me, holding her scarf up as she whispered. "The commander wants us to go home. He says that the American devils want civilians to cause chaos, and the sooner we stop running around, the faster the soldiers can end this war."

Though Pastor Pak wanted an excuse to turn back and find familiar ghosts in mountain graves, Imo was in a foul mood. She had her own scarf tied over her nose and mouth to protect her lungs from the cold, but she yanked it down and began to argue with the commander.

Emma whispered in my ear, "The pastor's wife is telling them that if they had ended the war faster we wouldn't have to run around at all."

Imo's rage triggered another fit of coughing. She raised her hand to signal that she wasn't done yelling, but she struggled to breathe as Jae-Min rubbed her back. Pastor Pak stepped between his wife and the commander.

At the Paks' house it had been difficult for me to believe that Pastor Pak was a fighter, because he always spoke so gently and held his bleeding heart out for all to see. When he began criticizing the commander, however, his posture and voice changed as though he had pulled a completely different man from his gut. I had never thought of Pastor Pak as large, but with his face unflinching and his eyes locked intensely on his target, he loomed.

I elbowed Emma, but she was too transfixed to translate. Though his words were incomprehensible to me, I too was captivated, and intimidated, enough to understand why a seemingly no-nonsense woman like Imo would give up her fortune, and possibly her family, to be his wife.

Scowling, the commander reached into his pocket for a small stack of cards. He handed one to Pastor Pak, disdainfully, and said something that could have been an insult.

All I picked up was *"gah"* and *"bbali"*—"go away" and

"hurry"—but Pastor Pak bowed and thanked him. Since Emma followed suit, I did too.

After we left the square, Emma explained that Pastor Pak had convinced the commander to allow Imo to rest at the military hospital overnight. All we had to do was present the card to the officer in charge.

I examined the card, which was heftier than the safe-conduct pass that I always kept in my jacket pocket—wriggled into a seam in case Imo went poking around again. On the KPA card, there was a drawing of Kim Il-Sung, triumphant under a halo of light, flanked by soldiers who had their heads tilted toward him in admiration. It reminded me of the framed Christian drawings Pastor Pak had left behind in his cellar.

"It says, 'Long live Korean independence and unification,'" Emma told me.

"He looks like Jesus," I said, mimicking his hands, which were up, with both palms open to the sky, "surrounded by his disciples."

"He does," snorted Emma. "Whoever drew this must have studied the Bible."

A giggle tumbled from my lips, as involuntarily as a hiccup. I was exhausted, with blisters on my heels and welts on my shoulders, but the urge to laugh trumped every discomfort. I clapped a hand over my mouth, trying to hold back the landslide that roiled at the tip of my tongue.

Jae-Min scrunched his brow in judgmental confusion. He was so stern, yet infantile with his earflaps, that I couldn't contain myself.

I succumbed as one might sneeze, an oafish guffaw bursting out like a gunshot. "That's why he banned religion!" I barked. "He can't take the competition!"

Imo glanced anxiously at the soldiers who were shoveling gravel by the square. "Shut up!" she hissed.

I wanted to, desperately, but the laughter wouldn't let go, my chest heaving so hard that I could barely stand. Covering my face, I pretended to cry, hoping that faking tears would hide the extent to which I had disintegrated.

"Ellie," Emma began, but her wrinkles twitched, betraying a hint of a smile. Fear was contagious, but insolence was too—as was madness. Whatever rebuke she had for me crumbled as she whispered, "You can't worship Jesus when you want to be Jesus."

I crowed and she doubled over, while Pastor Pak frantically tried to shush us. We were almost on our knees, shaken by a delirium that tickled like the bubbles in champagne. A warm wave spread throughout my body, sending feeling surging back into my numbed extremities.

Oh, Emma. Neither of us knew that one day North Korea would reset its calendar so that year zero aligned with Kim Il-Sung's birth. Neither of us expected that everyone here aged twelve and up would be required to wear a badge with his face on it, and that he'd have his own ten commandments. Who would have thought that this "puppet" would end up becoming more than the sun? That entire mountains would be carved with his name, and that decades after his death people would bow before his embalmed corpse?

The old will die, and the young will forget.

"Enough!" Pastor Pak snapped, his eyes glistening, the whites as round as coins. The soldiers' shovels grated loudly, but there were a few civilians who were too close for comfort.

Imo wheezed, her voice barely audible over yet another plane overhead. "The bird listens during the day and the mouse does at night. We have to be careful! It's bad enough that we're speaking in Japanese. Do you know how much people here hate that language?"

Jae-Min's resemblance to Imo was uncanny when he shot me his version of her scathing glare. "Stop being an idiot or you'll get us all jailed—or worse!"

I choked down my mirth, but it fought me like a fish might a gull. I didn't dare look at Emma, afraid that I might lose it anew.

"What are they going to do," Emma scoffed, "kill me? I'm already dead."

Jae-Min rolled his eyes, but her sentence sobered me up faster than any scolding could.

We went back toward the station to find the KPA's temporary medical facility, which was in an unmarked concrete warehouse. Absently, I reached into my pocket and pinched a dried anchovy, normally used for seasoning. I slipped the prickly fish onto my parched tongue and sucked on it like candy.

At this rate, it was going to take us more than a month just to get to Pyongyang. So much could change in that time! The lightness from our laughter, which I had wanted to harbor like rations, had evaporated. Disgruntled, I turned to Emma while the Paks approached the soldiers at the facility. "Do you still want to make our own trip?" I asked. "Because we could. The Paks are going to rest here, but the two of us could keep going."

As if she had been making the same calculation, Emma said, "You and I can walk faster and for longer. We could probably reach Pyongyang in a week if we pushed ourselves."

"I don't think we have to walk. There are going to be jeeps and trucks coming through here to bring supplies down south. Maybe we can get a ride."

"You think?"

"That's what I did as a correspondent. I just kept asking people for rides until someone said yes. Eventually someone does."

"What if they think we're loose women, and they try to do . . . something nasty?"

Something nasty. No one ever wanted to say "rape" out loud, no matter how much it dominated our thoughts. It was a pornographic crime, shrouded in silence. I wondered if men knew just how much women worried about rape, even in times of peace.

"The longer we are out on this road, the more likely it is to happen," I replied.

Emma chewed her lip, which had taken on a deep shade of cranberry. "Where will we go to ask? The side of the road?"

"Yes, where else? Every jeep driver from the North has no choice but to take this path."

"But we'll look like prostitutes if we stand there beckoning men!"

"Oh, Emma. What's worse? Looking like a hooker or walking three hundred kilometers in the cold?"

She paused to consider, a hesitation that astonished me.

"Emma, are you seriously thinking about going to Pyongyang on foot just for modesty's sake? Didn't you just say you were already dead?"

"Well, it's—"

"Then who cares about what a bunch of strangers think? The sooner we get to your house, the safer we are, don't you think?"

Emma sighed. "You're right. My goodness, you are like those tanks. You just roll over people."

"Thank you," I said, taking it as a compliment, knowing that Emma meant it with at least a modicum of admiration.

At the warehouse entrance, a soldier fiddled with a heavy padlock that had rusted around the keyhole. Imo coughed and leaned on Jae-Min's arm as metal clicked and the door swung open.

"Let's talk to Pastor Pak," said Emma, turning to the warehouse.

Relieved that the soldiers were letting us in, I followed her. I was so intent on savoring a respite indoors that I didn't think to question why a medical facility had to be locked.

19

NO CHARITY

December 18, 1950

Inside the warehouse, it was so dank that the windows were fogged, and condensation dripped in gray rivulets. Light was dim through the filthy glass, and though it was warmer than outside, our breath still came in clouds. There was a wire fence dividing the space, with the shadowy forms of dozens of men behind it. The stench of urine and feces overpowered everything.

Soldiers were right beside me, so I couldn't speak to Emma in Japanese, but I reached out for her hand as my fear bubbled up like bile. She squeezed back. My eyes watered, and Imo gagged. When I blinked, the faces behind the fence came into focus. Among them, there was a bloodshot blue eye gleaming from between wires.

I gasped, the air so fetid that I could taste it.

These men were American and South Korean prisoners of war. Dirt was smeared on their faces, and their clothes were blackened and crusty. Most had winter coats and hats on, but some of them wore nothing but lightweight summer uniforms. The former might have been captured at the Chosin, while the latter might have been taken months ago and forced to march up north. A few of the summer soldiers were crouched underneath a filthy, threadbare blanket, staring at me with an uncertainty that made me squirm.

Could they read my face? Would a true Communist supporter react with this much distress? I felt naked and porous—guilty for being on the wrong side of that fence, even as a civilian.

Emma sputtered like a kettle, her Korean volcanic as she chided the soldier with the padlock. All I caught was the word for "daughter," "*ttal*," and the word for "scared," "*museowo*." I wasn't prepared for Emma to grab my arm, and my head bobbled when she yanked me to the door. She huffed before slamming it shut, cutting us off from the Paks' and the KPA soldiers' bewildered faces.

It was windier than I had remembered, and I sucked in the blustery air, panting like I had been trapped underwater. Through my breath, I wanted to flush the putrid warehouse from my lungs, even as I became lightheaded.

"Let's go," said Emma. "I told Pastor Pak we were going back to the station and on to Pyongyang. It's time we catch our ride, don't you think?" She sounded chipper, as though we had just finished an unpleasant errand, but the prisoners' faces had imprinted on me in a sickly way.

Kneading my forehead, I squatted. "I need a minute."

"Take it when we're by the road," Emma said, unrelenting. A line of soldiers filed behind the warehouse, toward the station. "I told those little twerps that you are terrified of foreign men and that they should have warned us before letting us inside. A bit odd for a person your age, but not unbelievable."

I stood up slowly. "I feel awful for them. I wish there were something I could do to help."

"There isn't. That hospital—at least that's what the soldiers call it—is for the prisoners who are too weak to march any farther. Supposedly they're getting treatment, but you saw how it was in Kanggye. There's barely medicine for our own. They're not going to waste it on invaders."

Invaders. I hated that title more than any other that the Communists had slapped on us, because it implied that we had started this war. History is often written by the victors, but Kim Il-Sung had gotten a head start in editing the narrative—and I despised him for it.

Seeing that I was upset, Emma said, "There are men in high places who cannot get along, and as a result, we have lost almost everything. Mourn if you must. Pray for their souls if you wish. Either way, we have to get away."

Nodding, I began to shove one foot in front of the other, though I'd worn off the skin on my heels. Emma and I swung to the other side of the train station, where the auto road widened into a plaza with military tents. Orange shingles were scattered over the remnants of a pagoda, and soldiers were removing the debris. The bottom half of a statue stood in the plaza's center, and it was impossible to tell who it might have depicted. It was just a robe, or perhaps a dress, and a pair of pointed shoes carved in stone.

Civilians formed sparse lines on either side of the road, begging from the KPA soldiers and cheering at incoming jeeps. Children ran to the trucks, their hands outstretched or pointing to their open mouths. Instead of food, however, the soldiers gave out leaflets that promised that rations were on their way.

Emma and I settled by the road too. Some of the jeeps had no passengers, only crates of ammunition that rattled over every bump. Beleaguered soldiers marched in staggered rows, bearing to the side so the vehicles could pass. These hollow-eyed men mostly ignored the beggars, but a few shook their heads regretfully and held out their empty hands to show that they had nothing to share.

"There are probably more bullets than barley here," I said, counting the jeeps in the convoy, which extended for as far as I could see. "Just look at how scrawny these soldiers are."

"Boys are rushing to enlist, though," said Emma, as she set down her bags and helped me untie mine. "For many of them, it's the only way to get fed at all."

I rotated my stiff shoulders, while Emma massaged the area beneath her collarbones, where she had crisscrossed her straps. Closer to the pagoda's rubble, there were people trying to hitchhike, including a couple who were so old that neither of them had any teeth. Most hitchhikers were waiting for cars heading to China, but several, like us, were trying to go south.

"I didn't think we'd have so much competition," I said, dismayed by my lack of foresight. Of course we weren't going to be the only ones trying to escape. Of course this wasn't going to be like an American base, where only two or three correspondents were bumming rides. "*Aigo*, there's no way anyone's going to stop for us if they're not even stopping for the babies or the elderly."

"*Aigo*," chided Emma. "You can't even say '*aigo*' without sounding like a foreigner. Just keep your mouth shut and let me talk." She was wearing one of her embroidered hanboks, which had gotten dirty, but the blue and purple butterflies hid the stains well. No one else around us wore such colorful or elaborate artwork so casually. It was certainly a risk when the Communists emphasized austerity, but Emma was a proud industrial worker, and a member of the new favored class. After smoothing out her skirt, she pushed past a cluster of teenagers who were dutifully waving North Korean flags.

I was always too impatient to wait on sidelines, but Emma had left her bags with me, and her savings and sewing machine were inside, along with Imo's millet and dried fish, which, in our haste, we had forgotten to return to the Paks. Though we should have gone back to the warehouse, my shame over this petty theft was easier to overlook because Emma and I could not survive without it.

Emma's shoes left sweeping marks in the mud as she dragged one leg behind her, her gait suddenly lopsided. Laboriously, she hobbled onto the road, hollering at the next jeep with her hands clasped in pathetic pleading. I had forgotten what a good actress she was and hadn't been expecting her to be so smart—or shameless.

The soldiers in the jeep puttered past her without a second glance.

Undeterred, Emma shuffled on to the next jeep with renewed vigor. Smacking her hand against her chest, she groaned, her eyes partially closed as though she might collapse. A vein in her neck pulsed and her hand twitched. I was impressed by her deliberate expressions, but the soldiers shooed her away. In another life, Emma could have been a star, but in this one, her audience had seen too much. She might as well have been a ghost begging the living for another chance at life, invisible to everyone but me.

Emma tried four more cars before a soldier yelled at her, spittle flying from his lips. Exasperated, Emma scuttled back to where

I was, her shoulders slumped. Even though she was faking it all, I felt sorry for her—sorry for us—and resented the soldiers for being so callous. I sat down on one of my bags, curling and uncurling my aching toes.

"They aren't allowed to take civilians—*mingan-in*—with them," Emma explained. "And they also want us to get away from the roads."

Under my breath, I repeated "*mingan-in,*" and added it to my budding arsenal. The more Korean I understood, the better my chances of getting home were.

"I'm so tired," I said, even though she was the one who had scampered beside the jeeps. The warehouse was far behind us, but I still felt submerged. There was nothing I could do but wait for the water to drain—hope that it actually would drain.

"Let's rest," said Emma, sitting on her bag and propping up her swollen feet, "and think." She rummaged through one of her coat pockets for some dried shrimp, and picked off the lint before handing me a few. They were each the size of my fingernail, pink and as hard as pebbles, but packed with flavor, like slivers of bouillon.

I drank from my canteen. The water helped soften the shrimp in my mouth, and once it got squishy, I could grind it into a salty pulp. "Are we horrible for leaving the Paks behind?" I asked. "Taking and eating their food after everything they've done for us?"

"No," said Emma, without any hint of remorse. "But we do owe them. It will be a debt that they can collect—maybe not now, but later. That is how the pastor's wife thinks. It is how her family became rich. There is no charity here, nor are their saints, but you and I will pay our dues when the time comes." In her other pocket she found more shrimp, and she held them out in her palm. They reminded me of pomegranate seeds, the kind that had bound Persephone to the underworld in Greek mythology.

I swallowed the shrimp whole, each morsel like a segment in a chain grating down my throat. "What about the Chinese?" I asked, and took another swig of water.

"What about them?"

"There are millions of Korean civilians here, but very few Chinese. Maybe their soldiers will be willing to help us—help me, if I speak Mandarin to them. Don't you think?"

My father often joked that Chinese people were much nicer to one another outside of China than in the motherland. Though there was gang violence in Chinatown, and there were other crimes between Chinese people, it was true that being far from home, missing home, could make people kinder to others who reminded them of it. I wasn't sure if this applied so close to the Chinese border, but it was worth a shot.

"I don't see any Chinese," said Emma. "Unless you plan to sit here, like it's a parade, and wait for them? Would you like a flag?"

I brushed off her sarcasm. "This is the only auto road between Kanggye and Pyongyang. It's just a matter of time before a PVA convoy comes through."

"We are losing daylight, though. We can't waste our walking time for nothing."

"Let's give it a few hours. And if nothing happens, then we'll go back to the railroad tracks and keep going."

"One hour."

"Fine." I stretched out my legs as the sun emerged from the clouds and bathed us with a fleeting benevolence. As if emboldened, the wind tumbled forth like a child from its hiding spot, bellowing and blowing gravel into our faces.

Another line of trucks appeared, loaded with American bazookas. These looked like stovepipes, except that they could launch rockets straight through a tank's hull. How the hell were the KPA so good at stealing our weapons? Or rather, how the hell were we so careless about our stock? At this rate, Washington was probably rivaling Stalin as Kim Il-Sung's greatest supplier.

At the pagoda's ruins, one truck heading south finally stopped. A soldier in the back leaned and held his hand out to a heavily pregnant woman who carried a toddler boy on her hip. She was young, her hanbok splayed like a bell over her stomach. When she lifted her boy, I saw that his arm had been crudely amputated, the swollen stump wrapped in crusty brown bandages. Her husband and daughter, who might have been five years old, and an elderly couple lined up too, but the soldiers refused to take them. There was not enough space for the entire family.

"*Bbali,*" said the soldiers.

This offer was not one that would wait, nor was this a choice she could dally over.

Resigned, the young mother scooped up her daughter and hugged her tightly—a single, searing moment before she climbed into the truck and wrapped her son in the folds of her skirt. Sometimes survival meant separation. I wasn't sure if her daughter was old enough to understand the significance of this goodbye, or its possible permanence. As the truck drove away, the girl watched quietly, while her father's shoulders shook.

THE GLOBAL TRIBUNE

Evacuation Has Begun

December 17, 1950

Enemy forces continue their onslaught against allied defense lines at Hungnam Port. Reinforcements have arrived, but the UN Command is still outnumbered. Divisions at the perimeter must hold until the evacuation is completed—at which point, the last of the rearguard will make a break for the airstrip, where planes will be waiting to save them . . .

20

A MOTHER'S GUIDANCE

December 18, 1950

Jae-Min was the first to spot us. From behind the remnants of the station, he ran, waving his arms with the *jige* bouncing on his back. All the chickens were already dead, and their stiff little bodies thumped in the basket as Jae-Min bounded over a mud-filled pothole.

"We've been looking all over for you!" Jae-Min cried. Sweating, he turned to signal to Pastor Pak and Imo, while I raised my brow at Emma.

"I thought you told them we were leaving?"

"I did," she said. "Mostly."

"Mostly?"

Jae-Min wiped his forehead, so irritated that when Emma greeted him he only grunted and said, "What were you two thinking, wandering off by yourselves?"

"You knew we were going," said Emma, defensively.

"Out of the warehouse," Jae-Min fumed, "not the entire town!"

"Well, how could you expect the foreigner to stay in a place like that tonight? It's like making a pig sleep in a slaughterhouse!"

"Well, if you had just waited, you would have known that we got permission to go to the soldiers' barracks. It'll just be for the evening, but at least we can get some proper rest."

"That's nice," said Emma. "Hopefully your mom will feel better, but the foreigner and I are fine. We're going to get a ride to Pyongyang."

"Pyongyang?" Jae-Min blinked, incredulous. "This isn't a bus station! If it was so easy to hop in a car, don't you think everyone else would have done it?"

Pastor Pak and Imo had caught up, agitated but not nearly as upset as Jae-Min. I bowed to them, but after a cursory acknowledgment, they all reverted to speaking in their own language. Some Korean words were similar to Mandarin words, and though I occasionally tried to match them, usually I just resigned myself to feeling infantile as everyone else discussed plans in front of me, without me. Emma often translated, but it was maddening to hear everything through her filter, especially since she frequently tweaked or omitted details.

This is why journalists shouldn't use secondary sources, I thought, melancholic.

Withdrawing into myself, I wondered what the headlines were back in the States. I had a story now—multiple stories—but no way to send anything out. A professor of mine had once asked, "If a tree falls in the forest and no one is there to hear it, does it make a sound?" That question applied to stories too. If there is no one to record them or read them, they disappear, and later people will ask, Did that really happen? Did that actually exist?

Imo was the first to switch back to Japanese, her pronunciation regal compared to the rest of us. "I will go with you to Pyongyang," she declared, head high like she was bestowing a favor. "My son and husband will move much faster without any of us holding them back."

"Really?" I asked. I was galled that Imo would lump Emma and me in with her, when Emma and I were much faster and more endurant than she was. "Are you sure that's a good idea, with your health as it is? I'm not sure how long it will take for us to get a ride, if we get one at all. So far no one has been willing to take us. I wouldn't want you to waste your time out here, in the cold."

"Yes, go rest," said Emma, as eager as I was to prevent her from joining. "The roadside is dustier than the tracks are, and it will be worse for your lungs."

Imo scoffed. "I am not so fragile."

Imo was younger than Emma, but I never saw her show any deference to Emma's seniority. She pushed at Emma's hip, and after Emma shifted, Imo bunched her skirt up and eased herself down between the two of us.

"Three is a large group," I said. "It will be difficult to get anyone to take us all, even if we are women."

Imo's dark eyes bored into me with the fervor of a raptor fixed on its prey. "Then I suppose you will have to walk with the men. You are young and strong. Perhaps you can keep pace."

Emma gave me a pitiful pout, her signal to surrender.

"Fine." I shrugged.

Truthfully, Emma was probably the strongest walker of us all. I would have gladly hiked with Pastor Pak and Jae-Min instead of riding with Imo, but I sensed that Emma didn't want to be stuck alone with her either. Leaning forward, I watched the road like it was a pot that I was willing to boil, hoping that the horizon would suddenly teem with men in quilted uniforms.

For at least half an hour there were no vehicles, just soldiers on foot, and a few unhappy, unlucky oxen. The civilians who were scattered around the pagoda gave up, group by group, as the sun began its retreat. When Imo shivered, Pastor Pak took out the cast-iron pot, which he used as a valiant little firepit. Jae-Min left to collect more wood. Beneath Pastor Pak's cracked and calloused hands, flames rose to attention.

I was worried that the armies had ceased their operations for the day.

When a line of jeeps appeared, Emma jumped up so quickly that her skirt swung over the fire. Smoke singed its hem, blackening a butterfly's wings.

"Don't be so frantic," Imo scolded. "You're like a crazy goat jumping around."

"Then you go," said Emma. "You're the one who's actually sick. Try coughing and see what they say."

"No, stupid. They'll think I have tuberculosis and definitely won't take us!" Imo succumbed to coughing again and motioned for Emma to carry on, waving like she was sending off a servant.

Leaving Pastor Pak to boil water, and me to prepare our millet, Emma headed for the first jeep. Under Imo's judgmental eye, Emma sprang from one vehicle to the next, imploring everyone in the line, with no success. Emma repeated this with a second convoy, and then a third, while Imo offered suggestions on her posture, tone, and opening lines. Pastor Pak and Jae-Min also attempted to convince the soldiers to stop, but a hostile commander demanded the reason why neither of them had enlisted when they both appeared able-bodied. After that, Pastor Pak and Jae-Min moved their fire farther from the road and lurked within the angular shadows of the pagoda ruins.

It wasn't until the porridge began to boil that a truck carrying crates and fuel barrels pulled over, nearly squashing Emma's foot.

A soldier in the passenger side leaned over the driver's lap. Instead of speaking to Emma, however, he called out to me: "*Nǐ zài zhèlǐ gǎo shénme guǐ?*" "What demonic antics are you plotting here?"

I paused midstir, my ladle dangling in the slimy porridge. The soldier who spoke had thick brows drawn tightly together, and his nostrils flared. He was dressed in a KPA jacket, but his fur-and-leather hat matched that of the PVA uniform.

It took me a moment to see the freckles on his nose—uncommon among Chinese complexions—and recognize him as the sullen soldier from the clinic in Kanggye.

"Brother Ling!" I exclaimed.

"Comrade Ying," he corrected, even more dour than before. "I thought your Korean auntie looked familiar, with all those . . . colors everywhere." He gestured to the embroidery on Emma's skirt.

Emma frowned questioningly, but I didn't want to risk using Japanese in front of anyone with a gun; George remained my swollen scar.

"You were supposed to go back to China," continued Comrade Ying. "Did you get lost?"

My mind swirled back to the clinic, and the conversations that I had had with the Chinese soldiers, mired within the haze of moonshine. The specifics were like minnows in the shallows—close enough to see, but not to catch. I thought Comrade Ying had agreed to ask around for my fake man, but his words were muffled by the blasts of the recent bombing, a memory so vivid that it had smothered everything else that had happened in Kanggye.

Focus, I told myself. *Did I say my fake man was from Beijing? Did I provide his Chinese zodiac sign? Height?*

"I'm here to bring my boyfriend home," I declared, chest

puffed to compensate for my gnawing insecurity. "He's in Pyongyang, fighting for liberation."

The driver, who was in a thick jacket that matched no known uniform, had one hand at the top of the steering wheel. His skin was fairer than Comrade Ying's, and he had voluminous eyelashes. In Mandarin, the driver asked, "How do you know your boyfriend is in Pyongyang? There is no postal service, no communication lines for civilians."

"How do you even know he's alive?" demanded Comrade Ying. "And I thought he was your fiancé, not just a boyfriend."

"We're recently engaged," I said, crossing my arms. "We'd be married now if he hadn't volunteered to serve his country. He is an only son! His mother is very ill and wants to see him one last time, so I must bring him home."

"*Aiya*," said the driver. "The worst job in the military is giving bad news to families. What is this poor woman sick with?"

"Nobody knows," I answered. "Perhaps a disease of the heart."

Though the driver softened, Comrade Ying said, "Well, you can't help her by wandering around in Korea."

"I'm twenty-eight years old!" I said. "Do you know how hard it will be for me to find another man at this age? This might be my last chance for a good marriage. I will walk to Pyongyang if I must, but if you are kind enough to let me ride in your truck, and I find my fiancé, I promise that we will name our firstborn child after you."

"Is something wrong with your mind?" asked Comrade Ying. "I don't want any of your spawn carrying my name."

The driver put a hand up to Comrade Ying's lips. "My name is Zhang Shou-Liu," he announced. "Of the Fortieth Corps, Thirteenth Army, 120th Division. And I accept your offer."

Comrade Ying smacked Comrade Zhang on the back of his

head. "Absolutely not! This is just going to cause us trouble." The Mandarin term for "trouble," "*ma fan*," encompassed being burdensome and annoying too.

"I won't cause trouble!" I cried, startling Emma and the Paks. Though Pastor Pak understood some Mandarin, he wasn't translating for the rest, and their eyes darted warily between me and the PVA soldiers.

"I can be useful," I continued. "My friend and I can mend clothing, and we also have some food to share. Good food too. We have chicken, and a little bit of dried fish. And we can cook! Please take us with you. I promise we won't be a burden; you'll barely notice that we're there—except when we are helping you."

"'We'?" repeated Comrade Ying. "We'd have to take both of you?"

"Three of us," I said, gesturing to Imo, whose expression was almost as sullen as Comrade Ying's. "But that's three times the amount of help."

"No. Definitely no," said Comrade Ying. "There is no space for three."

"We can sit on the crates," I proposed. "We can squeeze together. We aren't very big; we just have many layers on at the moment."

Comrade Zhang leaned farther out the window. "What kind of chicken do you have? Do you have rice too?"

"Only millet and barley, but our chicken is very fresh! Raised in mountain air. Very recently dead."

"We cannot take three," Comrade Ying repeated, shoving Comrade Zhang from the window. "This is not a rickshaw. Civilians cannot ride with us, but since you are Chinese I can pretend you came with our army if anyone asks. No Koreans."

"Please," I said, clasping my hands together. "These people let me stay with them when I crossed the border by myself, with nothing but the clothes on my back. If it wasn't for them, I'd be dead. At least let me take one of them. I can't actually cook or sew, so I'm not as useful by myself."

"Eh?" uttered Comrade Ying. "Then what business do you have getting married? Your mother should have taught you some basic skills before you got engaged!"

"My mother died when I was a girl!" I exclaimed. "I was raised by my father, but I'm doing my best to learn to be a good wife."

Comrade Zhang's hands flew to his cheeks. "Oh heavens, I'm so sorry. How awful."

Unfazed, Comrade Ying leaned back in his own seat. "That explains why you're out here running amok. A girl really needs a mother's guidance."

"Yes," I said somberly. "Her only wish for me was to marry a good man. I will forever regret that she cannot be at my wedding, and that she will never know my fiancé, but maybe, wherever she is, she can be happy that I have found love."

Comrade Zhang nodded. "Certainly! She must be protecting you from afar. Let's hope she's watching over your fiancé and keeping him safe for you too."

"No!" interjected Comrade Ying, like he was scolding a dog. "We don't believe those old traditions anymore, remember?"

"Ah yes. Sorry," said Comrade Zhang.

Comrade Ying cleared his throat and said, "You may take one friend, as long as you can both fit in the back, behind the crates, so no one can see you. We don't need you to cook; we just need you to stay hidden."

"I'm sure three of us can—"

"One friend!" Comrade Ying snapped. "And in exchange, we want your chicken and your boots."

"My boots?" I asked. "How am I going to walk around without my boots?"

"And whatever millet you have," added Comrade Zhang. "And don't forget to name your son after me! If I die before I can have children, at least I know—"

"Chicken, boots, and millet," interrupted Ying, reciting each item sharply, like a recipe. "If you agree, then hurry up and get in. We've already wasted too much time, and we will get in trouble if we fall too far behind."

My heart drummed. Did I dare push again? If it was only two, could I convince them to take Emma and Imo?

From behind me, Pastor Pak stepped onto the road, loose pebbles crunching beneath his feet. I hadn't noticed him unpacking anything, but he cradled a bag of millet in his arms. In Mandarin, he said, "Agreed. My wife is very ill, and she will not survive on this road. Here." With a bow, he handed over the bag. "I will get the chickens. There are only three, but as our Chinese sister said, they are fresh and will make a good, warm meal."

Comrades Ying and Zhang inclined their heads before accepting the millet and stowing it in their footwell.

"Hurry up," called Comrade Ying.

Pastor Pak untangled the knots that secured the basket of chickens to the *jige*, while Jae-Min hugged his mom and guided her to stand. After passing the basket to Comrade Zhang, Pastor Pak jumped back to help his wife, and he and Jae-Min enveloped her in their arms, as sturdy as boughs. Together, they lifted her up into the truck.

Emma remained by the roadside like a lone candle left unlit. Something about how she watched the Paks, her shoulders hunched, cut me deeply.

I swallowed and said to her, in crude Korean, "You go. I walk."

I wasn't sure how I was going to do it with no boots, but I couldn't bear leaving her here. I pointed to Emma, and then to the truck. "You go."

Emma's lips, a hard line, softened before parting. She swatted me on my butt, as though I had done something wrong. "No," she said in Korean, careful to pick short, simple phrases. "It will be okay. Go. You go." Forcing a smile, she squeezed my shoulder. From inside her bag, she took out a set of keys and pressed them into my palm, then formed a triangle over her head with her two hands pointed.

Home. The keys to her home.

"Imo," Emma said, tapping her temple. *Imo knows where it is.*

I nodded in confirmation, and strung together, "See you soon. See us there."

"Hey, hurry!" called Comrade Ying.

As quickly as I could, I rearranged our bags, taking the heavy sewing machine myself so Emma wouldn't have to journey with it. Then I scurried to the back of the truck, where the Paks were saying their goodbyes. Emma fumbled through a stack of papers that she had in her satchel, and found a small red book that looked like a diary. After holding it to her heart, she tucked it into my jacket, where Clara's letters used to be, and called out to Imo to make sure that Imo saw that I had it.

I wondered what it was, since Emma had held it so reverently.

Imo leaned over and kissed Pastor Pak on the lips, an unexpected display of affection that made Jae-Min turn away. When I clambered past them, Pastor Pak said to me, in Mandarin, "Thank you. On the day you arrived at my home, I thought the Lord had sent me a trial, when he really sent me an angel. Thank you."

"You're welcome," I mumbled, but it singed like a lie. I felt like

I had made a pact with the Devil and hadn't even gotten what I had bargained for.

Imo crawled over the crates and settled into one corner of the truck with nothing but a large, gray bag of grain, which she clutched protectively. With a wet, guttural cough, she leaned against a barrel, while I moved to the opposite corner, where crates were piled high enough to press into the truck's canvas roof. A splinter lodged in my thumb when I tried to move them. Giving up, I wedged my bags into what little space there was, and climbed on top of the fuel barrel, my head behind Comrade Zhang's and my leg dangling beside Imo's shoulder.

As we drove off, at a pace close to a jog, Comrade Zhang began to sing in a low, melodic baritone. It was a song that I recognized as a Chinese lullaby about mothers—the kids who had them, and the kids who didn't: *"In the world, only mothers are good. Children with mothers are treasures, and in mother's arms there is endless happiness . . ."*

From where I was, I craned my neck but couldn't see Emma, Pastor Pak, or Jae-Min. Between the cargo and the canvas, there was just a slab of sky, a slice of road, and a foreboding feeling that I had erred. Emma's keys were in my pocket, the metal still warm from when I'd clenched it in my fist. Her giving these to me was a type of faith, though it was more like a gamble—a bet that *home* still stood, and that I'd make it there, that she'd make it there, and that the two of us would meet again.

21

MEANINGFUL SACRIFICE

December 18, 1950

It was pitch-black inside the truck, and my bottom was numb from being plastered to the metal barrel. The cold seeped into my flesh and bore into my bones, until finally I stood up and rubbed each cheek.

"Anja," said Imo, hoarse from coughing. Dust from the road billowed over the crates and remained trapped beneath the musty canvas, saturating our air. I had forgotten what *"anja"* meant, but I figured that she was just territorial of her space. Imo had spent the past hours pretending that I was part of the cargo, and I had done the same to her.

Shifting away from her, I stretched until my spine popped, then climbed closer to the truck's open back. Now that it was dark, we didn't need to hide so thoroughly. Out of caution, I still crouched, and tucked my hair beneath my hat so that my wool-wrapped face wouldn't be so different from any of the comrades'.

I peered out behind us, undeterred by the wind. My skin had

thickened, and what used to feel like a whipping was now more like a playful slap. The road lolled out like a tongue. Ours was the last vehicle in this caravan, with only pedestrians plodding behind us. Comrade Zhang drove slowly over craters that had been patched with a sloppy mix of sand and gravel. Despite fretting about falling behind, Comrade Ying made us stop whenever there were refugees camped around bonfires—so he could scold them.

"The bombers are hitting the roads well enough as it is!" he hollered in Mandarin, even though it wasn't clear that anyone understood him.

As we swerved into a field, a detour to bypass an area that had been heavily bombed, I wondered if Emma was still walking. Had she eaten? It was a miserably bumpy ride, but if Emma were here, the two of us might have laughed about it. Time would have flowed a bit faster. We would have sat with our heads together, whispering over our last morsels of shrimp, and I could have told Emma what I had overheard while perched on the fuel barrel.

Comrades Ying and Zhang were anxious, and their superiors were afraid, because Chairman Mao was losing his patience. The chairman had been asking about his oldest son, Mao An-Ying, who had volunteered to fight in Korea. The Chinese generals had refused to answer him, passing Mao's request around like a hot potato. Meanwhile, every Chinese soldier in Korea knew that An-Ying was dead—killed in an air strike at the end of November.

Prior to this ride, I hadn't heard anything about An-Ying at all. Did the Americans even know that Mao's heir had been in Korea? Given the lack of media coverage, the strike was either a secret assassination or a complete accident, and my bet was on the latter. My fingers twitched just from thinking about the story I could write, which had yet to break even in China.

Closing my eyes, I pictured Mao, with jowls drooping and

head grayed, ensconced in Beijing with his hand on his phone—pleading for it to ring. Did powerful people grieve like we did, or did they just get angry?

"It's the chairman's own fault," Comrade Zhang had said, indignantly. "None of our commanders wanted his son, but the chairman forced us to take him. The chairman can only blame himself!"

Comrade Ying's reply had been solemn: "It doesn't matter who he blames. The chairman has given a son to this war. He will not allow any of us to go home unless we bring back a victory that makes that sacrifice meaningful."

"We will," Comrade Zhang had said. "The imperialists are struggling. If we do a good job at Hungnam Port, they might give up on ever coming back. Right?"

Comrade Ying had declined to answer, and the two of them had settled into a precarious and weighted silence, like the one that Imo and I shared. Shoving my hands into my armpits for warmth, I shrank farther behind the crates. "Victory" was a nebulous term, and here in Korea, it was constantly changing.

Comrade Zhang decelerated to a crawl as we approached Pyongyang.

I had lost track of time. In Korea I had begun measuring the hours based on the frequency of the planes overhead. Without lights, it was impossible to pinpoint where they were, but we could always hear them. At dusk, there was usually a lull in their activity. Closer to midnight, there'd be a steady rise in droning.

In the gunpowder sky, a gibbous moon floated, an ominous eye that watched us roll into the capital. Shadowy figures, slouched and round, mushroomed along the road, but I could see them only when they moved. They appeared to be fixing potholes, perhaps clearing debris. There were several military checkpoints, which were nothing more than clusters of sleepy soldiers who smoked cigarettes while waving the convoy onward.

Pyongyang's central streets, wide and lined with telephone poles, were smoothly paved and bisected with tram rails. While there was extensive damage in many neighborhoods, the areas that we drove through were mostly intact. Uniform, multilevel buildings were desolate above deserted sidewalks. Rows of houses were as somber as gravestones, their walls mottled with dull, shuttered windows. Only soldiers were out, with machine guns pointed, patrolling what looked like an unfinished ghost story.

Though I had read that the industrial North had been more prosperous than the agricultural South, this was my first time comparing the two capitals. I was apprehensive, but also in awe, my curiosity its own compulsive force. This wasn't just a place; it was a setting, the backdrop of a multitude of stories. Even if it was controlled by people who'd arrest me if they knew who I really was, it was still akin to a stockpot of wrapped candy that I was excited to open and examine.

Hundreds of questions twirled in my mind. Were there any Americans here at all? Did the UN Command make any sort of impact during their short occupation? How did the remaining inhabitants feel about yet another change in authority?

Our truck jostled past a sprawling brick complex that might have once been a factory, or housing for industrial workers. Now it was surrounded by sandbags piled waist-high, and dozens of military vehicles that blocked the guarded entrance. Tires squelched as other vehicles in our convoy parked on a muddy lawn. Comrade Zhang pulled up at the farthest end, one of the crates tilting precariously when he braked.

"Wait," Comrade Ying called back to us. "Don't move."

Imo was slumped beside the fuel barrel, as limp and disheveled as a well-loved doll. Her chest moved, laboriously but steadily, and her bag of grains rested on her belly. She had hugged it for the duration of the trip.

"Chuang-Chuang!" yelled Comrade Ying. "Get over here."

"What is it?" asked another man, several cars away.

I ducked back behind the crates, uncertain why Comrade Ying would draw anyone's attention our way. "Chuang-Chuang," however, was a *xiaoming*—a childhood nickname given to infants to confuse evil spirits. It was uncommon for anyone to use these names in adulthood unless they were family or childhood friends.

"I told you to come, so just come," said Comrade Ying, warningly.

Comrade Zhang spat on the floor and lit a cigarette, the smoke wafting into the hold. Imo wrapped her scarf over her mouth, glaring at me like it was my fault that he was smoking.

"I have to unload," whined Chuang-Chuang. His footsteps thumped toward us. "What do you want, *Guh*?"

So they were brothers. Less worried now, I ventured out by the first row of crates.

When Comrade Ying came around to the hold, he grunted with disapprobation. "Didn't I tell you not to move?"

"I thought you meant *don't leave the truck*, not *don't move at all*," I said.

Comrade Ying might have admonished me more, but then Chuang-Chuang appeared—a soldier who wasn't even five feet tall. Perhaps he was a teenager, but he looked prepubescent. His quilted uniform was split at the shoulder, and his face was as round as the moon overhead. Even in the low light, I could see that he had the same thick brows and spattering of freckles as Comrade Ying.

Chuang-Chuang recoiled at the sight of my skirt. "What's a girl doing here?" he whispered. "Are you in trouble?"

"She's here for you," Comrade Ying snapped. "Now, switch shoes."

Along the line of vehicles, men were jumping out and slamming their doors, chattering in a mix of languages. Though their uniforms did not always match, the Chinese soldiers, including Chuang-Chuang and Comrade Ying, invariably wore cotton sneakers. Chuang-Chuang's were frayed at the tongues, and smeared with mud. I didn't want them, but a deal was a deal, so I started unlacing my boots.

Chuang-Chuang hesitated. "Aren't those hers? Doesn't she need them?"

"She doesn't need them as much as you do, dummy," said Comrade Ying.

"But I can't steal shoes from a girl!"

"You aren't stealing. I traded for them. Now, stop wasting time, and change. The sooner we unload, the sooner we can eat."

Obeying reluctantly, Chuang-Chuang hopped into the truck. "All right," he said, wincing as he slipped off his sneakers. His bare feet were engorged, the skin stretched taut and shiny.

I grimaced too. Back in Tachikawa, I used to joke with Barbara that everyone on base was obsessed with feet, but proper care of them—proper soles—was a life-and-death matter for a soldier. Just looking at Chuang-Chuang was painful, but I also felt sorry for myself as I exchanged my thick boots for a flimsy mess that was like a wet roll of toilet paper.

Chuang-Chuang struggled to squeeze his swollen feet into the sturdy leather, and Comrade Ying bent to help him.

"These are nice," remarked Chuang-Chuang. "Where did she even get these?"

"Black market," I replied stonily.

"You speak Chinese?" asked Chuang-Chuang, gawking at me anew.

"The less you know, the better," scoffed Comrade Ying. "Now go back and help your comrades unload. When you're done, I'll have another surprise for you."

"Oh, really? Is it a warmer hat?"

"You'll see."

"I hope it's a hat."

"It's better than a hat."

"A new jacket?"

"You'll see. Just go!"

"Ah, you don't need to yell!" cried Chuang-Chuang. He eased himself out of the truck, flexing his ankles in my boots, marveling at how the leather was hefty yet supple. Turning to me, he smiled shyly. "Thank you, miss."

Comrade Ying swatted the back of his head. "I'm the one who made the trade! You should be thanking me."

"Okay, okay," huffed Chuang-Chuang. "Thanks, *Guh*!"

As Chuang-Chuang clomped back to his own vehicle, I yanked off my second layer of socks. "Take these too," I said, though they were unwashed and covered with lint. "For your little brother."

Comrade Ying shifted away, suspicious. "Is there something else you want?"

"No, I just saw that he has no socks. It's a miracle that he still has toes, but he won't always be so lucky, even with my boots. Here." I held my socks out farther.

Comrade Ying examined me astutely. He had the type of features that could clench like a fist, his brows so tight that they matched the V-shaped silhouette of a bird in flight. "You are a liar," he declared.

I lowered my hand. "Excuse me?"

"You are a liar," he repeated. "From the moment I met you in Kanggye, I could tell that you were hiding something. You are still hiding something."

Alarmed, I glanced at either side of the lawn. There were so many soldiers around, and I didn't have shoes on, but I was prepared to run, dragging Imo if I had to—potentially ditching Imo if I had to.

Comrade Ying was shrewd enough to see my discomfort, but he took my socks and shoved them deep into his pocket. "But I suppose the less I know, the better. In the end, you are one of us, and that's all that matters. If we don't look out for our own kind here, who else will?" Extending his arm, he offered to help me climb down from the truck.

I was able to jump myself, but I accepted his support, while Imo crawled clumsily over the cargo.

"I hope you find what you are looking for," said Comrade Ying. "And I hope that you and your Korean friends remain safe."

"You as well," I replied. "I hope that you get to go home soon."

"I do too. But I have a feeling that I will never go back to China."

"Nonsense," I said. "You are just tired. No one can know their own fate, or anyone else's."

His words, from such young lips, were too disturbing to accept. And yet when Comrade Ying turned away and Comrade Zhang tossed the glowing end of his cigarette into the mud, I saw it too—as though the barrier between our world and the next had thinned into a veil, then flickered. Whether by instinct or something else, there was a message that I could read, like a headline caught in the corner of my eye.

Comrade Ying is going to die in Korea, along with his younger brother.

The two of them were loosed arrows flying on a one-way journey that I could witness but could not alter. I preferred to believe that we made our own fates, but I wondered to what extent theirs was set upon birth, when their souls had crept into the wrong womb, in the wrong country, at the wrong point in our contentious history. Perhaps I too was simply overtired, but I could not shake this preemptive sense of regret.

Washington, December 3, 1950: Memorandum of a Telephone Conversation, by the Assistant Secretary of State for United Nations Affairs (Hickerson):

[India's Prime Minister Jawaharlal] Nehru believes that it is a matter of absolute necessity to avoid use of the atomic bomb. Such use would make [world] war inevitable. There is a wide-spread feeling in Asia that the atomic bomb is a weapon used only against Asiatics. (*Foreign Relations of the United States*, 1950, Volume VII, p. 1334)

Washington, 8 November 1950, Memorandum by the Planning Adviser, Bureau of Far Eastern Affairs (Emmerson) to the Assistant Secretary of State for Far Eastern Affairs (Rusk)

We must consider that, regardless of the fact that military results achieved by atomic bombardment may be identical to those attained by conventional weapons, the effect on world opinion will be vastly different. The A-bomb has the status of a peculiar monster conserved by American cunning and its use by us, in whatever situation, would be exploited to our serious detriment.

(*Foreign Relations of the United States*, 1950, Volume VII, p. 1099)

22

LIKE EVERYONE ELSE

December 19, 1950

Sirens were stationed throughout Pyongyang, and they blared before curfew each evening. We had arrived well past midnight, and on every other block harried soldiers stopped us for an interrogation. They wanted to see our identification, but Imo told them that our house had been bombed and all our paperwork destroyed—at least that was what I guessed. Unlike Emma, Imo refused to translate anything, and when I tried asking her for an explanation, she just said, *"Dakchyeo."*

On some of the streets, downed power lines lay like dead snakes, limp but still unnerving. The first few soldiers we met allowed us to continue toward Emma's home, but eventually a stout officer directed us, at gunpoint, to a canning factory that functioned as a general shelter. Thousands of people were packed inside—refugees from the countryside as well as residents of the city who had nowhere else to live. Laundry hung on the machinery, and sleeping mats were spread on the floor as everyone waited for curfew to end.

It stank of fish, but I was so exhausted that I unrolled my mat and claimed the only empty space left, which partially blocked a set of stairs. I scrunched myself up to make room for Imo, who draped herself protectively over our bags. After hooking her leg over Emma's sewing machine, Imo whispered to me haughtily: "I don't want to be with you either, you know, but I was holding my family back with my illness. I am here for my son, not for myself—or you."

I pretended not to hear her. Squeezing my eyes shut, I let sleep seduce me into a realm of dark alleys where sad dead men followed me, tiptoeing in the imprints of my bare, bootless feet.

At first light, the factory inhabitants repacked their belongings and elbowed their way out, spilling into the streets, families splitting up strategically to meet their collective needs. The military had set up ration centers, but even at dawn they were so crowded that I couldn't see where the line began. Homeless women cooked in the open air, while family members waited for their allotment of grain or scavenged for supplies.

We had no water to wash with, but Imo combed her fingers through her hair and twirled it into a greasy bun. Before we left, she patted my chest to make sure that I had Emma's little book. I had flipped through it quickly, but aside from a few scribbles and a stamp on the first page, it was entirely empty.

"What is this book for?" I asked Imo.

"Emergencies," she replied. "Don't show it to anyone until I tell you to. Don't do anything or talk to anyone until I tell you to. Understand?"

"But what—"

She pinched my lips shut. "People here are not mountain bumpkins. You do not speak Japanese like a Korean, or like a Japanese. Most people won't care, but enough will notice, and too many will wonder. City folk have standards, you know."

Keeping quiet, I nodded. I never thought I had a strong accent in Japanese, but I had learned from my parents, who probably spoke it with their own respective accents from when they were under colonial rule.

Past the canning factory, there was a shopping area with wide raised walkways, but the stores were closed and the windows barren. Not even banks were operating; people had raided them early on, stashing away fistfuls of won that ultimately became worthless. Armed KPA soldiers were everywhere, monitoring the endless lines in which both adults and children stood in hungry obedience.

Imo's breathing remained ragged, but she was oddly energetic. I walked three paces behind her, carrying our provisions while she held her sack of grain daintily, as though it were a purse. Occasionally, she waved to the men in uniform, confidently, like she could purchase them along with whatever trinkets she imagined to be on display. She had been born and raised in Pyongyang, but it never occurred to me that she might have missed it—that she might have any emotions other than anger and irritation.

Much of Pyongyang's industrial area had been bombed, but Emma's textile factory lay along the fringes of the city center. The complex was similar to the one that the Chinese soldiers were garrisoned at, and though it was undamaged, there was no electricity to run the machinery. Behind it, there was workers' lodging, row after row of squat cinder-block houses with stucco walls, some of which had been punctured by stray artillery. A North Korean flag fluttered languidly from the mildew-streaked gate, with signs in Russian and Korean.

Imo heaved a deep sigh. "Thank heavens it's still here," she said, and she slouched as though she had taken on more baggage. Lifting her skirt, she trod cautiously over the stagnant puddle blocking the entrance. Many of the workers had probably left, but the central walkway was swept clean, and smoke trailed from some of the chimneys. There was a large noticeboard with a framed portrait of Kim Il-Sung, and faded prints of women courageously linking arms, their red scarves flapping in the wind. In Kanggye, Emma had complained that red was a difficult color to dye fabric, and even harder to maintain, but everyone, including the young and the poor, had to keep their scarves pristine or risk a public shaming.

"It's this one," said Imo, stopping in front of a weathered door. The house, like all the others, was the color of an old bruise, with a sloping shingled roof. Though modest, it was modern compared to the thatched huts in Kanggye. A note was tacked onto the door frame, which Imo barely read before tearing it off. "Give me the keys."

I hesitated, wary that Imo might slip in herself and slam the door behind her. She kept looking over her shoulder, swiveling her head from one end of the street to the other. "Hurry," she added, "before anyone sees us."

I wasn't sure what had happened to the version of her that had sashayed past submachine guns in the shopping district, but I pulled the keys from my pocket and dropped them into her cupped hand, which she held out not like a beggar but like she was confiscating contraband.

Imo flipped to the correct key and jiggled the door open, then shut it frantically as soon as we crossed the threshold. Inside, the stale air carried the pungent scent of mothballs. There was a single narrow glass window, with an orange curtain that was as fantastically embroidered as Emma's skirts. The entire house was one room, with a raised alcove for sleeping, and a potbellied stove for heat. Cramped in the corner was a Western-style dining table, which had schoolbooks and scraps of fabric piled on top. The bathroom facilities must have been shared; there was a bucket of water beside the stove, mostly evaporated, but no sink or tap.

I marveled at it all. Even though it was spare, I was jubilant to have shelter again. Out of habit, we removed our shoes, the clay tiles so chilly that our feet left moist prints of condensation on them.

Imo wheezed disapprovingly, noting the jackets that dangled from the wall, and the shoes lined up by the door. "It looks exactly the same," she remarked. On the table, there was a dusty ceramic dish filled with candy, and Imo picked up a piece. "She didn't even throw away Yun-Hee's sweets. These are sticky, and bad for your teeth, you know."

The candy's wax wrapper was so old that it disintegrated as Imo rotated it between her thumb and forefinger. When the paper fell away, the amber candy caught the light, glistening like a jewel. Imo closed her fingers over it, squeezing so tightly that her knuckles turned white. "I think about her every day," said Imo, to her own pale fist. "I watched her grow. I loved her too."

I lingered by the window, unsettled by Imo's sorrow, and the speed and extent to which her moods swung. Recalling what Jae-Min had told me about Emma and his mother, I said, "I heard you were all very close when you lived in Pyongyang."

"At one point, yes. I was Yun-Hee's godmother. Her Japanese name, Machiko, was taken from mine." Imo opened her hand, the shreds of wax paper sticking in the creases of her palm. She put the candy back reverently, as though it were a shard of bone. Picking through the fabric, Imo said, "Moon Hwa-Ja has this house because of me, you know. She got this job because of me. This factory was built by a Japanese cotton company, and the owner was my brother-in-law's business partner. I even helped Hwa-Ja improve her Japanese, so she could get a better-paying position. I gave her my own books, from Tokyo. How else would a person like her speak it so well? How else would she have become a supervisor?"

I hadn't been expecting Imo to give me such a detailed answer. "Well, I think—"

"Don't interrupt," said Imo, though I had only been answering her question. "When Hwa-Ja left her husband, no one, not even her own family, was willing to help her. She became a Christian because my husband used to give out cereal! She stayed in my home for a *year*. I gave her all of Jae-Min's old clothes and diapers. If it weren't for me, Hwa-Ja would have had to beg her husband to take her back. She probably would have had to kneel before his concubine too!"

"So you were friends?" I asked, uncertain.

"We spent a lot of time together." Imo began separating the silk and woven prints from the cheaper fabric into distinct piles on the table. "My husband wanted Hwa-Ja and her husband to reconcile. I was the one who convinced him that she needed to live on her own, because I know what it's like to fight with your family. In that sense, Hwa-Ja and I understood each other. In a rare way, that made it worth overlooking our differences."

I thought back to what Emma had told me about her marriage. Until now, I had assumed that her husband had left her, not the other way around. It took courage to defy convention, and knowing this about Emma made me admire her even more. "What happened, then?" I asked. "Why aren't you close anymore?"

Imo draped her chosen fabric over her wrist and left the rest on the table. "She asked me for a favor, and I said no. Hwa-Ja can be very entitled, you know."

The way Imo sat, with her nose tilted up, made me want to laugh at the irony, but I held back. "What was the favor? Did it have to do with her daughter?"

"It had to do with my son," said Imo. "I don't know how much Hwa-Ja has told you, but she wanted my son to marry Yun-Hee. My son is a very popular boy, of course. He is kind, strong, well educated. From a good family! Hwa-Ja wasn't the only one who asked me about Jae-Min, but she was the only one who took my rejection personally." Her cheeks flushed, as if the mere recollection of this appeal had rekindled her indignation.

"Auntie Moon never told me about this."

"Of course she didn't. People don't like to talk about things that make them look bad."

"But I thought Jae-Min liked Yun-Hee?"

"He did, but he was a *child*," said Imo. "Hwa-Ja married young, but I did not. Hwa-Ja married a man her parents picked for her, but I did not. I gave her the same response that I gave everyone else: 'After my son graduates from university, he can decide who he wants to marry. I will not choose his wife, but I forbid him from marrying anyone until he is done with school.' Jae-Min was only sixteen when she asked me. Sixteen! Far too young to be engaged these days. Unless you're a bumpkin."

I calculated the ages. Jae-Min had been two years older than Yun-Hee, so Emma must have tried to arrange their match when

Yun-Hee was fourteen. Quietly, I connected the dots between the accounts that I had heard. "Auntie Moon must have been pushing for the marriage so Yun-Hee could avoid the draft . . . the *cheong-shindae* . . . since the Japanese military only took unmarried girls, right?"

Imo's eyes narrowed. "It doesn't matter why she did it. Jae-Min is my son. I try to be a generous person, but not with his future. I have saved Hwa-Ja on multiple occasions, but she only remembers the time that I refused to give."

She was already aggravated, but another question burned in my mouth. It was none of my business, but I had built my career by inserting myself where I didn't belong and prodding until a stranger's story became my own. Within the short time frame that I had known Emma, she had claimed too much of my heart for me to be impartial, so I scrutinized Imo's face. "Did you know the truth about the labor drafts? About the comfort stations?"

The silk fabric slipped from Imo's wrist. She stiffened, and instead of bending to retrieve it, she crossed her arms protectively. "I only knew what everyone else did." Though she was offended by the question, she seemed to be weighing her words, like one might pick unbruised fruit at a market. "I knew, like everyone else did, that the Kempeitai abducted and purchased girls specifically for the comfort stations. It was happening years before the Second World War—here in Korea, where women were forced to serve the Japanese authorities. Because there was a system already in place for the comfort stations, I didn't believe that the labor draft would include them. Like everyone else, I thought the labor draft was only for factory work. Like everyone else, I didn't realize how many girls were routed for sex until after the war, when they could finally come home."

Imo kept her gaze on the table as she continued. "I thought Yun-Hee would go to an assembly line, like Jae-Min and his classmates. Hwa-Ja assumes that I knew more than everyone else because I have Japanese friends and relatives, but the Japanese only talked about how awful life was in Japan—how the Imperial Army was on the verge of surrender, and how it was already negotiating terms that could protect the emperor. I assumed that Yun-Hee would work for a few months at most when she was drafted. I never imagined that we'd never see her again."

Tears beaded in Imo's eyelashes, and she flicked them away before they fell, with a sweep of her finger that was so casual that I would have missed it if I hadn't been focusing on her face.

"Do you think Yun-Hee ended up at a comfort station, then?" I asked.

"I hope not. If she did, I understand why she wouldn't want to come back. There is no future here for women like that, unless they are willing to work as prostitutes. Or lie. Otherwise they just end up being burdens to their families, and if there is anything about Yun-Hee that I am certain of, it's that she would not have wanted to be a burden on her mother. Had I truly known the risks, I would have agreed to the marriage, at least for the paperwork. Of course I would have, but Hwa-Ja doesn't believe me."

Imo covered her face with her hands and rubbed her eyes. I pretended not to notice that her palms were wet when she folded them together, but the ache of being the *other* was one that I empathized with deeply.

Leaning closer to Imo, I said, "I believe you."

She lifted her chin, stunned. For a moment, she seemed younger, less severe, maybe even pleasant. Her effervescent expression, however, promptly devolved into her usual brooding.

"I don't care if you believe me," she sneered. "It's not your opinion that matters."

I sighed, disappointed by how quickly our momentary connection had been severed. "All right. I'll boil some water. Perhaps drinking something warm will make you feel better."

Though Imo only grunted, I felt culpable for making her cry—like I had broken something that I didn't even think was fragile. I suspected that for Imo, service was a form of care, so I examined the stove and its multiple compartments. This model was strange to me, and I wasn't sure where to light the fire.

"I will make us breakfast," Imo said. "You don't know what to do."

"I can figure it out." There was a bag of coal against the back wall, along with some matches, brushes, and spades in a tin bucket.

"No, I'm too hungry. I have no patience for your errors." With a single wipe, Imo smoothed away her distress like one might flatten the wrinkles in a bedsheet. "Go see if Hwa-Ja has any food. And check if the water pump outside is still working. It's hard to go from rich to poor, but you do get used to it." She swatted me to the side and yanked out the stove's bottom tray, soot scattering over the floor.

I would never have described myself as rich, but I supposed that my middle-class Californian living standard was comparatively high for Korea. As for Imo, she certainly wasn't poor, but Pastor Pak's mountain house was probably a steep decline from whatever mansion she had grown up in.

I picked up the fabric pieces that she had dropped, some so fine that they might have been used for formal hanboks or kimonos. While I didn't regret asking about Yun-Hee, I wished that I hadn't begun that conversation expecting her to lie. In Korea I was desperate to hold on to my sense of self, but I wasn't here as a correspondent anymore. Regardless of what I did, or thought I was doing, I was simply fighting to survive, like everyone else was. If we were lucky, maybe we could escape and claim a different life:

My old life.

23

SEEING RED

December 19, 1950

Someone was watching Emma's house. As soon as Imo lit the coals and smoke drifted from the chimney, a young woman with a red scarf banged on our door. She didn't wait for us to open it. Since she had a spare key, she burst right in, sending Imo's asthma flaring.

"Hello, hello!" she greeted, with the exuberance of someone who wholeheartedly believed that it was darkest before the dawn. "I'm Kim Miho, Youth Pioneer!"

My Korean was getting better, but I couldn't understand the rest of what she said. Miho was animated, reciting what might have been a Party slogan. Her hair was cropped to her jawline, and she wore a navy student's uniform. Though she seemed welcoming, Imo turned as white as chalk, choking on phlegm as she buckled into a bow.

Imo and Miho spoke, but all I caught was "Kanggye" and "Moon Hwa-Ja." When Miho tried to ask me a question, Imo held up her hand and shook her head, rasping some excuse. Though Imo had scrupulously hidden her tears from me, she threw herself on the ground in front of Miho and began to bawl, pounding the floor with her fist. It was so uncharacteristically undignified that I was embarrassed on her behalf, but Imo only blubbered more loudly, wailing a story and beckoning to me. I knelt beside her, wondering if I was supposed to cry too, but then she pawed at my jacket for Emma's red book.

I almost screamed when Imo handed it to Miho, my mind flashing back to Clara's letters burning in the fire. Though I didn't know why Emma cared so much about an empty booklet, she had entrusted me with it, and I couldn't let anyone take it away.

Stunned, Miho flipped the book open and stared at the first page, and then at me. I noticed that her neatly trimmed fingernails were stained with red ink, which matched the book's binding. Miho murmured, regarding me hesitantly, as though my exterior was an eggshell and one wrong move could crack me. People tend to think you're stupid when you don't speak their language, but Miho seemed to have concluded that I was incapacitated in another way. She returned the book not to me but to Imo.

Still wheezing, Imo hustled to the table, snatching up the silk fabric that she had separated out earlier. She pushed the bundle into Miho's arms, and though Miho initially refused, eventually she accepted, with an exaggerated groan. Both of them transitioned to variations of "*annyeonghi*" and "*neeh,*" bowing back and forth until Miho retreated across the threshold, embracing her colorful silk.

Imo closed the door and leaned her back against it, deflating with relief as Miho's skipping footsteps faded.

"What happened?" I asked quietly, conscious that sound could carry beyond the house.

Imo's breath rattled. Holding the red book out to me, she said, "Your name is now Song Yun-Hee."

I hesitated before taking it back. "I don't understand."

"It's a life-review book, for writing self-criticisms," Imo explained. "Many people don't have identification documents, but every citizen has one of these books. You have to present one at Party meetings in order to get your ration stamps. Our village in Kanggye was never strict about checking our entries, since many farmers can't write, but here in Pyongyang people take life review very seriously. City people have standards."

"There's no photograph in it, though."

"Of course not. Do you know how expensive photographs are?"

"But without them, anyone can just take someone's book and pretend to be them."

"No one would do that. Who wants to steal another person's self-criticisms? That's like claiming someone else's sins. Maybe if there are unredeemed ration stamps it would have some value, but it's not worth the risk. Meddling with these books is a highly condemnable act, you know!"

"How does Yun-Hee even have a book? She wasn't here when the Communists took over."

Imo covered her mouth, hacking up a glob of mucus. She was comfortable enough with me, or perhaps she cared so little about my opinion, that she spat into a handkerchief in front of me. "Because Hwa-Ja insisted on getting her one. Ridiculous, right? She kept telling everyone that her daughter was coming back, and no one believed her. Miho said the other workers all thought she was crazy for keeping that book, until now. You get to prove Hwa-Ja right, I suppose."

Poor Emma. It must have been lonely being surrounded by such discouragement, especially since many of these neighbors must have been Yun-Hee's friends. Another fear popped into my head. "Don't people here know Yun-Hee?"

"Some might. If they've worked here long enough to have seen her, then they might also recognize me, which is a much bigger problem. I don't know what to do about that yet, but I'll think of something. In the meantime, we both have to contribute. There is no electricity to run the machines, so we can't make our own textiles, but the Soviets have sent us fabric, and the women here are sewing uniforms."

"Are you joking?" I asked. "The last time I sewed anything was in high school. I can't make a uniform. Can you?"

"Maybe. I've never tried, but I know how to use a sewing machine. Don't you?"

"Sort of. I've forgotten most of it by now."

"Well, can you at least knit?"

"Badly."

"Oh heavens," said Imo, wheezing again. "Yun-Hee has been knitting since she could hold a pair of chopsticks. She was like a machine! People will definitely know you aren't her if you can't make anything at all."

"I think my inability to speak Korean is more telling than my inability to knit," I said, dryly.

Imo began pacing in the small space in front of the threshold. With every two steps, she had to whirl around. "I told Miho that you are mentally unwell. That's not uncommon for women who came back after the war, even the ones who were in factories."

"Yes, but I don't think any of them were so traumatized that they couldn't speak their own language."

"Well, I didn't have much time to think of an explanation!"

"Why didn't you just tell her that I'm Chinese, like we've done this entire time?"

"Because this is Hwa-Ja's house!" she snapped. "Random people can't stay here, but Yun-Hee is a registered resident. Miho is going to note that Yun-Hee—you—are back, and register me as your guest."

I clutched my head, digging my nails into my scalp as my own airways constricted. "This isn't going to work. Someone's bound to figure out who we are, or at least that we aren't who we say we are. Maybe we should just go to one of the shelters before we get caught."

"Our families are meeting us here," said Imo. "And you saw the shelters. They're dangerous and unsanitary! Full of disease too. At least here we have a stove, and a door we can lock."

"What good is a lock when we don't know who else has the key? Is Miho the only one who can barge in here?"

Imo cast a nervous glance at the window. "This is a compound of women. About a quarter of the workers are still here, and none of them are men. We are far safer in this house than in the open, with homeless, desperate men. You may go to the shelter if you want, but I am staying."

Leaving the entrance area, Imo skirted past me to the pantry, a narrow cabinet that was about the size of a high school locker. Like a raccoon, she poked at every jar and canister on the two shelves, opening and examining them before rearranging them entirely. I didn't know what the punishment was for impersonating someone and lying to a Youth Pioneer, but I did know that the North Korean justice system was as vicious as it was unpredictable.

"We have some time to think," Imo added, sniffing a ceramic pot. "Between the two of us, we should be smart enough to come up with a story."

"Between the two of us, only one of us truly has a choice," I muttered.

I couldn't speak Korean, so my risk of exposure would be far greater without Imo to help me navigate—at least until Emma arrived. Though I hated to admit it, my safety right now depended more on Imo than on anything else. She counted out sheets of dried kelp and stacked them beside a bag of buckwheat noodles, gleeful when she found a tawny bottle of sesame oil. Acquiescing, I went to unpack the provisions that I had carried.

Miho gave us instructions on where to find the factory's storage facility, which functioned as its air-raid shelter. Dutifully, she also warned us not to touch unexploded ordnance and listed the streets that were closed due to land mines.

The water pumps weren't working, so Imo ordered me to go to the river, in a pair of rubber boots that might have been Yun-Hee's. They were loose on me, and I clunked past the bland factory housing with a stockpot balanced on my hip and canteens over my shoulder.

I followed a group of bucket-toting women to a frozen bank that was lined with gingko trees and knotted weeping willows. The lowest willow branches, blond and bare, grazed the ice along the shore. In the center of the river, people had sawed out holes. Copying the women before me, I glided onto the ice, removed my gloves, and plunged my canteen into the dark water.

I squealed and recoiled, my hands redder than my drunken

face had been. Children on the bank giggled, and their mothers scolded them for pointing, though some adults chuckled too. After huffing on my hands to warm them, I dangled the canteens in by their straps, and the stockpot by its handles. When rising, I sloshed gallons of water over my coat and skirt and shrieked again.

"Be careful!" yelled a woman.

Additional moisture made the ice more slippery. If I fell into one of these holes, I'd drown with my face pressed against a frozen wall.

My wet skirt clung to my boots as I skidded back to the shore, my body bent over the stockpot while the canteens clanged against it. By the time I'd trudged back to Emma's house, my teeth were chattering and I had a new pair of blisters. Never in my life had I been so cold! I expected Imo to criticize my ineptitude, but she rushed to help me shed my soaked layers, hanging everything beside the stove. She had made barley tea, sweetened with dried dates, which she poured for me without her usual grimace.

In a closet by the sleeping alcove, there were spare blankets, yarn, dishware, several bolts of fabric, and extra clothing. I selected a plain navy sweater, which reeked so strongly of mothballs that it must have been stored for an extended period. Though I had worn Yun-Hee's boots, touching the clothes that once warmed her body reminded me of the Communist soldiers who had stripped coats from the fallen marines.

"You're going to catch a cold," said Imo, heaving the stockpot onto the stove. "Do you not know how to tie a hanbok?"

"Of course I do, but these must be Yun-Hee's. I'm not sure if Emma would want me to wear them."

"Yun-Hee is gone," Imo declared, without a modicum of her initial chagrin. "Everything is meant to be used, and standing around like a naked fool doesn't help anyone. Besides, I don't want to keep looking at your skinny, shivering butt!"

Suddenly conscious of my goose bumps, I whispered an apology to the closet and picked the oldest items I could find—a pair of badly pilled pants and the navy sweater, which had been patched at the elbows. At least I felt more like a beggar than a thief.

Imo scattered corn into the stockpot. "By the way, it turns out there is a well a few streets away from us, so you won't have to go all the way to the river next time. Isn't that nice?" Nonchalantly, she broke apart a few sheets of kelp.

I wanted to throttle her. When I had questioned her about an alternative to the river, she had chided me for being lazy and pushed me out the door.

Imo didn't seem sheepish at all, but she did refill my tea without my asking. The steam from the simmering soup filled the room with a moist, savory warmth. Content, Imo covered the pot and proceeded to mop the floor tiles with a hand rag. Just a few hours of rest in Emma's house seemed to have alleviated her cough.

Outside, rain began to peck at the roof. It was gentle at first, but soon it became hail that snapped like tap shoes overhead. Dense flurries of snow spiraled before splattering in popcorn-sized chunks, clinging on contact. Within minutes, the window was sheathed in white.

---

20 December 1950
Dear Yun-Hee,

Forgive me for not writing for so long. To be honest, I am surprised that I am still alive to write you now. The pastor and I are sheltering in an empty church, but it is so cold that I can barely hold this pen. The ink is frozen, and I used my saliva to thaw it.

There are about forty others here, waiting for the blizzard to pass. We have a fire, but its warmth is not enough. Wherever you are, pray for us. Pray for Jae-Min.

I don't know how we are going to tell his mother.

Mom

24

FOOLS LIKE ME

December 19, 1950

The rain and snow alternated, dropping in sheets, endless white flags, as though the sky itself had capitulated and collapsed onto the capital. I wasn't a person who prayed often, but that evening I knelt by the window and gave the Guanyin bodhisattva a list, not unlike what children send to Santa Claus. Instead of toys, however, I asked for protection for my loved ones in the States; for Barbara and the former WASPs in Japan; and for Emma, Pastor Pak, and Jae-Min, who were still on the road.

Imo pointed out that many in North Korea were safer with the storm, because none of the bombers could fly in it. The two of us set up our mats by the stove and plugged the house's drafty cracks with paper scraps.

I wasn't sure whether Imo had stopped hating me or she simply had a compulsive need to be heard, but she prattled on about Pyongyang—the city that she knew, the home that she lost, and the paradise that she dreamed of still. She competed with the weather, her voice ringing above the percussive sleet. "When I was a girl, I lived in a house with three floors. I can't remember how many people were in that home. There were so many servants. We had a swimming pool and a garden, and our own automobile. And a piano!"

Upon her mentioning the piano, her fingers cycled like mine often did when I thought about my typewriter. "My siblings and I each had our own nanny," she continued. "My father only hired Japanese people, so my nanny was from Osaka. But she spoke too much Osaka slang. When I was six, he replaced her with another woman, a former teacher from Tokyo. My father used to say that early learning matters most. You can't build anything on a sloppy foundation, you know."

Into the evening, she described her mother's Chinese porcelain, the imported silk from Kyoto, and her father's bars of gold, stacked like bricks in his office safe.

"How did he become so rich?" I asked.

My question startled her, as though I were a pet that she was speaking at instead of a person she was speaking with. "Oh," she said, "he worked very hard. I suppose he was lucky, at least early on, but he had a good instinct about the right people to work with. He was always willing to adapt and learn new skills. He could drive, you know!"

With a velvety laugh, she launched into stories about how her father took the whole family for drives along the coast, how she stood up in the back seat and her hair caught the wind and whipped like a flag, how he bought her and her sisters matching pearls, and about the time they drove all the way to Busan and back.

I didn't mind her chattiness, but this golden past was as irrelevant to us now as my California hills. There was a page, or maybe several pages, that she seemed to have ripped out of her own book—and those were the ones that I wanted to read.

"How did you meet Pastor Pak?" I interrupted.

She paused, allowing the rain to hammer its interlude. "That is a very long story." She yawned. "I will tell you another time."

December 20, 1950

Imo's symptoms continued to improve, and the storm was beginning to abate. I hoped this meant that Emma and the Pak men were able to travel again, and maybe pick up their pace. The sooner Emma returned, the sooner she and I could set out for South Korea.

In preparation for the Party meetings, which often took place regardless of the weather, Imo announced that she was going to shave her eyebrows.

"Why in the world would you do that?" I asked.

"Eyebrows are the most important part of your face," she explained. "They show our thoughts, so others notice them. If I take off my eyebrows and redraw them with coal in a different shape, anyone who used to know me might not recognize me—especially if I wrap my scarf around my nose and mouth."

After setting aside a portion of soup for Miho, and a variety of gifts scrounged from Emma's closet, including spools of embroidery thread, Imo lathered her brow bone with soap.

I watched her with the gobsmacked dread that one might reserve for traffic accidents. Having spent two full days with her during the blizzard, and learned the minutiae of her formerly entitled life, I found Imo more baffling than ever. Imo valued her dignity so much that she preferred to swallow her phlegm rather than spit on the street, and yet here she sat, determined, at the table, holding a hand mirror and a kitchen knife.

"Maybe we should just go to a public shelter," I said. "Then neither of us will have to worry so much about getting caught."

Imo balanced the mirror against Yun-Hee's old books and stretched her skin taut in preparation. "Ellie-yah, how is it that you still do not understand? My family was very, very famous in Pyongyang. There are people all over the city who might recognize me, not just here at the factory. I will have to disguise myself no matter where I am."

She was lamenting, but there was a hint of pride too.

"Yes, but you left your parents decades ago, didn't you? Surely no one would still consider you a Japanese collaborator."

"You underestimate our leaders," she said, focused on her reflection. "Even in war, the noose does not loosen."

With steadfast precision, she began shaving, head tilted so the suds wouldn't drip into her eyes. "I've never shaved anything before," she remarked. "Well, actually, when I was younger one of my father's dogs got injured trying to jump over a fence. We had Akitas, purebred—very expensive, very elegant, taller from snout to tail than I was! An ordinary man would have shot the dog, but my father insisted on treating it. We had to shave him to stitch up the wound. Can you imagine such a fuss?"

Her hair stuck in a sudsy patch at her temple. "Then, just a few years later, the authorities confiscated all our dogs for the war effort. Akitas have very fine, fluffy pelts, you know. The military used them to line the soldiers' winter jackets. Oh, how painful that was!" She sighed, dabbing her face with a towel before going back for stray hairs. "I've always wanted to have another Akita, but they are very hard to find now."

Triumphantly, she wiped her knife. Without her eyebrows, she resembled an egg. I had never paid much attention to Imo's brows before, but in hindsight, they had been abundant, with a graceful arch that accented her fine bone structure. Her hairless forehead seemed gigantic. It was unnerving and certainly shocking, but I wouldn't have considered her unrecognizable.

Still, she nodded confidently and said, "This will do."

She changed into one of Yun-Hee's hanboks—a plain pink top and a hefty skirt embroidered with songbirds from hip to hem, which actually fit her better than her own plain hanboks. After braiding my hair, Imo said, "When in doubt, just cry. Remember, our house has been bombed, and you . . . well, you won't need to worry about anyone asking you about *that*. It's not something to talk about—not if you have manners, anyway. We have been through a lot, and the women here have too. The crawfish is on the crab's side. They will understand."

Imo drew on her new brows, feather strokes with her fingernail, smudging to change their shape in a way that was more convincing than I had anticipated.

In the afternoon, Miho came to visit us again, and this time she brought an elderly woman, whom she introduced as her maternal grandmother, Granny Cho. The two of them had slush spread like icing on their hats and shoulders.

Miho, impervious to the weather, was her same bubbly self, but Granny Cho had a scowl that rivaled Imo's. From what I understood, Granny Cho was the head supervisor at the factory and had been one of the first workers here. Her tan cheeks were puffed like coin purses, her skin so leathery that creases cut through her wrinkles. Once she might have been tall, but now her neck was almost horizontal, her chin jutting out and her spine curving to follow. Over her coat, she wore a red armband with a star sewn on it.

Imo ushered Miho and Granny Cho inside like she was elated to see them, and fussed as she wiped their faces with the same towel that she had used earlier to mop the rainwater that had leaked in through the roof. I brought them their soup, which was tepid, the bean paste having settled at the bottom. When I gave them each a spoon, Imo clucked her tongue. Snatching the ladle from the main pot, Imo made a show of picking out additional chunks of kelp for them.

Granny Cho left her bowl untouched and examined me with eyes that were cloudy with cataracts.

Imo tapped my shoulder, reminding me to bow, while Miho chewed complacently on her kelp.

I bent forward, and Granny Cho's lips melted into a frown so deep that it dragged her jowls down. *"Yun-Hee neun aniyah."*

Dread prickled across my skin. Any mention of Yun-Hee with such disgruntlement could not be good. Imo, however, laughed and patted Granny Cho teasingly. *"Hwakshilhi Yun-Hee yeh-yo!"*

Miho gulped down the rest of her soup and giggled, stroking Granny Cho's hand. From her patronizing tone, I guessed that she was agreeing with Imo, possibly insinuating that Granny Cho was either mistaken or incompetent.

Granny Cho slammed her fist on the table, sending Yun-Hee's candy jumping from its dish. *"Song Yun-Hee neun aniyah!"* Directing her attention to me, she asked a question that I couldn't decipher, and Imo tried to placate her by rushing to the alcove to retrieve my red book. Imo flipped open to the first page and pointed to Yun-Hee's name, as well as the accompanying government stamp.

Granny Cho howled in frustration. Grabbing my arm, Granny Cho ripped open the top of my coat and pulled down my shirt. I tried to wriggle free as she exposed my collarbone, but Granny

Cho's gnarled hands were like Emma's, strengthened by decades of needlework. The old woman shouted, jabbing at my skin like she was trying to puncture it.

Only then did I remember Emma weeping on Kanggye's frozen road: *There's a birthmark on her collarbone, shaped like a gourd.*

Granny Cho's nail left scarlet crescents, stamping me for the liar that I was. Yun-Hee dominated Emma's world so completely that I often forgot that Yun-Hee had belonged to anyone else, even though Imo and Jae-Min had explicitly told me she had. Emma's daughter was a single thread, but she had been woven so tightly into the fabric of her community that her disappearance had led to a collective unraveling.

"I am sorry," I said, in Japanese. "You are right, Granny. I am not Yun-Hee." I avoided eye contact with Imo, whose furious glare hit me like a searchlight that could sunburn. "I am a Chinese woman. I met Moon Hwa-Ja in Kanggye after I crossed the Yalu River. I was badly hurt, and I needed help. She took me in so I could heal, but then we had to evacuate."

Granny Cho released me, the imprint of her fingers still pressed into my sleeve. Switching languages, she asked, "If you are Chinese, why can you speak Japanese?"

"My family is from Taiwan," I explained. *The crawfish is on the crab's side.* "It was a Japanese colony for even longer than Korea was—fifty years for us, thirty-five for you."

Telling the truth after days built on lies was clean and refreshing, like I had rinsed myself a bit. Imo, however, was sending me dagger eyes.

"How did you end up here, then?" asked Miho.

I took a breath, swinging back to fiction. "I found a man and fell in love. I followed him to China, but he went to war. I didn't want to wait, so I came to Korea to bring him home."

At least this story had rolled off my tongue so many times that it was reflexive. Love was the best kind of lie, because it had no rules—it was a believable excuse for almost anything, from the irrational to the insane. Almost anyone with a heart had, at some point, been deafened by its fervent, urgent beat.

"Oh, poor thing," said Granny Cho, with more judgment than sympathy. "No wonder Hwa-Ja took you in; she knows all about bad decisions. Is she coming to join you soon?"

"I hope so," I said. "She gave me her house key, so she must be meeting us here."

Miho perked up for more gossip. "Do your parents know you're in Korea? Where is your man now? Is he still alive?"

"My parents have no idea where I am," I replied. "And as for my fiancé, I suspect he's here in Pyongyang. I haven't found him yet, though."

"Well, you'd better find him soon," cautioned Granny Cho. "None of the Chinese are staying here long. The Women Workers Association set up their garrisons as temporary facilities only. Most of them will be gone in the next few days."

"That soon?" Time here was distorted, as if we were in another realm—so much changed in the blink of an eye. "I thought they'd be fortifying Pyongyang."

"Bah! We don't need them in Pyongyang," said Granny Cho. "We need them to chase down the puppet army and drive out the invaders!"

I stifled a groan. What had I missed having been cooped up with Imo for two days?

"So they're going to Hungnam?" I asked, fear snaking its way around my throat. "Does that mean the Americans—the imperialists—are counterattacking?"

"Oh, Hungnam is safe," said Granny Cho. "Don't look so

scared! The invaders have given up the port. They're sailing away as we speak."

I'd been anticipating this news, but it still hit like a crowbar to the shins. There were essentially no more Americans in North Korea. Any hope that I had of a UN counterattack pushing north to meet me was but sea foam on the shore . . . unless Granny Cho was mistaken?

"How are you so sure they've given up?" I asked. "If the imperialists are truly gone, why is there a need to chase them?"

"Because they're still occupying our land," replied Granny Cho. "The marauders are holding our brothers and sisters in the South."

Still confused, I questioned whether there was a language barrier. Imo had her lips pressed together, itching to intervene, but she was too afraid to give herself away with her impeccable Japanese.

Miho set her empty bowl down. "We have to unify the country—now, while the imperialists are running. We can't give them time to rebuild their strength."

Blood rushed to my head, dredging up a horrifying sense of déjà vu. Two months ago, I had been at a press conference, debating whether MacArthur would really send our troops past the 38th parallel, into North Korea—when Mao had warned him not to. Ultimately, MacArthur's calling that bluff was what brought the Chinese into this war in the first place. That cursed boundary, which had begun as a pen mark on a map in Potsdam, was now sealed with blood on Korean soil.

"So the Chinese army is going to cross into South Korea?" I asked, hoping I was wrong. It was one thing for America to get kicked out of the North. It was an entirely different matter for it to lose the South.

"The volunteers are already amassing at the thirty-eighth parallel," said Granny Cho. "How did you not know? Didn't you come here with Chinese soldiers?"

"I only asked them about my fiancé," I muttered, trying to conceal my alarm. I was utterly flabbergasted that Mao would venture to make the same mistake that MacArthur did, when neither of those men had spent a single night in Korea since the war began. "We never talked about military matters."

"Women need to care just as much about military matters as we do about marriage!" chided Granny Cho. "Didn't your chairman say that we women hold up half the sky? It's much easier to find a new man than a new country! The imperialists are fighting for domination, but we are fighting for our very existence."

Outrage mounted in me at the prospect of another cycle of devastation. "If the Chinese attack Seoul, the Americans are going to go berserk," I said. "Berserk! They're going to escalate to a whole other level. They're going to send more men! They'll get more bombs, worse bombs!"

"The Americans are weak," piped Miho.

"No, they're not!" I said. "They are arrogant. They aren't going to make the same mistakes, especially in the South. Our men are going to die for nothing if they cross that border."

"Our men *and* women are going to die for freedom," said Granny Cho. "It's much harder to fight when there is a yoke around your neck. We learned this under the Japanese. We must give everything we have, and do everything we can, to prevent anyone else from putting one back on us. If we cower now, we will become a colony again."

"Mao is risking a third world war!" I cried. "A nuclear war!"

"Korea is our world," said Granny Cho, unfazed. "And it is already at war. The Americans think they can own us because they defeated our Japanese colonizers. People like us will never have peace until the colonizers of the world realize that our land is not their rice bowl and our people are not their slaves. A person from Taiwan should know this well."

Imo faked a noisy cough, sending me a message with her eyes, which had shifted from a look of authoritative anger to one of pleading desperation. *Dial yourself down.*

Both Miho and Granny Cho had furrowed their brows warily, so I stepped back, almost laughing as their perspective sank in.

Who was I fooling? Here I was, with tens of thousands of Chinese troops, in Pyongyang, hoping to go south, where the American army waited in full force. All the while, Soviet pilots flew overhead, and Stalin and Truman flooded the peninsula with arms. The dogfight between two Korean dictators had already escalated into a global conflict, and it was irrelevant to Granny Cho whether it remained within her borders. I had once thought that there would be fewer wars if every leader had to send their own children into battle, but I saw now that war was a wager, and there were people willing to gamble everything on one big bet.

"All I want is to find my lover," I said, as simply as I could. "I've worked hard to get here. I've done some favors, and I've had some luck. If what you say is true, then I need to hurry before he sets off again."

"Ah," said Granny Cho. "I know you've come a long way, but if I were you, I'd turn back while you can. There are so many men, but you only have one life; it's an insult to your parents to waste it."

"My one life is worth little without my one love," I declared, burrowing deeper into my disguise.

Granny Cho threw up her hands and let out a sputtering puff of air. "He is lucky! And you are foolish. But for your sake, I hope you find him." Reverting to Korean, she made some disdainful remarks to Miho, perhaps highlighting me as a cautionary example of what not to do and who not to be.

Miho regarded me with sympathetic foreboding, as though I had a disease that she hoped to be immune to later. I wanted to tell her that love, whether romantic or familial, had no vaccine or antidote—and instead of looking down at "fools" like me, she should be looking up, with grave concern, at the men in high places who succumbed to heartache in the same mad way. As silly as I seemed, at least I didn't have an army or an arsenal at my disposal.

With another cough, Imo clapped her hands together. She offered Miho more soup and urged Granny Cho to finish hers, then chattered while passing them each a gleaming spool of embroidery thread. Undoubtedly, Emma had been saving that thread so she could needle birds into flight and buds into bloom. I hated how casually Imo tossed Emma's possessions away, but I also knew that it was not without calculation.

A brilliant mind was an asset, but it took skill to wield it like a weapon. Among the myriad of uncertainties around me, there was one fact that had become crystal clear: Imo was one of the shrewdest people I had ever met, and she was as terrifying as she was extraordinary.

December 20, 1950
Dear Mom and Dad,

I've been scared for my life, but now I am scared for our world.

The more I see in the North, the less confidence I have that this war can lead to anything but mutually assured destruction.

For us Americans, Korea is a barrier against Communism, but for Koreans, this land is their home. Though many Koreans are fleeing the bombs, there are others, so many others, who have made it clear that they will die before they allow "imperialists" to take it.

They will let their blood soak this earth.

There is Communist propaganda in spades, but there are also indisputable kernels of truth. The North Koreans see us as colonizers, and this is not unfair—for when Japan annexed Korea, America recognized that claim in exchange for Japan's recognition that America ruled the Philippines. We cannot trade other countries like playing cards and expect their citizens to forget about it—at least not so soon.

America will not win this war. I am sorry to write with such a poor attitude, but I feel more helpless than I ever have and miss you more than you could possibly know.

With all my love,
Ellie

25

EVERYTHING

December 24, 1950

I wondered when American intelligence was going to figure out that Mao was planning an attack on Seoul. From a journalistic perspective, this would have been a life-changing, career-making kind of story, but behind enemy lines, I was impotent. This irony made me want to snap Emma's pencils and shred the paper on the table, but instead I forced myself to write—to channel my frustration into Yun-Hee's old notebooks. The correspondent in me had to be quiet, but it couldn't be silent.

Imo usually woke after I did, so I spent my early mornings scribbling notes that I could elaborate on when I returned to safe ground, and hiding them among Yun-Hee's school supplies. *I will return to safe ground,* I repeated to myself, though lately there was another voice chiming in that said, *I can survive here too, if I have to.* It was a consolation prize for my heart, which, like any muscle would be, was strained beneath the load I was forcing it to carry.

Imo started teaching me Korean, and I filled my empty hours

with its syllables, memorizing the most important words: "revolution," "*byeogmyeong*"; "liberation," "*baebang*"; "victory," "*seungli.*"

The storm grew bored enough to break, and as it flounced to the west, the sun pirouetted over the clouds. Our neighbors greeted these clear skies with disapprobation, and the streets around us remained hushed and desolate. Within hours, the soul-shaking thunder of near-supersonic jets sounded overhead. American reconnaissance missions had resumed, which meant that soon, bombing would too.

"There seem to be even more planes than before," said Imo, mixing acorn powder with water and seasoning. She licked the spoon with just the tip of her tongue, before adding more soy sauce. "I hope they aren't bombing people on the roads. God willing, my husband and son are safe."

"And Auntie Moon too," I added.

Sometimes when the jets dipped low, we could feel the vibrations in our teeth. Contrary to what everyone hoped, the war seemed to be getting worse, and I was inwardly torn. There was a patriotic part of me that was proud that the Americans weren't giving up, and that there was some truth to the claim that the marines refused to retreat. As a human, however—a soul with no race and no nationality—I was gutted by death, by the obscene, staggering piles of bodies that everyone was too busy to bury.

Bihaeng-gi, taengkeu, pogtan. "Airplane, tank, bomb."

Imo and I went to our first Party meeting, held outdoors, in the compound's rain-drenched courtyard. Almost everyone in the factory housing was in their late teens or early twenties, and many were knitting hats for soldiers as we gathered. Miho was in charge of taking attendance and stamping our red books, but Imo had given her a fake name. It turned out that Imo's storm of tears upon Miho's first visit was because she insisted that her red book had been destroyed in a bombing. Normally, losing one's red book was a punishable offense. Though Miho had accepted the excuse, Imo was ineligible for ration stamps until she got a replacement, even though that was impossible now, due to the ongoing war.

Granny Cho, who led the meeting, introduced me as a Chinese revolutionary, prompting the women to cheer for me like it was a homecoming. Several of the workers thanked me for my solidarity in what little Mandarin they knew, while others threw their arms around me in gratitude, and also in grief. Within Korea, there were now 175,000 North Korean soldiers, and a whopping 300,000 Chinese "volunteers," coalescing at the 38th parallel. Nearly a million more Chinese troops were in Manchuria, amassing at the Yalu River. What the Communists lacked in arms, they made up for in manpower, a transfusion of young blood pouring from one war-torn country to the next.

I wondered to what extent the American government had tried to understand the people we were fighting. For all Stalin's faults, when Korea was liberated in 1945, he had closed the Japanese-run political prisons and freed the Korean rebels immediately. The Americans, meanwhile, had first tried ruling South Korea through Japanese intermediaries, and brutally suppressed the Koreans who protested. We considered the Communists to be brainwashed, without examining the history of their subjugation and what it meant for them. There was a cultural and psychological component to this war that I wished that I could write about, because our failure to consider it was costing us dearly.

I stood in a circle along with the factory workers, our breath rising like a ring of smoke. The meeting was entirely in Korean, and incomprehensible to me, because Imo, as usual, refused to translate. It was annoying, but I wasn't angry at her. Since our arrival in Pyongyang, the hatred that I thought she harbored had shifted shape enough for me to realize that it was just the shadow of a different beast: fear. Her surliness was often more about herself than about me, and knowing that made it easier for me to let go of my own resentment.

At the end of the meeting, Miho passed out bolts of burlap. The fabric was thin and as scratchy as twine, but supposedly it was enough for each of us to make 120 sandbags, which the KPA would fill with dirt and rubble for barricades. Though Imo couldn't receive credit without her red book, she still had to meet her quota; women were enlisting in the KPA as well as men, and if we weren't willing to fight, we had to work. If we weren't willing to work, and work well, we had to leave the compound.

Imo hugged her roll, and when everyone dispersed, she trotted away like a bandit with her spoils. I slung my bolt over my shoulder and caught up to her.

"It's all in the eyebrows," she whispered to me, with a triumphant smile. "Some of the women there are clever foxes, you know. I'm glad none of them recognized me."

"Good job," I said, though I wasn't convinced that her eyebrow disguise had worked. I suspected that she simply wasn't as remarkable as she thought she was, but she was so pleased with herself that she hummed all the way back to Emma's door.

It was cold inside, because we were low on coal, and there was nowhere for civilians to buy it. We had to save our fire for cooking, and for nights when the temperature was especially extreme. While I unwrapped the pieces of Emma's sewing machine and tried to remember how to assemble it, Imo portioned out some pickled radish and icy kelp soup.

The two of us spent the rest of the day working on our sandbags, with all our blankets piled on our laps and around our shoulders. We made an assembly line of two, with me measuring and marking based on Miho's instructions, and Imo cutting. Given her good spirits, I decided to prod about Pastor Pak again.

"Tell me about your husband," I said. "He was originally a pastor here in Pyongyang, wasn't he?"

"Oh," said Imo, beaming, "my husband wasn't just a pastor. He was a very famous pastor. There were almost a thousand people in his church at one point. It was like a small kingdom."

"Is that how you met? You went to his church?"

She paused, her scissors still biting the burlap. "No. We met because he came to my demonstration."

"What kind of demonstration?" I asked, bracing myself for a soporific story about whatever flower-arranging or dance show she had prestigiously been a part of.

"It was a demonstration against the imperial authorities," she said, resuming her cutting, the blades scraping together.

My chalk snapped between my fingers. "Wait. What?"

"It was a demonstration following the death of Emperor Taisho. Everyone in Korea was mandated to mourn him, but I decided not to." She spoke flippantly, like she was talking about turning down a slice of pie, as opposed to defying an imperial regime.

I'd left a white residue all over the table, but I was too stunned to care. "So you were at a protest? A protest?"

"I organized a protest," Imo clarified. "So yes, of course I was at it."

"*You?* Organized a *protest?*" I repeated. "Against the colonial authorities?"

"I organized several protests," said Imo, getting churlish. "But this was long ago. I don't even remember it, really."

"I thought you just fell in love with Pastor Pak. I didn't know you were also a rebel."

"Why would I have fallen in love with a rebel if I myself wasn't a rebel?"

"I don't know. Maybe you thought he was handsome and charming?"

"Ha!" She scoffed. "I'm not as foolish as you are! Pak Sung-Ho was indeed very handsome and charming. He is still very handsome and charming. But that wasn't why I fell in love with him, and certainly not why I married him."

She dropped her scissors with a clunk. "You might find this hard to believe, but I used to be a difficult woman. Pak Sung-Ho was one of few men who were strong enough to be with me, because his commitment to Korea's independence was unwavering. He didn't mind that I cared more about my protests than about learning how to cook or sew. He loved me for who I was, instead of what kind of wife I might be."

I slid to the edge of my stool, my elbows jutting onto the table. "Why would someone like you care so much? Your family worked with the Japanese authorities and did very well, didn't they? What made you want to change that?"

"Everything."

"Everything?"

"Did you become an echo?" she snapped. "Or a pet bird?"

"Well, 'everything' is very broad!"

Her eyes rolled up, then to the side, as she thought. "Maybe not everything, but it was many things. I grew up in a home that was like a castle. I ate like I was royalty, and went to specialized Japanese schools, but that didn't mean that I didn't notice how everyone else lived—how the Koreans here lived. But every injustice was like a ghost that only I could see, haunting me, when the rest of my family didn't believe they existed. I used to think there was something wrong with me. Koreans used to have to bow toward Tokyo each morning, where the emperor was, and students got expelled for refusing. One girl was hung upside down outside her school, and the teachers poured hot sauce down her nose."

"That's awful!"

"It was. But when I told my parents about it, they said it was her own fault. People would get their tongues cut out for speaking Korean in public, and that was their own fault too. The Kempeitai were never wrong. My family believed in order, and they taught me that Korea needed Japan's protection because people here were too hotheaded to govern themselves. I used to swallow that explanation, but after forcing it down so many times, I choked. I just couldn't go along with it anymore."

"But wasn't your father Korean?" I asked. "And your mother half Korean?"

"Oh, they weren't like the other Koreans," she said with a wistful smile. "At least that's what they believed. My father tried harder to be Japanese than the Japanese. He struggled to get rid of his accent, and made our mother take us to pray at Shinto shrines every day. He even donated money to build a new shrine in Pyongyang's center! He gave so much to many different charities here."

I had never asked my parents about their childhood in Taiwan, and they didn't like to talk about it, but from the bits and pieces they offered, I knew that there was a strong policy of assimilation, and that resistance often had swift and violent repercussions. Many of my friends were impressed that I spoke three languages, but most people from a colonized country, and immigrants to a new country, will be fluent in at least two. It isn't always a choice; often it is simply a matter of survival.

"Did your father know about your protests?" I asked Imo.

She shoved her hands underneath our blankets. "Not at first. But eventually, he found out because I got arrested."

"Oh my God, you got arrested?"

"Multiple times! But it wasn't so dangerous for me, because the police knew my father. They loved my father. In that sense, I cannot claim that I was as brave as the other protesters. Even ethnic Japanese got executed for supporting Korea. My family was powerful, so I was never detained for long."

The image of a younger Imo glowering in a cell was too absurd to picture. "Your father must have been furious."

"Oh, he was livid. But I was his favorite daughter, and no matter how angry he was, he would never let anyone hurt me. When he got fed up with bribing the police, he decided to arrange for me to marry a businessman in Tokyo. He thought that if I left Korea I'd stay out of trouble, but a week before my wedding—my very expensive wedding—I eloped with Pak Sung-Ho."

My jaw could not drop any farther, but it hung open as I shook my head. "So, that's why your father disowned you?"

Imo's eyes narrowed. "How do you know so much about my family? Were you and Hwa-Ja talking about me?"

"I heard from Jae-Min."

Her belligerence subsided at the mention of her son. "Oh. Well, my father had no choice. He lost face, and the more famous you are, the worse it is when that happens. It's one thing to argue with the Kempeitai in Pyongyang. It's another to embarrass a prominent family from Tokyo." She picked up her scissors and stabbed at the burlap until it frayed and her blades sliced through.

"I was a terrible daughter. I don't regret what I did, but I wish that I hadn't been his child. We would both have been happier, I think."

I dabbed at the chalk powder and used my finger to mark lines on my fabric. Despite Imo's remorse, her father sounded awful—arrogant and bigoted—and that made me more sympathetic to her, and the decisions that she'd had to make between being a good person and being a good daughter.

"Have you spoken with your father since then?"

"Not as much as I should have," she said, piling her crudely cut rectangles in a stack on the table, and then tapping harshly at the roll of burlap remaining. "What have you been doing? Do your hands and ears not work at the same time? We only have two days to finish, you know!"

Hastily, I unfurled another length of fabric while she jabbed into the part that I had marked. "Where is your family now?"

"Not in Pyongyang," she said. "Otherwise I wouldn't be here in this shack, doing both of our work for us."

"Okay, okay." I had never met anyone who could slam a verbal door shut like Imo could. I reached for Emma's measuring tape and began marking again. Now that I had gotten a glimpse of Imo the activist, I had more questions. She had dedicated so much time to outlining her father's and her husband's accomplishments, but now I speculated that her anxiety about being identified was due to her own notoriety, as opposed to either of theirs. There certainly were female rebels in Korea, but not many of them were part Japanese, or affiliated with the colonial regime.

For the rest of the evening, Imo remained uncharacteristically quiet, tossing out one-word answers to anything I asked. We sewed to the sound of jet engines, stopping periodically to warm our hands, until it grew too dark to work. Only then did Imo start a fire, our reward for eighty-seven sandbags completed.

Emma's small space heated up quickly, and I basked by the stove. My arm was sore from cranking the sewing machine, and Imo had blisters on her palms from gripping the scissors. It was only our first day with our assignment, and I dreaded the possibility that this was long-term work. Pyongyang was supposed to be temporary, a stopover on my way to Seoul. I also worried about Emma constantly, and missed her too. Every plane that passed made me wonder if she had been hit by a bullet or a bomb, and a question lurked in a corner of my mind, as needling as a pebble in my shoe: How long was I going to wait for her?

I didn't know the answer. I knew only that I wasn't ready to give up on her yet. Emma saved my life, and if I had a chance to reciprocate, I had to take it.

While we waited for our soup to boil, Imo presented me with a grayish brown dome molded into the shape of a bowl. "It's Christmas Eve," she announced, setting it on the table with flourish. It wobbled like an opaque Jell-O.

"Is it really? I thought today was the twenty-third."

"No, it's the twenty-fourth. I've been keeping track. It helps me stay sane, you know."

"I've been keeping track too, but maybe I missed a day." I thought about MacArthur's impetuous promise. Were any of our soldiers going home for the holidays intact and alive?

"Even with the war, today is still a special day," said Imo, drizzling a soy sauce mixture over her blob. "This is *muk*. Acorn jelly. It's not a special dish, but it's one of the few that I can make well. I learned from our neighbors in the mountains. I didn't have all the ingredients, but it should still be tasty, and very nutritious."

She sliced the *muk* like it was a cake. Though it was slightly bitter, the silky texture melted on my tongue, coating it with a smooth, nutty flavor. We ate it along with a small feast of boiled corn and pickled vegetables, then chased it down with our savory seaweed soup. It had been a while since I was satiated, and my stomach so rotund.

"Oh dear," said Imo as we set down our empty bowls. "We forgot to pray. My husband would be very upset, especially on such an important day!"

"Well, it's not over yet. Do you want to say something now?"

"Why don't you go ahead? You're the American."

"I'm American, but I'm not Christian," I said. "I'm Buddhist."

"Oh, that's funny. I assumed all Americans were Christian." Imo laughed, the first sheerly joyful expression that I had gotten from her. "I am not Christian either."

"What? I assumed *you* were Christian."

"Because my husband is Christian?"

"I mean, he's not just a Christian. He's a pastor."

Imo laughed again. "I was raised Shinto. There were many things I decided to let go of from my childhood, but that wasn't one of them."

"Does Pastor Pak know?"

She shrugged. "Maybe one day I will convert, but doubt is as personal as faith. It doesn't mean I love him less. My husband has always said that being Christian isn't about saying you are Christian and demanding that others do the same. It is about acting Christian, about emulating and modeling the teachings of Christ. His family converted because there were missionaries who did so much for the rebels in Korea, even risking their own lives. This is why Sung-Ho will never hate America. He has met good Americans—kind Americans, and selfless Americans. He knows that not all of you are evil."

Does he still? I wondered. *After so many bombs, and so many bodies bereft of proper shrouds?*

"Go ahead," said Imo, shifting impatiently.

"All right, then." Clasping my hands together, I bowed my head. "Dear God, please protect our loved ones. Please help—"

"No, no!" she interrupted. "You can't just start off by asking for favors, you know. You need to say your thanks first!"

"Oh, sorry. Do you want to say the prayer? Maybe you should just say the prayer."

She waved her hand and shook her head.

"Okay, fine. Dear God, we are grateful to be safe and sheltered. We are grateful to have food, to have health, and to have made it to Pyongyang. Please help Auntie Moon, Pastor Pak, and Jae-Min reach us soon. Please keep them safe, along with all our other loved ones within and outside of Korea." I looked up at Imo, whose eyes were closed, a wrinkle deep between where her brows would have been. "Was that acceptable?"

"Ask for the war to end."

I rolled my eyes. "Well, that's obvious."

She pursed her lips. "If there is truly one God, and he is truly a man who reigns with only his son, then it might not be."

Relenting, I bowed my head again and added, "Please end the war. Please help our leaders find an agreement and send all our soldiers home safely."

"Amen!" declared Imo.

Christmas had never been a holy day for me, but there was something lovely about a Buddhist and a Shintoist creating a prayer for a Christian holiday—two women in between, who agreed that one did not have to exclude the other.

"Amen," I repeated.

WESTERN UNION TELEGRAM

Mr. Clark Pembroke

The Global Tribune

830 East Broadway, New York, NY

URGENT

Gen. MacArthur has requested 26 atomic bombs for a list of targets. Also requested another 4 for invasion forces and 4 more for enemy air power. God help us all. Story to follow.

Mr. Joshua Sterling, Special Correspondent (Tokyo)

December 24, 1950

THE GLOBAL TRIBUNE

MacArthur Gave Truman a Miracle for Christmas and Wants an Atomic Bomb in Return

December 25, 1950

President Truman is calling the evacuation from Hungnam, which was completed yesterday afternoon, a miracle, but Seoul is not rejoicing. Communist forces have gathered in great strength at the 38th parallel. Invasion is imminent, and a red Christmas in Korea is inevitable . . .

26

STOLEN MISFORTUNE

December 31, 1950

On Christmas Eve, the Americans completed their withdrawal from North Korea by blowing up Hungnam Port and heavily bombing eastward of Pyongyang. It was unclear to what extent that destruction had worked, because one week later, on New Year's Eve, the Chinese army launched a massive offensive in South Korea.

The sky, which was once loud, was now deafening as fighter jets clashed in packs—sometimes more than fifty planes at a time, the best of the best—tearing at one another at harrowing speeds that made it impossible to be outside. When jets took damage, their metal parts hurtled down onto the towns and cities below. Having lived through World War II, I was astounded by how drastically warfare had evolved in the past five years.

Imo and I rarely left Emma's house, not only because of the jets but also because we were behind on every assignment. We rushed to catch up, but making up our previous quota meant we began each new task with a delay. We had started keeping the stove door open so we could work at night, squinting under the flickering firelight. Initially, the sound of the sewing machine was a soothing substitute for the tapping of my typewriter. Now that infernal whirring made me want to grind my teeth to nubs.

In between our assignments, I had to fetch our water, and with the coal supply dwindling, I also had to search for wood. After our second Party meeting, I went back to the riverbank and saw that of the willows, only stumps remained, and the gingko trees had shrunk. People must have taken their branches to burn in their homes. When I told Imo this, she clucked her tongue and sent me back with a cleaver, the closest item Emma had to a hatchet.

"We'd better collect some too, before it's all gone," she warned, even though we had enough coal to tide us over for a few more days. "Only a fool waits until he's starving to think about his next meal."

Though the gingkoes were the only trees left, it felt sacrilegious to hack at their bark and chip through the rings that belied their age. Koreans and Chinese both apportioned respect based on seniority. No matter how old you were, your elders could still call you by your milk name, as if to show that they had been around long enough to know who you once were, and that through their care they could claim credit for who you had become. These gingkoes had survived centuries of transition, witnessing the capitulation of dynasties and the rise and fall of subsequent governments.

I climbed to harvest their branches, convincing myself that it was a haircut rather than a butchering, and I steadily filled my bag with pieces of these ancient sentinels. As I trudged back through the workers' compound with my comparatively paltry collection of bark and twigs, there was a brief lull in the activity of jets. In that evanescent calm, I heard a muffled argument coming from Emma's house.

Someone was crying—weak and needling, *"Mianhae. Mianhae."*

Pausing in my tracks, I tilted my ear toward the door. It couldn't have been Imo. She wasn't capable of such a pathetic noise, almost like the mewling of a kitten. Or was she?

This anguished keening set the wheels in my head spinning like dervishes. Someone must have discovered who we were and confronted Imo—maybe it was Granny Cho. I bent my knees, ready to run, the spicy scent of freshly cut wood filling my nostrils as my breath quickened. If I gently let my load down, I'd be agile enough to sneak away, but my feet remained rooted.

Imo was in trouble, and I couldn't leave her. She was a thorn in my side that had morphed into an inextricable barnacle.

Swearing quietly in English, I dropped my wood and prepared to fight. I didn't want to hit anyone as old as Granny Cho, but if she was trying to arrest Imo, then I just had to do it, and quickly, before Granny Cho had time to counterattack—forcefully, so she'd be less likely to chase us.

Remember, I thought to myself, *you also have a cleaver, if you need it.*

With one fluid motion, I flung open the door, ready to kick out some knees.

Imo jumped back with a shout, bumping into the table. Since there were no meetings today, she hadn't bothered to draw on her brows; I was getting used to her new look, but it was still jarring sometimes, especially when she was angry. Another woman sat hunched on a stool, with multiple bags bulging like tumors on her body. She was sniffling, in such distress that she had forgotten to remove her boots. One of her ankles was swollen enough to stretch the rubber. The hem of her skirt was crusted with dirt and salt, but against a clean patch on her right side I recognized a lavender butterfly.

"Emma?" I said, tentatively.

The woman lifted her head, her eyes sunken into puffy, inflamed pouches. She had lost weight, yet she seemed to have more provisions to carry than I remembered. Two lines of loose skin hung from her chin, while veins snaked across her hands. Her hair was matted along her temples, and her coat was torn at the shoulder.

"Oh, I'm so glad to see you!" I exclaimed. Without caring how filthy she was, I wrapped her in a hug so tight that I lifted her off her seat. Her cheek against my neck was like a slab of ice. "You've walked such a long way, oh my goodness! Why are you crying? Are you hurt?"

"She is fine," Imo snapped, throwing her rag over Emma's wet footprints. "She's just crying because that's the only thing she knows how to do!"

Appalled, I stood between them. "Imo, what is wrong with you? Just look at her ankle!"

"Just look around the room!" Imo yelled back. "Where is my son? And my husband?"

My blood ran cold as I realized that Emma was alone, while Imo's shoulders heaved from rage. I had been so excited to see Emma that I had neglected to notice the blank spaces beside her, where Imo's love was supposed to be.

Emma squeezed the folds of her skirt and wept more loudly. "I'm sorry! I'm so sorry!"

Imo used her foot to mop the muddy floor, furiously, like she was smashing an insect. "Moon Hwa-Ja! Stop acting like they're dead, and in the name of Jesus Christ, stop your damn crying!"

"What happened?" I asked.

"The army took Jae-Min," Emma croaked, her tears dissolving the grime under her nails. "We came across a checkpoint just a few days after you two left, and it was blocked with tanks. There were dozens of soldiers there, picking out the young men. They took anyone who could walk, and forced them to get into a truck."

"And she did nothing!" cried Imo.

"They all had guns!" said Emma. "I tried talking to them. The pastor did too, but they said that if Jae-Min didn't go with them they'd shoot him for dodging his service."

"My son never dodged service! He is a registered student!"

"They didn't care! Jae-Min showed them his university card, but they know the schools are all closed now."

"You should have bribed them!"

"We would have gotten into even more trouble if we did that."

"Not if you did it right! Not if you were smart about it!" Imo pointed at all of Emma's bags. "How can you have the nerve to tell me you tried your best when you still have so much?"

"They had guns," Emma repeated, meekly. "They were already angry. We couldn't push them more. The pastor followed the truck to see if he could help Jae-Min sneak away. I was supposed to wait for them past the checkpoint, and I did for as long as I could—two whole days! It was freezing, and I was afraid that I'd run out of food. I had to leave without them. I'm so sorry!"

Imo exhaled a hiss like the opening of a shaken soda can. "Can you believe it?" she asked me. "We should have never separated, when you and I are the brains and spine of this lot. What's an old man like Sung-Ho going to do running after the army? Those commanders have no meat to eat, but more than enough flesh to sacrifice!"

"I told him that," said Emma. "I cried! I yelled! I said that you were waiting for him, and that you need him, but he insisted on finding his son."

Imo unleashed a string of Korean curse words, which might not have had a Japanese translation. "He should have trusted Jae-Min! No matter how strong my husband thinks he is, Jae-Min is stronger now. How could Sung-Ho possibly have thought that it would be better for me to lose them both?" She pulled at her bun in frustration, loose strands of hair slashing across her face.

"You're not going to lose them!" I tried to bring Imo into a hug, but she backed away toward the stove. Letting my arms drop, I said, "There's a good chance that Jae-Min will be routed through Pyongyang if the army sends recruits south. Jae-Min and Pastor Pak will have a plan. Have some faith in them."

I nudged Emma, expecting her to echo my positivity, but she began to blubber again. "I'm so sorry to arrive with bad news!"

"Oh, for the last time," cried Imo, "I don't need you to apologize! I just need you to shut up!"

Emma slapped her hands over her face and rocked back and forth, moaning. It had been nearly ten days since Emma and I had parted ways. What else had Emma seen along the road? I wanted to comfort her, but I felt split between her and Imo, the rightful owner of this pain.

"I'm going to lie down," seethed Imo. "I'm so angry, I could go crazy!" She stomped, disgusted, to the sleeping alcove. Without bothering to unroll any of the mats, she lay down on the bare floor, her body bent like a willow branch.

Emma hiccuped and wiped her nose on her sleeve, smudging a line of dirt over her lip. Quietly, like an intruder in her own home, she picked up the blankets by the stove and draped them over Imo, who did not stir or say her thanks.

After days of incessant, occasionally mind-numbing chatter, Imo's mute stillness frightened me.

"She needs to have a conversation with herself," Emma whispered, wincing as she returned to the table. "In the end, she is the only one she will listen to."

"What about you, Emma?" I asked. "Are you all right?"

"It doesn't matter how I am," she said. "I am alive."

"What happened to your ankle?"

"It's not severe. I slipped and twisted it, but luckily it isn't broken."

"It looks like more than just a twist." Kneeling, I pulled off her boot, worried about the extent to which this injury could affect our plans to continue southward. It was difficult to see anything through all the mud caked below her knee, but there was a wound on her calf that had bled through her thick wool stockings. "Let me make you some tea. After you warm up, I'll fetch more water so you can bathe."

Emma muttered a response, but I couldn't hear it clearly. The jets had started up again, and they weren't just flying; they were firing. Even the older children could identify some of the planes, not just by the sound of their engines but by the ammunition they carried.

I went to build a fire, and only then did I remember the gingko wood that I had left outside. Uncertain how it would fare in Emma's coal stove, I went to retrieve it but found the stoop bare. Frantically, I searched the area around Emma's housing while rage flooded through me. My only contribution to our group was my ability to work, and now I had lost my morning's labor, and our evening's comfort.

"*Shibal!*" I shouted. I had seen Korean parents whack their children for saying that word, but it didn't feel as good as swearing in my native language. Under my breath, I muttered every English profanity I could think of, but still couldn't alleviate the pressure spiking in my chest. I wanted to scream until my throat was raw, and tear through the compound with a cleaver.

Dejected, I returned to Emma's house, only to have her scold me for swearing, because apparently I couldn't even say *"shibal"* without sounding like a foreigner.

"If you get arrested for such foul language, you'll deserve it," she said after I explained what had happened. "And what possessed you to hurt those poor trees? They are older than all of us combined!"

I expected Imo to pipe up and admit that cutting the gingko had been her idea, but she remained silent and immobile beneath her blankets, rounded like a freshly filled grave. "We're almost out of coal," I said. "I had to get wood for the fire."

"So forage first," said Emma. "And cut elsewhere if you must. My grandparents used to say that trees that live past a hundred years become spirits with powers. Killing them can curse your household! It's a blessing that someone took your bag. They stole away our misfortune."

"I'm sorry." I didn't expect that Emma, a Christian, would care so much about tree spirits, but then again, my own Buddhism was often enigmatic and inconsistent. "For what it's worth, I didn't kill any trees. I just chopped off some of the branches."

"Still unlucky," she huffed.

If it wasn't for Emma's reprimanding, I might have devoted everything I knew about investigative journalism to tracking down the criminal who stole my wood. Instead, I dipped into the remainder of our coal to boil water for Emma to bathe in, ruefully calculating the hours of warmth before the cold reclaimed us.

31 December 1950
Dear Yun-Hee,

It's good to be home, but no matter how many years have passed, it is not quite home without you. It was such a long walk from Kanggye, and I met so many people. I asked them all about you—if they'd seen you, or perhaps heard of you. I wasn't the only one doing this. So many families have been separated during the bombings and are looking for their loved ones.

Pray for the Pak family, Yun-Hee. They are like us now, and, as angry as I have been at your Imo, no one deserves this kind of grief. I hurt my leg, but as soon as it's better I will visit the new refugee shelters and see if there are any leads as to where you might be. Even in war, there is opportunity.

Stay warm, and though these are desperate times, remember to be careful of strangers. Bad people are opportunistic too.

Mom

Washington, 27 December 1950, Memorandum of Conversation, by Mr. Lucius D. Battle, Special Assistant to the Secretary of State:

The President agreed that we should not pull out of Korea and leave our friends there to be murdered.

(*Foreign Relations of the United States*, 1950, Volume VII, p. 1601)

27

TEN THOUSAND YEARS

January 1, 1951

Emma refused to talk about her lone journey to Pyongyang, except to say that it was grueling and mercilessly cold. I could tell she guarded a secret, but I chose not to push. She would tell us when she was ready, and until then I would pray for Jae-Min and Pastor Pak. Though I had been waiting for Emma, now I was hesitant to leave Imo alone, especially in the state she was in. Once Emma's ankle healed, could the two of us convince Imo to come with us? Lately I had been praying more than I had at any point in my adult life, because even simple matters seemed so uncertain.

Emma's house took on new life upon her return, as if awakening for its mistress. With her ankle compressed in burlap, Emma limped from one corner to the next, greeting her furniture, caressing items as though she were taking attendance. Inanimate objects became inhabitants, and through Emma they introduced themselves to me. There were hidden crannies that Imo and I had missed, including loose tiles in the floor that Emma normally hid her jewelry in, and a compartment in the alcove where she had stored dried fruits.

"I'm so grateful it's all here," Emma said when she finished perusing her closet. She rearranged items that Imo and I had misplaced, and though she must have noticed that fabric and thread were missing, she only smiled. Even with her injury, Emma stood taller here, as confident as a turtle diving back into the sea. With fiery pride, she told me stories about when she and a neighbor laid the tile floor down, and about how she had worked overtime to pay for the stove.

Dramatically, she wailed at the clumsy sandbags that Imo and I had stitched, as if the fabric had been murdered and mutilated. Once she recovered from her shock, Emma picked up her scissors and went to her machine. Without bothering to measure anything, she single-handedly flew through the rest of our quota, redoing some of our particularly crooked pieces.

"It's like eating rice cake lying down," she said smugly, smoothing out her finished pile of perfectly symmetrical bags. "Speaking of which, I might have a bit of rice flour left. Maybe we'll be able to have some rice cake for New Year!"

With Imo seemingly comatose, Emma sifted through the pantry. Even with the incessant jets, Emma was our hostess, and she had to give us a good meal. All of us had lost weight since leaving Kanggye. There was no longer any fat on my belly to grab, and my hip bones had turned into handles, but any excitement I had for rice cake was tempered by my anxiousness to leave.

"Let me help you," I said as she hobbled to the stove. "You need to rest your ankle. It's going to be another long trip south, and we need you to recover as soon as possible."

Emma only shooed me away. "I'll be able to walk in a few days. Don't worry."

But I *was* worried. Both Emma and Imo were part of this city in a way that I was not, and I could tell it had a hold on them—a hold that might become harder to break the longer we stayed.

Late afternoon on New Year's Day, Imo finally stirred. She had refused to eat or drink anything for almost twenty-four hours, grunting whenever Emma or I went to check on her, and rising only to use the latrines.

By the time Imo lumbered to the table, with blankets hooded over her disheveled hair, Emma had brought her a steaming bowl of rice cake soup. The broth was the same seaweed stock as before, but the addition of the glutinous rice cake elevated it into a real meal—one that could actually stick to the ribs. Emma's supplies were sparse, but she was an expert with what she did have. Even something as basic as barley tasted better when she added the right amount of sesame oil and cooked it just long enough for the grains to soften yet still retain their springy texture.

From her compartment in the alcove, Emma brought out dried persimmons, chewy like caramel and grainy like a pear. They were vibrantly colored, and redolent of the idealized memory of summer. When I took a bite, fireflies winked behind my closed eyelids. Summer was sure to come again, but in Pyongyang I was finding it hard to believe that the mountains of ice would ever yield to spring.

Imo perched on her stool reluctantly, and sipped her tea resentfully. Upon our encouragement, she took the tiniest of nibbles, like eating was a chore.

Emma swallowed her rice cake whole, then inhaled her own portion of barley. "There's something I've been wanting to ask you, *Sahmonim*," she said, addressing Imo as "Pastor's Wife" in Korean. "I didn't want to do it right when I got back, but I think we've settled long enough that it would be fair to do so now."

"Aigo," sighed Imo, as though she were still in charge of Emma's house. "What do you want, Hwa-Ja?"

Emma grinned innocently. "I want to know what in God's name happened to your eyebrows."

Imo's fingers flew to her brow bone. She seemed confused, as though she had forgotten about the shaving. It was hard for me to discern whether she was mad or just surprised until she reverted to Korean, each syllable punctuated and as percussive as a drum.

"Don't swear!" cried Emma, suddenly frantic. "The foreigner can't even speak Korean, but she's already picked up your bad language!"

"Oh, really?" Imo shot me a flaying glare. "You're too forgetful to remember the various forms of 'please,' but you can swear now?"

"She can't do it very well," Emma admitted. "Poor pronunciation, but still rude."

"So rude!"

"I only swore once!" I said.

"You shouldn't swear at all!" snapped Imo. "Didn't your parents teach you that? Swearing is a right that must be earned. When you yourself are a parent—when you have squeezed a baby out from between your legs—then you have suffered enough to speak as you wish."

"That's not true!" exclaimed Emma. "Don't listen to the pastor's wife. Look at what she did to her own face. She can't give advice."

"Eyebrows are a guide to your emotions!" said Imo, defensively. "And your identity! You know all the nosy bitches here. I had to disguise myself. To survive!"

Emma snorted. "That's the most absurd thing I've ever heard. Do you know how busy these women are? They all work long hours and then volunteer for the Women Workers Association, not to mention caring for elders and sometimes children! No one is going to waste their time chasing you, you paranoid loon."

"It's easy for you to say when the Party loves people like you," said Imo. "Have you already forgotten what happened to my father? Maybe for you he is just one of thousands, but not for me."

Imo's eyes flashed, but Emma's darkened severely when she said, "You make him sound like a victim."

I was taken aback by Emma's tone, which was uncharacteristically threatening.

Imo lowered her head. The veins in her neck pulsed blue. "He is still my father," she murmured. "I know what he did, and what he deserved, but he still raised me. As much as I love Pyongyang, I cannot be here without mourning."

Curiosity was an itchy kind of pain, and I desperately wanted to know Imo's father's history, but I could tell that Imo was skirting the brink of a sordid memory. Any prodding might send her crawling back to the alcove, under the worn-in safety of Emma's old blankets.

Emma huffed and waved her hand, fingers flapping. "As long as you agree that he deserved it, we don't need to discuss it any further." Her kettle had burn marks along it and the teacups were mismatched, but she refilled each of ours with hot water. "The first cup is for aroma," Emma explained to me, with forced levity, while Imo remained curved in shame. "The second is for flavor, and the third is for health."

I thanked her, though this was my fifth refill and my tea was so diluted that it barely held its scent. Steam rose, resplendent, as the bloated tea leaves sank to the bottoms of our cups.

Emma cleared her throat and put a hand on Imo's shoulder. "You must learn from your Imo," she said to me. "Her ideas aren't always sound, but she is brave enough to think outside of boxes. She is weird, but that's what makes her a better person than almost everyone I know."

The tension in Imo's jaw softened, and she blinked, uncertain. When she blushed, her marble cheeks became rose quartz. "It's not weird if it works! I've gone to two Party meetings already, and no one has recognized me—not even that snooty grasshopper Granny Cho! She's as insufferable as ever, you know."

"You've changed a lot since the Japanese left," said Emma, gently, giving Imo an additional slice of persimmon. "It's not the eyebrows that disguise you."

"It's definitely the eyebrows," Imo said, then took a wolfish bite. "They are the key to our expressions."

Emma chuckled and dropped the subject. "*Mokja!*" she said, pushing Imo's plate closer to her, and mine to me, even though it was empty except for a few corn kernels. "There's more rice cake in the pot, and I can prepare more barley if you're still hungry."

My stool scraped the floor as I jumped to serve myself more soup. Emma smacked her lips and blew on her tea while Imo tore into her meal. Rice cake stuck to Imo's teeth, and warmth radiated from inside my belly until a sudden knock on the window jolted us from our meal.

Imo was so apprehensive that she shrieked, but Emma patted her back and said, "Relax—it's probably just an announcement, or maybe a drill." Careful to avoid putting weight on her ankle, Emma rose and pulled open the curtains.

"It's not another evacuation, is it?" asked Imo.

Outside, women were running down the road, banging on everyone's doors and windows. They didn't sound scared, but their shouting was frenzied. I focused on Emma and Imo, trying to read their faces as one might a letter with poor penmanship. Were we supposed to be happy? Sad?

Emma cupped her cheeks in disbelief, while Imo sagged against the table, her eyes losing focus as if in reminiscence.

"What is it?" I asked, unable to glean anything from their vague expressions.

Emma met my anxious stare. "They're saying that Seoul is ours."

She used the word "ours," which confused me at first. *Of course Seoul is ours,* I thought, before I remembered that in the context of this war there was no "our," because there was no "we"—not for a North Korean and an American. Every ounce of soup in me boiled along with my blood.

"No, that's not possible," I said, angrily. "The Communists just launched their attack yesterday."

There was a part of me that had thought, wishfully, that the battle at the border could goad the Americans into pushing north again. Even if that didn't happen, there was no way Seoul would have fallen so quickly. If it did, it would be the third time that the capital had changed hands in the last six months. This was probably just propaganda to improve morale for the New Year.

I refused to believe it.

Miho tapped on the windowpane and waved at us from outside. "Come," she shouted jubilantly, "to Granny Cho's!"

"Araso!" Emma called back, donning her scarf. "Let's go," she said, collecting our empty plates.

"I'll stay here," I decided. "I'm not used to eating this much anymore, and I feel ill. I can watch the house."

Emma's eyes bulged reproachfully. "You must come. It will look suspicious if you don't, especially since you've told everyone that you're Chinese. This is just as much their victory as ours!"

"We all have to go," Imo insisted. "There is always attendance, even if it's an unofficial event. After everyone has seen you rejoice, you can come back and rest." She plaited her uncombed hair and went to get coal for her brows.

I thought about Emma's story, about the Sun saying the people were his eyes. In Pyongyang, that phrase took on a heightened potency, and within Emma's home I began to see faces on the walls—water stains curving like ears, cracks gaping like mouths. Every dent was an iris, all seeing, all knowing. Here, even emotions were rationed, and today I was not allowed to have despair.

Mechanically, I bared my teeth into a grin.

Granny Cho's home was twice the size of Emma's, but it also served as temporary lodging for new and short-term workers. A few dozen women were gathered on the walkway, and the older ones squealed and greeted Emma with tender embraces. While they laughed, a teenager with a red scarf opened a bottle of *makgeolli*. I had never seen Emma so radiant, like a missing puzzle piece that had clicked into its whole. I shouldn't have been surprised that she had her own circle, but I was envious and somewhat territorial. Here, Emma wasn't just my only friend; she was my life raft in a sea of hostility.

A small but solid force smacked into me, almost knocking me off my feet. Miho had wrapped her arm around my shoulders, in a hug that was more like a choke hold. "The puppet army is in full retreat!" she cried, releasing me so she could clap her hands, bouncing with delight. "The imperialists are preparing to leave Seoul. Word is, they're going to run all the way to Busan! Long live Marshal Kim! Long live Chairman Mao. Long live our revolutionary allies!"

"Long live Korean independence!" shouted Emma.

"*Manseh!*" cried Imo, throwing her arms up.

"Manseh! Manseh!" echoed the others.

Do not cry, I warned myself, flinging my palms together so that I was clapping too. *"Manseh,"* in Korean, was the same as *"wansui,"* in Chinese. They both meant "ten thousand years," and served as a blessing, a wish for long life. Emma danced with her friends, but Imo, more than anyone else, shocked me, shouting slogans in Korean as though she were in rapture, twirling as if possessed.

Everyone else congratulated one another, and though I concentrated on clapping, my ability to keep my body on automatic was coming undone. Busan was at the southernmost tip of the Korean peninsula, and a retreat that far practically ceded the entire South to the Communists. The journey from Kanggye to Emma's house had been difficult enough. How the hell was I going to get back home when my goal had moved so far, and there was no guarantee that the Americans would be there when I arrived? It was at least another six hundred kilometers from Pyongyang, and more than double the distance from where I was to Seoul.

I didn't have it in me to pretend anymore, even with my wonderful meal, and even if I doubted this truth. Imo's nails dug into my wrist, tethering me. She pulled me away before anyone else could see me cry, and she called over her shoulder, "We will be back with drinks!"

"Hurry," she whispered, rushing me to Emma's house.

The compound looked distorted through my tears, the path a mess of wavy lines. "It's just not possible," I said. "There are multiple UN divisions at the thirty-eighth parallel. There's been nonstop surveillance. We must have had time to prepare for the attack. This has to be propaganda. I don't know why people here are naïve enough to believe it."

Imo only held on to me more tightly and said, "Oh, Ellie, I

know how hard it is to be happy when you are afraid that you have lost everything. It will be easier as time goes on. Or, at least, you will get better at putting on your mask." Her lips quivered, and she bit down on them.

I thought that Imo was thinking about her father, but when she began to weep, with the same gut-wrenching sounds that Emma had made when she had realized that I wasn't her daughter, I understood that Imo was talking about her son—her only son—who was now in uniform.

We had no way of knowing where Jae-Min was fighting, but war made it clear that human life had a hierarchy, and the young and inexperienced were almost always at the bottom. The 38th parallel was heavily fortified on both sides, and sown with more land mines than crops. If what Granny Cho said was true, and what I knew about the American defense was true, then this advance must have come at the cost of tens of thousands of Chinese and North Korean boys.

Oh, Jae-Min, I thought, while Imo's knees buckled, *for your country, you are a hero, but for your mother, you are everything. Please stay alive. Please come home.* As I clung to Imo and her tears dotted my coat, the other women's voices continued to resound in exultation: *"Manseh! Manseh! Manseh!"*

28

THE FLAG WE SALUTE

January 1, 1951

In the relative safety of Emma's home, I pulled out a stool for Imo to sit on, but she remained plastered against the door, blocking it with her body as if she were afraid that someone would try to intrude. Staring at the wall, with her hands pressed on the wood behind her, Imo spoke. "My son does not know that my father was killed. My son does not know who my father was, or what he did to his own people. My son does not know that I was in touch with my parents, secretly, up until the end of the war. Though I was publicly disowned, in private I went home once a season, entering through the back garden. I'd walk past the pool and slip in through the servants' door, and spend an evening in my childhood home."

I sat in front of her, my condolences at the tip of my tongue, but she didn't look at me. Something about the crowd, something about the chanting, had rattled her, more than the bombs and the jets that had become our backdrop.

Her fingers began to move, slowly and rhythmically. "If I had time, I played the piano," she said. "One of my father's favorite pastimes was listening to me play sonatas. My teacher used to say that I had a golden ear—perfect pitch."

As if breaking from a trance, she looked straight at me and said, "I grew up believing that my father was a patriot who worked to make Korea safe and Asia great. Parents always worry about what their children don't tell them, when it's really parents who hide so much from their children. Even now, I wish it were all a misunderstanding, but I have seen too much—and heard even more—to be able to pretend."

"I'm sorry," I said, thinking back to what Emma had told me about the very rich *chinilpa*. "I don't know your father or what he did, but I know from your stories that you loved him."

"I shunned him," said Imo, "but I was never strong enough to cut him off completely. There were many Koreans like him, working for the Japanese authorities, but few were as determined to succeed. I didn't see him much when I was a girl, because he was always traveling to Japan, but eventually the governor-general rewarded him with a post in Pyongyang, managing procurement for the military police." She smiled, and lowered her eyes again. "That was why I was never imprisoned, no matter how many times I was arrested. My father didn't just obey the colonizers. He befriended them. He did whatever the Japanese asked for, and did it well, without questions or arguments. Because of him, the authorities had enough arms to quell Korean rebellions, and confiscate crops for Japan, even when people here were starving. My father got the Kempeitai everything they needed. Everything."

I kept my face neutral, but my hands began to tremble and I had to press them against my lap. In my conversations with Imo about her past, I was aware that she had self-censored, but I never expected the rot beneath the glamour to be this hideous. "Your father took girls too, didn't he?" I whispered.

Imo was so ashamed that she seemed to sink into the worn wood behind her. "He purchased them from traffickers and kidnappers, but he was just as evil as the Kempeitai who raided homes and stole girls from their parents. I used to think my father was a progressive man, because he let me go to university. He didn't expect that at school I'd end up learning how to uncover who he truly was."

Outside, the other women were still celebrating, but the pall between Imo and me was so somber that their chanting had become ominous. Now I understood that Imo must have truly believed that the labor drafts wouldn't feed into the sex stations, because there had already been another system in place—a system that her father, and others like him, had managed. "How could you possibly keep seeing him after that?" I asked.

"Because he is my father," said Imo. "And I felt it was my duty, as his daughter, to change him. To make sure that if there is a hell, he does not burn there. I never let Jae-Min speak to him, but I was determined that one day my father would repent. Whenever we met, I told him about everything I did to fight for Korea's independence. I told him that it was never too late to redeem himself, that the money he had could be used to support the resistance—to save lives. It wouldn't erase his sins, but at least he wouldn't be an abomination."

I shook my head. "I don't think people like that can change—at least not in the time frame that you want them to."

She exhaled, as if forcing herself to squeeze out the rest of this story. "Our last conversation was right after the Japanese emperor surrendered to America. I remember the pressure on the streets then. Everyone was excited that Korea was about to be liberated, but for my father, it was judgment day. He was obligated to support the Japanese administration until the Soviet forces arrived, but he sent my mother and the rest of our family to Japan. He told me that regardless of how I had shamed him, I was still his daughter, and if I wanted to go there'd be space for me and my son. There were no promises that the Americans would be merciful, but he knew that the Koreans would tear us apart. That was the first time he ever said anything to indicate that he knew his own people hated him. It was also the first time he ever admitted that he was afraid."

Before I could say anything, she added, "He didn't deserve pity. I know that."

Though I was sitting and she was standing, she managed to appear small, as vulnerable as a hermit crab without its shell. "What did you say to him then?" I asked.

"I told him that a free Korea was a dream that I had claimed, and my place was with my husband in Pyongyang. We were going to rebuild our country, you know. I said goodbye, with the understanding that I wasn't going to see my parents again, but I was wrong. One week later I saw my father, but it wasn't in his fancy house. He had been arrested and thrown into the same prison that he'd helped put Korean activists in. It was awful."

I raised my brow. My religion emphasized compassion, but I was not a devout enough Buddhist to be able to muster any sorrow for this man's death, let alone his incarceration. "So . . . you went there to get him out?"

"I wasn't supposed to go," said Imo, weakly. "My husband isn't the type of man to forbid me my freedoms, but he ordered me to stay away. People were still rounding up the collaborators, but I thought that I had contributed enough to the movement to have leverage. My father didn't deserve help—I know that—but he and my mother gave me life, so I went to the prison alone, without telling my husband or son. Outside the gate, people were celebrating Japan's surrender—they were shouting, '*Manseh, Manseh,*' just like they are now—but inside, it was a mess. All the cells were packed, and I couldn't find my father until I yelled his name. He had been beaten so badly that I could only identify him by the sound of his voice, when he shouted that he didn't know me. The ground was disgusting, but I got on my knees and begged the guards to let him out. I touched my head to the floor."

She sagged against the door, and slid down until she was on her haunches, arms wrapped around her knees. "I went to that prison worried that the men in charge might say no. I wasn't expecting to meet a boy whose sister had been raped by Japanese policemen, or a man whose daughter had disappeared in a comfort station. I wasn't thinking when I told them all that I was my father's daughter. I just wanted to save him, even if I knew that he didn't deserve it. I—" She stopped.

I had been hanging on every word, and I held my breath in anticipation of her next one. The sudden silence that ensued, however, was its own, dreadful confession.

Though I was American, by virtue of my heritage I was aware that East Asians, whether Chinese or Korean, thought in terms of the collective, and the crimes of any person extended to their immediate family. I stood up so quickly that my stool clattered to the floor. "What did they do to you, Imo?"

"The details are not important."

"They punished you, didn't they?"

"They punished my father," she clarified, her voice barely a whisper.

I slammed my fist on the table. "Damn it! God, Imo, if those men hurt you, if those men—" I paused, that word too barbed for me just to spit it out.

Imo did not say "rape," for some women never do, and some women never can, but I read it on her lips, in her breath, in the clouding of her eyes, in between the careful lines that gave her enough leeway to claim that I had simply misunderstood if she regretted confiding in me. If her punishment had been a beating, or anything else but rape, Imo would have told me. There is no crime that chokes people into silence quite like that one.

Apoplectic, I threw the last of our coal into the stove, breaking our rule about conserving the fire for nighttime and cooking. "How many men violated you?"

"My father was executed that same day," she replied.

"I'm not talking about your father," I said. "I'm talking about you, Imo. *You*. What those men did to you, whatever it was—it was abhorrent. I hope you know that you didn't deserve it, that no one does, regardless of what their family did or what mistakes they made. Please tell me you know that."

"Oh," she said, vacantly, "of course I do."

Her response only made me feel stupid. I'd interviewed enough women to know that many would say what they were "supposed to," even if it didn't match their inner conviction. I shouldn't have fed her a line, but I wasn't speaking to Imo as a journalist. I was speaking to her as a friend.

Taking the poker, I stabbed at the fire until it blazed, then slammed the iron door shut so hard that it bounced back open. The warmth from the flames, normally soothing, only made me more agitated as I pushed the door shut again. "Does Auntie Moon know what happened?"

"Why would she? She wasn't there."

"I thought you might have told her."

"And have her tell me that I should have listened to my husband?" asked Imo, incredulously. "Or that I shouldn't have tried to spare my father from what he deserved? We weren't even speaking to each other then, and even if we were, there would have been no reason for me to tell anyone."

"But what those men did was a crime! They should have been prosecuted!"

"By what court?" Imo scoffed. "No one would have faulted them, and even if they did, what justice could I have with a lifetime of shame, not just for me but also my husband and son? I don't want everyone discussing the details of what happened, pitying me or deciding whether I deserved it or not. I'd rather it be over in the prison than have it drag on forever. Even after death, I'd be remembered as a victim, and that is not who I am."

"What about Pastor Pak? Does he know?"

"No," she said, with guilt. "My husband knew something was wrong, but I hid the marks on my body and told him that I was grieving my father, as any woman would. I ate very little, though, and I jumped at every sound. I often couldn't sleep, and when I did, I woke everyone else up with my nightmares. I used to wet myself if there was a rally and it got too loud. Eventually, Sung-Ho decided that we had to leave the city, even if he had to give up his church. He took me to his parents' home in Kanggye, because he thought the mountain air would help my health. There, I could start over. I improved, but even now I often feel like an actress who had to learn how to be the real Machiko. I've gotten adept at it, but I still haven't mastered it, you know."

She smiled wanly, with a quiet acceptance that flooded me

with sorrow. Never would I have imagined that someone as strong, bold, and outspoken as Imo could decide to endure such a secret. Perhaps suffocating was preferable to bearing the weight of judgment, but I was livid. I thought about the military sex slaves Emma had interviewed, many of whom had never spoken at all about the violations before Emma found them.

"It might help to talk to someone," I said. "It doesn't have to be a friend. It could even be a doctor. Did you at least see a doctor?"

Imo held up her hand. "Stop," she said. "I did not tell you about my father because I want your outrage or your advice. I told you so that you can understand that people everywhere are the same. Regardless of their nationality, they can be brave and they can be kind. Regardless of their religion, they can be cruel and they can be depraved. There are some people who will always do the right thing no matter what, and there are some people who will always choose wrong. Most people, however, fall somewhere in between, where their actions depend not only on their circumstances but also on their leaders."

Taking a deep breath, she glanced out the window to make sure no one was on the street. "I am a proud Korean woman," she said. "I love my country, but I am afraid of the men who are leading it. I am afraid of where our people are headed, and I am terrified of this war. My husband and I have given everything we could for an independent and unified Korea—our youth, our tears, even our blood. There is one thing that I will not give for this goal, and that is my son. I told you my story not for me, but for Jae-Min. I know that you are going to return to American-controlled territory, and eventually to Japan." She bowed her head and clasped her hands together. "I want you to take Jae-Min with you. Vouch for him when you find your people. Help him, as I have helped you. Provide him with shelter and food until he finds my family in Japan, please. My son must leave this country."

There was a desperation in her voice that stunned me as much as the request itself. I was so accustomed to her arrogance that I didn't know how to react to this humble vulnerability. Mostly, I was surprised that Imo thought I had so much power.

"There are so many ifs, Imo," I began. "I'm not sure if I will survive, let alone make it back home. And I'm a correspondent, not part of the military, so I don't know if I can just bring someone with me to Japan. Maybe he could stay in South Korea if we cross the thirty-eighth parallel, but even then . . . I'm not sure if there will be a South Korea in a few months—or even a few weeks."

It scared me to say this out loud, because it sounded far more daunting. Imo probably thought I was being obstinate, but the biggest if, which I didn't dare list, was whether her son was alive.

"Jae-Min must leave this country," she repeated, firmly. "I don't care if that means Jae-Min calls himself Japanese or even American. Kingdoms fall, and boundaries change. It doesn't matter which flag my son salutes. I just want him to finish his studies without the fear of bombing. I want him to have his own family without the fear of starvation, and to plan a future without the fear of war. I want him to live—I just want him to *live*—in whatever country he is safest in. I don't care if that makes me a traitor or a coward."

She squared her shoulders to underline her position, but I knew Imo well enough to understand that she was proud, and that she definitely cared about being labeled as anything other than the activist that she was.

"You are not a coward," I said. "It takes courage to go to a new country. It's a different kind of courage than staying to fight, but it takes strength. Immigration is not for the faint of heart. Sometimes it takes courage just to persist amid the ugliness of this world."

Imo stood straight, checking the lock on the door before heading to the alcove. "Life in Japan is hard for Koreans. They are second-class citizens there, and often treated like animals. I don't know if that has changed, or if it will ever change, but Korea as we know it is going to be torn to shreds."

She picked up her bag of grain, the one that she had carried with her when we had left Songgan. I had found it odd that she had never stored it with the rest of the food, but I had assumed that she had been squirreling it away for herself.

"I will stay here, and my husband and I will continue to fight," said Imo, opening the bag and brushing the grains aside. A package emerged, wrapped in several layers of shirts. "I do not know if I will live to see an independent and peaceful Korea, but perhaps one day my son, or my grandson, will be able to return to one."

Within the first shirt, there were two black-and-white photographs, one of a young woman dressed in an elaborate silk kimono, and a second of that same woman in a plain hemp hanbok, seated next to Pastor Pak, with Jae-Min standing behind them.

"This was taken a few weeks before my engagement," said Imo, pointing to the first photo. "My father sent a copy to the man he had wanted me to marry, in Tokyo, and he kept one for our family. This other one, with Jae-Min and Sung-Ho, was taken in 1940."

"This woman is you?" I asked, picking up both photos.

The woman pictured was corpulent, voluptuous, with a soft face and obsidian hair that fanned out like a mane. Her eyes had more fat around the lids than now, and the corners of her lips pointed upward, as though she was tempted to smile but the photographer had told her not to. Imo must have lost at least forty pounds since then—so much weight that her bone structure was now defined and her eyes had deep folds. While her hair used to be dark, short, and curled, now it was mostly silver, and almost always worn in that unbearably tight bun.

I handed the photos back to her. No wonder Granny Cho hadn't recognized her.

"Sometimes I can't believe it either," Imo said, setting the photos aside. She continued unwrapping the package, hemp layers peeling like cabbage leaves to reveal a porcelain peony bowl. It was the same one that I had seen Imo cherishing in her kitchen, before she put it back into her cabinet.

I covered my mouth to avoid decrying hypocrisy, as she had been so harsh to Pastor Pak about his items.

"My father asked me to take our family piano," said Imo, admiring the peonies, which were so exceptionally shaded that they appeared three-dimensional, "but I couldn't, because there wasn't enough space in our house. So instead, I took this bowl. My mother loved it, but their luggage for Japan was full, and she thought it was too fragile to bring. This is the only item that I have from my parents, along with my mother's address in Tokyo." She flipped her engagement photo over and pointed to a block of Japanese text. "Between this bowl and the photographs, Jae-Min should have enough to prove to my mother that he is my son."

If he can find her, I thought. *If he is alive, and if he can escape from the army.*

The parade of ifs stretched onward, a line of dice that all had to land the same way for Imo's wish to be granted. It was a line that I couldn't wait for either. Over the next few days I would have to find a way south, regardless of whether Jae-Min arrived in Pyongyang, and regardless of whether Emma or Imo was willing to come along. The prospect of leaving Emma behind depressed me, but after seeing her reunite with her friends, I doubted that she'd want to depart again—for me, or for a part of Korea that was becoming increasingly foreign to her.

Imo rewrapped the bowl, concealing its opulent peonies in hemp. After putting her bag back in the alcove, Imo rummaged through the closet for a pitcher. Emma had no liquor, but we filled the pitcher with tea, freshly brewed and heavily diluted. Outside, the women of the compound were still raucous. It was time for us to put our masks back on and rejoin them.

THE GLOBAL TRIBUNE

U.S. Embassy Evacuates as United Nations Forces Prepare to Withdraw from Seoul

January 2, 1950

Allied troops are regrouping in Busan, while military advisors are considering a full-scale withdrawal to Japan . . .

29

PRETTY WHEN WRITTEN

January 2, 1951

Refugees from the rural North were streaming into Pyongyang, which seemed to be the only city with any functioning services. Ragged and cold, they filled the shelters, spilled onto the streets, and crowded around every ration station. The Women Workers Association managed to keep a semblance of order at the textile factory, and as much as Imo disliked Granny Cho, Granny Cho skillfully leveraged her Party connections to prevent the neighborhood from being overrun by squatters.

Granny Cho had no qualms about marching to the nearest police station to kick out any man, woman, or child whom she deemed unworthy. Since my arrival, only three abandoned houses had been opened to newcomers, and exclusively to seamstresses. Everyone received a quota, and assignments were adjusted based on ability. Imo and I only made sandbags, but Emma churned out shirts with pert collars and pants with extra lining. Her fine work pleased Granny Cho so much that both Emma and I got extra stamps in our red books, which Imo took to the ration stations.

While waiting in the woefully long lines, Imo kept her ear tuned for news to supplement what Granny Cho told us. Both North and South Korea had hemorrhaged soldiers fighting for Seoul, with units largely comprising new, untrained recruits. Boys with deadly toys chased one another over frozen rivers, past shattered bridges that both sides had demolished when it was their turn to defend the capital. Carnage was everywhere, not just from combatants but also from refugees. Earlier in the war, hordes of civilians, desperate to follow the American retreat, had stampeded onto the remaining bridge. UN troops, desperate to stop the Communist pursuit, had detonated that bridge, along with the people who were packed like sardines across it.

I had my methods of coping with gruesome news, but I had never been numb to it like I was now. The armor that I used to wear had chipped away, leaving just a shell, similar to what a turtle or mollusk might have. It was protective, but in a far less powerful way.

One wears armor to fight. One wears a shell to hide.

Imo's description of becoming an actress to play herself was the closest to my own sentiments. In the past weeks, I had forgotten how to be Eleanor Chang. I wanted to believe that identity was as ingrained as riding a bicycle and that I'd pick mine up as soon as I crossed the battle lines, but I was scared that I had amputated part of my humanity.

Gore no longer made me want to vomit. There were no bombs or bullets around me, but people were dying from starvation and displacement in extreme cold. Every day, soldiers carted frozen corpses to mass graves outside the city. I walked by them without flinching, like they were nothing more than roadkill, unpleasant but not extraordinary.

Prior to being stranded here, I used to joke that there was something wrong with me, because I chased stories instead of suitors. Now I knew there was something wrong with me, but there was nothing I could do about it. Of all the wounds that we can suffer from, those of the mind are the most difficult to treat, for they are invisible, and often dismissed as imaginary. A strong mind is supposed to heal itself, and regenerate in ways that no one would ever expect a limb or organ to.

I focused on preparing for my own journey, and the tasks needed just to scrape by. Without coal, I had to forage farther for wood than before, and there were more civilians competing with me now. Men from the countryside ventured into the city with *jiges* piled high with logs for barter, but with rations declining, every grain was worth more than its weight in gold. Yet nothing was edible when it was frozen solid. It was impossible to choose between food and warmth, so I compromised my morals.

I returned to the gingko trees on the riverbank with the detachment of an experienced executioner, because in war there was no magic, and no tree spirits to protect this city. All the branches were gone, so I gripped my cleaver tightly and hacked away at the trunks. Swing after swing, I squeezed my eyes shut to protect them from the splinters that sprayed off the bark. The exertion left me sweaty, panting, and starving.

Upon returning, I mumbled a greeting to Emma, who was hunched over the sewing machine, its wheel a blur as she cranked it. Her leg was healing well, but she kept it crossed on her lap like a broken wing.

After throwing the wood beside the stove, next to the textbooks that served as kindling, I chugged cold water to fill my clamoring belly. Emma was so fixated on the pant leg that she was feeding through the machine that she didn't seem to notice when I sat down beside her. Ever since the fall of Seoul there had been a wedge between us, stymying the camaraderie that we had shared in Kanggye. I wasn't sure where the tension came from, that feeling of having to tiptoe when I talked to her, and vice versa. Was she resentful that Imo and I had left the celebration? Or had it simply sunk in for her that we were on opposite sides in this war?

The skin of my fingers was cracked from the dry air and scratched from foraging. Emma had a jar of petroleum jelly, and I slathered a glob over my knuckles, which were as rough as elephants' knees.

"Don't touch any fabric," Emma warned, watching her line of thread, "for at least ten minutes. Oil stains are a headache to wash out."

"I know," I said, leaning away from her pile of finished work.

Emma had as many rules about sewing as Imo had had for her mountain home. "I'm going to finish this pair," she said, "and then it's your turn. We'll do it together. You need to start making more than sandbags, or Granny Cho isn't going to let you stay. Only factory workers can live here, and women more skilled than I am are begging for work. It doesn't have to be perfect, just presentable, so that I can show Granny Cho that you're improving."

"All right." I rubbed my hands vigorously, willing my skin to soak up the moisture.

Emma could make an entire uniform in less than forty-five minutes, and she measured her fabric by holding it against her arm. Her scissors flashed as she snipped her thread when she was finished. "If all goes well, we can get you and the pastor's wife new red books. Do you remember when I told you that I was going to come up with a Korean name for you?"

I nodded, not only because I did remember that conversation but also because I had no words to explain politely that the last thing I wanted was my own red book.

"I had a lot of time to think about it on my way here," Emma continued. "I came up with a few that fit nicely with your surname, but my favorite one is Eun-Ha." She pulled the completed pant leg from her machine. "What do you think? It means 'Silver River,' which is what Koreans call the Milky Way. It's pretty when written. Chang Eun-Ha. I can show you later."

"Chang Eun-Ha?" I repeated. My tongue struggled to bend for the vowels.

"Almost. Your accent is getting better, but you still use too much of your nose. There are many Chinese here, though, and even some Americans who have adapted to our language. You will too."

Saliva pooled in my mouth. Here, I had been getting a glimpse of what my life might be like if I were trapped in North Korea long-term, and it was as surreal as it was terrifying. The situation in Pyongyang was deteriorating, yet the women in the compound were optimistic, or at least appeared to be, despite the lack of fuel and the diminishing rations. Granny Cho told everyone that the shortages were temporary sacrifices to support the KPA's offensive, and that once Grand Marshal Kim unified the country there'd be plenty of food from the agricultural South. Everyone would have warm rice again, the good grains that the Japanese used to confiscate for export, firm and pearlescent.

I didn't need to ask Emma to know that she no longer wanted to flee, for she had reunited with her true flock and was nestled once again among Yun-Hee's earthly possessions. Here with her friends, Emma was going to continue waiting for her daughter. All that was left for me to do was to commit to saying goodbye and find the courage to depart—alone.

Swallowing, I said, "Emma, I am grateful for your help, and everything that you and Imo have done for me. My entire family owes you a debt, and I will try my best to repay you by finding out what happened to Yun-Hee when I get home. As much as I will miss you, I have to leave Pyongyang, and soon. If I don't catch up with the Americans in Busan, I might never see my parents again."

"Nonsense," Emma said, lining up the inseams of the pants to make sure they were even. "When Korea is unified, ships and planes will be running again. You'll be able to go to Japan, or maybe directly to America. Just be patient. Better to arrive later, in one piece." She tossed the new pants onto a stack of nearly fifty pairs, which needed only to have buttons sewn into the waists.

I wiped my hands on a rag to take off any excess jelly. "Emma, America wants to contain Communism. Washington still hasn't recognized Mao's government. If Grand Marshal Kim controls all of Korea, we won't have diplomatic relations with him, which means I can't go to Japan from here, let alone America."

"Ah, it won't be that bad," she said. "There will be a way. You are a determined girl, and very smart. You will get home."

"It's not just about being smart or trying hard!" Yun-Hee had also been smart and determined, from what I'd heard, but here her mother was, alone. "It's not about one Korea winning over the other either. The world is sitting on a powder keg. Even if Korea is unified, there are still two Chinas. There are still two nuclear powers who hate each other enough that they might not be satisfied with proxies anymore. You and I discussed this in Kanggye, and my opinion hasn't changed. America will not withdraw from Korea before bombing the North beyond recognition. And they can do that with or without atomic weapons."

Emma threw up her hands, almost knocking over the bowl of buttons. "The Lord has a plan, and we all have our fate. If I must die, I'd rather be here, in my home, with people I love, than on the side of the road somewhere in the South. The women here are already fond of you, and I'm sure they will only grow to love you more. When Yun-Hee comes back to us, she will welcome you like a sister. She always wanted a sibling. I won't stop you from leaving, but I want you to know that you do have a place here too—in my house, and in my city." Smiling, she handed me a brass button, recycled from an old police uniform.

I grabbed it from her, along with some thread, a sense of bittersweetness welling up within me. All this time, Emma had been thinking of making a way for me to fit in, even if it meant remolding my edges. There was no doubt in my mind that I would have been able to adapt to a new language and a new land, for I was a daughter of immigrants. Emma, however, had said aloud the reasoning that swung my own heart.

"Thank you," I said, "but if I have to die, I want to be as close as possible to my home, and the people I love. I'd rather go knowing that I tried my best and did everything in my power to find them again."

Emma patted my hand. "I understand. You are a good daughter. I hope the Lord will help you find your way, but if you change your mind, we are here, and you are welcome."

"Same for you, Emma. If you change your mind, you can come with me."

I threaded my needle, careful not to prick myself when I poked it through the buttonhole. Just as I never needed to ask Emma whether she was going to stay in Pyongyang, she must have known that I was going to leave it. Perhaps the wedge between us was simply a placeholder for a separation that we had both accepted as inevitable.

30

JUDGMENT OF SOLOMON

January 3, 1951

I lay awake in the dark, listening to Emma's snoring and Imo's deep, rattling breath, wondering if I was being irrational. The more I mulled over my plans to go south, the more it seemed like a suicide mission. There wasn't enough food in Emma's house to spare for an extended trip, nor would I be able to carry enough to sustain my needs. For shelter, I'd have to rely on the generosity of Korean civilians, but I didn't speak their native language. Had I left earlier, I could have tagged along with Chinese soldiers, but there weren't any of them in Pyongyang anymore.

If Yun-Hee was alive somewhere, was she also trying to go home, and ruminating on the same fears as I was? Unlike me, she had had at least five summers to figure it out. Stalin once said that his greatest generals were General December, General January, and General February—and here we were, suffering the wrath of winter acutely. I despised the cold more than any mortal foe, and regretted having waited for Emma when I should have just latched onto Comrade Ying and hitchhiked onward. Admittedly, part of me was peeved at her for changing her mind, so that I had missed my ride for nothing.

A whistle cut through the sounds of sleep. I thought it was a person's, perhaps Miho's, but it became extended, louder, and more high-pitched. No human or animal made that kind of noise, but my twilight brain was sluggish, until the curfew sirens erupted into wails—low, then shrill, cyclical and hair-raising.

Bolting upright, I slammed my palms over my ears. "Get up!" I screamed, though Imo had already popped out of her blankets. An explosion rippled through the earth, shaking our mats, a force that resonated in the cavity of my chest.

Emma was still tangled in her bedding when more whistles screeched overhead, blending into a sadistic chorus.

"We're being bombed!" Imo cried, ripping Emma's blankets off.

This wasn't like Kanggye, where we had been in the mountains, miles from the targets. Bombs were hurtling down on us, so many that I couldn't distinguish each one. In the blinding light that washed through the window, Imo's eyes were replete with terror. Dark pellets descended through cloud cover like locusts, to consume us. The ground pulsed with each impact, smoke saturating the air when Emma stumbled to her feet.

Panicked, I knotted my blankets around my neck and Imo seized her special bag. Emma, however, made a mad dash to the pantry and proceeded to pack.

"Leave it!" Imo yelled, shoving Emma to the door just as Emma grabbed the last of her millet.

Linking arms, we bounded outside to the path, Emma like a bandit with her sack thumping over her shoulder. It was so bright that it might have been day, the cries of our neighbors strident as everyone raced to the air-raid shelter. I was too scared to register what anyone was saying as bombs thundered relentlessly in the city center.

Red.

A cadmium wave crested across the river, blasts shattering brick walls like they were sheets of glass. Anguished people on the other side flung themselves onto the frozen water, some sliding into holes in the ice. Columns of fire sucked up those who were on the bank, the human screams lacerating what remained of my composure.

I shrieked too, despondently, maniacally, while I struggled to keep up. The corners of my lips cracked. My eardrums split and throbbed from the deafening crackle of conflagration. Napalm crashed over the river, igniting the debris on it until the water itself seemed to burn, writhing like a serpent on fire—a serpent in agony.

This wasn't precision bombing; it was revenge. If America couldn't have Seoul, then its enemies couldn't have Pyongyang. Whole blocks were disappearing in tunnels of smoke, and houses were melting in flashing bursts of light. I shut my eyes as heat singed my lashes and brows, ash surging up my nostrils.

Ahead, Miho and another young woman crouched outside the dilapidated shelter, shouting and rubbing soot from their faces. Their red scarves flapped in the wind while they urged everyone to hurry inside. This two-story unit, with glass windows and a shoddy tiled roof, was not built to withstand bombs, but workers flooded past its barbed-wire gates anyway, dropping their possessions in the bedlam. Emma clapped Miho on the shoulder, proud of her for holding herself together, as we staggered into the stairwell.

I clung to the wobbly railing, my knees threatening to give

way as we descended into an unlit and unventilated basement. The walls were moist, but thick enough to muffle the bombing when the door slammed shut. Someone was wailing, "Mercy, mercy," over and over again.

It was pitch-black at the bottom of the stairs. "Who's there?" croaked Granny Cho, groping at us. My Korean had improved enough to understand such a basic phrase.

"Moon Hwa-Ja!" Emma shouted.

"Kim Chu-yin!" added Imo, using her fake name.

I was going to give my Chinese name, but Emma cut me off. "Chang Eun-Ha," she said.

"Four more," Granny Cho rasped anxiously. Though she had no paper list, she knew the workers well enough to rattle off the names and house numbers of the women who were still unaccounted for.

"I'll go find them," said Emma.

"No!" I exclaimed, my lips bleeding where they had cracked. "It's too dangerous."

"They aren't far," said Emma, switching to Japanese. "I'm just going to check their houses."

"No, I'll go," I insisted. "Your leg has barely healed. I'll be faster."

"Don't be stupid," hissed Emma. "You don't even know what they look like, or where they are! You'll only cause more trouble if you get lost."

Granny Cho pushed between us. "I'll go. They are my responsibility."

"With your old, knobby legs?" cried Emma. "You can barely climb up and down these stairs!"

At the top of the stairway, Miho threw open the door, light from above illuminating the petrified women around me. Two more workers clomped down to the basement, with wet rags over their mouths, one with a bundle balanced on her head.

Granny Cho barked at them to remove their rags or say their names. As soon as Granny Cho identified them, Emma charged up the stairs before anyone could object.

"Wait!" I cried, but Emma didn't stop. I snatched the wet rags from the women who had just arrived, and ran after her.

"Stay with your Imo!" Emma commanded when I caught up to her outside. "She'll be scared, and she'll need those wet rags more than I do."

Black clouds smothered our side of the river as the wind shifted.

"Just take one," I said, pushing a rag into Emma's hand. "Come back quickly, all right? If you don't see them right away, just turn around!"

Emma gave no indication that she had heard me over the explosions, her hunched form bobbing as she sprinted past the barbed-wire gate.

"You can't block the door!" Miho exclaimed. "Go down. I will wait for Auntie Moon!"

Acquiescing to the orders of a teenager, I lunged back to the basement.

Imo accosted me at the base of the stairs. "Don't just run off," she wheezed, struggling to enunciate as her breath faltered. "I know you want to do something, but sometimes the best way to help is to make sure others don't have to worry about you."

It wasn't as smoky belowground as it was outside, but it was cloyingly humid, and Imo's asthma was always worse when she was stressed. Each blast overhead was flanked by sobbing around us, and that one woman was still sniveling, "Mercy, mercy," even with her friends trying to calm her.

Granny Cho repeated the names of everyone present, as assertively as a headmistress. I gave Imo the rag and fumbled along the wall until I found a space for us to sit and wait for Emma. Threading my fingers through Imo's chilled ones, I had us both sit, hip to hip, leaning against what might have been a boiler.

One way or another, it will be over soon, I told myself, another blast rocking us. My throat tightened, like terror could seal it shut, drag and drown me in plain air. Tears leaked from the corners of my eyes to my lips, but I didn't feel the same guilt that I did before. The divisions that I previously maintained had become so blurred that I couldn't think in terms of "us" and "them" anymore.

"We" were in a basement.

"They" were bombing us.

I despised this war and the men who had started it. Not just Kim Il-Sung and his associates, but the Empire of Japan that had colonized Korea, and the men in Potsdam—my own leaders included—who had cleaved it in two. My anger was so overwhelming that I trembled, but I had no hate left for the ordinary people, not even the low-level soldiers dying for the freedom their rulers had promised them.

Imo coughed, so forcefully that she doubled over, trying to eject the soot from her lungs. I untied my blankets and draped them over us both, hoping that keeping warm would help her. I measured time by the number of explosions we heard, and after eleven more, the upstairs door cracked open, light racing against the walls.

Miho and Emma struggled to carry a limp woman down to the basement. They accidentally banged her head on the railing as they balanced on the stairs, but she didn't wake up. Another woman filed in after them, a cast-iron kettle swinging from the crook of her elbow.

"Move!" Emma cried, as Granny Cho rushed to support the comatose woman's head. The other workers parted to make space, and as soon as the upper door slammed shut, we were rendered blind again.

Women chattered frantically. The kettle scraped loudly against the floor, and someone yelled.

"What are they saying?" I asked Imo.

"That woman has a blood sugar disorder," said Imo. "She's been rationing her medication over the past months, and she fainted when she got up from her sleeping mat."

"Is she alive?"

"For now, yes, but we need to take her to a doctor when the bombing stops. How long do you think it will last?"

"I have no idea."

Imo coughed again, before clearing her throat. "Are they going to annihilate Pyongyang?" she asked hoarsely.

"Not if the leadership has any hope that the UN forces can recapture it," I said. "No one wants to rebuild a city as big as this one, but if they no longer believe that they can come north again, then they won't hold back."

The woman who had arrived with the kettle moaned. Everyone shifted in the dark around the woman who had fainted, worried because she wasn't waking up. I wanted to care more, but I didn't know her face any more than I knew the thousands of others burning in two-thousand-degree heat. No one was just a number, but if my heart wasn't tethered it simply couldn't hurt anymore. Did my detachment mean that I was ready to die?

I thought of my family, beginning with my mom. She preferred Coca-Cola over tea, but ate spaghetti with chopsticks. My dad never liked reading, but he had subscribed to the *Global Tribune* to support my work, even if he mostly used it to line his cockatiel's cage. My elder brother played baseball, while my younger brother was in the 4-H club. The former married a girl from Hong Kong, and the latter the daughter of Italian immigrants. My mom disapproved of both choices, but did her best to hide it, except when she and I went shopping. Then she would let loose and complain about skinny bitches who couldn't cook, even though I too was a skinny bitch who couldn't cook.

Yes, I still wanted to live.

Of course I wanted to live, to see them again, in all their endearing dysfunction, their sacrifice, and their judgment; to watch my nieces and nephews grow, even if it meant fielding their well-meaning questions about my spinsterhood; to have time with my friends, and maybe the chance to find love again, the kind that stuck—the kind that made it clear that every other encounter had failed precisely so that this one could flower.

It was getting smokier in the basement, and warmer too. "Oh, Imo," I said, on the brink of a breakdown, "if I'm meant to die young, I hope it's quick at least."

She had her rag pressed over her face, but she removed it and said, "Aren't you almost thirty? That's not very young."

Her sardonic response startled me so much that the pressure in my chest abated ever so slightly. "Fine, then. If I'm meant to die unwed, I hope it's quick at least."

Imo laughed, low and raspy, shuddering as she held back another cough. A tremendous boom resounded, close enough to rattle our entire bodies, knocking our cheeks together. I couldn't see where Emma was, and the only person audible was the one still saying, "Mercy, mercy."

Imo kept her head leaned against mine. "When I was young,

my mother prayed often. So did the other women around me. I used to hate it, you know. I used to think that women, more than men, must pray because no one else will listen. I didn't want to be a woman who prayed; I wanted to be a woman who made people listen. It wasn't until I met my husband that I changed my mind and understood it all in a different way. He had a gift, you know. I miss him so much."

"I miss him too," I said, remembering Pastor Pak's altruism and envying his steadfast faith. "I hope he's safe, wherever he is." It was close to dawn, and I couldn't help thinking of Pastor Pak's early-morning prayers, which aligned with the sun's light splitting the horizon.

"Me too," said Imo. She sniffled before clearing her throat and sitting up. Alert, she abruptly switched to Korean, as if she had forgotten I was there. The lines that she began to recite were the same ones that Pastor Pak had repeated so often in his mountain home that I recognized them right away, and knew the English translation. "Our father, who art in heaven, hallowed be thy—"

Shocked, I slapped my hand over Imo's mouth as another explosion sounded, vibrating in our marrow. Warm wind rushed in through the cracks in the building. "What are you doing?" I hissed. "Have you lost your mind?"

Many of the women in the basement had taken care to save their red armbands and scarves before fleeing their homes.

Imo grabbed my pinkie finger and yanked it back so hard that I yelped and let go. "Most of these girls are from Pyongyang," she said, "and were raised Christian, if I had to guess, even if they couldn't worship openly. I've been married to Sung-Ho long enough to have learned how to speak when his people feel alone, to reassure them that they haven't been abandoned."

"But Granny Cho is going to report you," I whispered, unsure where the old woman was lurking, "or strangle you with a red scarf. Just stop and think before you say more."

"I am not afraid of Granny Cho," declared Imo, even though she had spent our entire time avoiding her as much as she could. "A prayer isn't everything these women need, but it is the only thing I can give them. And probably the only thing they can have."

When I tried to cover her mouth again, she moved to bite me, her teeth grazing my palm before I yanked it away. I pulled my hands tightly over my own belly.

"Our father, who art in heaven!" Imo called out, projecting with intention. "Hallowed be thy name!"

A scattered hush settled over the women in the basement, and stretched into a cavernous silence, amplifying the explosions overhead. In the darkness, people swallowed their sobs, and the woman who kept saying "mercy" stifled herself midword. The ground still trembled, and I did too, frazzled by the bombs and terrified for Imo, who had abandoned all logic.

I braced for Miho or Granny Cho to decry her as a counter-revolutionary, a crusader for the opiate of the masses, but Imo seized the emptiness around us and continued. ". . . thy kingdom come; thy will be done on earth as it is in heaven." She wheezed as another boom dislodged fragments of plaster from the ceiling.

In the brief interlude between the bombs, Granny Cho cut in, "Give us this day . . ."

". . . our daily bread," said Imo, matching her, as Emma and other women who knew this scripture joined in, word for word. ". . . and forgive us our trespasses, as we forgive those who trespass against us." Their sonorous voices reverberated off the damp concrete walls, rendering the basement an echo chamber. ". . . and lead us not into temptation, but deliver us from evil. For thine is the kingdom and the power, and the glory, for ever and ever. Amen."

Amen.

Though Pastor Pak was not here, I heard him too in these lines, in this dissent. Imo began a sermon that I couldn't understand, but I was in utter awe of her magnitude—in awe of Machiko, the protester and activist, the woman who saw similarities based on shared humanity, over the artificial divisions of religion and nationality. Even as she paused to cough, she held court, held silence, bringing comfort from nothing but her ability to think beyond boxes and her courage to cross lines.

There was still despair, and fear, ever present, but there was also a power in having a voice and being free to exercise it. I did not worship a singular God, but I recognized that the divine, whether in the form of tree spirits or a kingdom of deities, often spoke in still, small voices, and hearkened them too. No matter how loud and insistent the bombs were, I believed that someone could hear us—not just our given words but those kept in the heart.

Soaking in Imo's fortitude and the assurance of her narrative, I prepared myself for the coming of dawn.

31

REMEMBER MY SON

January 3, 1951

At daybreak we crawled out of the basement, disoriented, as if we had been transported to another land, another realm, where plumes stretched up to meet a hideous orange sky. The scenery was foreign, and so grotesque that it was otherworldly. As I stepped over cinders, I questioned whether we had died below the storage building and this was our hell—an expansive, gut-wrenching ashtray. Gray and yellow clouds, mottled like bruises, blended with the tarry smoke of bonfires that smoldered throughout the city center.

When I was a child, I feared the dark for what it hid. Now I dreaded the morning light for what it revealed. Napalm left human-shaped pieces of coal and twisted bodies burnt to the bone. In basements close to the infernos, heat had sucked the oxygen from the air, desiccating people into mummified husks. The river had thawed from the intensity of the blasts, and charred remains floated to the water's surface. Corpses marred the incinerated banks.

A third of the buildings had been reaped overnight, like Kanggye all over again, but everything was taller and broader, the ruins staggering to behold. Our throats were parched, and our legs cramped from crowding together, but the factory was far enough from the city center that it was mostly intact. Though exhausted, Granny Cho and Miho made rounds through the entire compound, checking every house. Emma's was unscathed, its drab walls proudly retaining its weathered roof.

I didn't know the name of the woman with the blood sugar disorder. All I knew was that her condition was treatable but there was no doctor to see her, and no medicine to purchase.

She had died in the basement. It had been as quick as a robbery.

Human fat and hair have a distinct, acrid stench when burned, and though I'd gotten a few whiffs in the MASH tents, I'd never stewed in it—inhaled it—and wondered how much of the ash in my lungs was bone. My blackened saliva, stained from soot, clung gelatinously to my tongue. Beside me, Imo panted, her chest rising and falling so rapidly that the collar on her jacket fluttered. Like a fish on land she gaped, her mouth open as if she were begging for food, when her body was really begging for oxygen.

As soon as we returned to Emma's home, we chugged freezing water straight from the spout of the kettle, my throat burning with each gulp. Ash had drifted in through the chimney, and the cracks along the door frame, covering everything inside. It was unseasonably warm, but cold enough that we couldn't shed our coats.

"We need to go to a hospital," I said, licking water from my salty upper lip. "Imo needs help. She can barely breathe."

Emma ran her index finger along the table, leaving a dash through a layer of sediment. "The hospitals are all in the city center, though. There are clinics closer by, but many of them closed when the Americans came."

Imo lowered herself onto a folded mat. "No," she croaked. "The doctors are too busy—if there are any left, that is."

Emma frowned. "We could try the barracks. They should have medical facilities. We can ask Granny Cho about them."

"Will they be able to treat her?" I asked, recalling the alleged hospital in Songgan that had been a wretched cross between a detention center and a barn.

"Maybe," said Emma, "though soldiers get priority there. I don't know if the medical staff will even look at the pastor's wife."

"She's the mother of a soldier now," I pointed out. "That must count for something."

"Maybe in times of peace," said Emma. "Maybe in times of plenty. No one thinks of mothers during war."

"*Everyone* thinks of mothers during war," I pushed back. "At least their own mothers. I know I do. I'm sure Jae-Min and almost every other soldier does too."

Emma shuffled to the window and peeled back the curtain. Over the city, gray particles swirled in place of snow. "The air is terrible. What if she gets worse when we take her outside?"

Imo slapped her hand on the mat, a muffled thump that was hardly threatening. "Stop talking about me like I'm a child," she rasped. "It's a waste of time to go anywhere. No one will look twice unless you're dying, and even then, they might not blink."

"We need to do something before you get worse," I argued. "What if the bombers come back tonight? This might be our only chance to get you medicine."

"In a military clinic?" asked Imo. "They're stocked to treat war wounds. Lung illness is for the weak. The rich. They won't have anything for me. What I need is clean air, but no doctor can clear the sky."

"We need to get away from Pyongyang, then," I said, "away from the smoke."

"Shall we go back to Kanggye?" asked Imo sarcastically, erupting into a fit of coughing.

"There is smoke everywhere," said Emma, drawing the curtain shut. "The imperialists are bombing everywhere. No place is safe."

"The South might be," I said. "Not safe, but safer. There will be raids, but not bombing at this scale . . . I think. The Soviets are still behind in that technology . . . I think." I'd been cut off from global media for so long that I had no idea where anyone was in the arms race now. For all I knew, the Soviets could have successfully tested a nuclear airdrop over Christmas. "America still has air superiority . . . I think."

"I'll have some rest and hot water," declared Imo, rising so she could unfold the mat that she was sitting on. "We've been awake all night. Once I sleep I will feel better."

"We can still go south," I insisted, shoving past my own doubts. "I am going to go south. I know you want to wait for Jae-Min and Pastor Pak, but we've dawdled for too long. We can't afford to hesitate anymore."

"The pastor's wife can barely walk!" interjected Emma. "She can't make it to the city center, let alone across the thirty-eighth parallel."

"We're going to hitchhike," I said.

"With who?" Emma demanded. "The Chinese divisions have already left. Our army isn't going to care about your boyfriend. No one will chauffeur you to the front lines to search for a single man among so many."

"I have a different idea this time," I said. "I've been thinking about options for a while, but I didn't have a breakthrough until earlier this morning, when we were in the basement."

Emma and Imo regarded me warily, even though it was Imo who had inspired me to venture beyond the walls I knew and consider alternative solutions. I had been telling everyone that my boyfriend was a soldier because in the American military women still weren't allowed in combat. In China, however, there had been multiple all-female units since the 1930s, including pilots, snipers, and foot soldiers. Women fighters were relatively uncommon, but they existed—and because of them, I had another cover.

"I'm going to pretend to be a Chinese soldier," I announced. "Not the girlfriend of a Chinese soldier, but a Chinese soldier. I'll say that I got injured and separated from my unit. Left behind, so I need to catch up. If you can let me have one of the KPA uniforms you made, I can explain that my own uniform was damaged and I borrowed one from an ally."

Imo cupped a hand over her ear, convinced that she had misheard me. "You can't just be a soldier," she sputtered. "What do you know about war? What do you know about the Chinese army?"

"Do you even know how to hold a gun?" asked Emma.

"I know enough," I replied, undeterred by their skepticism. "I am not a soldier, but I have studied war in more detail than most soldiers have. Writing about war is different from fighting it, but I've learned about Mao's strategy. And if I do 'forget' anything, I am 'only a woman,' after all. The Communists are desperate for more bodies. Are they really going to cross-examine someone who is willing to fight for them?"

"You might as well jump into the river!" Emma cried. "The army isn't going to drop you off at a hotel or a train station. They're going to take you straight to a trench or a foxhole!"

"I'll adjust as I go," I said. "As long as I can get to the battleground, I can find a way to reunite with UN troops."

"Who will shoot you because you're in a KPA uniform," Imo said.

"Or throw a grenade at you," said Emma.

"Run you over with a tank!" huffed Imo.

"Or strafe you with a plane!" added Emma. "You are tired, Eun-Ha. Have some soup, and then go to sleep. Think about it again when your head recovers."

Perhaps we were pecking at one another in exhausted irritation, but it was clear to me that this was our end. None of us were puppets, yet each of us had strings that pulled us in different directions. I couldn't let mine stay entangled with theirs anymore; I had my own family, and they were waiting.

"I am going south," I repeated with emphasis. "Emma, I understand that Pyongyang is your home. Imo, I understand that you are tied to your husband and son. You are both welcome to come with me, and I would be happy if you did, but I understand why you won't. I am grateful to you both, and I will always remember you both. And maybe, when this war ends, we will find a way to meet again."

Imo, though worn, smiled fleetingly at me, before forcing her lips back into a stern line. That brief, gentle expression, as vibrant as a firefly's glow, resembled that of the woman I had seen in her two old photographs. Even with her age and scrawny frame, she was, once again, Machiko—a woman who, in spite of her surroundings, had to fight joy to maintain her serious countenance.

Emma waved her hand. "Enough, Eun-Ha. Take a nap, and then we will talk. I will go out and see if I can find any medicine for the lungs. Take care of the pastor's wife while I'm gone. Boil water for her and make sure she is comfortable."

"I am not a child," Imo reminded us, but Emma disregarded her.

After rummaging for empty cups and items to barter, including a bronze pin and a beaded floral necklace, Emma wrapped a scarf around her mouth and charged out into the ash storm, hands up to protect her eyes from the grainy wind.

Obediently, I brought Imo the kettle of water and propped another mat underneath her torso to keep her upright. Though I was cold, I took all the blankets we had and draped them over her birdlike body.

"Stop fussing," wheezed Imo. "I can't relax with you making a mess. I'll be fine, really. I know my own body, more than the two of you nosy birds do!" Adjusting herself on the mat, she motioned for me to lie down.

I stayed on my haunches by the stove, arranging our gingko wood in a pyramid with kindling underneath. "Think about Busan, Imo," I said, stuffing another sheet of paper in. "Please. I am afraid of the distance too, but in the span of a lifetime, it's not so far. And the journey will only become harder as the war goes on. If the two of us go now, your family can find us later, or you can find them. Please think about it, Imo. Jae-Min and Pastor Pak would want you to."

She chuckled, but it morphed into a wet, raucous cough. "Perhaps 'almost thirty' is still young after all," she said, hoarsely. "I appreciate your care, Chang Eun-Ha—truly, I do—but if you wish to help me, then don't give up on my son. Whatever kind will you have for me, extend it to my son. I do not want to die, but I am not afraid to either. I have an heir, and through his line I will persist, as immortal as any of us can hope to be." She pulled her blankets higher, over her chin, then crossed her arms beneath them.

Flustered, I said, "I will help Jae-Min if I can, but that doesn't mean I can't help you too. It wouldn't even be me helping you; it would be us helping each other. I don't want to be alone either, you know. I'm scared too, you know."

Imo's hair slipped over her brow bone as she gave me an impatient side-eye. "Don't be so dramatic. You won't be alone, at least not for long. I am grateful to have met you, but my place is not by your side. I will wait here for my husband, and when he comes we will leave together. Be brave, Chang Eun-Ha. You don't need to remember me or my husband. All I ask is that you remember my son, Pak Jae-Min. Please remember my son, Pak Jae-Min."

She swallowed noisily, a glob of mucus shifting down her sinewy throat.

Pak Jae-Min.

"I will," I said, picking up the matchbox. It was a simple enough promise, but in my mind Pak Jae-Min was no different from Song Yun-Hee. To their mothers, they were eternal and everlasting, death-defying in the convulsions of war, but that didn't mean that either of them was alive. I hated to think that both Emma and Imo were waiting in purgatory for children who were never coming when I was certain that the bombing of Pyongyang had only just begun.

With a bitter taste on my tongue and a hollowness within my chest, I struck a match. Its light was tepid, but it leaped to the kindling in the womb of the stove. Tendrils of smoke curled over the remnants of a girl's cherished books and a river's sacred trees. Steadily, a pearly haze inundated Emma's steadfast home, enveloping us both.

January 3, 1951
Pyongyang

Dear Mom and Dad,

I am still alive, but I am worried about my friend Machiko. She has asthma, I think, and it's gotten so much worse with the bombing. She's so proud that it's hard for her to admit any kind of weakness. I both hate and love that about her.

I didn't expect to make friends in North Korea, and now I have two. Buddhists say that attachment is suffering, and I understand that keenly now. While I don't want to abandon my friends to this war, to the bombs, I have done everything I can to convince them to come with me, to no avail. Their hearts are here, but mine remains with you.

I hope you won't have to wait for much longer.

With all my love,
Ellie

32

DO NOT STARE

January 3, 1951

I didn't realize that I had fallen asleep, curled in a ball on the floor, until an excruciating headache cleaved my dreams in two. The blankets were piled on top of me, and the untended fire had dwindled to a handful of cinders. My throat was like sandpaper, and though it was still light outside, I was alone by the stove. Imo had moved to the alcove, perhaps to distance herself from the smoke.

She lay flat on her back, staring up at the ceiling with no quilt or jacket, with her porcelain bowl and photographs beside her. Oddly, she had changed to a lightweight hemp hanbok—a plain white skirt and *jeogori*. Her silver hair was neatly combed and tied up in a bun, and her fingers were stained with soot.

"Imo?" I called out, unsure what this stunt was. I had given her all the pillows and mats to keep her torso upright and make it easier for her to breathe. "You aren't supposed to lie down like that. It's bad for your asthma."

She did not even turn to acknowledge me as I approached,

and I wondered if I had upset her somehow. If Imo was displeased, certainly she'd give me a tirade instead of the silent treatment, but she wasn't moving. Only when I'd noticed her eyebrows—drawn shakily but almost exactly like her natural ones—did I realize that she wasn't blinking.

I froze.

In life, there is no way to rewind, to redo, but I stepped backward as if I could reverse time by curling on the floor again and closing my eyes. Sight is only one sense, and maybe if I lay still, I'd hear Imo's voice chiding me for being lazy, urging me to get up and sew. I had become accustomed to death, to its stench and its prevalence, but despite its capriciousness, I still hadn't expected it to steal from me. This was a robbery, vicious and brazen, but it was my own fault for letting my guard down, when this was a war zone and not a fairy tale, when Korea was in contention and nowhere was safe—when no one was safe, especially not ordinary people like Imo and me.

Koreans, North and South, were dying for freedom, but whose?

With two fingertips, I closed Imo's eyes, a tremor radiating through my wrist from the chill in her skin and the pliability of muscle gone limp. I pushed on her chin to stop her mouth from hanging open, because I couldn't let her stiffen with that fishlike gaping, howling in suffocation. That way I could pretend that it was peaceful. That way I could contain my rage.

One isn't supposed to blame the dead, but Imo was a fighter, and as I touched her coiffed hair I knew that she had chosen to let go and leave on her own terms—with dignity even in death. I understood her desire to control her fate to the extent that she could, but I still had a selfish urge to grab her and scream, *What about me?*

Imo had abandoned me to this war, to these bombs, and though she owed me nothing, how could she depart without saying goodbye? There was no note, only her bowl and the photos to remind me of my obligation. It saddened me to think that maybe we weren't really friends, that maybe the warmth between us was simply because she began to see me as an asset instead of a liability.

I hoped not.

I picked up the peony bowl, and with it a promise. "Goodbye, Imo," I said, my head bowed, my voice raw. "Thank you for sharing your food with me. Thank you for cooking for me and taking care of me. Thank you for being my friend, regardless of the reasons, because without you, I would have been lonelier here. I would have been more scared, and I'm not sure if I would have made it this far."

I definitely wouldn't have made it this far.

Under Chinese Buddhist tradition, it is forbidden to move the dead for at least eight hours—to allow time for their soul to detach, to accept that it must pass on to a new life. In reincarnation, a spirit is like a ball of yarn, knit up with each birth and unraveled with each death. I wasn't sure what Christians or Shintoists did for mourning, and as a Buddhist I was too young, and too lucky, to have performed any rites on my own. Without guidance, I knelt beside Imo's body, whispering, "*Namu amituofo,*" and wondering where the hell Emma had gone. It must have been at least a few hours since she had left for the medicine, and I worried that the city, rendered rabid by war, had swallowed her too.

The fire succumbed to ash, and the house invited the cold. Even without warmth there was still smoke, relentlessly cloying, and the occasional bellow of jets. I couldn't tell how long I had knelt in the alcove any more than I could have guessed how long

I had slept. When Emma finally returned, my shins and knees felt like they had crystallized and molded to the floor.

Emma was smeared with soot, cradling a cup like it was a baby bird, or a handful of elusive white rice. A torrent of emotions surged when I saw her, a cataclysm of contradictions—relief that she was alive, ebullience that she was back, and fury that she had taken so long. Coursing beneath it all was a consummate sense of shame, because I had been in charge of the pastor's wife, and under my watch, we had lost her.

It wasn't my fault, I wanted to say, but I was responsible, and so I slathered over my guilt another accusation. "It's late," I said as Emma closed and bolted the door.

Haggard, she set down the cup, which contained several tablespoons of a dark, gummy liquid. "I had to walk to two clinics and three different barracks before I could get this syrup," she said. "It's for throat pain, but there wasn't anything else. Medics don't even have bandages. They're using paper to wrap wounds."

Emma slouched to remove her shoes, and she was so exhausted that she left them clumped in a pile. When she saw Imo in clean summer clothing, she frowned in confusion. Like me, she must have thought Imo was being eccentric, but then she set down her cup as the truth sank in. Sorrow fell like a shadow over her face. "Did you change her clothes?" she asked.

"She did it herself," I said, but with that answer came an acrid revelation.

The hemp hanbok that Imo had put on was the same one that she had been wearing in her family portrait ten years ago. White was the color of mourning, but in Korea it was also the color of resistance. During colonial rule, the Japanese had forbidden Koreans from wearing white, so it became a symbol. And so the rebels wore it.

With lead in my chest, I said, "She put it on because she is meeting her husband."

Love is a language, unspoken and unwritten, but even in chaos it can grasp at the soul. I didn't know when or how Imo had discovered the truth—whether it was in the basement, or only hours ago—but now I too was certain. When death had stolen my Imo, it left an ephemeral trail, footprints shaped like the ones that Pastor Pak used to leave in the snowy forest when he went to chop wood. Invisible. Obvious. Illogical, yet irrefutable.

The phantom smell of fresh pine wafted above the smoke. "You lied to us about Pastor Pak, didn't you?" I said. "He died on the road, didn't he? That's why you were crying so much when you got here."

It was a silly thing to say, and I willed Emma to scold me for being morbid. Instead, she sucked in her breath like a parent who was about to whip out her switch. "Why should you care?" she demanded. "The pastor was not yours to claim in any way."

Another piece of my heart snapped in two. "I care that you lied to me."

"I lied to the pastor's wife. You just happened to be there—not that you have any horse to ride on, when your tail is longer than anyone else's."

Heat rushed to my cheeks. "I lie when I have to, to strangers, in order to survive. You and I are supposed to be friends. Pak Imo was your friend. We're supposed to be able to trust each other!"

"No," she corrected, "we are supposed to protect each other. Honesty without compassion is cruel, but maybe you are too young, or too foreign, to understand."

"It's a matter of respect," I said, unconvinced that this was cultural rather than personal. "Imo deserved to know what happened to her husband. Maybe if she had, she would have given up on staying in Pyongyang. We could have left for Seoul earlier, maybe before the bombing. Maybe—"

"Or she would have died sooner, of heartache," said Emma, her tone softening even as I clenched my fists. "Eun-Ha, life is a river that only flows in one direction. It carries us in its current, and only God knows where it will take us. None of it is fair, nor does it make sense. It simply *is*. You can look back, but do not stare. You'll go mad if you do. Trust me—I know."

I threw my head back, trying to blink away tears, only to have them sear down my temples. "Did you lie about Jae-Min too?"

"No," she said, passing me a handkerchief blotted with soot. "Army officers took Jae-Min at a checkpoint. That is true, but the pastor didn't follow him. He didn't want to leave his wife alone, so the two of us kept going toward Pyongyang, as quickly as we could. It was horribly cold, though, and there were many people frozen to death along the road. We pushed ourselves, but we got caught in a blizzard. By the time we found shelter, the pastor already had frostbite. He hadn't been eating enough, I think. There were maybe forty people packed into an old church with us, and seven died, including a baby."

Emma began to cry too, and reached for her moistened handkerchief. "I couldn't tell his wife," she said, mopping her eyes, "not when her health was so bad, and when there was still Jae-Min to live for. Oh, poor Jae-Min. May the good Lord bless him and keep him safe. Two parents in less than a month . . ."

She blew her nose and I unplugged my grief, letting sorrow slice me bare as I bawled. "What are we going to do, Emma?" I cried, with the urgent, frenetic abandon of a child. "We have nothing to bury her with, and even if we did, the ground is frozen. Can we at least find a priest, or a holy person?"

Emma sniffed. "A holy person is even harder to find than a

doctor is. The pastor was one of the few who didn't flee south when the purges began."

"I don't want to put her in a mass grave," I said, remembering the soldiers who had carted bodies outside the city. "Imo would hate that."

"From dust we were made, and to dust we will return," said Emma, darkening as she lay her handkerchief out to dry. "I had to leave the pastor behind the church, with no marker, no funeral, not even a change of clothes. He is holding a baby, because that is the best arrangement the baby's parents could make. Choice is a luxury, now more so than ever, and we all must make do, including the dead—especially the dead."

"Are there more of the dead in this city than the living?" I wondered aloud.

"Not yet," said Emma, "but if we don't focus on ourselves, there will be. The pastor and his wife are with the Lord, and they are safe. As for you and I, we are not done here—not with this world, and not with this war. Look back if you wish, Eun-Ha, but do not stare, as I have said. You will go mad if you do. Mad."

January 4–5, 1951

Granny Cho convened an emergency meeting to discuss what to do with the dead. We moved Imo and the other woman to the unheated factory, where their bodies could freeze while the rest of us scrounged for a solution.

Imo had been right about the predominant religion in the compound. Most of the women were Christian, because Granny Cho herself was Christian and generally refused to hire anyone who didn't share her religion—with exceptions for girls from the countryside, whom she converted aggressively when they came to live with her. Because of the dearth of priests, Granny Cho improvised a Christian service, and vowed to get the authorities to help us dig graves around the factory. She was supposed to meet with a public health officer tomorrow, but then tomorrow never came.

Just past midnight, blaring sirens shattered our already fractured sleep. The Bomber Command had returned, invisible above the cloud cover, sending thousands of explosives streaking toward the earth.

Like thousands of shooting stars.

Like fireworks, I told myself, and then I lost control of my bladder as Emma and I gathered our blankets and ran breathlessly to the air-raid basement. I thought I was getting braver, but it seemed I was only breaking, unable to feel or respond in any consistent manner. Embarrassed, I sat on my wet skirt while Granny Cho did her head count, and I called out, "Chang Eun-Ha!" when it was my turn. People often said that two is company and three is a crowd, but Imo was my missing limb, with a phantom pain that cut to my core.

I was certain that I couldn't breathe, that my mouth was filling with ash, and smoke was billowing into the basement. Only when Emma wrapped her arms around me did I realize that I was shaking, teeth chattering like castanets. Granny Cho shouted the Lord's Prayer, augmenting her voice above the clatter of bombs, but it wasn't the same without Imo. It would never be the same, and I would never be the same.

Decay.

The city had become a carcass, cavernous, the beams of partially bombed buildings jutting like ribs when we braved the sunlight once more. Fire crackled, a steady cremation. In residential districts, only chimneys remained, row after row of chimneys as stark and repetitive as the bars on a prison cell. Pyongyang's center was obliterated, leaving scattered rings of survivors along its fringes, ambling with no homes, no food, and with a ticking clock until the next raid.

Some houses in the factory compound had been split into jagged fragments, with charred cracks along their earthen foundations. Emma's home had remained stalwart, but there was something sinister about it. The air was heavy with the heartache of hungry ghosts, angry ghosts who still had too much to say. Unable to rest, they howled with the ashen wind.

I fed our stove pieces of a neighbor's broken door frame, buying us a few days of life with another's destitution. Emma's shadow flickered forebodingly against the wall as she counted out the items left in her pantry. The well was damaged, which meant we had to fill our canteens at the river, where there were corpses bloated in the water. I was scared that their fingers might graze mine when I dunked my containers below the surface. I imagined that they'd pull me in.

"Let's go," Emma said, staring at the empty stockpot. Her black eyes, as unyielding as cast-iron, seemed to suck in light, while bluish spider veins cracked beneath her lashes.

"I'll go," I volunteered. "You walked so much the other day. I can get us our water while you stay here and rest."

"I meant, let's go south," she said, "to Seoul, or Busan, while we still can, while we still have food and some strength. I wish we had left sooner, but I was afraid before. I am still afraid now, but nothing, not even the journey or the unknown, scares me more than staying in this place."

South.

The skin on my fingers split as I squeezed them shut, and I let out a throaty cackle, abrupt and maniacal. I thought about Pastor Pak, and his stubborn desire to stay in Korea despite being so close to the Chinese border. For a moment, I wandered backward to Kanggye, envisioning all of us pivoting on the main road and following the flow of refugees to Manchuria. Perhaps we should have known better than to swim against the current when the alternative was so far and the conditions so deplorable. In China, we might have found another way.

Don't stare, I told myself, trying to tear myself from the past. I focused on the dull silver sides of the stockpot and the dents beneath its handles. Raising my head, I met Emma's resolute gaze and soaked up the encouragement that I needed to break the grip of regret. She and I were alive, and for now that was all that mattered. That was enough.

"As soon as we pack, we can say goodbye to Granny Cho," I said, collecting my calm. "As soon as we bury Imo, we can leave."

Picking up the stockpot and the canteens, I headed for the river, remembering that there was no need to be afraid of ghosts or the flesh of the dead, of missing eyes or detached limbs. They were harmless compared to the terror of living men, throughout history, with maps and pens, drawing lines across land they'd never been to and forcing them on people they did not know.

---

4 January 1951
Dear Sahmonim,

I don't know what to say to you, because I am still in disbelief that I survived this bombing and you did not. You've always had such a strong mind that I was sure it could carry your body. Regardless of everything that has happened between us, I am grateful to have had you during some of the most difficult moments of my life. I am sorry I couldn't get back in time to see you off, but I take comfort in knowing that you are with the pastor, and will soon be with the Lord.

Please watch over Yun-Hee from where you are.

Trust that I will do the same for Jae-Min here on earth.

With gratitude,
Moon Hwa-Ja

33

THE GIFT OF LIFE

January 9, 1951

The horizon was brown, milky through sheets of snowfall, glazed like a salve over the burnt sky. This most recent blizzard, fierce and thick, put our plans on hold. I pressed my forehead against the windowpane, barely making out the house across the road. Fat snowflakes tackled the ash, grounding the jets again and blessing us with silence that gave us back our sleep and part of our sanity.

Tanks rolled into Pyongyang, taking advantage of the relative safety of bad weather to transport heavy weaponry southward. KPA soldiers trudged alongside them, and occasionally wandered into the compound on their way to nearby barracks. If Granny Cho saw them, she'd shoo them away with the ferocity of a gander.

"Perverts!" she'd scold. "This is a women-only facility!"

We were all supposed to reprimand officers with the same indignation, but modesty was a fine mesh, not barbed wire. So much of the city had been destroyed that it was only a matter of time before the military commandeered the compound and converted it to use as their own facilities—if bombs didn't claim it first.

I continued peering outside, my hair standing on end as the snow accumulated on the sloping rooftops. The visibility was so bad that I couldn't see anyone turn down our street, and a darkened silhouette emerged seemingly from nowhere. He wore a KPA uniform, and a fur hat with earflaps.

Emma was stirring corn and millet porridge, so diluted that the kernels swirled like autumn leaves around her spoon. The ration stations had closed since the bombings, and we ate with the assumption that Emma's pantry would have to tide us over until spring.

"There's a man from the army outside!" I cried, pointing frantically at the glass. "We're supposed to tell him to leave, aren't we?"

Leaving her spoon in the pot, Emma bounded for her rubber shoes. Before she could pull them on, the soldier popped up by our window, his face an inch from the glass.

I screamed, extended like a siren, until I noticed the soldier's deep-set obsidian eyes and his gracefully arched brows. It was as if Imo had been resurrected and had donned a soldier's garb. "Jae-Min?" I said in disbelief.

Emma gasped, and thumped her chest with her palm. "Oh, good Lord, Jae-Min!"

We raced each other to the entrance, colliding in our haste before slamming against the door and fumbling at the lock. My hands found the latch first, but it was Emma who wrestled him in like she was kidnapping him from the storm, kicking the door shut to prevent any pursuit.

Snow had rushed in, leaving arrow patterns on the tile; lingering snowflakes brushed my lips when I unhinged my jaw and laughed. In ecstasy, I tasted the smoky undertone of ash, dislodging slush from Jae-Min's shoulders as I hugged him.

"You're alive!" Emma cried. She squeezed his arms and pulled at his cheeks to prove that he was here and that he was whole. "You must be starving! And thirsty! *Aigo*, you are so thin, so thin! You were always too thin, but now you look truly awful!"

Jae-Min bowed and removed his hat, his hair gelling into greasy stripes when he ran his fingers through it. Ice had frosted the tongues of his boots and settled in the folds of his scarf.

Emma scurried for a stool, but he remained by the door, craning his neck to survey the room. "I have enough food, thank you," he said, bowing again. "I can't stay. I just wanted to check to see if you made it here. Are my parents with you? I assumed that you'd all be together. Their old neighborhood is nothing but rubble."

I chewed the inside of my cheek as Jae-Min's eyes flitted to each corner of the house, to the alcove, and to the closet and pantry. "Oh, Jae-Min," I began, but Emma cut me off.

"South!" she said, quick as a bullet. "Oh, Jae-Min, we're so sorry. They wanted to wait for you—they did—but your mother's health was getting worse. They left just before the bombing, and thank God! There's no way your mother would have survived this much smoke, not with her weak lungs." Leaping back to the kitchen, she fussed with the pot on the stove, hiding her face behind the steam.

"Oh," said Jae-Min, disappointed.

Bowls clinked as Emma ladled out three portions of millet. The dried corn kernels, which hadn't softened yet, floated to the surface.

Emma's lie clamped me like a pillory, but Jae-Min forced a

smile and said, "I suppose that is for the best. Did they say where? Seoul?"

"Yes," said Emma, blowing on his millet to cool it. "Your father has many friends who moved to Seoul when our government shut down the churches. There are many Christians there now, I hear. I'm sure there are people helping them, just as the pastor himself has helped so many."

"I hope so," said Jae-Min, before turning to me, perplexed. "Why didn't you go with them, Ellie? Aren't you trying to go back to America?"

"I promised your mother that I'd wait for you," I blurted, sounding more aggressive than I had intended. The lie slid out easily but clipped my insides, tearing at my own fresh wounds. I could utter the right words but couldn't hold back how much they hurt. A sob erupted from my chest. *When in doubt, just cry,* Imo had told me, but I wasn't crying intentionally. These days, my eyes leaked like a broken faucet, and my nose and cheeks were inflamed from constant rubbing. I was sick of feeling helpless, as though my soul were in a pressure cooker, building with intensity as people around us perished.

"Oh dear God!" Jae-Min cried. "You didn't have to wait for me! What if I had gotten sent to the front lines and you were stuck here forever? You both should have gone with my parents when you had the chance!"

"I owe your mom." I sniveled. "It was the least I could do."

As Jae-Min regarded me with tenderness, I bawled, racked by remorse, not just for covering up his parents' deaths but also for pretending that I cared enough to wait for him. If it weren't for the blizzard, Emma and I would have set out already.

Emma sighed. "Eat." She pushed the bowl that was intended

for Jae-Min into my hands. "I'm sorry, Jae-Min. Please excuse her. She's lost her nerves. It has been terrible here."

"I know," said Jae-Min. "I was praying the entire way to Pyongyang. I was scared that it'd be nothing but ashes. I have to get back to my unit, though. I'm not supposed to be here, and if I'm gone for too long they'll think I'm trying to desert."

"You're not trying to desert?" asked Emma.

"They'll kill me if I do," said Jae-Min.

"You'll die if you don't!" exclaimed Emma. "You aren't a fighter!" She squeezed his lean arms again, even though he didn't have to be a bodybuilder to pull a trigger.

"I'm not fighting," said Jae-Min, brushing her away. "When the officers took me from the road, they asked why I wasn't in the army already. When I showed them my student ID and told them I was studying civil engineering, they separated me from the other new recruits and sent me to the engineering battalion. While everyone else headed south, I ended up all the way back north—right at the Yalu River!"

"Oh, so you are not going to battle?" asked Emma.

"Not for the moment. I'm helping to rebuild bridges and reinforce the supply route from China. But after the imperialists bombed Pyongyang, some of us were reassigned to assess the damage here. We just got in this morning. I'll probably be here for the next few weeks, at least."

"Weeks?" repeated Emma, alarmed. "What kind of son are you, Pak Jae-Min? We just told you that your parents are in the South. How could you possibly think about staying here when your first duty is to those who gave you life? Your parents need you! You have to go find them. Take care of them, especially your *eomma*!"

She elbowed me to support her, but shame had stolen my voice. I nodded my agreement, cementing my complicity.

"You need to go south," said Emma, firmly. "Work hard. Set yourself up for a good job and a good life so your parents can rely on you. Maybe one day we can all come back to Pyongyang, or Kanggye, but until then, there will be more air raids. Please, Jae-Min, for your parents—and for us! If you don't come, we will have stayed here for nothing. We would have waited through the bombings for nothing."

The snow on Jae-Min's shoulders was melting, running down his uniform and seeping into the bunched fabric at his elbows. When his lips parted and his eyes widened, he was an amalgam of his parents, their features alive in the canvas of his face.

His dimples flashed as he clenched his jaw. "So many of the roads have been bombed, though, and we haven't been able to repair them because of the snow. There are comrades heading to Seoul, but I'm not sure if they'll be able to pass through. Even if we were to get there, how would we find my parents?"

Emma blinked rapidly, as if there were flash cards in her eyelids that she could sort through for an answer.

"Your mom left us an address," I piped, reassuring myself that this technically was not a lie, "on the back of a photo that she brought from Kanggye. It's to your grandmother's house in Tokyo. You are to meet there if you can't find each other in Seoul. If the war worsens in South Korea, you are to go there directly."

Emma bobbed her head emphatically and leaped right in as if we were in a dance. "Your parents left before the battle for Seoul began. They might actually have headed to Japan already. God has a plan, Jae-Min, but he only helps those who help themselves. So help yourself, and us too. Eun-Ha and I are ready to leave Pyongyang when you are."

Jae-Min raised his brow at my Korean name. I myself still hadn't gotten used to it, but he didn't inquire any further. Nervously, he raked his fingers through his hair again. "I have to go back to my unit," he said, with a light stutter. "I need time to think. I'm not even supposed to be here, you know. I could get in a lot of trouble, you know."

I'm not supposed to be here either, I thought, hoping we could trust Jae-Min not to report us.

"Tomorrow, then," urged Emma. "Think, and come back tomorrow. We will be here, God willing."

"I'll try," he mumbled. Leaving his millet untouched, he threw his wet hat back on, the earflaps flopping limply. Clumps of slush had formed a halo around his boots. As soon as Emma unlatched the door with reluctant acceptance, Jae-Min dove outside. He seemed to take flight as he ran down the path, into the dark and into the wind, fragile like a paper plane, when the snow engulfed his form.

"I feel awful for lying," I said to Emma, cupping my millet with both hands. The corn was plump and inviting now that it had had time to soak.

"Don't," she said. "We told him exactly what he needed to hear, and exactly what his mother would have wanted."

As we watched the storm, shoulder to shoulder, I tried to take comfort in Imo's unequivocal last wishes and justify what I had done, but I couldn't stymie my sense of obligation to Jae-Min and his own free will. Worst of all, the second air raid and the blizzard had kept Granny Cho in the compound, so she hadn't been able to meet with anyone who could remove our dead. Imo was still on the floor of the textile factory, only a few streets away from Emma's house. On his way in, Jae-Min had walked past his own mother's body. He would do so again on his way out.

Perhaps one day he would hate us.

9 January 1951
Dear Yun-Hee,

Jae-Min is home! Still in the army, but alive. Skinnier than ever, but alive. An orphan, but alive.

I had faith that he would return. Why? Because that mother of his is probably moving heaven and hell to protect him. Wherever she is bound for in death, I know she won't go until she sees that he is safe. If anyone can bribe the Devil, it's that one. If anyone has the nerve to keep God waiting, it's her.

Pray to the Lord, Yun-Hee, and ask your Imo to watch over you too. Some people have guardian angels, but you might be able to get a guardian warrior. I believe, this time, she might help us.

Mom

34

SURRENDER

January 15, 1951

Prior to Jae-Min's return, I had assumed that the North Koreans were blindly throwing people to the front lines. I never imagined that they had an engineering unit. Despite everything that I had observed about the Communist forces, I was still underestimating them. Perhaps the Americans were too.

Jae-Min's team in Kanggye had designed a new type of bridge that could be rapidly assembled, then disassembled and hidden when not in use. Since American reconnaissance couldn't spot them, bombers couldn't destroy them. This kind of work was sorely needed around war-torn Seoul, so when Jae-Min volunteered to transfer to the South, his superiors quickly agreed. They even lauded his bravery, given that so many of his peers were deserting to avoid the front lines.

A convoy was scheduled to leave this evening, and Jae-Min had promised to sneak us in. Emma collected a bunch of uniforms so we could claim to be delivering them. After packing the sewing machine, Emma's meager valuables, and every morsel of food in the pantry, we had little room for anything unessential. Still, I picked up Imo's porcelain bowl and said, "Imo wanted Jae-Min to have this. It's from her family."

Emma recoiled as though I had presented her with an urn full of ashes. "We can't pack that," she said. "It'll crack like an egg if we breathe on it the wrong way."

"But Pak Imo managed to bring it all the way from Kanggye."

"We won't coddle it like she did. Leave it here. Maybe lay it to rest with her. The photographs will be proof enough for Jae-Min if he meets his mother's family." She stuffed her notebook into her satchel, but I continued cradling the bowl.

It had been eleven days since Imo died, and still no one had come to remove any of the bodies. Word had spread that Granny Cho had space for the deceased, so people from surrounding neighborhoods had bartered with her to store theirs temporarily. I never wanted Imo in a mass grave, and now she was in a mass crypt. There was no way anyone would let a dead woman keep such an expensive item when the entire city teetered on the brink of famine.

Oblivious to my chagrin, Emma unfolded two uniforms that she had adjusted to our size. She had packed several useless, sentimental trinkets, but I had none of my own. Why couldn't she just let me have Imo's?

"Have you forgiven her yet?" I asked, bringing the bowl closer to my chest. "Or are you still angry?"

Emma balanced on one foot, about to thread a stockinged leg into her pants. "What are you talking about, Eun-Ha? The pastor's wife still?"

"Yes. You used to be friends, right?"

I had tried asking Emma about Imo before, but each time she

had brushed me off, saying that they went to the same church and nothing more.

Emma wriggled into the pants, then tucked her sweater into the waist, the camouflage pattern clashing with her colorful wool. "We spent a lot of time together," she said, "but we drifted apart after Pastor Pak moved to Kanggye."

"So you were friends."

"Like I've told you, we went to church together. Everyone has to be friendly at church."

"Oh, come on." If there was anything that every religion had in common, it was that houses of worship had their own dramas and rivalries. "Imo thought you were friends. Even from your description, and what I've seen so far, it seems like you were."

"I know what she must have told you," Emma said, putting on her coat, and the KPA uniform over it. "I didn't think she'd complain to you, but maybe the two of you became *friends*." She said "friends" like it was an accusation.

"I'd like to think all of us became friends," I said, tentatively, "that we are *still* friends. Friendship, like any kind of love, does not end with death. It doesn't necessarily end with fights either. Even if you are angry at someone, you can still care for them, right? Why else would Imo let you stay in her home, and you let her stay in yours?"

Emma stopped in the middle of buttoning, but she hadn't lined up the side of the uniform correctly, and it hung lopsided. "Your Imo and I became close at church, even though we came from very different backgrounds. Family is everyone's center, but she and I had both been disowned by our parents. Her parents didn't want her to marry her husband, and my parents didn't want me to divorce mine. For women like your Imo and me, friendship is even more important, because it must fill the holes that family leaves."

She began to falter when she said, "I didn't think of your Imo as my friend. I thought of her as family. But when I asked her to help save my daughter, I realized that she didn't feel the same about me."

"Do you really think that Imo knew the full scope of the labor draft though?"

"I can't say," said Emma. "I will never know what she actually knew, but if she was ignorant about the draft, it was because she chose to be. Everyone with a daughter feared the worst. It's not that I blame her for what happened to my Yun-Hee, but her response changed how I saw her. She didn't think my daughter was worthy of her son, and she preferred to gamble with Yun-Hee's life than to let her join the Pak family."

"Yun-Hee and Jae-Min were children, though—quite young to marry, don't you think?"

"That wasn't the issue. Christians aren't supposed to care about class, but in the end, it still matters. My lineage is decent, but I am a single mother with a broken family. The pastor's wife was descended from nobility and never suffered any kind of shame, aside from being disowned by her criminal of a father. People like her can be kind to people like me. They can give charity to people like me, but they don't wish to be in-laws with people like me. Do you understand?"

I didn't answer, even though conventions of class and status were ubiquitous in America too. Ultimately, Imo's secret wasn't mine to tell, but I questioned how many of each woman's assumptions about the other were correct. Did Imo really look down on Emma to that extent? And would Emma really have reacted poorly if Imo had confided in her about the rapes? Though I considered both of them my friends now, I knew only the present versions of them, and too briefly to discern the truth from their respective interpretations.

"Everyone says that a tree with bad roots cannot bear good fruit," Emma continued. "The pastor's wife was a mother, and she did what she thought was best for her son. I understand her decision, but in turn I made my own. I don't want a friend who does not consider me an equal, because that kind of relationship will always have teeth."

"Oh, Emma," I said. "I can't say how Imo felt in the past, but from what little she told me, she loved Yun-Hee and regretted what happened—immensely. She said she would have agreed to the marriage if she had known what the labor draft really entailed. I don't know if she ever told you that, but I do think it's something you should know."

Emma fingered the buttons on her uniform, undoing and refastening them when she realized that they were crooked. "Well, it doesn't matter now. My daughter is gone, and the pastor's wife is dead. And that bowl is useless." She tucked her hair beneath her hat and turned away, deliberately hiding her face from me. "Get dressed. Jae-Min is coming soon."

I set the bowl down, wishing that I had tried to compel the two of them to talk while Imo was alive. This grudge was not mine to resolve, but I was dismayed by how much had been lost in the fissure between them.

I changed into my uniform, the collar scratchy against my neck. The material was thin for winter wear, but Emma had lined each pant leg with a full-length skirt, sewn loosely so we could rip it out if we had to blend in as civilians again.

"Do I look like a man?" Emma asked, rubbing her nose. "Best if no one knows we are women. Perverts are everywhere."

"Good enough," I said. "Jae-Min said we'd be alone with the cargo, and hopefully no one will pry."

As I twisted my hair up to hide it, Emma tore a page from one of Yun-Hee's notebooks and began writing with slow, careful strokes. Her characters were so neat that they could have been printed on a press.

"I already left a letter for Yun-Hee with Granny Cho," Emma said, "but I should put another one on my door just in case."

"Still?" I asked, brushing my hair from my forehead.

If Yun-Hee was alive and abroad, she wasn't going to come to Korea with the war ongoing. If she was already on the peninsula, it was unlikely that she'd venture to Pyongyang, so freshly and brutally bombed.

"Emma," I said, "the bombers are coming back, and with the city center gone, they're going to start hitting the outskirts. I think you should leave your house with the understanding that you might never see it again—not because you won't return here, but because it won't be standing when you do."

Smiling, Emma signed the note. "I will not surrender any earlier than I have to. So long as I am alive, I will never give up." After blowing on the ink, she went outside to tack the message onto her door.

While she was distracted, I snatched up Imo's peony bowl, relief flooding through me. Swiftly, I cocooned the porcelain within my lightest bag, cushioning it between Yun-Hee's hanboks and Emma's stockings. Love, as heavy as it was, existed in illogical and fragile places; and war, as brutal as it was, required more than food and shelter for survival.

Jae-Min took Emma and me to a loading zone disguised between mounds of dirt, where vehicles were covered with burlap that had been painted to resemble foliage. Along the road, decoy targets, such as fake tunnel openings and broken radio towers, were stocked with antiaircraft artillery. North Koreans were shooting down American planes, and getting better at it each day. Communist militaries were innovating and adapting to this war, but the civilians couldn't do the same. Since the last bombing, another wave of refugees was fleeing the capital, many of whom had been displaced multiple times. Everyone was thinner, dirtier, shuffling to towns where ration stations were rumored to be in operation.

We passed a young couple who were shouting at each other by an oil drum because they had found a small boy shivering inside it. The man wanted to take the boy with them, but the woman wanted to survive. She told the man that he had no idea how much work it took to care for children, and they barely had enough food as it was.

"Oh, what a shame," said Emma, as Jae-Min approached an open-bodied cargo truck with only planks of wood for the sides. "Jae-Min-ah, can we take him? Maybe he can join the army?" She grabbed Jae-Min's arm hopefully, as though becoming a child soldier was a lucky outcome.

"I'm not even supposed to be taking the two of you," said Jae-Min, refusing to look back. "And he's too little to be useful. At that age, they are better off dying with their parents." He heaved Emma's bags into the back of the truck. Other soldiers were loading the convoy, and Emma and I let our uniforms speak for themselves. No one stopped us from climbing in and huddling between a set of smoke generators.

Jae-Min gave us a blanket. "I've been thinking more about who my parents know in Seoul. I bet my father would turn first to Han Tae-Won. Did he say anything to you about him?"

"He mentioned a few names," Emma bluffed, pulling the blanket over our laps. "That one does sound familiar. He's a devout Christian, right?"

"Oh yes," confirmed Jae-Min, even though almost everyone in Pastor Pak's circle was Christian and this detail didn't narrow anything down. "Uncle Han moved to Seoul because he got a job at the Christian college."

"We'll go to the college, then," said Emma. "If your uncle Han lived there before the war, he should be well set up. That'll be good for your mother. It'll be easier for her to adjust if she's in a nice house." She smiled and patted Jae-Min's cheek, so convincingly that it set me on edge. I wasn't sure how much of Emma's apparent optimism was skillful acting or delusion. Propagandists say that if you repeat a lie often enough it becomes the truth, and this mentality applied to heartache too.

I shoved my hands into my pockets, poking the bump where the safe-conduct pass was hidden. So many people were gone, and though I remembered faces, holding on to names was like clutching an armful of wineglasses. When they slipped and shattered, I couldn't piece them back together. No matter how hard I tried, I couldn't recall the name of that Chinese driver whom I had promised to name my firstborn son after, but I never forgot his voice, singing folk songs as we drove through the night.

Ahead of us, engines rumbled.

The convoy left in clusters, olive beads rolling across a scorched land. Our cargo truck was paired with a Soviet jeep merging onto the road to match pace with the foot soldiers who walked with the refugees. Even after so much destruction, the Communist army didn't seem diminished. In addition to the forced recruits, there were volunteers who had nothing to lose and no one to live for, no other source of food and no other outlet for their anger. Trying to eliminate the KPA by mass bombing was like trying to kill a tiger by setting the entire forest on fire. Perhaps America could win this war by making North Korea utterly unlivable, but when the plumes from our bombs obscured the sky, Kim the Sun began to shine brighter.

I kept my scarf over my mouth as we jostled over potholes, following the railroad. What disgusted me most was the existence of leaders, on either side, who preferred to reign over ash rather than allow the other side to declare victory.

Occasionally, we caught up to refugees who had passed us earlier, during loading. As people scattered, I recognized the couple we had seen by the oil drum. The man was hunched forward, with the boy's little arms knotted around his neck. The woman had unbuttoned her coat and was chastising them loudly.

Emma leaned over and chortled. "She says that her husband is carrying the boy wrong, and that he might drop him. She says he'd better let her carry him, because she will do a better job."

The woman reached for the boy, swung him onto her hip, and pulled him up so he could rest his head against her chest. After tucking his skinny legs into her coat, she rebuttoned it over him, enveloping him in a cocoon of warmth.

"Victory and peace in Korea [cannot] be achieved unless the population of Korea is convinced that we do not come merely to bring devastation, unless these simple, primitive and sometimes barbaric peoples are convinced that we—not the Communists—are their friends and offer the hope of a better life."

—Hanson W. Baldwin, *The New York Times,*
August 21, 1950

"The Chinese and Korean comrades should unite as closely as brothers, go through thick and thin together, stick together in life and death and fight to the end to defeat their common enemy. The Chinese comrades must consider Korea's cause as their own."

—Mao Ze-Dong, Directive to the Chinese
People's Volunteers, January 19, 1951

35

SPARE CHANGE

January 18–21, 1951

We drove at night to avoid air strikes. Jae-Min shared his meals with us, mostly pickled turnips, soybeans, and pre-cooked potatoes, and after three days of travel we stopped at a partially bombed train tunnel, eager to rest behind its walls. The soldiers jumped out, joking with one another as they carried their bedding and canteens. Emma and I took our stockpot and followed them, but suddenly Jae-Min stopped short.

"Don't look," he said. "Go back."

Another soldier dropped his canteen, which banged resonantly against the rail.

A dark mound was blocking the tracks.

Though Emma backed away, I kept walking. At this point, there was nothing that Jae-Min had seen that I hadn't, and I was still a correspondent. Amid the uncertainty and propaganda in this war, my best source of news was my own eyes, and refusing to look was akin to lying to myself. Tuning out Jae-Min's protests, I pushed past the soldiers and stepped into the shadowy entrance.

Cold smothered rot, but the metallic scent of blood lingered in this cramped space. Amid the tangle of overlapping limbs, wrists bound with communication wire poked out from South Korean uniforms. There were Americans and others from the UN Command, but it would be hard to identify anyone, because most of them had been shot in the head.

I was numb to many things, but I still found myself trying to guess the age of every corpse that I saw. It wasn't that the death of the elderly was irrelevant, but the murder of a young person wasn't just a theft of a life—it was a theft of a lifetime. Sound echoed against the tunnel walls, amplifying each drop of water from the icicles overhead and the crunch of gravel as I pivoted on my heels.

Exhaling, I shut my eyes and took myself back to my arrival at Tachikawa and my first set of interviews there. Barbara had invited me to a barbecue, and I had gotten a glass of lemonade before whipping out my notebook to get a sense of who these American soldiers were. There had been a boy from Oklahoma who was barely sixteen, dapper in his fatigues. Proudly, he had told me that he had forged his parents' signatures so he could enlist when he was fifteen. He had been eager to join because his best friend, a seventeen-year-old who used to work on the same farm as he did, had been making seventy-five dollars a month in the military. It had sounded like a good deal and a fair gamble.

Many of the boys I had interviewed weren't in Korea for the money, though. If asked, they often replied that they were here to protect their country, here to protect freedom—here to stop Communism and help a people whom they had never met, in a land that they didn't know.

I looked at Emma and Jae-Min through the tunnel. They stared as though I might faint, but I summoned my resolve and mimed a necklace on my chest.

Dog tags.

For their parents. If I could get back to UN territory, I could send these tags to their rightful place, where they might bring closure—answers for families who might otherwise continue waiting and wondering. There was a point at which hope could be as toxic as a narcotic.

I returned to the pile of bodies, and prodded at necks until I found the slim chains holding tags. Earlier, I would have been afraid to show sympathy for the "other side," but now I understood the KPA soldiers better. Like us, they were human, and like ours, they were mostly boys. They feared death, as our own troops did, and oblivion, as anyone would.

Jae-Min and a few others came to help me, kneeling next to their enemies to unsnap their chains. With several hands working, I collected all of the tags, and they clinked like spare change in my pockets. Emma made no comment when we finally returned to the truck, but she used her own handkerchief to wipe the dried blood from my fingers.

After leaving the tunnel, the soldiers drove faster than we ever had, as if tailed by a curse. Closer to the South, there were more terraced rice paddies, marred by the steps of men who had climbed to peer across at their former compatriots on the other side. It was too dark for me to see any signs demarcating the 38th parallel, the infamous, contentious border between the two Koreas. For all the fanfare, I had expected there to be some kind of gravitas when we crossed that line, but I was unaware that we were in South Korea until we arrived at a brick building capped by a green dome and a monumental spire—the Kaesong train station.

Kaesong was a South Korean city, but it had been captured by the Communists and held since December. It hadn't been bombed as badly as the North Korean cities, but now it was akin to a refugee camp, with tents sprawled around the train station and refuse covering its streets.

"This used to be the capital of the Goryeo Kingdom," said Emma, reverently, at the remnants of a palace complex.

Despite the unsanitary conditions, I marveled at the pagodas that still loomed, lovely. Their sweeping eaves and latticed windows were far more fragile than concrete buildings, and yet they remained—a tenuous thread to the past and a reminder of who the people in Korea once were, before colonization and before the bombs.

With all the Communist officers in uniform, it was hard for me to believe that we were truly past the 38th parallel, but there was a subtle yet unmistakable optimism here. Civilians hoping to flee the North and soldiers withdrawing after fighting in the South converged at this hallowed junction, and I felt that clarion thrum—a jump start of my beleaguered confidence that brought my hope to bud.

I wasn't home yet, but at least I was finally on the right side of the peninsula. Here, I could see the light at the end of the tunnel, and the dawn that Miho was so sure would come.

While Jae-Min and his comrades prepared for the next portion of our journey, Emma took me to the Confucian Academy, which now functioned as a medical facility. So far, no one had questioned us, but we still maintained the pretense that we were repairing and delivering uniforms.

I thought back to the press briefing that I had been rejected from. It was so much easier to access these spaces as a woman who sews than as a woman who writes. A needle mends, while a pen exposes, and the mere existence of a woman who wields the latter is a threat. I used to worry about being discovered whenever Communist soldiers were around, but that fear had subsided slightly. Like a wolf in sheep's clothing, I was hiding but I wasn't necessarily prey. Did crossing that artificial line do that much for my self-esteem? There was still a risk that I'd be arrested or killed because of my nationality, yet I couldn't help feeling like I had become dangerous—stronger—simply by virtue of surviving.

The North Korean flag flapped over a fortress that had been converted into a mixed North Korean and Chinese garrison, and patients waited in the small courtyard behind it. As I handed new uniforms to the nurses, Emma offered to patch up soldiers' clothing. She too seemed energized by the buoyancy of this city, and said, "The more I think about it, the more it makes sense that Yun-Hee is in the South. If she wasn't able to cross the border, then maybe she settled here. Kaesong was probably as close to home as she could get, don't you think?"

"Maybe," I said, "but we don't have much time here to look for her. Jae-Min said we're leaving in the morning, remember?"

"That's enough for me to at least try."

Outside of the clinic, nurses were burning medical waste. After handing me a half-finished project, Emma went to greet each woman, bowing and repeating her standard lines. "Have you seen a girl named Song Yun-Hee?" she asked. "Her Japanese name is Machiko. She is one hundred sixty centimeters tall and has eyes like mine. She was born in the year of the horse and is from Pyongyang. There's a birthmark on her collarbone, shaped like a gourd."

The description, even with these details, was too vague.

"I should have had Yun-Hee sit for a picture," said Emma after all the nurses shook their heads. "But there were so many other costs—school supplies, uniforms—and many pebbles make a landslide. Sometimes I regret sending her to school. It was expensive, and if I hadn't registered her, the authorities wouldn't have known her age. They might not have even known she existed."

When Emma moved on to questioning refugees, I hurried to sew up the project she had given me, a pair of pants with torn knees. My work was inelegant, but my stitches would hold. By the time I finished the pants, Emma had disappeared behind the refugees' laundry lines.

Annoyed, I went around to the academy's garden, where a cluster of Chinese soldiers sat on a stone wall. Several of them had crudely stitched lacerations, and one was missing an arm. They shared a single cigarette, passing it back and forth. I was supposed to be sewing, but if Emma was conducting an investigation, why should I waste time doing something that I wasn't even good at?

Pinning my needle into my front pocket, I went to the soldiers. "Excuse me," I said. "I'm looking for a Korean woman named Song Yun-Hee. Have any of you met her?"

A Chinese soldier with a swollen leg smirked. "A Korean woman? In Korea?" He poked the man beside him. "Ah-Huang, have you seen a Korean woman anywhere around here?"

They laughed, and I regretted asking such an absurd question. Chinese soldiers probably didn't speak much to civilians, given the language barrier. "Never mind," I huffed.

"Wait," said the man whose arm had been amputated. "What was her name, again?" He took his turn with the cigarette, inhaling so deeply that the soldier after him protested and yanked it from his mouth.

"Song Yun-Hee," I repeated. "She's twenty years old, and a bit taller than me."

"Ah, doesn't sound familiar at all," said the man with one arm. "But we can barely keep track of our own comrades, let alone Koreans we don't know."

Swollen Leg reached for the cigarette. "Our division was ordered to charge across the Imjin River, but no one told us that the banks were packed with land mines. Those of us here in Kaesong got hit before making it across. Anyone who got hurt on the other bank will probably be in Seoul. That probably applies to civilians too. If you don't find your friend here, try the South."

"Thanks," I said, though this advice wasn't helpful at all. "I guess she could be anywhere, really."

"Yes," answered Swollen Leg, coughing and fanning the smoke from his face. "Including the heavenly palace."

The one beside him, Ah-Huang, slapped him in the stomach reproachfully.

"Sorry." Swollen Leg shrugged. "But it's the truth." Their cigarette had burned to the butt, but the soldiers passed it around one last time, sucking out every bit of nicotine.

I left them, offended by the suggestion that Yun-Hee was dead, even if that was the most likely outcome. Sniffing indignantly, I went to ask another group of soldiers about Yun-Hee, and then another. By the time I found Emma again, I was grouchy, but she had only become more cheerful. It was like she had morphed into Miho.

"Hello, hello!" said Emma. "Did you fix more uniforms? Or meet anyone handsome?"

I rolled my eyes. Only Emma could think of matchmaking in a place like this. "I didn't do much. Did you find anything out about Yun-Hee?"

"Nope, but I've got a feeling that I'm getting closer."

"How?"

"Because of what you said, Eun-Ha. If Yun-Hee was anywhere in the North, she would have come home already, so she *must* be in the South. And if I keep talking to people here, eventually I'm going to come across her trail. I know it!"

I didn't have the energy to contradict her or try to temper her enthusiasm. After all, I too had wasted my time butting at that dead end. Why did I even ask those soldiers about Yun-Hee? I used to cringe when Emma spoke of her daughter like she was still alive, but now I was also getting upset when anyone else implied otherwise. Certainly the strain of leaving Pyongyang again was affecting Emma, and maybe her newfound zeal was a manifestation of that—but I had to remain realistic, for both of us.

The next morning, Emma and I snuck back onto our truck. This time, the convoy we traveled with was larger, with valuable enough supplies—anti-tank mines, field telephones, switchboards, and radio receivers—that it departed with a fighter-jet escort.

The highway between Kaesong and Seoul was badly torched, and UN troops had burned the nearby airfields. Warped vehicles cluttered the road, and sabotaged tanks lay tilted in ditches.

Emma elbowed me when we passed some soldiers who were scavenging for parts. "Maybe Jae-Min can introduce you to some of his friends in the engineering battalion," she said. "They might be a little young for you, but no man needs to know your real age. I think you could pass for twenty—still on the older side, but not so bad."

"Oh heavens, Emma," I said. "I'm not here to find a husband. Can you give it a rest?"

Emma let out a throaty cackle. "You don't have to find him. Maybe he will find you."

Jae-Min swiveled around. "Can you two be quiet?" he hissed, pointing to the jet above us. Its metal belly gleamed. "Everything can change in a second. If the wrong truck gets hit, our entire convoy will go up in flames. The highway to Seoul is more dangerous than any road we've traveled on before, you know."

He gave us a condescending glare before whirling forward again, which sent goose bumps prickling along my arms. For a moment, Imo was *there*, like a bulb behind a lampshade—invisible until it flickered on.

When we reached the Imjin River, soldiers disembarked to carry supplies on foot, for the ice wasn't strong enough to hold the trucks. The broad riverbank was mostly gray, and mottled with copper dents—frozen remnants of the bloodshed that had opened New Year's Day. Most of the carnage had been removed or covered by the subsequent blizzard, but in patches where the snow had recently thawed, stiff hands reached for the sky.

"There might be uncleared land mines," warned Jae-Min. "Stay within the markers."

This ground was too solid to bury bodies, but military engineers had managed to rig explosives underneath it. It was easier to slip a mine into the soil than an entire human, but this dissonance sickened me. The war machine was voracious, overwhelming and insatiable.

We trod single file on a narrow path demarcated by rocks and logs. Sweat poured from my hairline as we stepped onto the ice, which was streaked with the same rusty blood as the bank. Snow had fallen since the battle, but no force of nature could cast a clean slate over this much misery.

My feet slid precariously. Though my ears perked for any whisper of cracking, the soldiers did not seem apprehensive. Many of them made this crossing multiple times a day, forming a human supply line that trundled over rough terrain. At the opposite shore, another set of rocks indicated safety.

I relaxed, but did not breathe more easily until we'd hiked up to the highway, where roofing nails poked out from the snow. UN troops had scattered the nails to puncture the tires of advancing Communist vehicles, and though most had been picked clean, the storm had washed some as far as the riverbed. The Americans had bombed the South too, leaving snowy open spaces where KPA rail depots had been. Subsequent battles had raged, so storefronts were riddled with bullet holes and rockets had blasted through factories. Tank treads had torn up the streets, while grenades had blasted homes. Around the hills, homeless civilians had erected tents, creating clustered shantytowns that swayed with the wind.

Seoul snuck up on us.

In the midst of this devastation, I realized that we were in the capital only when we reached the Northwestern Gate, a stone arch wedged into the old city wall. The gate's colorful pagoda had red columns and ceramic tiles, and a wooden chicken was perched in the rafters—supposedly to ward off evil. Above the arch, portraits of Mao, Stalin, and Kim now hung in ostentatious frames. Beyond, the streets were completely deserted, though it was the middle of the day.

If I hadn't stood here for a photograph before, I might have believed this was a different city. Seoul used to be a center for art, where people made movies and went to the theater, held concerts and visited museums. Back in October, cars were still running here. Children scampered through alleys while their parents frequented the remaining shops. Families waved American flags outside Seoul National University, which had served as the headquarters for the US Army, where soldiers distributed powdered eggs and milk.

"I always wanted to go to Seoul," Emma said, pensive as we passed dilapidated stalls, "but I never thought it would be like this."

It was as though both sides had despised this city. The UN troops had strategically burned their supplies, leaving charred, unrecognizable piles of garbage and sandbag barricades everywhere. Communist soldiers had taken over the government offices, and—possibly out of spite—had torched the capitol building and converted it into stables full of manure.

"I heard that everyone left with the Americans," said Jae-Min, our footsteps audible on the granite street, "even though it was the middle of winter and they had to walk to Busan."

"There must be some people here still," said Emma, peering through the broken windows. "Busan is so terribly far."

"It's about the same distance from here as Kanggye is to Pyongyang," Jae-Min pointed out.

"Yes," said Emma. "That was terribly far! I wouldn't be able to do it again. Once was more than enough!"

I was exhausted too, but I hoped that Emma wasn't serious. She and I were supposed to go to Busan, and the sooner the better.

"I did a few interviews in Seoul after the UN Command recaptured it," I said as a rat scampered out from under ruined brickwork. "Everyone I spoke with said that they were terrified of being arrested by the Communists. People would disappear without warning, and it wasn't even clear why."

Jae-Min scrunched his forehead. "Maybe my parents didn't end up staying with my uncle Han after all. The Communists would never have allowed a Christian college to keep operating."

"Do you know where the college is?" asked Emma.

"No," Jae-Min replied. "I've been to Seoul a few times, but I don't remember the streets."

"Well, perhaps we can find a map," said Emma, brightening. "There might be neighbors who have seen your parents."

I cleared my throat and tried to catch Emma's eye, but she refused to look at me. Lying to Jae-Min about his parents was bad enough. Sending him on a wild-goose chase was just cruel.

"Your parents are probably in Busan or Japan," I piped up. "I wouldn't bother going to the college now. If I were you, I'd just head to Japan."

"I might as well check, since we're here," said Jae-Min.

"I will check for you," offered Emma. "You are busy. Once Eun-Ha and I rest a bit, I will start asking for your parents, maybe at the field hospitals."

"No, you should be careful," Jae-Min protested.

"I will be asking about my daughter anyway. The more I think about it, the more certain I am that Yun-Hee got stuck in the South. She probably settled in Seoul. It's the biggest city, after all! This is my chance to find her. I might as well ask about your parents too, while I'm looking."

"Wait! No!" I said, unprepared for how quickly a lie and a side quest had obscured our main objectives. "Seoul isn't our destination, remember? We don't have to go all the way to Busan, but we have to get to UN territory. The Bomber Command might still hit here. Everyone else in Seoul was smart enough to leave. We can't be foolish enough to stay!"

"I am a member of the army now," said Jae-Min. "The only duty that can surpass my obligation to the army is the one that I owe to my parents. I will not leave Seoul until I am sure they are not waiting here."

Emma nodded emphatically. "I came south to survive, but my life is built around another. I will not leave Seoul until I am done searching for Yun-Hee."

I groaned, but quickly clamped my mouth shut.

Emma clung to her home, yet upon arriving in a new place she convinced herself that it made complete sense for her daughter to have been there all along. *Kanggye is close to the border; Yun-Hee must have settled there from China! Kaesong is close to the border; Yun-Hee must have settled there from the South!* It was becoming infuriating. Unlike Emma, I didn't have this endless vigor for Yun-Hee, nor did I want to scour Seoul for ghosts. I just wanted to go home, but everything we did in life was for the heart, and I had hitched mine to Jae-Min's and Emma's ill-fated ones.

At the next corner, a man with one leg leaned on an empty *jige*, the first person we had seen in civilian clothing inside the city wall. He glowered at us before disappearing into the cramped space between two houses, his *jige* clunking.

Emma rushed after him and wiggled, as slick as a minnow, into the alley. I heard her call excitedly, "Hey! Hey, sir! Have you met a girl named Song Yun-Hee? Her Japanese name is Machiko and she is one hundred sixty centimeters tall . . . eyes like mine . . . She is my daughter, born in the year of the horse!"

36

GHOST HUNT

January 21–31, 1951

The KPA's engineering battalion operated out of a movie theater, but Jae-Min spent most days camped along the Han River, beside the bridge that he was repairing. Emma and I had expected Seoul to have public shelters and ration stations, but there were no government-run facilities or services, no rule of law or public order. There weren't even Party meetings anymore. Many of the homes had been looted, and the remaining civilians kept themselves hidden. The Communist officers were confiscating food and valuables for the war effort, and no one had anything left to spare. Occasionally, women slunk to open manhole covers and collected water with gourds dangled down from ropes.

None of them had met a girl from Pyongyang in her twenties named Song Yun-Hee.

Refugees squatted around the former shopping district, most of which had been demolished, but cramped commercial spaces remained in the surrounding alleys. At the end of one block, there was an abandoned haberdashery, its moniker in Chinese swinging overhead. The door was broken and the windows were boarded up, but it was in better condition than most of the other stores. Aside from a stack of magazines on the counter, and a hat rack, everything, including the stove, had been packed away or stolen. There was a cramped storage room, in which Emma and I finally laid down our belongings and donned civilian wear once again.

I didn't intend to stay in Seoul for long, regardless of Emma's or Jae-Min's plans. Even as I wiped the floors and laid out our mats, I plotted paths to Busan like a chess player strategizing against a stronger opponent. Though I was outmatched, I had to find a ride, or a map so I could start walking. While Emma renewed her search for Yun-Hee, I looked for soldiers heading to the front lines. There weren't many Chinese speakers, however, and the few I met had all been assigned to stay in Seoul.

Jae-Min visited us every other day, usually with coal and occasionally with soybeans or corn. About a week after our arrival, he came, seeming shaken, with a handful of nails pilfered from his unit.

"My bridge is gone," he said. "My work was for nothing. It has all been for nothing."

"What do you mean?" I asked, holding the nails while he examined our broken door.

"The UN Command has begun a counteroffensive," Jae-Min replied. "You might not have to go to Busan after all. For all we know, the Americans will be here next week and you can just open your broken door to meet them." He sounded just like his father had in Kanggye.

Apparently, the Americans were pushing north again, and clashing with a concentration of Chinese troops merely fifty miles away.

Once again, the tide was turning.

Once again, there was going to be a battle for Seoul.

Once again, engineers who had rushed to repair bridges were ordered to detonate them. Jae-Min's unit was now charged with laying land mines in the opposite bank of the Han River, and all he had left of his bridge was the fistful of nails that I cupped in my hand.

Over the next days, Communist soldiers began staggering into Seoul with their wounded comrades on their backs. They left bloody footprints in the streets, and the city without chatter became the city of wails as Chinese ambulances barreled past us. Their patients moaned, reluctant to leave this hideous world, even for the promise of the heavenly palace.

"Mom!" they called.

"Mom," I heard.

Mom. It echoed.

Did these mothers know what was happening to their children? Were there women who could feel when a life that they had brought into this world was forced to leave it?

In Seoul, I needed a battle. I needed the UN Command to return so I wouldn't have to go to Busan, but it was hard to rejoice in a rising tide when it was going to crash down on us all, sweeping away any life left in this city.

Tsunami.

Emma and I brought our remaining uniforms to the medical stations, where we received soap and biscuits from intercepted American rations. We visited often enough that the health care workers recognized us and promised to watch out for a Song Yun-Hee. To my relief, Emma never actually asked about either of the Paks, but she always assured Jae-Min that she did.

Did the families of the disappeared ever accept that they

could rest? I used to assume that after a certain number of people asked, places visited, and years passed, the families had to let go, but after meeting Emma I understood that some people could never give themselves permission to move on. We needed to tell Jae-Min the truth about his parents, but I wasn't sure when.

In Japan, I promised myself. *Once we're in Japan, I'll do it.*

On the last day of the month, Emma and I headed to the only hospital that was still in operation, where she spoke with the Korean administrators and I checked in with the Chinese medical staff. There were two Chinese physicians and a veterinarian, with assistants who had trained on the go. The vet treated dysentery and parasitic infections, which had mushroomed when the sanitation structure collapsed, but he also delivered babies. It had been several days since the vet had changed his shirt, and the splotches of blood and bile on it were as distinct as a human face.

"No Song Yun-Hee!" he said when he saw me, "but a little girl was born yesterday. The father offered to let me name her, and I don't know many Korean names, so I said, 'How about Yun-Hee?' They loved it, so now there is a baby Yun-Hee in this neighborhood!"

"That's nice," I said, handing him a set of new uniforms. I didn't begrudge the vet the satisfaction of a birth amid so much death, but I struggled to stave off my own pessimism when I wondered what kind of country these children were going to inherit—what kind of world all of our children were going to inherit. The staff here were using mattress covers as shrouds, and running low on those too.

In the stairwell, a skinny girl, perhaps ten years old, clomped loudly down in leather boots too large for her. Her winter jacket was moth-eaten and her pants threadbare.

I frowned, because these boots, though scuffed, were of

exceptionally high quality, and looked remarkably like the ones that I used to have. "Stop, please," I said to the girl in Korean, and crouched down.

She obeyed, but shifted uncomfortably when I touched the familiar laces. "These are mine," she whined, then pointed at the vet. "He gave them to me."

"No worry," I said, in broken Korean. "I take from you no. Where you get shoes?"

The girl leaned away.

Chuckling, the vet patted her back. "It's all right. Go find your mom." He nudged her toward the room where the female patients recovered. She clunked away in a hurry, glancing over her shoulder as though she was afraid that I might chase her.

Turning to me again, the vet said, "I took them off a boy yesterday. His brother had carried him in, but he was already dead when he got here. Probably dead for several hours, but his brother wouldn't let him go. Went into a frenzy when we took the boots."

The blood drained from my face, and I swayed on my feet. "What was the boy's name?" I asked. "The boy who was wearing those boots?"

"Oh, I don't know," said the vet. "There have been so many boys, but his brother is still upstairs, if you want to ask him. He's in bad condition, but not so bad that he can't talk, or fight. Once he gets a bit of rest, he's going back south, though, so you—"

"Which room?"

"First one on the right. Why? Do you know him?"

"I'll be back!" I cried, whirling on my heels and leaving the vet dumbfounded.

I dashed up the stairs, racking my brain for memories that were as scattered and infinitesimal as crumbs. *Think.* I pushed myself, shushing the bombs that blared on, at full blast, whenever

I recalled Pyongyang. A single name floated to the front of my mind, like driftwood that had snapped off of a sunken ship, rising out of the abyss to take form on my tongue: Ying.

Comrade Ying! Yes, that was it! Could he really be here, in Seoul?

Two soldiers carrying an empty stretcher bumped into me. It was grimy upstairs, with a rankness that I had grown accustomed to. Aside from the burning of flesh, I no longer noticed bodily odors. The groans of the wounded rumbled through the walls as I trudged into the room on the right, which was full of bamboo mats.

About twenty men were crowded together, their skin flecked from so many cuts that they looked like they had measles. Most of them wore Chinese quilted uniforms stained reddish brown like the snow along the Imjin. Soldiers coming back from Wonju had warned us about a new type of bomb that burst in the air, showering everyone with steel fragments. There were too many swollen lips and eyes for me to identify anyone on sight alone, so I yelled out his name. "Comrade Ying!"

Every head turned toward me.

Was it wrong for me to want him to live when his sole purpose in Korea was to kill my countrymen? I had raced up here so desperately, for the mere chance of catching him in the flesh. Perhaps it was because I was grateful that he had helped me, despite suspecting that I was hiding something. Or perhaps it was because in the entire duration of this war, he had been the only one to say *You're one of us*, when "us" had always been such an elusive term for me.

A soldier in the center of the second row winced and pushed himself up. His jacket was badly soiled, the batting seeping out from every small tatter. He was missing an ear and part of his cheek, and bandages held the rest of his shrapnel-studded face together. Even his hands had been sliced, scabs forming in lines like tigers' stripes.

"You again," he said hoarsely, as his eyes struggled to focus. "What are you doing here?"

I stepped into the sliver of walking space between the patients, careful not to trip on anyone's limbs. "So you remember me."

"There aren't that many Chinese girls wandering around in Korea," he said. "Did you find your fiancé?"

"I'm still looking," I lied, "but I came here because . . ."

What was the right excuse now? I struggled to recall what I had told him before. The other soldiers were still staring, but their attention didn't scare me anymore. Grief itself is a wound, and it had scarred so many faces, lodging in the wells of their eyes.

"Aiyo," said Comrade Ying, growing impatient. "You're here to get your boots back, aren't you? My brother always felt bad that I made you give them to us. He probably would have wanted you to have them, but someone else has already claimed them. Sorry."

Comrade Ying glowered, as though he had figured out my scheme, without realizing that he had squeezed my heart. My chest throbbed with a suffocating kind of pain that radiated through my body like a well-placed punch, but it also reminded me that I was still alive, still human.

"I'm sorry about your brother," I said, trying to visualize the younger brother's face, yet only recalling his swollen feet. "But I'm not here to take anything from you. I'm here because I have something that belongs to you." Digging into my pocket, I poked at the lining until I pinched the safe-conduct pass.

Perhaps it was because of hubris, perhaps it was because of hope, but I maintained that none of us could know the outcome of our lives. Maybe it was true that Comrade Ying would never return to China, but even such a destiny had a myriad of pathways. If fate was a thread, then I wanted to pull it loose, so I unfolded the pass, the creases still crisp. "Take it."

Comrade Ying strained to read the Chinese characters, while soldiers nearby leaned over to look. As soon as Comrade Ying realized what I had given him, he crumpled it in his fist.

A soldier beside him, similarly pockmarked with wounds, asked, "What is it?"

"Nothing," Comrade Ying replied. "Women's matters." He clamped his other hand over his closed fingers, as if the paper could fight to unfurl.

"Don't be stingy," said the soldier. "Show us!"

"It's private," I said, stepping back to the door.

I was about to leave, but Comrade Ying said, "Did I ever tell you where I am from, or why I am here, in Korea?"

I halted, as the soldiers watched us intently. "No, you didn't."

"I am a Southerner," Comrade Ying said, with the same pride that Pastor Pak had when speaking of the North. "I was born and raised in Nanjing."

Nanjing, the former capital of a unified China, should not have been famous for the mass rape of its women by Japanese soldiers, but in the aftermath of World War II that stigma was difficult to shake. "I see" was all I could say.

"I never planned to join the army," Comrade Ying continued. "I was supposed to be a teacher, like my father, but then the Japanese invaded our city. My brother and I were home with our mother when the soldiers came to our neighborhood. Surely, I don't need to tell you what happened to her. All you need to know is that I was there, and I couldn't stop them. The soldiers broke her neck, but even then they did not leave her alone. I was eight, and my brother was five."

Other men murmured, a few saying that they had heard similar stories—that they had enlisted after similar stories.

I thought of Emma, and the "comfort" stations, which had expanded rapidly after Nanjing made international headlines. The Japanese commanders told their soldiers that they couldn't rape civilians anymore, but they could rape Emma's daughter as many times as they wanted to, however they wanted to. History was a chain, and too often it was wrapped around women's necks. In every country, there were monuments dedicated to men who waged wars. How many had anything to honor the women who suffered through them, or survived them?

"China has been weak," Comrade Ying said, "but we are learning from our failings—many lessons, but the most important is this: Imperialists will take small bites before they try to swallow you whole. Japan took Korea and Taiwan first. If they didn't have a colony in Korea, they would never have been able to invade China. What do you think will happen if America controls this land? They will keep bases here, won't they? Korea is the gateway to Manchuria, and to all of our homes. We cannot allow a hostile power to control it again. We fight now to safeguard our future, so that the children today won't suffer like we did, and the children of tomorrow can prosper."

Solemn faces beside him nodded, and I ached for each one, at a loss for words when there was such a kaleidoscope of anguish. This room was a mere sampling of the Chinese boys who had come of age witnessing invasion and atrocities. Mao had harnessed that agony in a way that Washington had yet to understand, and I wasn't sure if they ever would. We were trying to fight Mao, but he wasn't mortal anymore. He was an ideology, and he thrived, not simply on Marxism or any other type of Communism, but on the sheer trauma of colonialism.

As a woman between worlds, I wanted to tell these men so much about my experiences, yet there was so little I could share without revealing who I was. I couldn't explain that even though I didn't always believe in American leadership, I believed in democracy, so ardently that I was willing to risk my life to defend it. Especially after what I had seen in North Korea, I was certain that no person should ever be *the sun*.

"People everywhere are the same," I finally said, channeling my friend Machiko. "Regardless of their nationality, they can be kind, and they can be cruel. The world has many selfish leaders, stupid leaders, and terrifying leaders, but it is largely filled with people who want to be good. It doesn't matter where you are in this life. Just pick somewhere where you can live and do good—where your nation does not depend on the ambition and whims of a single man, where you can change your leaders when they fail you."

Even in a democracy it was hard to pry power from the fists of a privileged few, but at least there was no mandate from heaven, no unrestrained king, emperor, or führer. At least we could fight with our presses, and sow words like seeds—to grow flowers from sea to shining sea, and hope for that fragile peace to spread. The greatest protection for our children would come not from chairmen or generalissimos, but from ordinary people committed to building more bridges than bombs.

I still believe this.

I will *always* believe this.

"You are one of us," I said, "and that's all that matters."

Comrade Ying's hands tightened around the paper, pressed to his chest like a second heart, a second chance. I had no control over whether Comrade Ying would use the pass, or whether the soldiers on our side would honor it, but giving it to him felt like closing a circle, awakening a new sense of purpose for me. On this earth, we must anchor ourselves in our shared humanity, for if we don't look out for one another here, who else will?

January 31, 1951
Dear Mom and Dad,

I know the question that you all are itching to ask.

Was it worth it, coming to Korea? Do I regret covering war when so many told me not to?

While I can't say if it was worth it, or that I have no regrets, I can say, with my full heart, that I would do it all again if I had to. I see, more than ever, that the stories we tell as correspondents—and how we tell them—are affected by our experiences. Each of these stories shapes the choices that Americans make back home, and the progression of the war itself.

The most prominent military editors right now seem unable to write about Koreans without calling them barbarians, and high-ranking generals seem unable to talk about Chinese without calling them laundrymen. What might be the outcome of this war if there are more journalists, on every side, who grew up between worlds, as you raised me?

I don't know yet, but I do know that I have an obligation to tell the story that others will not, even if it is one that many do not wish to hear.

With all my love,
Ellie

37

SUNRISE

January 31–February 8, 1951

When I told Emma that I'd found Comrade Ying, she shrieked, anticipating a romantic story. Upon hearing about the safe-conduct pass, she grabbed my shoulders and shook me so hard that I almost had whiplash. "You gave him a piece of paper?" she cried. "That's it? He probably has a dozen of those tickets already!"

I rubbed my neck. "He can share it with a friend, then."

"Ah, what a waste," she sulked. "You are good at finding things, though—much better than I am."

"Oh heavens, Emma, I wasn't looking for him. And even if I was, this kind of thing depends on luck more than skill."

"Then you are luckier than me. Now that you've found your man, send your luck my way!"

Comrade Ying was certainly not my man, and his situation was entirely different from Yun-Hee's, but Emma latched onto him like he had been sent by the Lord—like he was proof that people did come back, and a sign that her daughter would too. Emma doubled her time in the clinics and knocked on doors throughout Seoul, while I began interviewing Chinese soldiers about the war. These conversations, though grueling, helped me remember who I was, and who I was still determined to be. Though the odds were low, I ended each of my own interviews with the same question: *Have you seen or met a Korean girl, one hundred sixty centimeters tall, named Song Yun-Hee, possibly going by Machiko?*

None of the soldiers had anything to say about Yun-Hee, but I learned that the Chinese forces moved at night and attacked in waves of three—the first with burp guns, the second with grenades, and the third without any arms, so they could pick up the weapons of the dead comrades before them. Their casualty rate was astronomical. And though Mao called his soldiers volunteers, many of them had been prisoners of war taken during the Communist Revolution, forced to fight in Korea or face execution.

I wrote everything down in the evenings, transferring pain to paper, injustice to ink, filling Yun-Hee's old notebook with my own observations. These were not the kind of stories that I could harbor without losing my mind, but the goal of sharing them—of setting them free—kept me afloat while I waited for the change that everyone knew was coming.

One afternoon, Chinese artillerymen told me the UN troops had recaptured Suwon Airfield, only twenty miles from Seoul. Morale was low in the hospital, but in Emma's alleys, where civilians hid, a cautious excitement simmered.

At night, flares ignited and streaked across the Han River, followed by rounds of shelling.

When I was a child, I read that lightning always came before thunder, and one could estimate a storm's distance by counting the seconds between the flash and the rumble. I knew that didn't apply here, but Suwon was my sunrise. Thousands of tons of supplies were landing in that airfield, which meant that medical evacuations were going out—and flight nurses were touching down.

Flight nurses. Several of them knew me, and many more knew of me. It was surreal to think that Barbara and my other friends might be less than a marathon away. If I could get to Suwon, then I could get back to Japan, but the way there was paved with explosives, and men who gunned down anything that moved. I wasn't ready to take that risk, but I stowed this backup plan, and it emboldened me to optimism. The Americans were advancing, and if we stayed put and held on, they would come to us.

Seoul, however, was essentially under siege. Supplies barely trickled in from the North, even as engineers scrambled to repair the roads. Hunger had become famine. Emma and I had exhausted our provisions from Pyongyang, and we subsisted off what Jae-Min smuggled to us, which was paltry. Communist soldiers were wary about intercepting American airdrops after encountering booby-trapped packages rigged to explode regardless of who opened them—military or civilian, adult or child. We ate bark chipped off of trees, and whatever grass we could find, but there were also rumors that people were eating the dead.

That would be my red line. When I was desperate enough to consider cannibalism, then it was time to steal a helmet and run to Suwon, mines and bullets be damned.

On February 6, Lunar New Year passed without a single cheer. There were no firecrackers, and even if they had been available, everyone would have been too scarred by war to revel in anything that sounded like gunfire. Emma and I had stopped washing our clothes, because there was barely enough water to drink. We only changed our socks and stockings and hung the dirty pairs in the sun. It didn't matter that they stank; as long as they were dry, we wore them. Jae-Min's visits had become less frequent, but when he showed up at the haberdashery, Emma and I scrambled eagerly to meet him. He was our lottery ticket for food, and it had been a while since we had won.

Now, however, he slumped against the wall, holding out his empty hands like we were hungry dogs who had to sniff them. "I've been transferred," Jae-Min announced, his cheeks gaunt. "The entire engineering battalion is going to Kaesong. We're moving out tomorrow, and Seoul is being evacuated in stages."

"Already?" I asked, though it seemed like ages since I'd first heard rumors about a battle. Good news almost made up for his lack of food, even if it was a double-edged sword. "Are the UN troops close, then?"

"No," Jae-Min answered, insulted by the hopefulness that I hadn't bothered to hide. "We're still fighting in Wonju, but Chinese support is wavering. Their generals are in Beijing, urging Mao to let them withdraw."

"What will happen if the Chinese leave?" asked Emma.

"Our soldiers will defend the Han River," said Jae-Min, "if only for pride's sake, but we are preparing to lose the capital. All able-bodied men aged fifteen to forty and women aged sixteen to twenty-five will come north with us."

"Sixteen to twenty-five?" I repeated. "Why twenty-five? Is that when a woman becomes too old to be useful?"

"Does it matter?" asked Emma.

I raised my chin. "On principle, yes."

She smacked the back of my head. "You don't even want to go north! No one in Seoul does. I've had many conversations with the people who were living here before the war started, and none of them want to be unified with us. They'd rather live under the imperialists than Marshal Kim!"

"They won't have a choice," said Jae-Min, coarsely. "If they fit the criteria, we're marching them north—at gunpoint if we must."

"Like prisoners of war?" I exclaimed. "People here are so weak from malnourishment. They're not going to survive a forced journey in the winter, even if they're young and fit. Do you even want to go back, Jae-Min? To Pyongyang?"

"Of course not," he said. "I have to find my parents!"

"Regardless of your parents. If it were just you, would you still go back?"

He shifted against the wall, the light through the window boards casting lines across his face. "Not anymore. Home as I knew it is gone. My university has been bombed and my family has fled. What else is there to go back to?"

"Then stay here with us," I pleaded. "That was our original plan, remember? You were supposed to leave the army once we got to Seoul. We can find a way to hide you so they can't take you back."

"We can't stay in Seoul," said Jae-Min. "The soldiers have orders to comb through the city and search for everything and everyone worth taking. Even if we manage to hide, there will be no food. The Americans won't be here anytime soon, because our soldiers will hold them off for as long as they can. We have to make it hard so the Americans will think twice about crossing into our territory again."

"You already did that at the Chosin," I said, unabashed with my bitterness.

MacArthur might have wanted a second shot at the North, but there was no way the American public would be willing to endure the cost—at least not if news of the war was making it back home.

"What do we do, then?" asked Emma, looking at Jae-Min and then at me. "You aren't going to Kaesong, are you, Jae-Min?"

"I am not," Jae-Min confirmed.

Emma and I both exhaled in relief.

"Suwon?" I asked, daring for more, daydreaming of flight nurses.

"Incheon," he answered. "It's about the same distance as Suwon, but it's under Communist control, so we won't risk crossing the battle lines.

"Seoul is important for morale," Jae-Min continued, "but it has no strategic value. The Americans will try to take Incheon first, since it's on the Yellow Sea. If we get there now, we can make it before the fighting moves westward, and be there for its . . . liberation."

I tried to rein in my expectations, which had spiked constantly with tidings from the front lines, only to free-fall after another cold, hungry day stretched into another flare-filled night. Could Incheon be my last step before I returned home, or would the Communist forces flip this war yet again?

"Do you know the way?" Emma asked.

"That's why I came to see you," said Jae-Min, putting his hands back in his pockets. "I don't know the South well, but I have a friend who does. He's planning to change into civilian clothing and leave for Incheon tonight. He invited me to go with him, but I told him that I had friends I had to bring. I told him that you two helped my parents when I couldn't be there for them, so I couldn't just leave you behind. I owe you both."

Guilt needled at me as he bowed.

"Of course we want to go," I said, trying not to blush with embarrassment. "If, as you say, Seoul is being evacuated, we'll starve if we stay."

"Who is this friend?" asked Emma, warily. "What if this is a trick and he reports you?"

"He's another engineer from my unit," said Jae-Min. "He invited me and two others only, one of whom was my senior at Pyongyang University. They are all good men and have seen enough to know that we're better off in the South—for now."

"Do you trust them?" asked Emma, still suspicious.

"With my life," answered Jae-Min. "And even if I didn't, we don't have many alternatives. We could find our own way to Incheon, but the fields around us are mined and soldiers are everywhere. Getting lost could get us killed." He weighed his next words. "Even if we don't get lost, we could still get killed."

Jae-Min meant to warn us, but neither Emma nor I could be fazed by the ordinary risks of war anymore. "Even if we do nothing at all, we could still get killed," I said.

"We saw that in Kanggye, and again in Pyongyang," added Emma, as wind whistled in through the crooked window boards. "I don't want us to fall for a trap, but if your friend is genuine, then of course we will go with him."

Jae-Min's brows loosened as he relaxed, as if he had been worried that we would refuse to depart with him. I was touched that he cared so much about us when he could have easily shed us as a snake would its old skin. Most likely, his decision depended on his affection for Emma, though a cynical part of me did consider to what extent he, a KPA soldier, thought it would be helpful to have an American with him when defecting. Regardless of his motives, I owed the Pak family an immense debt, and it was now time to pay my dues.

38

MILKY WAY

February 8, 1951

Jae-Min had no civilian clothing, so Emma laid out two of her cleanest skirts and worked like Cinderella's fairy godmother, scissors flashing and wheel spinning, until she had a hanbok made to his measurements. It fit him perfectly, and though it was made of a blend of hemp, the pale fabric shone like silk when it caught the feeble evening light.

"You look like a scholar," said Emma, proud of her work.

"I am a scholar," Jae-Min reminded her. "I don't have a university anymore, but my mind carries more books than my arms can."

"How confident you are after a change of clothes!" Emma teased.

Jae-Min's friend's house was at the outer edge of Seoul, close to where the Southern Gate used to be. Before the war, that area had been a hectic market, but it was eerily stagnant now. Railroad tracks ran through a massive arch, the standard portraits of Mao, Stalin, and Kim Il-Sung dominating the two-story pagoda. Much of the surrounding area was in shambles, with so much debris that it was no longer possible to walk through the arch itself.

A group of about twenty men had congregated in front of the wall, half of whom were dressed in KPA uniforms and slinging guns. One man, in slacks and a parka, waved at Jae-Min.

"That's Mr. Oh Jang-Soo," Jae-Min explained. "He studied engineering in Tokyo, and briefly in Hawaii, before he started teaching in Wonsan. He is from the South, though; this house belongs to his brother, who went to Busan with the rest of his family."

With the sharp division of this war, I often forgot that only five years ago Korea was a single country, and people often had relatives in both Pyongyang and Seoul.

Jae-Min surveyed the faces. "My other two friends are back there. I recognize some comrades from our unit, but I don't know most of these men."

"I guess all of you brought friends," I remarked, concerned by the number of strangers. "And the friends brought more friends."

"They should have at least gotten rid of their uniforms," said Emma. "We look like a military squad!"

"They might not have had time to," said Jae-Min, sympathetic even though the men in civilian dress were casting resentful side-eyes at those in uniform. "It's cold, and most of us only have a uniform, and nothing else. Some could also be soldiers on patrol, joining right now. We'll go all together, but if something isn't right, the three of us can continue on our own. Just stay with me, all right?"

"Agreed," I said.

As soon as we got our bearings, I intended for us to leave this crowd, which was large enough to be glaringly conspicuous on these empty roads. One man had been so desperate to blend in with the refugees that he had fashioned himself an outfit of sheets and blankets tied in knots around his waist and shoulders. His socks were loose on his skinny ankles and sagged over his sneakers.

Jang-Soo took the lead, and Jae-Min made the three of us walk directly behind him, almost nicking Jang-Soo's heels as we slipped past the rubble. The new moon had been two days ago, leaving only a timid crescent winking overhead. It was so dark, but above us the Milky Way flared, defiant and demanding. In the heavens, I saw a river, persistent in its beauty, refusing to succumb to the barbarism on earth—untouchable and incomparable.

Divine.

Beyond the hills, explosions pulsed from the battles that were just beginning today. Planes zoomed from Suwon Airfield, and helicopters puttered overhead. Outside of the city, there were no buildings to shield us from the gusts, and downed power lines lashed from their poles.

"You know," said Emma, linking her arm through mine, "Incheon is across the sea from China. If Yun-Hee came back to Korea by boat, she might have landed there. Maybe she settled there too. Maybe she's still there now, don't you think?"

Though Emma had named me after the Milky Way, she was the one who managed to cut through the dark and draw happiness from this trip that everyone else had been dreading.

"We will find out soon," I said. "And if your daughter is not in Incheon, we can try other cities. When I get back to Japan, I will go to every news station that's still running and put out advertisements in every language I know. Somewhere in this world, someone who has met a Song Yun-Hee will see it."

I wasn't sure when, during these weeks of searching and asking, I had decided to believe that Yun-Hee was alive. Perhaps

Emma had worn down my doubt, as an ever-flowing river carves through granite mountains; as forests grow, seed by seed, to dominate once-barren territory. Statistics about the women trafficked during World War II didn't matter to me anymore. All I knew was that there was a girl out there waiting to go home, a woman now, waiting to be found.

Past the outskirts, Jang-Soo led us away from the main road to avoid any checkpoints, though from what I had heard, Communist soldiers had been abandoning their posts. Jae-Min and the other engineers threaded us along footpaths between newly laid minefields until we reached the Han River, wide and frozen. Shells flashing farther south illuminated the curvature of a bridge, its steel beams torn asunder, gnarled like chicken claws. I felt every pebble through the soles of my rubber boots as we headed to where the ice was thick and solid.

There was no way that I would have made it past the Han River myself, with the multitude of hidden traps embedded in the land. We were supposed to return to the road, but the other side of the river was a blanket of snow and wreckage. Weaving through a field, we searched for telephone poles that might indicate where the highway was. The ground was craggy and uneven, with drops so sharp that a few men tripped and rolled headfirst into shrubbery.

At the bottom of one hill, a set of wooden steps popped out from the vegetation, extending up to the peak. I had seen these stairways around American camps before. Our engineers often built them into mountainsides for more efficient movement, but the effort was worth it only if there was a supply route nearby—but we seemed to be in the middle of nowhere.

"There's no snow or ice on these steps," I said, touching the damp wood. "Someone must have used them fairly recently."

Jang-Soo overheard me. "Yes," he said. "We should stay away, even if we have to circle up north again. There might be scouts at the top, and they all have orders to shoot deserters."

"Will they really?" I asked.

"Sometimes," said Jae-Min. "I never do, but there are officers who take pride in killing traitors."

"I never do either," added Jang-Soo, "but if either of us was the type who would, then we wouldn't be here now, would we?"

I stared at the hill, the stairs blending into the murky top, framed by starry sky. Jang-Soo made us retrace our steps, so we wound around the base of the previous hill, ducking back to find tree cover. We shrank underneath spruce and other evergreens, down steep terrain, hoping that we'd smell the sea. It had been more than an hour since we had found any distinct road, and I was beginning to worry that we were moving in circles. Aside from those stairs, every hill had seemed identical.

Emma yawned noisily. "Do you think we're lost?"

"We are not lost," said Jae-Min. "This is just a detour."

Men cursed when they stubbed their toes on roots that arched above the soil. Within the woods, shadows stretched from trunk to trunk. I thought my tired eyes were failing me until Jae-Min whispered, "Oh no."

While I froze midstep, it took a moment for the entire group to hush. Twigs crunched beneath someone's shoes. Though I could barely see the bark on the tree beside me, I sensed that we were being watched. There were footsteps, skillfully soft, like faint static beneath a song on the radio.

Channeling the acumen of a prey animal, I strained to listen, ears begging for clarity as I debated which way to run.

"Chinese soldiers," whispered Jae-Min. "But they're moving away from us."

"Did they see us?" asked Emma.

"Of course," said Jae-Min, "but they don't seem to care. They're heading north, which is strange. Maybe they're traitors too. Either way, they're pretending not to notice us. Let's extend them the same courtesy."

I let out a long, loud breath, which hung opaque in the evergreen-scented air. My second pair of gloves was worn through, and I snaked my hands inside the sleeves of my jacket for warmth.

As we shifted back southward, we came across several more Chinese soldiers, all of whom were traveling in the opposite direction. None of them appeared to be injured, and they never bothered to stop us or ask where we were going. They probably didn't speak Korean, but I still found it odd. Surely they weren't all deserting? And if they were, shouldn't they have been going to surrender to UN troops, the other way?

39

THE RIGHT THING

February 8, 1951

The forest dwindled into a clearing, which widened to meet a raised dirt road lined with young cherry trees, their branches nude and delicate compared to the hefty spruces'. Someone had tried to plant beauty here in recent years, possibly after World War II. In contrast, there were wooden boxes stacked at the edge of the field, and land mines that were just left out—an unfinished job. Mounds of soil nearby covered freshly buried mines, poorly concealed.

"Stay close to the trees," instructed Jae-Min. "There are less likely to be mines where there are roots."

The hills had faded in the distance, and we walked on protruding roots like we were on a tightrope, and leaped into a ditch that hugged the road.

"I think that's Route Twenty," Jang-Soo said, holding his compass at the tip of his nose and squinting at the needle. "That should lead directly to Incheon. We can't stay on it for long, but we should try to keep it in sight so we don't get lost again."

Emma leaned over and cupped her hand close to my ear. "We might still be lost," she whispered. "Maybe we should go our own way. What do you think? If it's just us and Jae-Min, no one will assume he's deserting. We can follow this road and just ask for directions openly."

"I don't think we are lost anymore," I replied, "but I agree with you."

Now that we were past most of the mines, there was no reason to stay with the other men and risk being spotted by KPA soldiers. Emma and I slowed, falling behind the others, but Jae-Min continued trailing Jang-Soo.

"We have to talk to Jae-Min," said Emma as heads bobbed past us and we lost sight of Jae-Min's earflaps. Climbing out of the ditch and onto the road, I pulled at my rubber boots, which were chafing against my ankles. I had had multiple blisters in the same place, yet my skin there still hadn't hardened enough to prevent new ones from forming. From the height of the road, the lowlands looked so flat that they resembled a snow-covered lake.

Ahead, there was a pop, as though someone had uncorked a bottle of champagne. It came from one of the trees on the right, its trunk hissing.

Suddenly, the sky glowed red and an orange dot hovered like an orb above the road. Terror drilled into my core.

"What's that?" asked Emma, squinting at the parachute flare, but the men in front had already whirled around.

"Domang-ga!" screamed Jang-Soo, shoving past us to get back to the forest. Others leaped into the ditch as a voracious wind snatched the flare, streaking it sideways like a comet.

"Run!" cried Jae-Min, darting between Emma and me and seizing our arms.

Men shouted and dove into the ditch, landing on their hands and knees. In their chaotic rush, someone kicked a trip wire, setting off a second flare, which sizzled before sputtering up to the sky. Another wave of crimson washed over our horrified faces.

Emma and I tumbled just as illumination shells burst in a crooked ring, spraying dirt into our open mouths. Jae-Min flailed and let go of us. The entire clearing flashed with bright yellow light that seared my eyes.

Where there was lightning, there was thunder, and here, the thunder was deadly. The flares enhanced the outline of each blade of grass, each twig protruding from the salt-and-pepper snow, but the trip wires had been strategically placed far away from the tree line. Even the fastest men were still hurdling over mounds of dirt in the open field. Those in uniform blended in better with the terrain, while those of us in civilian dress reflected every kind of light. Jang-Soo tore off his jacket, then ripped the buttons on his white shirt and flung it above his head in surrender.

Emma sagged, her weight nearly dislocating my arm from its socket, as she tried to climb out of the ditch. "My ankle," she yelped. She slipped on a patch of mud and slid down on her belly, knocking my legs out from underneath me.

"We have to hurry!" I cried, yanking at her. "Please!"

Moaning, Emma forced herself to stand. Together, we lunged and, arms and chests soaked, clawed ourselves up to the field.

"What are you doing?" yelled Jae-Min. Everyone else was running away, but he was careening toward us, struggling to untie his belongings. Sacks tumbled to the ground as he tackled Emma and scooped her onto his back. The three of us trailed the rest of our group by at least fifty yards, in a field that might as well have been a stadium full of floodlights.

Bullets hissed and snapped, clattering as they picked up pace. Men shrieked as soil and ice shot up in columns. The rounds came too rapidly to be sniper fire, but they were precise enough that people collapsed like they were being mowed. Soldiers landed with guttural wails, arms and legs splayed in the snow.

My lungs burned as I kept my eyes on the forest, gritting my teeth as another round of shells and bullets exploded in an arc. Our skirts were silver bells, obnoxiously conspicuous.

"Zigzag!" I said, in English.

I wasn't sure if Jae-Min knew what that meant, but I took the lead and sprinted from side to side, moving erratically to throw off anyone who might be trying to mark me. A sniper in one of the MASH units had given me this advice. I never imagined that I'd actually use it, nor was I confident that it applied when there were bullets everywhere.

Panting, Jae-Min mimicked me, Emma's head jerking back and forth as he shifted. Several of the men had reached the tree line where we had first seen the unburied mines. One man stumbled and landed on top of a mound, only to bounce back unscathed.

With sinking dread, I realized that nothing about this field had been an unfinished or sloppy job. There were likely no buried land mines at all, just a deliberate trap, shrewdly calculated. The war machine was ingenious, savage, and unrelenting.

Just as the men were about to disappear into the forest, mortars dove, squealing like fowl. I threw my arms over my face as a series of blasts, booming one after another, catapulted me forward. Air slammed from my lungs when I hit the ground, and Imo's bowl shattered with a crunch.

My eardrums rang but there was no longer any sound, only the harried vibration of the earth beneath me. I struggled to inhale, digging my fingers into the slush, ripping a nail in my frenzy to anchor myself. Clumps of dirt and broken rocks scraped my cheeks. Within my bag, shards that once were peonies stabbed me.

Dear Mom and Dad, I'm sorry I didn't write earlier.

Dear Clara, I'm sorry I never delivered your letters.

I thought about the salty ham that I ate from the military C rations and the fish-and-chips at San Francisco's wharf.

I thought about Imo and that blob that she made for Christmas, and garlic sizzling on my mom's stove at home.

I thought about George holding mochi in his outstretched palm.

What country are your parents from?

Flipping over onto my back, I hacked out a glob of dirt. Saliva dribbled down my chin and neck as I coughed to clear my throat. When I finally forced my eyes open, I was staring straight at the sky, neon from the flares, smoke rising to obscure the Milky Way. Slowly, my ears picked up on popping. I thought about butter, the movies, until Jae-Min's voice grew louder.

"Hear me? Eun-Ha? Do you hear me? Don't move. Be dead until the flares go out! Do you hear me? Don't move. Be dead until the flares go out. Eun-Ha? Ellie!"

"Yes," I croaked, interrupting his distraught loop, a broken record.

I thought about my high school prom.

"Do you hear me?" Jae-Min repeated. Unlike me, he was prone, with his face against the ground.

"Yes!" I shouted. My mind was a merry-go-round, of snapshots instead of horses, but it was reducing its dizzying speed. *Focus.* Keeping my neck stiff, I tried not to retch. There was nothing in my belly, but I still gagged at that abhorrent smell of burnt flesh. I wiggled my fingers and toes to confirm that I could, and called out, "Emma?"

"I already said I'm all right!" she snapped, on her side, with her legs open like scissors. "My back hurts, but I don't think anything is broken."

"Don't move!" Jae-Min said again, through clenched teeth.

"I won't!" she assured him.

We lay, immobile and unflinching against all instinct, through two more rounds of flares, limbs tingling as the ice imparted its own kind of burn. There were no more gunshots, but I was still scared—plastered to the ground with my arms out, a specimen under that sinister glow.

In my mind, I retraced our steps, beginning from when we had crossed the Han and wandered, bewildered, past where the highway was supposed to be. We might have gotten mixed up, but even if we had walked straight south, it was unlikely that we had gone far enough to reach UN territory—unless Jae-Min's intelligence was wrong. When I examined those wooden steps, I had assumed that they were leftovers from the last time the Americans had occupied this area. Could it be that the UN troops had advanced farther than Jae-Min thought?

I was nearly certain that the flare trap had been set by Americans, or another UN contingent. No one else had this kind of equipment, and even if the Communist forces had stolen these supplies, they were far more conservative with their arms. The KPA might have shot deserters, but they would never have wasted mortars on them.

The flares winked out like eyes closing, plunging us into a darkness saturated with sound. Survivors whimpered, shells hissed, and shoes smacked against the mud. I was still afraid to move, anticipating another round of shells to illuminate the sky once more.

When my pulse slackened from its manic hum, I inched myself to sitting, rubbing crust from the corners of my lips. "There is a UN Command unit on one of these hills," I rasped, a film on my tongue. "That way, based on where the bullets came from. They can't be that far—maybe a mile?"

Jae-Min pushed himself onto his hands and knees. "People are dead," he said, caustically. "Can we at least take a moment to acknowledge that? Take their identification? Or does it only matter when it's your own?"

"Of course it matters," I said reflexively, and yet, if I was honest myself, it really didn't. The dead weren't supposed to blur together. It was supposed to be shocking each time, but I'd seen so many bodies that even faces had become as identical as the hills we had wandered in. Often, I grappled with remorse over my inability to feel, but in that pitch-black field, all I could summon was fury.

"They shouldn't have been in their uniforms," I said, adrenaline resurging in my veins. "It was stupid of them not to change their clothes, and stupid of us not to leave them behind earlier! Do you think we would have gotten shot at if it had been just the three of us under those flares?"

Jae-Min slammed his fist into the ground, the earth swallowing his knuckles with a squelch. "What is wrong with you? Soldiers here don't have ordinary clothes! The men who stayed in their uniforms probably didn't want to steal from civilians—they wanted to do the right thing. What kind of people would we be if we just excluded them?"

"Alive people!" I screamed.

"Jang-Soo surrendered!" Jae-Min shouted. "He waved his

white cloth, but we still got shot—in our backs, while we were running away!"

"It would have been different if there weren't men in goddamned uniforms!"

"Would it?" yelled Jae-Min. "You people kill civilians all the time!"

Gloves grazed my arm. Emma had rolled onto her stomach and crawled toward me, stretching until she hooked her fingers into the crook of my elbow. "Stop, you two," she rasped. "We can't make noise, and we can't stay here."

I wanted to take another swipe at Jae-Min, but Emma was right. "Who else in our group is left?" I spat.

"Jang-Soo *hyeong*?" called Jae-Min, with a mix of hope and dread.

There was no reply from Jang-Soo, but other men groaned feebly for help. I had no doubt that some had managed to bolt into the forest. Those lucky few were unlikely to return for their comrades, and I didn't blame them.

Jae-Min stood, wringing out his wet robe, which was blackened on the front. He came to help Emma to her feet.

"Aigo," she grunted as he lifted her abruptly, and she leaned against him, clutching the opening of his coat. With the fabric of their hanboks pressed together, I noticed a subtle difference in color that I otherwise might have missed. All of us were muddy, but Emma's skirt had a cardinal tint sweeping like embroidery around her waist and hips.

I reached out and lifted the hem of her coat. "You're bleeding."

I removed my gloves, and touched gently until I found a tear in her coat. Her lower back was wet, but no more than the rest of that side of her body, which had been nestled against the slush.

Jae-Min's breath quickened as he knelt and brushed my fingers aside. "What happened, Auntie?"

"I fell," she said, confused, as she pulled at her skirt. "Maybe I cut myself when I landed."

There were rocks on the ground, but Jae-Min sucked in his breath. "This is not a cut," he said, his face nearly touching the tear that I had found. "It's a bullet wound. You've been shot."

"Really?" asked Emma, wobbling without Jae-Min to lean on. "Are you sure?"

"What do you mean, are you sure?" I asked. "Shouldn't it be obvious?"

"I didn't feel anything," Emma wheezed. She tried to stand straighter, but winced and buckled over. "At least it wasn't what I thought a bullet would feel like. My waist was hot—burning hot—and it did hurt, but not that badly. By the time I noticed the burning, I was on the ground."

"Is there an exit wound?" I asked, trying to recall what I had heard from the nurses, palpating for additional openings in her clothing. In the end, I knew nothing about medicine and couldn't do much, regardless of the severity of her injury. "We need to get you help. We need a doctor!"

"Is it still bleeding?" asked Jae-Min.

"I can't tell," I said. "Can you?"

"No, it's too dark."

"We have to get her to a medic."

"Where?" he asked. "There's nothing around here. I think we're closer to Incheon than to Seoul, but it will still take us hours to get there—longer if we have to carry her."

"It's not that bad. I can walk," Emma said, but from how she wavered on her feet, I knew that was a lie.

I pointed to the forest. "If there is an American unit nearby, there will be medics, maybe even a field hospital. I'll bet they are on the hill with the stairway, the one that we took the detour around."

"I'll go," said Jae-Min. "You stay here with Auntie Moon, and I'll go get help."

"Are you stupid? If anyone should go to an American camp, it's me—the American."

"We'll go together," decided Jae-Min. "I'll carry her."

There were others in the field who needed care. They heard us speaking, and called in Korean, but if Jae-Min wasn't going to acknowledge them, I wouldn't either. I couldn't understand what they were saying, and they sank into the savage, sorrowful background. They were cogs, just like me—cogs spinning in the war machine. Though I wasn't military, I was trapped in it too.

"I'll come back for the others after we get Auntie Moon somewhere safe," said Jae-Min, without realizing that I was on the verge of tears. "Get her onto my back." He squatted, with his arms held out.

Some people are better at holding on to their humanity than others. These are often the same people who can help you find yours when you think you've lost it—who remind you that a soul is like a shadow, occasionally hidden or forgotten, but never discarded.

"Come," I said to Emma, easing her arms around Jae-Min's neck and steadying her as Jae-Min rose. "It'll be all right. We're taking you to a doctor." When he straightened his knees, the muted starlight shimmered on Emma's skirt, revealing a gradient of shades of red. What I had thought was mostly dirt was entirely blood, seeping beyond the darkest ring around her waist to soak her stockings.

"Run," I said to Jae-Min. "Quick. We don't have time."

"Is it that bad?" he asked, fear creeping into his question.

"Just run," I said.

Jae-Min's steps had been labored, but he picked up his pace as we went back to where we had come from, stepping over bodies, ignoring the soldiers who continued to mewl for us to take them too. Our large group had left messy tracks through the forest, and we followed them, hoping that the trail hadn't gotten mixed up with that of the Chinese soldiers.

Jae-Min began to slow, his chest heaving, as Emma's head lolled on his shoulder.

"Stay awake, Emma." I pinched her arm, terrified now that the bullet had hit an organ or an artery. "Stay awake. That's all you have to do." I refused to let my guard down. I refused to be robbed again. Maintaining my grip, I repeated myself, shaking her every few steps. "Stay awake. Stay awake."

Her wound was treatable. *She is not going to die.*

It is difficult to pinpoint when or why a single person stands out and becomes a special person. Emma had saved me, but our friendship was based on more than that. We had been outsiders in Kanggye; women who wrote; women who were, in our own ways, on the outskirts of what was acceptable in our countries and cultures. She wasn't just a friend. She was me in another life, a home behind enemy lines, and mercy in the midst of so much suffering.

"Eun-Ha," said Emma, her words slurring together, "I've been looking for a very long time."

"I know," I said, fighting to remain upbeat. "And you have new places to look now, new people to talk to. I'll help you; just hold on and stay awake." She didn't answer, and I couldn't tell if her eyes were open, so I shook her again, hard. "Stay awake!"

"I'm worried about you," Emma mumbled. "This world is not a safe place for a girl by herself. A girl alone."

"I'm not a girl, and I am not alone. Jae-Min is here too. Just worry about yourself."

"I can't," she sniffed. "It is my duty to worry about you. I will always worry about you. Always."

I refuse to let her die.

People often talk about a sixth sense, as much as I talked about being a woman between worlds. In the span of my life, I had never hovered so much or felt so untethered as I had in Korea, but perhaps that was what allowed me to catch the glimmers in the side of my eye and know, with certainty, that which I could not explain.

I didn't want to let her die, but in war, in life, sometimes all we can do is to watch—to bear witness as our hearts unravel.

It was fast, and it was unfair. It was unacceptable, and yet I had to accept it. This pain was mine, but this moment was not about me, so I summoned the strength to tell Emma not what I needed to say, but what she needed to hear.

I was a foreigner, and I sounded like a foreigner, but there was one word that I knew well now, one word that was so easy that even babies could say it.

Taking a deep, excruciating breath, I filled my lungs with icy air. "*Eomma,*" I said, trying to capture each vowel. "It will be okay. I will be okay. I survived the last war, and I will survive this one too. I will live well, I promise. Please don't worry. I will have a good life. A very good life."

Was this a gift? Was it better than a prayer? I didn't know, but it was the only thing I had to give, and the only thing I could possibly do. Around us, the trees grew sparse, thinning as the forest broke around the bottom of a hill. My knees were about to buckle as we reached the stairway, steeper and taller than I had remembered. Emma's shoulders shuddered as we began to climb with no railing, steps shaking precariously.

There wasn't enough time. Pumping my arms, I shot past Jae-Min and cupped my hands around my mouth. "Help!" I shouted in English. "We need help! A woman is badly hurt! She needs a doctor! Help!" My words reverberated despairingly along the slope, the surrounding mountain echoes mimicking my call. With my hands for support, I began scaling the stairs on all fours, hoping that I was right and I hadn't just alerted Communist soldiers to our presence. Through my fingertips, I felt the wood quiver as heavy feet clomped from the peak and headlamps flickered on.

They were here.

8 December 1950
Dear Yun-Hee,

I met a girl, older than you, by accident. She is a Chinese, but from America. I brought her to Pak Imo's house, and Imo is unhappy. I don't know if she will be able to stay—you know how Imo is, a bad Christian, really. You would like this girl, though. She has a strange name that is hard to say, but sometimes she reminds me of you.

The world is such a large place, and remembering that gives me more hope than anything else. Perhaps you are now a Korean in a foreign city across the sea. I imagine that you are happy in a land I do not know, speaking a language I do not speak. Maybe you have found a husband. Maybe you have built a new life. It doesn't have to be with me, as long as you are living well.

I will always worry about you.

Mom

40

THE PROMISE

American infantrymen thundered down the stairway with headlamps on and submachine guns out, shouting for us to put our hands up. They were afraid it was a trap, and I was terrified that they had had too much coffee and too little sleep. Too many men with debilitating trauma had been dusted off at the MASH and thrown back into the field with their finger on a trigger. Jae-Min still had Emma's legs pinned under both arms, and he knelt slowly to put her down. Was it moronic of me to come running to the people who might have shot her?

"I'm American!" I said, raising my hands, that motion a lever that brought me back to my landing in Kanggye.

What country are your parents from?

"My parents are American too!" I shouted. "I'm Eleanor Chang, from California! I am a correspondent with the *Global Tribune*. I got stranded—"

"Just shut up!" yelled a soldier, thrusting his gun at us. His brown eyes were close together above his crooked nose, which looked like it had been broken in a fight. "Shut up and let me see your hands!"

My hands trembled as I stared down that silver barrel. Bias is as personal as faith and doubt, and it is nearly impossible to know where a person falls along that spectrum, even if they tell you. Part of growing up "different" is understanding that critical moments in your life will depend on this mercurial, hidden attribute—on whether the person with the upper hand has ever had friends who look like you.

Jae-Min positioned Emma's head with care, then put his arms up, while six men staggered along the steps above us, guns locked on his face. The lights from headlamps roamed the surrounding hillside as they scanned for enemies hidden below the stairs.

"I am South Korean," Jae-Min said, in English.

Broken Nose's brow softened, his jaw easing open as he licked his lips. He might or might not have had a Chinese American friend, but he certainly had South Korean military counterparts. While three of the soldiers kept their guns on us, the rest leaped into the snow, sweeping the hill. Emma remained curled by Jae-Min's feet, the blood on her skirt a brilliant ruby red under the headlamps' incandescent bulbs, defacing her embroidered butterflies. I didn't need to check her to know that she was gone. I had seen it all coming, like lips puckering before blowing out a candle.

I kept my pain in, each unshed tear another layer calcifying in my core. Since leaving Pyongyang, I had lost my ability to cry, and it was excruciating to have no outlet for my anguish. I had been ransacked, so suddenly and thoroughly, yet I wasn't able to explain to these men what I had lost, and what Emma had meant to me.

Perhaps I appeared apathetic when the soldiers patted me down, lifting my skirt and peering into my shirt for grenades. One of the soldiers, with cauliflower ears and a chin full of stubble, announced that we were clear, and lowered his gun. "We just had to be sure you weren't a Red," he said, motioning for the others to swivel their barrels away from us.

Broken Nose bent over Emma. "Let's see what we can do. Are you all South Korean?"

"I am American," I said, enunciating to prove my English fluency. "I am a correspondent. Eleanor Chang."

He looked skeptically at my jacket, which still had Kim Il-Sung's face on it. It had been hard enough to convince soldiers to listen to me when I was wearing pants and combat boots, let alone a mud-stained hanbok, so I said, "Call the *Global Tribune*. Or, better yet, call the Air Evacuation Squadron in Tachikawa. Pak Jae-Min here is my interpreter, and this woman is my . . ." I trailed off, because "friend" did not seem sufficient. She had been my protector, my lifeline, a well of hope, and a kindred spirit.

"She is my aunt," said Jae-Min, firmly. "We were in Seoul, but went to Incheon because we heard it was going to be liberated before Seoul was."

"We got caught in cross fire on our way," I cut in. I didn't think Jae-Min would be careless enough to mention his KPA comrades, but I also didn't want to take any chances when the American soldiers still gripped their guns tightly.

"Well, this is a war zone," said Broken Nose. "You all shouldn't have been on the roads in the middle of the night. We don't have a surgeon here, but there's a medic who might be able to help. He's taken care of a lot of bullet wounds—that's for sure."

"Thank you," I stuttered, while Jae-Min heaved Emma into his arms, her limbs and head limp.

I couldn't bring myself to admit aloud that she was dead.

Broken Nose led us up the rest of the stairs, to a campsite of foxholes and a crude log bunker that was covered with foliage. On the reverse side of the slope, small tents were spread among the shrubs. From this vantage point, we could see the frozen Han, its bank rounding like a woman's hip.

The medical tent was empty except for a kerosene lantern and two cots. Jae-Min and I arranged Emma on one of them, and though her exposed skin was already cold, I sat on the ground beside her. I extended her time through my refusal to acknowledge what everyone, even the American soldiers, had already realized was the truth. Blue flames undulated behind the lantern glass while Broken Nose and the others walked away, their conversations snatched by the same wind that ruffled the tent flap.

Agitated, Jae-Min removed his hat and dug his fingers into Emma's neck for a pulse. It made me hopeful, but when he let go, his face broke into anguish.

"I failed," he said, running his hands in his hair and sinking into a crouch at the head of the cot. "I didn't notice that she got hurt. I think I know when she got hit too. I felt the push, but I didn't realize what it was. I made us lie still. I told her not to move while she was bleeding out."

"Oh, Jae-Min," I said. "You are a soldier. You know how this is. We are responsible for each other, but this was out of our hands."

I didn't really believe that, though. Did I end up making Jae-Min zigzag into a bullet? Perhaps we should have played dead in the ditch straightaway. Better yet, I could have made us stop at the stairway the first time we came upon it, and we would have never gone to that damned field at all.

"No," said Jae-Min. "I was responsible, and I failed her." Pulling his hands down, he pressed his thumbs beneath his jawbone and turned away from Emma's body.

"You didn't fail her," I said. "You did your best. Auntie Moon would never blame either of us, least of all you."

Jae-Min lifted his head. "I'm not talking about Auntie Moon. I'm talking about Yun-Hee."

I flinched at the name, which I hadn't expected to hear now that Emma's voice had been extinguished.

Shadows wavered against the canvas. "I never told Auntie Moon everything," Jae-Min continued. "I couldn't, not right away. It was always on my mind, and I was going to, but then too much time passed. The secret itself began to feel like a crime, and I couldn't confess it anymore."

"What do you mean?" My palms grew clammy beneath my gloves.

He remained hunched, wavering when he said, "The Kempeitai went to the textile factory and took all the girls eligible for the draft. Auntie Moon thinks that she was the last among us to see Yun-Hee alive, but that isn't true. At my school, I was in charge of loading cargo bound for the train station. On the day that Yun-Hee was drafted, I was moving ammunition crates for the front lines—Manchuria—when the Kempeitai arrived with a group of girls, maybe twenty, some without their socks or shoes on. The car wasn't meant for passengers, so I was surprised when the officers ordered the girls to get in. My friends and I were watching them, and I recognized Yun-Hee because of her coat. It was gray, but her mom embroiders everything—everything."

I covered my mouth as Jae-Min began to cry.

"I called her name," he sobbed, "screamed it. When she turned and saw me, I panicked. I broke away from my classmates and rushed to her car. I told the policemen that they had made a mistake—that she was my wife, and they weren't allowed to take married girls. They called me a liar and threatened to arrest me, and one of them started beating me with his gun. I was going to hit him back, but my friends pulled me away. Yun-Hee was crying, and I was useless. I told her that I was sorry, and that I loved her. I told her that I would wait for her."

I bit down on my knuckles in utter disbelief that Jae-Min had witnessed Yun-Hee boarding a train to China with his own eyes—Jae-Min, who had so vociferously claimed that she probably went to a factory in Japan. Perhaps Yun-Hee had another role along the front lines, but that was unlikely, given her age and ethnicity. My teeth cut through my gloves, into my flesh, until it hurt. "What did Yun-Hee say?" I asked, thinking about how scared she must have been, and trying to imagine what I might have done.

Jae-Min kneaded his eyes and let out a bitter laugh. "She said, 'Please take care of my mom. If you love me, please take care of my mom.' That was all. It was the only thing she asked for, so I promised her that I would. I don't know if she heard me, because the doors closed, but I yelled that I would. I kept yelling, even when the policemen took me away."

"Did you go to prison?"

"No. My mom came to the police station as soon as my classmates told her I was arrested. She wasn't speaking to her parents anymore, but she still used their connections to get me out."

A shiver jolted through me. "So . . . Imo knew too?"

"Everyone knew, but we had to protect Auntie Moon. At first it was because I wanted her to have hope that Yun-Hee would come back, and we all knew that girls who went to the front lines rarely did. Later, it was because I didn't want Auntie Moon to worry that her daughter suffered in a comfort station. Not many *cheongshindae* talked about what happened there, but some did, and it would have tortured Auntie Moon if she found out. That's why I never told you until now. I didn't know if you'd be able to keep a secret."

The irony pierced my gut, and I hung my head. "I can keep a secret all right," I said, my chest weighted with all the lies that I had accumulated. I rested my chin on my knees, reeling from a betrayal that wasn't even mine to resent—outrage at all the times the Paks had insisted that Emma was just assuming the worst. Even without confirmation, Emma had made deductions and trusted her own instincts. Would certainty have brought her comfort?

I believed that it would have. Admonishments lined up on my tongue, but I kept them gated as Jae-Min wept, crestfallen, by the cot. How could I possibly rebuke him when he was now an orphan, and I had withheld that truth?

Outside, men's voices rumbled, low like the roll of thunder before a storm.

"You took care of Auntie Moon to the best of your ability," I said, with as much clemency as I could. "Wherever Yun-Hee is, I'm sure that she would be grateful."

"Maybe she and Auntie Moon are finally together now," he said, eyes cast down at a spot between his boots.

"I hope not," I said, standing up to meet the soldiers who were returning to the tent, "because I'm going to keep looking for Yun-Hee here on earth, and I don't want to waste my time."

"Still?" asked Jae-Min, rising too. "Even with Auntie Moon gone?"

"Yes. I promised Auntie Moon that I would."

Helping Emma find her daughter was a commitment that had become sacred. It had been a goal that Emma and I had pursued together, and now I was bound to carry forth alone. While I was indebted to Emma for her kindness, this wasn't just about her. Everything she had accomplished on military sexual slavery had taken on its own importance. Emma's satchel remained tangled around her shoulder, a wet rectangular lump on the cot. Within it, her notebook had survived, and a part of her was preserved. Her work could be passed on, and I refused to fail her.

41

THE OTHER SIDE

February 9–12, 1951

It had snowed overnight, coating the tents in a gossamer white. Corpulent flakes clumped on the stubs of my eyelashes, which still hadn't grown back since being singed in Pyongyang. There was no air support, because of the weather, and the sky was briefly serene. Soldiers smoked their morning cigarettes and shaved with leftover coffee as they prepared to advance once again.

The UN Command had taken over several hills in the area, cutting Incheon off from the Han River. Apparently, the Chinese troops we had seen last night had been withdrawing, and any surviving KPA soldiers had been taken as prisoners of war.

American officers gave Jae-Min and me orange juice powder and some dense fruitcake in exchange for information about everything we had observed in Seoul. Though the officers remained skeptical that I was a correspondent, they took a liking to Jae-Min, whom they treated as one of their ROK allies. I salivated while tearing open the ration pack, so enchanted by the food that

I only thanked our interviewer when he'd remarked that Jae-Min's English was excellent, and mine was pretty good too.

With help from the soldiers, Jae-Min and I wrapped Emma in a poncho and buried her in a shallow grave on the hill, marked with a cross fashioned out of sticks and twine. I borrowed a map and copied our location into Yun-Hee's notebook. While overlooking the Han, Jae-Min and I said goodbye to Moon Hwa-Ja, but for him the farewell wasn't just to a beloved person—it was to a country, a childhood, and a home that he could never return to.

I wasn't innocent before this war, but now pieces of my whole lay with the people I had lost, in old churches and factories, beneath riverbanks and frozen earth. The prospect of my own homecoming was bittersweet, for these bombs had destroyed me too.

The next day, Jae-Min and I rode behind the American tanks to Incheon, where civilians gathered along the street to welcome the UN Command. Some of the braver children ran to the soldiers, with their small hands outstretched for chewing gum. There were so many refugees that I rarely remembered any one in particular, but I recognized a woman's shouting as she hustled through the crowd. A man behind her was carrying a boy on his shoulders, whose skinny legs were crossed at the ankles.

I smacked Jae-Min's arm. "That's the couple with the boy by the fuel barrel in Pyongyang!" I exclaimed freely in English. "Do you remember them?"

"No," Jae-Min replied, unimpressed, but he listened and translated for me anyway. "The woman says that her son is shy, but he's as hungry as the others. And chewing gum isn't really food. Does anyone have powdered milk?"

The American soldiers couldn't understand her, and other

civilians were also begging, so I took the biscuits that I had saved from breakfast and tossed them into her open arms. It wasn't much, just an acknowledgment that I saw her, and heard her too.

When the weather cleared up enough, Jae-Min and I hitched a flight from the recaptured Kimpo Airfield onward to Tachikawa. As soon as I stepped into the plane, however, I envisioned it crashing. During takeoff I braced myself for flak, and during landing I swore I heard burp guns. What had happened in Kanggye was tattooed over every recollection I had of being airborne, so vividly that I decided then and there that I would return to the United States by sea. Not even the glorious sight of Mount Fuji from above could convince me that flying was worth it anymore—that it could be anything but terrifying.

It was bright when I stepped shakily onto the tarmac. I inhaled the familiar mix of fuel, asphalt, and coffee, relieved by how comparatively warm the weather was. Though chilly, it was nothing like Kanggye, where icicles had formed on the fringes of my hair. A group of flight nurses were gathered in front of the office, clapping and whistling hysterically. I thought perhaps there was a high-ranking general whom I hadn't recognized on our plane, or maybe a visiting celebrity. Only when Barbara led the charge, curly hair bouncing as she sprinted, did I realize that these women were here for me.

I stiffened, dumbstruck, because it was too lovely to be real. If it wasn't for Emma's death, I would have wondered if I too had been shot in that rigged field, and the entrance to heaven was a hangar instead of a gate.

Barbara slammed against me. Her perfume was overwhelming when she kissed me on the cheek, leaving a sticky lip print. She nearly had me in a headlock when she said, "Heavens to Betsy, we all thought you were dead!"

Unsteady, I leaned against her, easing myself into the safety of her embrace like one might slip into warm bathwater. As the other women joined to hug me, I pictured my parents, still an ocean away, and imagined that I was holding them too. "Yes, I'm alive," I whispered. "I am here, and soon I will be home."

WESTERN UNION TELEGRAM

Mr. and Mrs. Shan-Wei Chang

1775 Cedar Drive, Daly City, CA

Alive and safe. Sorry to keep you waiting. Love you, letters to follow.

Ms. Eleanor Chang

February 11, 1951

International calls were prohibitively expensive, so I sent my parents a telegram and dropped my letters in the mail before picking up the pieces of the life I left behind. Returning to Japan was like emerging from a time machine. Everyone else had continued bustling, the world careening onward, while I had been away. Someone had taken the room that I was renting, and my belongings had been sold because I hadn't paid my bill. Someone had taken the job that I had worked so hard for, and I was off payroll because the *Global Tribune* had assumed that I was dead.

Barbara lent me money to tide me over until I got my accounts in order, and other women on base gave me some clothes. Despite the danger at the Chosin Reservoir, the flight nurses had returned to their planes, saving tens of thousands of our soldiers.

This heroism, however, was not without sacrifice. Two nurses had died in service, and that loss remained raw. In the nurses' quarters, there was a wall with photos of fallen comrades, the women and men who had given their lives for the mandate of their country. George was there, preserved at twenty-four.

There were rashes on my body from malnutrition, but a hot shower had never felt so promising. I slathered myself with cold cream while Barbara combed through the knots in my hair, which came out in clumps.

"What in God's name happened to my jacket?" she asked after I washed it.

"I had to blend in" was all I answered. I wasn't ready to describe everything that I had seen on the other side.

There was something wrong with me, but on base I wasn't alone. There was something wrong with almost everyone, from the nurses who had to stand in for mothers and watch boys die so far from home, to the pilots who vomited upon emerging from their cockpits, sickened by yet another round of bombing. In war, there are undeniably people who are eager to kill, to bring glory at any cost, but from what I have seen, most of us must contend with the impact of violence, and the ghosts that come with it.

While I stayed with Barbara, I borrowed money so Jae-Min could rent a room by the bathhouse. It didn't take long for him to get a job offer, though. There was a shortage of Korean-to-English interpreters, and the American military had been relying on Japanese interpreters with significant limitations. If Jae-Min wanted to, he could return to Korea as a member of the UN Command, but I knew that he wouldn't truly be free to decide until I told him the truth.

A few days after we were both clean, coiffed, and fed, I took Jae-Min for a walk in the market, past the food stands where the mochi granny still had lines that wound around the corner. His eyes wandered over the densely packed signage of stores stacked on top of one another, block after block. It was surreal to see such long stretches of commercial buildings with neither rubble nor ash.

I wore Barbara's coat, without the Kim Il-Sung pin and red patch, while Jae-Min had a peacoat and pants borrowed from an officer. Across the street, a man sold roasted chestnuts, their shells splitting around golden nuggets of meat. Children pulled their parents toward him, lured by a buttery aroma that tempted me too.

We reached a military housing complex. When my courage finally coalesced, I said, "I'm sorry, Jae-Min. I've been lying to you for some time."

"About what?" he asked.

I directed him to sit on a bench, preparing myself to absorb the grief that I had delayed by manipulating his fate—and the additional anger that was due like interest on a loan. "I told you that your parents had escaped to Seoul, but they never did. Your mother died during the bombing in Pyongyang, and your father died in a blizzard on his way there." With my hands gripping the bench, I recounted the smoke that had smothered the compound and Imo's last days, as well as every detail Emma had told me about Pastor Pak. "I am so sorry Auntie Moon and I weren't honest earlier. We were afraid that it would upset you too much. We wanted to focus on getting out of North Korea first."

After presenting him with Imo's photographs, I bowed deeply, as I had seen my Chinese relatives do.

Jae-Min didn't even look at me. Since he had cried so much over Auntie Moon, I expected him to crumble and beat the ground like Imo had during Miho's first visit, but he only stared at his family portrait, at his parents dressed in white. Only then did it occur to me that even though Jae-Min had survived, I could still end up losing him too.

The thought that he might never speak to me again was unbearable.

"Are you angry?" I probed.

"Yes," Jae-Min said softly, "but not at you." He touched the portrait, then met my gaze. "Auntie Moon and Yun-Hee have such similar expressions. Their eyebrows get stiff when they're uncomfortable. They stand much straighter when they lie. I knew Auntie Moon was hiding something from the moment I entered her house, but I chose not to think about it. In any case, I could never blame her. I understand that she was just trying to protect me."

Farther on, at an intersection, bicycles whizzed past cars at a red light, and I let out a quiet sigh. "Your grandmother's address is on the back of one of the pictures. Your mom said she doesn't know if she is still there, but since you're so close to Tokyo, you could try to find her, and maybe your aunts and uncles too."

Jae-Min turned over the family portrait and caught his breath. He became ashen, as though someone had stabbed him, his eyes wide like those of a deer in headlights.

"Look, I get that your maternal grandparents were not the best people," I said, before wincing at that understatement. "Okay, they were pretty terrible, from what your mom told me. But I guess she wanted you to have options. Since you have a job lined up, you probably don't need to reach out, but you can keep it for emergencies, all right?"

Jae-Min swallowed, tracing his finger over the writing. "It's not that. My mom left me a message." He showed me the back of the photo, where there were some lines in Japanese. I hadn't noticed them before, but I hadn't thought to check either of the pictures. Since Imo's passing, I had kept them hidden away.

Jae-Min pressed the picture to his chest, crinkling it under the force of his palm. "My parents are gone," he said, "but what I told you before still stands. You and Auntie Moon helped my mother and father when I couldn't be there for them. I will always be grateful for that."

I shifted on the bench, and dug my fingers into my own pockets. It had become a force of habit to poke at the seams where the safe-conduct pass had been. Jae-Min would probably never be as forgiving to himself as he was to me, so I said, "Yun-Hee probably feels the same way, you know. Until the very end, you were there for her mom too."

He smiled wanly as traffic picked up at the intersection and began to jam. "I hope she does. One way or another, I'll have to face her someday."

---

3 January 1951
To my son, Pak Jae-Min:

No mother can protect her child forever, this I knew, though I held on for as long as I could.

Please do not be sad. Study hard and finish school. Honor me by living well.

I am, and always will be, so proud to be your mom.

42

SEA LIONS

March 15–30, 1951

I left Japan on an ocean liner in March 1951, and spent most of the trip belowdecks, writing in Yun-Hee's notebook, and deciphering what Emma had written in hers. There were a few Korean passengers on the ship, and I showed them Emma's entries, hoping for an organized account of the interviews that she had conducted with former military sex slaves.

"These aren't interviews," said a young Korean student who was on his way to study in San Francisco. "These are all letters—hundreds of letters to someone named Yun-Hee."

"Are you sure?" I asked. The edges of Emma's notebook were worn, and several pages were water stained. "My friend said that she wrote down all the conversations she had with *cheongshindae* here."

"Some of the letters are about the *cheongshindae*," said my translator, flipping through the notebook, "but most of them are just ordinary things that a mother and daughter might talk about.

This one, for example, is about how you should soak short ribs in water to remove impurities before you make your stew." He turned the page. "This one is about how she thinks the pharmacist is having an affair, and how a man who cheats once will cheat again."

He gave the notebook back to me, and I closed it, perplexed. Had Emma recorded her interviews somewhere else? Or had something been lost or censored in translation?

When we approached the Californian coast, I raced to the deck. I knew I was home when I heard the sea lions barking, their black flippers sleek as they dove beneath the waves. Along the pier, thousands of people waited, some with American flags waving, as our ship pulled into the harbor. Clustered together at the front of the crowd was my family, anxiously watching as we dropped anchor. Everyone—my parents, my brothers and their wives, and my nieces and nephews—was pressed up impatiently against the wire gate.

I had never seen my father cry before, but he did when I stepped off the gangway, with Emma's satchel and a small bag of my own belongings. He was bawling too hard to speak, but my mom managed to yell, "You are never allowed to leave the country again!"

The rest of my family started shouting at once, wrestling me from the gate and into our car, piling in with fresh buns from my favorite bakery. Oh, they had warned me that it was dangerous to go to a war zone! What had I been thinking, going to North Korea? Why didn't I just become a doctor, like my brothers? And what the hell did I mean when I said I would do it all again? Didn't I know that it was a sin to die before one's parents? A sin! And did I at least come back with a nice man from a good family, or the possibility of having one in the near future?

My mom opened Tupperware container after Tupperware container of food she had packed, because, according to her, I looked *ghastly*, and now she did too, because of all the gray hair I had given her.

I didn't mind my family's comments, as relentless as they were. Their voices were no different from the barking of sea lions—a little loud, somewhat obnoxious—but in this cacophony, I knew that I was home.

43

THE TORCH

> "I would have dropped between 30 to 50 atomic bombs on [the enemy's] air bases and other depots strung across the neck of Manchuria . . . between 30 to 50 atomic bombs would have more than done the job!"
>
> —Douglas MacArthur, on being "deprived" of waging a "proper" campaign in Korea, 1954

April 1951–August 2019

The Korean War, as we knew it, ended with an armistice agreement in 1953. South Korea was shattered, but in the aftermath of the war there were no longer any North Korean towns or cities. Over the course of two days, January 3rd and 5th, 1951, the US Bomber Command dropped more than 2.6 million pounds of incendiary bombs on Pyongyang alone. It was a miracle that I survived that raid. Though I am not a mathematician or a scientist, I know there is a point at which the cumulative effect of napalm and explosives surpasses the devastation of an atomic weapon. I kept in touch with Jae-Min, and learned that the rest of Emma's compound had been obliterated in Operation Insomnia, during which America bombed Pyongyang continuously—for ninety days.

Back in the Bay Area, I wrote incessantly about the people I had met in North Korea: soldiers with nothing left to lose, because everyone they loved was dead; civilians who were angry because they no longer had their homes; and parents who could not see a safe future for their children until those who had bombed them were eliminated. When people are in complete and utter despair, they turn to their Gods and the otherworldly for answers for a world they no longer understand. In some places, that holy person is Jesus Christ. In some others, it is Muhammad. In North Korea, it is Kim Il-Sung.

In war, it is common to think of the enemy as less than human, as a puppet or animal, but it is impossible to bomb our way to peace. History is a chain, and humans, unlike animals, remember it. Though we look with pity at the NASA map showing the stark contrast between the two Koreas, it would be remiss not to acknowledge that we too had a role in that darkness.

I was never a Communist, but with Joseph McCarthy's Red Scare raging, no publisher wanted to touch my work on North Korea unless I was willing to "sanitize" it. Men more powerful than me were getting blacklisted for telling truths that I had seen. Following that war, the lines were black-and-white. In many ways, they still are. Throughout my life, I would continue to wonder about the men and women who had shared in my journey back south. Did Miho and Comrade Ying survive? Did the boy in the fuel barrel ever grow up?

Contrary to my parents' wishes, I went back to work as a journalist. I could have become a correspondent again, but Emma's project had become an obsession, so instead of joining another newspaper, I took a position with a nonprofit that assisted refugee survivors of sexual violence. For most of my career, I documented testimony from and wrote articles about women in war—those who survived, and those who did not. Through those connections, I continued to search for Emma's daughter.

There were records of people who were at refugee camps in

China, and Japanese military documents about the labor drafts, but none of those sources provided a complete picture of all the women and girls trafficked into the rape stations. I contacted every organization that worked on sexual slavery, and asked, in multiple languages, whether anyone had found a Korean woman named Song Yun-Hee or Machiko, born in 1930, about 160 centimeters tall. She didn't exist—or, at least, no one seemed to have met her.

Jae-Min had connected with his grandmother, but, true to his father, he chose to return to Korea, and work there as an interpreter for the American air force. True to his mother, he finished his studies, in Seoul, and became an engineer for the South Korean government. Though Jae-Min pored through the government's records on women repatriated following World War II, he too met only dead ends. I didn't want to give up, but there were days when I was resigned that Yun-Hee, like her mom, was in a shallow grave, but one that was unmarked and unknown.

With scant other resources, I delved back into Emma's notebook and had it translated. It turned out that the entries were indeed a series of letters to Yun-Hee, but many of them had extraordinary details about the survivors Emma had spoken with—how they had been deceived, abducted, or drafted, and the torture they had endured. I made copies of the relevant entries and mailed them to organizations and historians around the world, but this didn't yield anything about the one woman I needed to find.

Jae-Min married and moved on. I started my own family too. Time is like an arrow, and decades passed.

It wasn't until 1991 that everything changed. That summer, on August 14th, a woman named Kim Hak-Sun came forward in Seoul, the first to use her real name in a lawsuit demanding that the Japanese government take responsibility for its organized sexual slavery. Lighting a torch can be frightening, and often it is lonely, but when that fire catches, it is brilliant. Hundreds of women joined her from all over Japan's former occupied territories, including Taiwan and the Philippines. Survivors started gathering in front of the Japanese embassy in Seoul, every Wednesday at noon, to demand a sincere apology from the Japanese government—one that did not try to minimize their suffering, place the bulk of the blamc on "private actors," or assert that the women were "volunteers"—and one that would not be retracted by subsequent politicians.

As these survivors and activists gained momentum, I monitored everything related to their advocacy, with newfound hope. Shortly after my ninety-seventh birthday, I watched a documentary about a controversial deal between the South Korean and Japanese governments that was meant to settle "the comfort women issue" once and for all—but it had been rejected by many survivors. The documentary implored people not to focus on the politicians but on the *women*, and what they had explicitly asked for.

On my television screen, Emma suddenly appeared, aged but unmistakable. Her hair was dyed brown, but she had the same tadpole-shaped eyes and apricot lips, her light eyebrows initially stiff, softening only when she began to speak.

I screamed from my sofa, at first thinking that Emma hadn't died on that hill, or that perhaps she had crawled out of her grave—until the woman said that she was eighty-nine years old and from Pyongyang. Her name was written as Yanxi Lin, but the collar on her shirt was wide enough to show a birthmark, barely visible on her suntanned skin. It was shaped like a figure eight, or perhaps a gourd.

I had found her.

Jae-Min had already passed away, and I wasn't in touch with his children. Who else could understand the magnitude of this moment? My own family had always thought of Yun-Hee as my strange hobby, akin to a fascination with UFOs. After all these years, I had found her, but we were in a whole new millennium, and the Korean War was largely forgotten in the United States.

I contacted the organization in charge of the documentary, and through them I learned that Yun-Hee was living in Taipei. During World War II, she had gotten a kidney infection in one of the rape stations and nearly died. She worked odd jobs as she tried to make her way east, but with few other prospects, she ended up marrying a Chinese Nationalist and fled with him to Hong Kong, and eventually Taiwan.

In Taipei, Yun-Hee could not register with her Korean name, so she used her husband's surname, Lin, and the Chinese version of her name, Yan-Xi. For most of her life, she had told everyone, including her own children, that she had been a nurse in the Japanese army. Yun-Hee had come forward only eight years ago, after her husband had passed away and she'd had the chance to speak with her children about what she wanted to do for the rest of her life.

My hands often quivered, due to my age, but when I picked up the phone and called the number that the organization gave me, my muscles were firm. When a woman whose voice was all too familiar answered my call, I didn't ask for Lin Yan-Xi; I asked for Song Yun-Hee.

The line went silent.

I thought she had hung up, for I could hear the blood in my ear whooshing, as though the receiver were a seashell.

Finally, the woman cleared her throat and said, "Who are you?"

"You don't know me," I said, breaking into tears, "but I knew your mother, and I've been looking for you for a long time—a very long time."

44

SILVER RIVER

> "The fact is, there is no evidence to prove there was coercion, nothing to support it."
>
> —Shinzo Abe, on "comfort women," March 1, 2007

August 14, 2019

A young girl in a hanbok, sculpted in bronze, sits on a chair, with a bird on her shoulder. Her hands, balled into fists, rest on her lap, and only her toes are touching the ground. Underneath, her painted shadow is the form of an elderly woman. Beside her, there is an empty chair indicating where a person should be. In the winter, people put a hat on the girl's head and bundle her up in blankets. In the summer, they lay flowers at her feet.

South Koreans call her the Statue of Peace, and eight years ago, activists placed her right across from the Japanese embassy in Seoul. She is staring at its doors.

Abrasive, no?

Women, however, rarely obtain justice by being polite. The bronze girl's lips are sealed, but her mere existence is loud, lending voice to the former military sex slaves who cannot or will not step forward, including the overwhelming majority, who died in captivity.

I hadn't been on a plane since I left Korea in 1951, but when Song Yun-Hee invited me to a protest, I couldn't say no. At the age of ninety-seven, I am old enough to know that some things are worth facing our fears for, and my remaining time is too precious to travel by boat.

My son and I are early, but it is already crowded. Today is the 1,400th Wednesday protest, and thousands of women and men have shown up despite the blazing heat. Activists have been doing this weekly since 1992, and it is now the world's longest-running rally for a single cause.

Sweat trickles down my back. Several survivors are clustered around the statue, and I spot Yun-Hee among them, in a plain white hanbok. She has some makeup on, but her eyes are unmistakable.

"Slow down," says my son, and only then do I realize I'm running, my gait awkward from arthritis.

"Catch up, George," I say back to him.

When Yun-Hee recognizes me, a smile flares across her face, her cheeks rounding as every wrinkle stretches upward. She beckons to a little girl, who dashes to unfold two plastic stools, for my son and me.

"Ellie *jiějiě*!" Yun-Hee exclaims, addressing me as an elder sister, in Mandarin. I clasp her hands, strong and calloused, possibly from decades of needlework.

The little girl gives me a bottle of iced barley tea and pats one of the stools.

"Is this your granddaughter?" I ask.

"No," says Yun-Hee. "My great-granddaughter." She points to two other women, closer to my son's age, who wave and bow. "These two are my daughters. They came with me from Taiwan."

One daughter looks so much like Emma that it gives me chills.

It steals my breath away, and I believe, so fervently, in the immortality that Imo once spoke of.

"Your mother never stopped searching for you," I say, still holding Yun-Hee's hands. "Everywhere we went, you were the first thing she thought about—before food, before shelter. To the very end, she was only worried about you."

Emma's satchel is on my son's shoulder, heavy because I have stuffed it with the red book that I carried to Pyongyang, the hanbok I wore when I snuck out of Seoul, and the rubber boots that I walked in for so many miles.

"I tried to go home," Yun-Hee says, slumped as she grips me too, "but I had no money. And by the time I got some, Taiwan was under martial law and I wasn't allowed to leave. I sent letters to my mother, but I never heard anything back. I don't know if any of them even got to Pyongyang."

There is a part of me that is afraid that Yun-Hee might disappear if I let her go, like a dream or leprechauns' gold, but I have to release her in order to open my son's backpack. "You might not have received any letters from your mom," I say, "but she definitely wrote to you."

I take out Emma's notebook, which I had laminated, the love in each page carefully preserved.

Yun-Hee's mouth falls open. She holds my arm to steady herself, though I too waver on my feet. I didn't tell her about this notebook when we spoke by phone, because I wanted to surprise her with it. An intense sense of triumph washes over me as her fingers brush mine to take back what is hers. When she pulls the pages, however, it's as if she unplugs a cork and unlocks a dam.

The regret that I've held in for so many years pours forth as I finally give myself permission to set it down. I cry, and Yun-Hee does too, with abandon, suturing the old wounds that others have never been able to see. Our children are alarmed, but they do not interfere. Yun-Hee's great-granddaughter takes out a packet of tissues and strokes Yun-Hee's hand.

"I thought perhaps, in my lifetime, the Korean War would end," Yun-Hee says, forcing a smile, "or at least the borders would open. I should have been there for my mom. I never stopped thinking about her either. I was always worried that she would be alone, without anyone to take care of her."

"She was rarely alone," I say, taking a tissue. "There were many people who cared for her, and loved her too; people who loved you, and missed you too."

I want to ask Yun-Hee if she has had a good life, if she has lived well, but as her great-granddaughter hugs her waist and her daughters wipe the mascara that has smudged beneath her lashes, I know that I do not have to. Though I wish that I had found her earlier, it is never too late to have a new friend. Together, we can go to a place that only I can show her, a place that I am obligated to return to—a grave at the top of a hill, between Incheon and Seoul, overlooking the wide Han River.

The clock strikes noon and Yun-Hee turns her attention to the rest of the crowd, while I ease back and crack open my barley tea. She joins the other protesters by the statue, linking arms to form a protective line in front of it.

There were various reasons for survivors to object to the controversial deal between the two governments, and one of them was because it required the removal of this statue—when this girl in bronze is no longer a statue. She is a memorial. She is a channel for grief, and a tribute to the survivors who spent the final years of their lives campaigning, in rain, snow, or shine, while politicians continued to claim that there was "no evidence to prove there was coercion."

Yun-Hee opens her mouth, and everyone around her stops speaking. Those seated in front of her swivel around to watch while her daughter begins to film her with a smartphone.

Yun-Hee takes a deep breath, then says, first in Korean and then in Mandarin, for her audience in Taiwan: "To all the women too scared to speak: I see you. To all the women too ashamed to speak: I understand you. To all the deceased who cannot speak: I will remember you. I continue to speak, not just for myself but for all of us, so that from wherever you are, you can hear the whole world say that what happened to you was wrong. That it was a *crime*. That we were not volunteers, and we will not be silent."

In Yun-Hee, I do not just see her mother. I also see Imo, in her gravitas, her courage, and her eloquence. The survivors with Yun-Hee are old, and there are only about a dozen of them still living. One of them is blind, and most need a cane or a walker just to move around this street. Some politicians are eager for them to die, but these women are no longer mortal. They are a movement. Surrounding them are young women holding up signs, several of which have the same slogan: *Cheer up, Granny. We will remember.*

No matter how hard some forces try to destroy the beauty in this world, it will persist somewhere. It will survive somewhere, cutting through the dark, untouchable and incomparable.

Divine.

The old will die, but the young will remember.

I have lived a long life, and as I squint in the blazing sun, I feel my age. I am tired, but it remains true that nothing inspires me more than abrasive women emboldened to organize. When I look out at this crowd of thousands extended around a girl in bronze, I see a river, defiantly beautiful—defiantly powerful. Art is subjective, and though the empty seat of the Statue of Peace is meant to represent the women and girls who died in captivity, I consider it a place for family members to sit beside an effigy of a person they lost, a love they were robbed of.

As the survivors pick up their signs, I see in the corner of my eye an embroidered skirt, a butterfly brushing the statue's bare feet. It is as though the barrier between our world and the next has thinned into a veil and flickered.

There, on the bronze chair, Emma is waiting.

She is watching.

I believe that she is smiling.

I will not surrender any earlier than I have to. So long as I am alive, I will never give up.

AUTHOR'S NOTE

The Young Will Remember is a work of fiction, but it was woven together with many threads of truth. I am a Taiwanese American Buddhist who is married to a half-Korean American Christian. My husband's grandfather was a pastor from Pyongyang, who met his Christian wife in a refugee camp during the Korean War. Their religion was an important part of their identity, and I tried to reflect that in Pastor Pak.

Many of the women in this book are human rights defenders, and this is because I myself am a women's human rights lawyer, with a background in international criminal law. Yun-Hee and Emma's storyline is drawn from my experience working on sexual violence in the context of torture and contemporary forms of slavery, and from speaking with the families of victims of enforced disappearances—many of whom spend the rest of their lives agonizing over the fates of their loved ones.

Kim Hak-Sun is a real person, and August 14, the day that she came forward, is the International Day for Comfort Women, commemorating the survivors of World War II military sexual slavery throughout East and Southeast Asia. Sexual violence remains one of the most difficult crimes to prosecute, because there are always people who will try to argue that the victims deserved it, or wanted it, or that the onus was on them to stop it. As of June 2025, there are only seven registered "comfort women" who are alive in Korea, and the Wednesday protests are still ongoing. I encourage everyone to listen directly to the survivors' testimonies.

In order to write Ellie, I researched war correspondent Maggie Higgins and pilot Hazel Ying Lee, to understand what she might have faced in a male-dominated field in the 1950s. Imo, meanwhile, was inspired by Kaneko Fumiko, a Japanese woman who joined the Korean independence movement as an activist and later died in a political prison. I am so grateful to both Maggie Higgins and Kaneko Fumiko for their memoirs, which were my windows into the past.

Ellie's friends in Tachikawa are based on the real-life flight nurses of the 801st Medical Air Evacuation Squadron, which won the Presidential Unit Citation for extraordinary heroism when evacuating thousands of wounded from Hagaru-ri. While there was indeed a single day in December 1950 on which nurses were forbidden from flying because of the danger, Barbara's protest was my own invention—which is why I must reiterate that this book is fiction, and not to be used as a historical text.

Still, I tried as much as possible to be accurate about real events. I have a passion for history, not just as entertainment but also because I believe in learning from it. Though 36,000 Americans died in the Korean War, it usually isn't taught in schools, and it is often called "the Forgotten War." The research for this book was a beast, because I had little prior knowledge about it. I soon realized that it was impossible to write about the Korean War without considering the impact of World War II on Korea, which in turn was impossible to do without understanding the Japanese occupation. Ultimately, I could not include everything I wanted to, but Ellie's story focuses on two issues that are close to my heart: justice for survivors of sexual violence, and the impact of mass bombing on civilians.

The use of collective punishment as a tactic of war continues to this day, galvanized by propaganda that dehumanizes others to justify their destruction. It is important to recall that ordinary citizens often have no control over their leaders, and that all military action must be weighted and proportional. Rampant bombing of civilian targets isn't just a violation of international law; it also tends to foment instability and extremism, at the expense of long-term peace.

For the purposes of this book, I relied on American military records, old newspaper articles, and foreign correspondence to piece together the details of the bombing campaign in North Korea. Though the US did not use atomic weapons, the discourse regarding the decision not to was chilling, because so much depended on international reaction rather than humanitarian impact. American advisors worried that using nuclear bombs would unite the people of Asia against them, drive people toward the Soviets, or prompt the Soviets to deploy their own nuclear arsenal. Eventually, it was concluded that America could achieve its goals with conventional weapons.

The US dropped 635,000 tons of bombs on North Korea, virtually wiping out all its towns and cities. Tarzon bombs, weighing in at 20,000 pounds each, were used for the first time ever on Kanggye in November 1950. Approximately 12.5 percent of the Korean population died in this war, but estimates go up to 20 percent for the North—a total of about three million people for the entire peninsula. It is important to note that many Koreans did not die due to being hit by explosives but because of the horrendous conditions created by indiscriminate bombing, like starvation, homelessness, and lack of sanitation and medical care.

It is terrifying to think that humans have hoarded enough bombs to destroy this earth many times over. I've read that there tends to be a massive war at least every eighty to one hundred years because that's how long it takes for those who remember the previous war to die. We are now at that point after World War II, and it is my sincere hope that all the records and resources that we have—video footage of war, written accounts of brutality, and international mechanisms designed for diplomacy—can help us avoid another global escalation.

In this climate, I think of my children, and all children, who deserve to grow up without the fear of violence or famine. Like Ellie, I believe that our greatest hope for peace in this world will come not from those in power but from ordinary people committed to building more bridges than bombs. Like Ellie, I consider myself a small cog who fights by amplifying voices that need to be heard. There are stories that keep me up at night, and I write them down—and with them, a part of my soul. I aspire to keep these histories alive, and through this work, I hope that the young will learn.

And the young will remember.

It has been my honor to share this story with you.

ACKNOWLEDGMENTS

There are many people who have contributed to this book, so I'll start from the very beginning. Thank you to my agent, Alexa Stark. When I was brainstorming ideas for this book, I sent her a list of proposals and she asked, "Do you want to think of one more?"

I contemplated saying no, but instead I said, "Okay, fine," and over the weekend, the seed for this book sprouted. In this regard, I owe an immense debt to the survivors of military sexual slavery, whose struggle paved the way for other women and girls to break the stigma of shame to demand justice and accountability. Through this book, I hope that I have helped to commemorate their courage.

Thank you to Amanda Bergeron, my phenomenal editor, for helping me pull the final story across the finish line, for all of her enthusiasm and love for these characters, and for her unwavering support for me as an author. I have an amazing team at Berkley, including Theresa Tran, Randi Kramer, Lauren Burnstein, Kim-Salina I, Jessica Mangicaro, Elise Tecco, and Anna Venckus, who have been pivotal in bringing my book to readers.

To write this story, I interviewed people who had relatives who survived the Korean War. I am grateful to my mother-in-law, who helped me with setting the scenes by telling me about her early childhood in 1950s Seoul and sharing snippets of her parents' lives during the Korean War and Japanese occupation. She taught me how to make *hobak-jeon*, and introduced me to Ken Choi, a linguist who generously agreed to read the first draft of my manuscript. I am also thankful for my friends Connie, Ji-Hye, and Esther, all of whom entertained my random text messages about Korea.

As always, I am lucky to have Katarina, Norine, and Zakiya, who have offered a safe space for my writing and are the first people to whom I show any of my work. In the past years, I've also had the privilege of making friends with other authors, and I am grateful to Eunice Hong, Karan Lee, and Rania Hanna for being my beta readers, to Sarah Hawley for asking her father my various questions about airplanes, and to Juhea Kim and Margaret Juhae Li for their kindness and advice in the final stretch.

This book required an extraordinary amount of research, which would not have been possible without the Queens Public Library; or my sister-in-law Jennifer, who sponsored my access to newspaper archives; or journalists like Maggie Higgins, who risked their lives to record history as it happened. I also appreciate the staff at various US military institutes and museums, who have made so much information available online, and who answered my questions via email.

And finally, I am beyond grateful for my friends and family, whom I leaned on for emotional support—especially my parents; my husband, David; and my knitting club. Though it can be challenging to write while parenting, as I said in my dedication, I could never have completed a book so rooted in motherhood without the love that I have for my children.

To Calvin and Katie: I am, and always will be, so proud to be your mom.